SANDRA BROWN

CHILL FACTOR

SIMON & SCHUSTER
New York London Toronto Sydney

SIMON & SCHUSTER
Rockefeller Center
1230 Avenue of the Americas
New York, NY 10020

SIMON & SCHUSTER and colophon are registered trademarks
of Simon & Schuster, Inc.

Manufactured in the United States of America

ISBN: 0-7432-4554-7

CHILL
FACTOR

CHAPTER

1

THE GRAVE WAS SUBSTANDARD.

The storm was forecast to be a record breaker.

Little more than a shallow bowl gouged out of unyielding earth, the grave had been dug for Millicent Gunn—age eighteen, short brown hair, delicate build, five feet four inches tall, reported missing a week ago. The grave was long enough to accommodate her height. Its depth, or lack thereof, could be remedied in the spring, when the ground began to thaw. If scavengers didn't dispose of the body before then.

Ben Tierney shifted his gaze from the new grave to the others nearby. Four of them. Forest debris and vegetative decay provided natural camouflage, yet each lent subtle variations to the rugged topography if one knew what to look for. A dead tree had fallen across one, concealing it entirely except to someone with a discerning eye.

Like Tierney.

He took one last look into the empty, shallow grave, then picked up the shovel at his feet and backed away. As he did, he noticed the dark imprints left by his boots in the white carpet of sleet. They didn't concern him overmuch. If the meteorologists were calling it right, the footprints would soon be covered by several inches of frozen precipitation. When the ground thawed, the prints would be absorbed into the mud.

In any case, he didn't stop to worry about them. He had to get off the mountain. Now.

He'd left his car on the road a couple hundred yards from the summit and the makeshift graveyard. Although he was now moving downhill, there was no path to follow through the dense woods.

Thick ground cover gave him limited traction, but the terrain was uneven and hazardous, made even more so by the blowing precipitation that hampered his vision. Though he was in a hurry, he was forced to pick his way carefully to avoid a misstep.

Weathermen had been predicting this storm for days. A confluence of several systems had the potential of creating one of the worst winter storms in recent memory. People in its projected path were being advised to take precautions, stock provisions, and rethink travel plans. Only a fool would have ventured onto the mountain today. Or someone with pressing business to take care of.

Like Tierney.

The cold drizzle that had been falling since early afternoon had turned into freezing rain mixed with sleet. Pellets of it stung his face like pinpricks as he thrashed through the forest. He hunched his shoulders, bringing his collar up to his ears, which were already numb from cold.

The wind velocity had increased noticeably. Trees were taking a beating, their naked branches clacking together like rhythm sticks in the fierce wind. It stripped needles off the evergreens and whipped them about. One struck his cheek like a blow dart.

Twenty-five miles an hour, out of the northwest, he thought with that part of his brain that automatically registered the current status of his surroundings. He knew these things—wind velocity, time, temperature, direction—instinctually, as though he had a built-in weather vane, clock, thermometer, and GPS constantly feeding pertinent information to his subconscious.

It was an innate talent that he had developed into a skill, which had been finely tuned by spending much of his adult life outdoors. He didn't have to think consciously about this ever-changing environmental data but frequently relied on his ability to grasp it immediately when it was needed.

He was relying on it now, because it wouldn't do to be caught on the summit of Cleary Peak—the second highest in North Carolina, after Mount Mitchell—carrying a shovel and running away from four old graves and one freshly dug.

The local police weren't exactly reputed for their dogged investigations and crime-solving success. In fact, the department was a local joke. The chief was a has-been, big-city detective who'd been ousted from the department on which he'd served.

Chief Dutch Burton now led a band of inept small-town officers—yokels outfitted in spiffy uniforms with shiny badges—who had been hard-pressed to catch the culprit spray-painting obscenities on the trash receptacles behind the Texaco station.

Now they were focused on the five unsolved missing persons cases. Despite their insufficiencies, Cleary's finest had deduced that having five women vanish from one small community within two and a half years was, in all probability, more than a coincidence.

In a metropolis, that statistic would have been trumped by others even scarier. But here, in this mountainous, sparsely populated area, the disappearances of five women were staggering.

Further, it was a generally held opinion that the missing women had met with foul play, so finding human remains, not the women themselves, was the task facing the authorities. Suspicion would fall on a man carrying a shovel through the woods.

Like Tierney.

Up till now, he had flown under the radar of Police Chief Burton's curiosity. It was crucial to keep it that way.

In pace with his footsteps, he clicked off the vital statistics of the women buried in the graves on the summit. Carolyn Maddox, a twenty-six-year-old who had a deep bosom, beautiful black hair, and large brown eyes. Reported missing last October. A single mom and sole supporter of a diabetic child, she had cleaned rooms at one of the guest lodges in town. Her life had been a cheerless, nonstop cycle of toil and exhaustion.

Carolyn Maddox was getting plenty of peace and rest now. As was Laureen Elliott. Single, blond, and overweight, she had worked as a nurse at a medical clinic.

Betsy Calhoun, a widowed homemaker, had been older than the others.

Torrie Lambert, the youngest of them, had also been the first, the prettiest, and the only one not a resident of Cleary.

Tierney picked up his speed, trying to outrun his haunting thoughts as well as the weather. Ice was beginning to coat tree limbs like sleeves. Boulders were becoming glazed with it. The steep, curving road down to Cleary would soon become unnavigable, and it was imperative that he get off this goddamn mountain.

Fortunately, his built-in compass didn't fail him, and he emerged from the woods no more than twenty feet from where he'd entered it. He wasn't surprised to see that his car was already coated with a thin layer of ice and sleet.

As he approached it, he was breathing hard, emitting bursts of vapor into the cold air. His descent from the summit had been arduous. Or perhaps his labored breathing and rapid heart rate were caused by anxiety. Or frustration. Or regret.

He placed the shovel in the trunk of his car. Peeling off the latex gloves he'd been wearing, he tossed them into the trunk as well, then shut the lid. He got into the car and quickly closed the door, welcoming shelter from the biting wind.

Shivering, he blew on his hands and vigorously rubbed them together in the hope of restoring circulation to his fingertips. The latex gloves had been necessary, but they hadn't provided any protection against the cold. He took a pair of cashmere-lined leather gloves from a coat pocket and pulled them on.

He turned the ignition key.

Nothing happened.

He pumped the accelerator and tried again. The motor didn't even growl. After several more unsuccessful tries, he leaned back against the seat and stared at the gauges on the dashboard as though expecting them to communicate what he was doing wrong.

He cranked the key one more time, but the engine remained as dead and silent as the women crudely buried nearby.

"Shit!" He thumped both gloved fists against the steering wheel and stared straight ahead, although there was nothing to look at. A sheet of ice had completely obscured the windshield. "Tierney," he muttered, "you're screwed."

CHAPTER
2

THE WIND HAS PICKED UP, AND THERE'S ICY STUFF FALLING OUT there," Dutch Burton remarked as he let the drape fall back into place over the window. "We'd better start down soon."

"I need to empty these few shelves, then I'll be done." Lilly took several hardcover editions from the built-in bookcase and placed them in a packing box.

"You always enjoyed reading when we came up here."

"That's when I had time to catch up on the latest best-sellers. Nothing to distract me here."

"Except me, I guess," he said. "I remember pestering you until you put your book aside and paid attention to me."

She glanced up at Dutch from where she sat on the floor and smiled. But she didn't pursue his fond recollection of how they'd spent their leisure time in the mountain retreat. Initially they had come here on weekends and holidays to escape their hectic schedules in Atlanta.

Later they'd come here simply to escape.

She was packing what remained of her personal belongings to take with her when she left today. She wouldn't be coming back. Neither would Dutch. This would be the last page written—an epilogue, actually—of their life together. She had hoped to make their final farewell as unsentimental as possible. He seemed determined to stroll down memory lane.

Whether his recollections of times past were designed to make him feel better or to make her feel worse, she didn't want to engage in them. Their good times together had been so eclipsed by their bad ones that any memory reopened wounds.

She steered the topic back to pragmatic matters. "I made copies of all the closing documents. They're in that envelope, along with a check for your half of the sale."

He looked down at the manila envelope but left it lying on the oak coffee table where she had placed it. "It's not right. My getting half."

"Dutch, we've been through this." She folded down the four sections of the box top to seal it, wishing she could close the argument as easily.

"You paid for this cabin," he said.

"We purchased it together."

"But your salary made that possible. We couldn't have afforded it on mine."

She pushed the box along the floor to the door, then stood up and faced him. "We were married when we bought it, married when we shared it."

"Married when we made love in it."

"Dutch—"

"Married when you served me my morning coffee wearing nothing but a smile and that afghan," he said, motioning in the general direction of the knitted throw on the back of the armchair.

"Please don't do this."

"That's my line, Lilly." He took a step closer to her. "Don't do this."

"It's already done. It's been done for six months."

"You could undo it."

"You could accept it."

"I'll *never* accept it."

"That's your choice." She paused, took a breath, brought the volume down. "That's always your choice, Dutch. You refuse to accept change. And because you can't, you never get over anything."

"I don't want to get over you," he argued.

"You'll have to."

She turned away from him, pulled an empty box nearer the bookcase, and began filling it with books, although taking less care with them than before. She was now in a hurry to leave, before she was forced to say more hurtful things in order to convince him that their marriage was, finally and forever, over.

Several minutes of tense silence were broken only by the soughing of the wind through the trees surrounding the cabin. Branches knocked against the eaves with increasing frequency and force.

She wished he would leave ahead of her, preferred he not be

there when she left the cabin. Knowing that it would be for the last time, he might have an emotional meltdown. She'd been through such scenes before and didn't want to experience another. Their leave-taking didn't have to be bitter and ugly, but Dutch was making it so by resurrecting old quarrels.

Although clearly it wasn't his intention, his rehashing of these arguments only underscored how right she'd been to end the marriage.

"I think this Louis L'Amour is yours." She held up a book. "Do you want it, or shall I leave it for the new owners?"

"They're getting everything else," he said morosely. "Just as well throw in a paperback book."

"It was easier to sell the furnishings along with the cabin," she said. "The furnishings were bought specifically for this place and wouldn't look right in any other house. Besides, neither of us has extra space, so what would I have done with it? Move it all out only to sell it to someone else? And where would I have stored it in the meantime? It made more sense to include everything in the sell price."

"That's not the point, Lilly."

She knew the point. He didn't want to think of strangers living in the cabin, using their things. Leaving everything intact for someone else to enjoy seemed to him like a sacrilege, a violation of the privacy and intimacy they'd shared in these rooms.

I don't care how sensible it is to sell the whole kit and caboodle, Lilly. Screw sensible! How can you bear to think of other people sleeping in our bed between our sheets?

That had been his reaction when she'd told him her plans for the furnishings. Obviously her decision still riled him, but it was too late for her to change her mind even if she were so inclined. Which she wasn't.

When the shelves in the bookcase were empty, save for the lone Western novel, she looked around for anything she might have missed. "Those canned goods," she said, pointing to the grocery items she'd placed on the bar that separated the kitchen from the living area. "Do you want to take them with you?"

He shook his head.

She added them to the last box of books, which was only half full. "I scheduled the utilities to be disconnected, since the new owners won't be occupying the cabin until spring." Doubtless he already knew all this. She was talking to fill the silence, which seemed to become conversely weightier the more of herself she removed from the cabin.

"I have some last-minute items in the bathroom to gather up, then I'll be out of here. I'll shut off everything, lock up, then, as agreed, drop off the key at the realtor's office on my way out of town."

His misery was evident in his expression, his stance. He nodded but didn't say anything.

"You don't have to wait on me, Dutch. I'm sure you have responsibilities in town."

"They'll keep."

"With an ice and snow storm forecast? You'll probably be needed to direct traffic in the supermarket," she said, making light. "You know how everyone stocks up for the siege. Let's say our good-byes now, and you can get a head start down the mountain."

"I'll wait on you. We'll leave together. Do what you need to do in there," he said, indicating the bedroom. "I'll load these boxes into your trunk."

He hefted the first box and carried it out. Lilly went into the next room. The bed, with a nightstand on each side, fit compactly against the wall under the sloping ceiling. The only other furnishings were a rocking chair and a bureau. Windows made up the far wall. A closet and small bath were behind the wall opposite the windows.

Earlier she had drawn the drapes, so the room was gloomy. She checked the closet. The empty hangers on the rod looked forlorn. Nothing had been overlooked in the bureau drawers. She went into the bathroom and collected the toiletries she had used that morning, zipped them into a plastic travel case, and after checking to make certain that she'd left nothing in the medicine chest, returned to the bedroom.

She added the bag of toiletries to her suitcase, which lay open on the bed, then closed it just as Dutch rejoined her.

Without preamble of any kind, he said, "If it hadn't been for Amy, we'd still be married."

Lilly looked down and slowly shook her head. "Dutch, please, let's not—"

"If not for that, we'd have lasted forever."

"We don't know that."

"I do." He reached for her hands. They felt cold in his hot clutch. "I take full responsibility for everything. Our failure was my fault. If I'd have handled things differently, you wouldn't have left me. I see that now, Lilly. I acknowledge the mistakes I made, and they were huge. Stupid. I admit that. But, please, give me another chance. Please."

"We could never go back to the way we were before, Dutch. We're not the same people as when we met. Don't you realize that? No one can change what happened. But it changed us."

He seized on that. "You're right. People change. I've changed since the divorce. Moving up here. Taking this job. It's all been good for me, Lilly. I realize that Cleary is a far cry from Atlanta, but I've got something to build on here. A solid foundation. It's my home, and the people here know me and all my kinfolk. They like me. Respect me."

"That's wonderful, Dutch. I want you to succeed here. I wish that for you with all my heart."

She did indeed want him to succeed, not only for his sake but for hers. Until Dutch had reaffirmed himself as a good cop, especially in his own mind, she would never be entirely free of him. He would remain dependent on her for his self-esteem until he was once again confident about his work and himself. The small community of Cleary afforded him that opportunity. She hoped to God it worked out well.

"My career, my life," he said in a rush, "have been given fresh starts. But that won't mean anything if you're not part of it."

Before she could stop him, he put his arms around her and pulled her tightly against him. He spoke urgently, directly into her ear. "Say you'll give us another chance." He tried to kiss her, but she turned her head aside.

"Dutch, let go of me."

"Remember how good we used to be together? If you'd ever let down your guard, we'd be right back where we started. We could forget all the bad stuff and return to the way we were. We couldn't keep our hands off each other, remember?" He tried again to kiss her, this time grinding his lips insistently against hers.

"Stop it!" She pushed him away.

He fell back a step. His breathing was loud in the room. "You still won't let me touch you."

She crossed her arms over her middle, hugging herself. "You're not my husband anymore."

"You'll never forgive me, will you?" he shouted angrily. "You used what happened with Amy as an excuse to divorce me, but that's not what it was about at all, was it?"

"Go, Dutch. Leave before—"

"Before I lose control?" He sneered.

"Before you disgrace yourself."

She held her ground against his mean glare. Then, turning away quickly, he stamped from the room. He grabbed the envelope on the coffee table and snatched his coat and hat off the pegs near the door. Without taking time to put them on, he slammed the door behind himself hard enough to rattle the windowpanes. Seconds later she heard his Bronco's engine start and the scattering of gravel beneath its oversize tires as he peeled away.

She sank onto the edge of the bed, covering her face with her hands. They were cold and trembling. Now that it was over, she realized that she'd been not only angry and repulsed but afraid.

This Dutch with the hair-trigger temper was not the disarming man she had married. Despite his claims to have made a fresh start, he looked desperate. That desperation translated into frightening, mercurial mood shifts.

She was almost ashamed of the relief that washed over her from knowing that she never had to see him again. It was finally over. Dutch Burton was out of her life.

Exhausted by the encounter, she lay back on the bed and placed her forearm across her eyes.

She was awakened by the sound of sleet pellets striking the tin roof.

Go-rounds with Dutch always had left her exhausted. The tense encounters they'd had during the past week, while she was in Cleary to finalize the sale of the cabin, must have taken more of a toll on her than even she had realized. After this last one, her body had kindly shut down her mind for a while and allowed her to sleep.

She sat up, rubbing her arms against the chill. The cabin bedroom had grown dark, too dark for her even to read her wristwatch. She got up, went to the window, and pulled back the edge of the drapery. It let in very little light but enough for her to see her watch.

The time surprised her. She'd slept deeply and dreamlessly but, actually, not that long. As dark as it was, she had expected it to be much later. The low clouds enwrapping the mountaintop had created a premature and eerie darkness.

The ground was now covered with an opaque layer of sleet. It continued to fall, intermingled with freezing rain and what meteorologists call snow grains, tiny chips that look more menacing than their lacy cousins. Tree branches were already encased in tubes of ice, which were growing discernibly thicker. A strong wind buffeted the windowpanes.

It had been careless of her to fall asleep. That mistake was going to cost her a harrowing trip down the mountain road. Even after she reached Cleary, weather would probably factor into her long drive back to Atlanta. Having dispatched her business here, she was anxious to get home, return to her routine, get on with her life. Her office would be a bog of backed-up paperwork, e-mail, and projects, all demanding her immediate attention. But rather than dread her return, she looked forward to tackling the tasks waiting on her.

Besides being homesick for her work, she was ready to leave Dutch's hometown. She adored Cleary's ambience and the beautiful, mountainous terrain surrounding it. But the people here had known Dutch and his family for generations. As long as she was his wife, she'd been warmly received and accepted. Now that she had divorced him, townsfolk had turned noticeably cool toward her.

Considering how hostile he'd been when he left the cabin, it was past time for her to leave his territory.

Acting hastily, she carried her suitcase into the front room and set it beside the door. Then she gave the cabin one final, rapid inspection, checking to see that everything had been turned off and that nothing belonging to her or Dutch had been overlooked.

Satisfied that all was in order, she put on her coat and gloves and opened the front door. The wind struck her with a force that stole her breath. As soon as she stepped onto the porch, ice pellets stung her face. She needed to shield her eyes against them, but it was too dark to put on sunglasses. Squinting against the sleet, she carried her suitcase to the car and placed it in the backseat.

Back inside the cabin, she quickly used her inhaler. Breathing cold air could bring on an asthma attack. The inhaler would help prevent that. Then, taking no time for even one last, nostalgic look around, she pulled the door closed and locked the dead bolt with her key.

The interior of her car was as cold as a refrigerator. She started the motor but had to wait for the defroster to warm before she could go anywhere; the windshield was completely iced over. Pulling her coat more closely around her, she buried her nose and mouth in the collar and concentrated on breathing evenly. Her teeth were chattering, and she couldn't control her shivers.

Finally the air from the car's defroster became warm enough to melt the ice on the windshield into a slush, which her windshield wipers were able to sweep away. They couldn't, however, keep up with the volume of freezing precipitation. Her visibility was sorely limited, but it wasn't going to improve until she reached lower elevations. She had no choice but to start down the winding Mountain Laurel Road.

It was familiar to her, but she'd never driven it when it was icy. She leaned forward over the steering wheel, peering through the frosted windshield, straining to see beyond the hood ornament.

On the switchbacks, she hugged the right shoulder and rocky embankment, knowing that on the opposite side of the road were steep drop-offs. She caught herself holding her breath through the hairpin curves.

Inside her gloves, her fingertips were so cold they were numb, but her palms were sweaty as she gripped the steering wheel. Tension made the muscles of her shoulders and neck burn. Her anxious breathing grew more uneven.

Hoping to improve her visibility, she rubbed her coat sleeve across the windshield, but all that accomplished was to give her a clearer view of the dizzy swirl of sleet.

And then, suddenly, a human figure leaped from the wooded embankment onto the road directly in her path.

Reflexively she stamped on her brake pedal, remembering too late that braking abruptly was the wrong thing to do on an icy road. The car went into a skid. The figure in her headlights jumped back, trying to get out of the way. Wheels locked, the car slid past him, the back end fishtailing wildly. Lilly felt a bump against her rear fender. With a sinking sensation in her stomach, she realized he'd been struck.

That was her last sickening thought before the car crashed into a tree.

CHAPTER
3

HER AIR BAG DEPLOYED, SMACKING HER IN THE FACE AND RE-leasing a choking cloud of powder, which filled the car's interior. Instinctively she held her breath to avoid breathing it. The seat belt caught her hard across her chest.

In a distant part of her mind, the violence of the impact amazed her. This had been a relatively mild collision, but it left her stunned. She took a mental inventory of body parts and determined that she wasn't in pain anywhere, only shaken. But the person she'd hit... "My God!"

Batting the deflated air bag out of the way, she released her seat belt and shoved open the door. As she scrambled out, she lost her footing and pitched forward. The heels of her hands struck the icy pavement hard, as did her right knee. It hurt like hell.

Using the side of the car for support, she limped around to the rear. Shielding her eyes against the wind with her hand, she spotted the motionless figure lying faceup, head and trunk on the road's narrow shoulder, legs extending into the road. She could tell by the size of his hiking boots that the victim was male.

As though skating across the glassy pavement, she made her way to him and crouched down. A watch cap was pulled low over his ears and eyebrows. His eyes were closed. She detected no movement of his chest to indicate breathing. She dug beneath the wool scarf around his neck, beneath the collar of his coat, beneath the turtleneck sweater, and searched for a pulse.

Feeling one, she whispered, "Thank God, thank God."

But then she noticed the spreading dark stain on the rock beneath his head. She was about to lift his head and search for the source of the bleeding when she remembered that an individual with a head wound shouldn't be moved. Wasn't that a strict rule of emergency aid? There could be a spinal injury, which moving could exacerbate or even make fatal.

She had no way of determining the extent of his head injury. And that was a *visible* injury. What injuries might he have sustained that she couldn't see? Internal bleeding, a rib-punctured lung, a ruptured organ, broken bones. And she didn't like the look of the awkward angle at which he was lying, as though his back was bowed upward.

She must get help. Immediately. She stood up and turned back toward her car. She could use her cell phone to call 911. Cell service wasn't always reliable in the mountains, but maybe—

His groan halted her. She turned so quickly her feet almost went out from under her. She knelt beside him again. His eyes fluttered open, and he looked up at her. She'd seen eyes like that only once before. *"Tierney?"*

He opened his mouth to speak, then looked as though he was about to throw up. He clamped his lips together and swallowed several times, containing the urge. He closed his eyes again, then after a few seconds opened them. "I was hit?"

She nodded. "By the rear quarter panel, I think. Are you in pain?"

After a few moments' assessment, he said, "Everywhere."

"The back of your head is bleeding. I can't tell how bad it is. You fell on a rock. I'm afraid to move you."

His teeth had begun to chatter. Either he was cold or he was going into shock. Neither was good.

"I've got a blanket in the car. I'll be right back."

She stood up, ducked her head against the wind, and labored back to her car, wondering what on earth he'd been thinking to have charged out of the woods like that, straight into the middle of the road. What was he doing up here on foot, during a winter storm, in the first place?

The trunk lid release on the dashboard didn't work, possibly because of damage to the electrical system. Or possibly because the lid was frozen shut. She removed the key from the ignition and took it with her to the rear of the car. As she'd feared, the lock was glazed over.

She groped her way to the shoulder of the road and picked up the largest rock she could handle, then used it to chip away the ice. In emergency situations like this, people were supposed to experience an adrenaline rush that imbued them with superhuman strength. She felt no such thing. She was panting and exhausted by the time she'd knocked away enough ice to raise the trunk lid.

Shoving the packing boxes aside, she found the stadium blanket zipped into its plastic carrying case. She and Dutch had taken it to football games. It was for warding off an autumn chill, not surviving a blizzard, but she supposed it was better than nothing.

She returned to the prone figure. He lay as still as death. Her voice rose in panic. "Mr. Tierney?"

He opened his eyes. "I'm still alive."

"I had a hard time getting the trunk open. Sorry it took so long." She spread the blanket over him. "This won't be of much help, I'm afraid. I'll try—"

"Save the apologies. Do you have a cell phone?"

She remembered from the day they'd met that he was a take-charge kind of man. Fine. This wasn't the time to play the feminist card. She fished her cell phone from her coat pocket. It was on, the panel was lighted. She turned it toward him so he could read the message. "No service."

"I was afraid of that." He tried to turn his head, winced and gasped, then clenched his jaw to keep his teeth from chattering. After a moment, he asked, "Can your car be driven?"

She shook her head. What she knew about cars was limited, but when the hood looked like a crumpled soda can, it was reasonable to assume that the car was disabled.

"Well, we can't stay here." He made an effort to get up, but she pressed her hand against his shoulder.

"You could have a broken back, a spinal injury. I don't think you should move."

"It's a risk, yeah. But it's either that or freeze to death. I'll take the gamble. Help me up."

He extended his right hand, and she clasped it tightly as he struggled to sit up. But he couldn't stay up. Bending forward from the waist, he fell on her heavily. Lilly caught him against her shoulder and held him there while she repositioned the stadium blanket around his shoulders.

Then she eased him back until he was in a sitting position. His head remained bent low over his chest. Fresh blood trickled from beneath the tight watch cap, eddied around the front of his earlobe, and dribbled down his jaw.

"Tierney?" She lightly smacked his cheek. "Tierney!"

He raised his head, but his eyes remained closed. "Fainted, I think. Give me a minute. Dizzy as hell."

He breathed deeply, in through his nose, out through his mouth. After a time, he opened his eyes and nodded. "Better. Think that together we can get me on my feet?"

"Take all the time you need."

"Time is what we don't have. Get behind me and put your hands under my arms." She released him cautiously and, when she was certain that he could stay upright, moved behind him. "A backpack."

"Yeah. So?"

"The awkward way you were lying, I thought your back was broken."

"I landed on the backpack. Probably saved me from a serious skull fracture."

She eased the straps of the pack off his shoulders so she could lend him better support. "Ready when you are."

"I think I can stand up," he said. "You're there to break my fall just in case I start falling backward. Okay?"

"Okay."

He placed his hands on either side of his hips and levered himself up. Lilly did more than spot him should he fall. She made as great an effort as he, lifting him until he was standing and then supporting him until he said, "Thanks. I think I'm all right."

He reached beneath his coat, and when he withdrew his hand, he was holding a cell phone, which evidently had been clipped to his belt. He looked down at it and frowned. She read the curse word on his lips. He wasn't getting service either. He motioned toward the wrecked car. "Is there anything in your car we should take back to your cabin?"

Lilly looked at him with surprise. "You know about my cabin?"

Scott Hamer clenched his teeth against the strain.

"Almost there, son. Come on. You can do it. One more."

Scott's arms trembled with the effort. Veins bulged to a grotesque extent. Sweat rolled off him and dripped from the weight bench onto the gym mat, making small splats against the rubber.

"I can't do one more," he groaned.

"Yes you can. Give me a hundred and ten percent."

Wes Hamer's voice echoed in the high school gymnasium. Except for them, the building was deserted. Everyone else had been allowed to go home more than an hour ago. Scott was required to stay, long after classes were dismissed, long after all the other athletes had gone through their after-school workouts as set out by their coach, Scott's father, Wes.

"I want to see maximum effort."

It felt to Scott like his blood vessels were on the verge of bursting. He blinked sweat from his eyes and expelled several puffs of breath through his mouth, spraying spittle. Tremors of overexertion seized his biceps and triceps. His chest seemed about to explode.

But his dad wasn't going to let him stop until he had pressed four hundred twenty-five pounds, more than double Scott's body weight. Five reps had been the goal set for him today. His dad was big on setting goals. He was even bigger on achieving them.

"Stop screwing around, Scott," Wes said impatiently.

"I'm not."

"Breathe. Send the oxygen into those muscles. You can do this."

Scott inhaled deeply, then expelled the air in short pants, demanding the impossible of his arm and chest muscles.

"That's it!" his dad said. "You raised it another inch. Maybe two."

God, please let it be two.

"Give me one more effort. One more push, Scott."

Involuntarily, a low growl issued out of his throat as he channeled all his strength into his quivering arms. But he got the weight bar up another inch, enough to lock his elbows for a millisecond before his dad reached over and guided it into the brackets.

Scott's arms dropped lifelessly to his sides. His shoulders slumped into the bench. His chest heaved in an attempt to regain his breath. His entire body trembled with fatigue.

"Good job. Tomorrow we'll try for six." Wes passed him a towel before he turned away and moved toward his office, where the telephone had begun to ring. "You shower. I'll get this, then start locking up."

Scott heard his father answer the phone with a brusque "Hamer," then ask, "What do you want, Dora?" in the deprecating tone he always used with Scott's mother.

Scott sat up and ran the towel over his face and head. He was whipped, absolutely spent. He dreaded even the walk to the locker room. Only the promise of a hot shower got him off the bench.

"That was your mother," Wes called to him through the open door of his office.

It was a messy space that only the brave dared enter. On the desk were stacks of paperwork which Wes considered a waste of time and therefore avoided doing for as long as possible. The walls were covered with season schedules for numerous sport teams. A two-month calendar was filled with his handwritten hieroglyphics, which only he could read.

Also taped to the wall was a topographical map of Cleary and the surrounding area. His favorite hunting and fishing spots had been highlighted with a red marker. In framed photos of the last three years' football teams, Head Coach Wes Hamer stood proudly in the center of the front row.

"She said it's beginning to sleet," he told Scott. "Get a move on."

The pungent odor of the high school locker room was so familiar to Scott he didn't even notice it. His own stink mingled with the stench of adolescent sweat, dirty socks, jerseys, and jockstraps. The odor was so pervasive it seemed to have soaked into the grout between the tiles in the shower room.

Scott turned on the faucets in one of the stalls. As he peeled off his shirt, he looked over his shoulder into the mirror and frowned with disgust at the outbreak of acne on his back. He stepped into the shower and put his back to the spray, then vigorously scrubbed as much of it as he could reach with an antibacterial soap.

He was washing his crotch when his dad appeared, carrying a towel. "In case you forgot to pick one up."

"Thanks." Self-consciously he removed his hand from his private parts and went to work on his armpits.

Wes draped the towel over a bar outside the stall, then motioned toward Scott's groin. "You take after your old man," he said around a chuckle. "Nothing to be shy about in that department."

Scott hated when his dad tried to get chummy with him by talking about sex. Like that was a topic Scott was just dying to discuss with him. Like he enjoyed the innuendos and suggestive winks.

"You've got more than enough there to keep all your girlfriends happy."

"Dad."

"Just don't make one *too* happy," Wes said, his smile inverting. "You'd be a real catch for one of these local gals looking to elevate herself. They're not above tricking a guy. That goes for any female I ever met. Never trust the girl to take care of birth control," Wes said, shaking his index finger as though this was a new lecture and not one Scott had been routinely subjected to since puberty.

Scott turned off the water faucets and reached for the towel, quickly wrapping it around his hips. He headed toward his locker, but his dad wasn't finished yet. He clamped a hand on Scott's wet shoulder and turned him around. "You've got years of hard work ahead before you get to where you're going. I don't want some gal to turn up pregnant and ruin all our plans."

"That's not going to happen."

"Make damn sure it doesn't." Then Wes gave him an affection- ate push in the general direction of his locker. "Get dressed."

Five minutes later Wes locked the gymnasium door behind them, securing the building for the night. "Bet anything school's out to- morrow," he remarked. Intermittent sleet was falling, along with a dreary rain that instantly froze on any surface. "Be careful where you step. It's already getting slick."

Cautiously they made their way to the faculty parking lot, where Wes had a premium space, reserved for the athletic director of Cleary High School, home of the Fighting Cougars.

The windshield wipers labored against the freezing rain on the tempered glass. Scott shivered inside his coat and pushed his fists deep into the flannel-lined pockets. His stomach growled. "I hope Mom's got dinner ready."

"You can have a snack at the drugstore."

Scott turned his head quickly and looked at Wes.

Wes kept his eyes on the road. "We're stopping there before we go home."

Scott sank lower into his seat, pulled his coat close around him, and moodily stared through the windshield as they moved along Main Street. There were Closed signs in most of the store windows. Shopkeepers had left early, before the worst of the weather moved in. But it seemed no one had gone straight home. Traffic was heavy, es- pecially around the grocery market, which was still open and doing a brisk business.

All of this registered with Scott, but on a subliminal level, until his dad stopped for one of Main Street's two traffic lights. He was staring vacantly through the rain-spattered window when his eyes happened to focus on the flyer tacked to the utility pole.

MISSING!

Beneath that bold headline was a black-and-white photo of Mil- licent Gunn, followed by a basic physical description, the date of her disappearance, and a list of telephone numbers to call with any in- formation as to her whereabouts.

Scott closed his eyes, thinking about what Millicent had looked like the last time he'd seen her.

When he reopened his eyes, the car was once again in motion, the flyer no longer in sight.

CHAPTER

4

ARE YOU CERTAIN WE HAVE EVERYTHING WE MAY NEED? BOT-tled water and nonperishables?"

Marilee Ritt tried to contain her annoyance. "Yes, William. I double-checked the shopping list you gave me before leaving the market. I even stopped at the hardware store for extra flashlight batteries because the market had already sold out."

Her brother peered past her through the wide windows of the drugstore that bore his name. On Main Street, vehicles were reduced to a crawl, not because of road conditions, which were becoming increasingly dicey, but because there was so much traffic. People were anxious to get wherever they were going to wait out the storm.

"Forecasters are saying this could be a bad one, lasting several days."

"I listen to the radio and TV, too, William."

His eyes moved quickly back to his sister. "I didn't mean to imply that you were inefficient. Just a little absentminded sometimes. How about a cup of cocoa? On the house."

She glanced outside at the slow-moving stream of cars. "I don't think I'd get home any faster if I left now, so all right. I'd love some cocoa."

He ushered her toward the soda fountain at the front of the store and motioned her onto one of the chrome stools at the counter. "Linda, Marilee would like a cup of cocoa."

"Extra whipped cream, please," Marilee said, smiling at the woman behind the counter.

"Coming right up, Miss Marilee."

Linda Wexler had been managing the drugstore soda fountain long before William Ritt bought the business from the previous owner. When he took over, he'd been smart enough to keep Linda in place. She was a local institution, knowing everyone in town, who took cream in their coffee and who drank it black. The tuna salad was made fresh by her every morning, and she wouldn't even consider using frozen patties for the hamburgers she cooked to order on a griddle.

"Can you believe this mess outside?" she asked as she poured milk into a saucepan to heat for the cocoa. "I remember when we's kids, how excited we'd get ever' time snow was in the forecast, wondering was we gonna have school the next day or not. You prob'ly enjoy a free holiday much as your pupils."

Marilee smiled at her. "If we have a snow day, I'll probably use it to grade papers."

Linda sniffed with disapproval. "Waste of a day off."

The entrance door opened, and the bell above it tinkled. Marilee swiveled around on her stool to see who'd come in. Two teenage girls rushed inside, giggling and shaking moisture from their hair. They were in Marilee's third-period grammar and American literature class.

"You girls should be wearing caps," she said to them.

"Hi, Miss Ritt," they said, virtually in unison.

"What are you doing out in this weather? Shouldn't you be getting home?"

"We came to rent some videos," one said. "Just in case, you know, we don't have school tomorrow."

"I hope there are some new releases left," the other girl remarked.

"Thank you for reminding me," Marilee said. "I may take one or two movies home myself."

They looked at her strangely, as though it had never occurred to them that Miss Marilee Ritt might actually watch a movie. Or that she would do anything other than give tests, and grade themes, and monitor the hallways during class changes, keeping a keen eye out for unnecessary horseplay. They probably couldn't imagine any kind of life for her outside the corridors of Cleary High School.

And, until recently, they would have been right.

She felt her cheeks turn warm at the reminder of her new pastime and quickly changed the subject. "Get home before the roads get icy," she cautioned her students.

"We will," one said. "I have to be home before dark anyway. Because of Millicent. My folks are freaked out."

"Mine too," the other said. "Totally. They've got to know where I am twenty-four-seven." She rolled her eyes. "As if I'd get close enough to some creep that he could grab me and carry me off."

"I'm sure they're very concerned," Marilee said. "They should be."

"My daddy gave me a pistol to keep in my car," the other girl said. "Told me not to hesitate to shoot anybody who tried to mess with me."

Marilee murmured, "It's become a frightening situation." Gauging their impatience to get on with their evening, she told them to enjoy the snow day, if indeed they had one, then turned back to the counter just as Linda was serving her cocoa.

"Careful, hon, it's hot." Looking after the girls, Linda said, "People have gone plumb nuts."

"Hmm." Marilee took a tentative sip of the hot chocolate. "I'm not sure which is more disconcerting. Five missing women or fathers arming their teenage daughters with pistols."

Everyone in Cleary was nervous about the disappearances. People were locking doors that previously had gone unlatched. Women of all ages were warned to be aware of their surroundings when they were out alone and to avoid dark and isolated places. They were advised to trust no one they didn't know well. Since Millicent's disappearance, it had been suggested that husbands and boyfriends meet their partners at their workplaces at the end of the day to escort them home.

"I can't rightly blame them though," Linda said, lowering her voice. "You mark my words, Marilee. That Gunn girl is as good as dead if she ain't already."

It was pessimistic to think that way, but Marilee was prone to agree. "When are you leaving for home, Linda?"

"Whenever that slave-driving brother of yours says I can go."

"Maybe I can influence him to let you off early."

"Ain't likely. We been doin' a land-office business all afternoon. People figurin' it'll be days before they can get out again."

A drugstore had occupied the corner of Main and Hemlock streets for as long as Marilee could remember. When she was a little girl and the family had come into town, she'd always looked forward to stopping here.

William must have had fond memories of it too, because as soon as he graduated from pharmaceutical school, he'd returned to Cleary and started working here. When his employer decided to retire, William bought the business from him, then immediately borrowed money from the bank for expansion.

He bought the vacant building next door and incorporated it into the existing store, enlarging Linda's work space and adding booths to increase the soda fountain's capacity. He'd also had the foresight to set aside room for video rentals. In addition to the pharmacy, he had the most extensive stock of paperback books and magazines in town. Women shopped here for their cosmetics and greeting cards. Men bought tobacco products. Everyone came to catch up on local gossip. If Cleary had an epicenter, it was Ritt's Drug Store.

Along with prescriptions, William dispensed advice, compliments, congratulations, or condolences, whatever his customers' situations called for. Although Marilee thought the white lab coat he wore in the store was a bit pretentious, his customers seemed not to mind.

Of course there were those who speculated on why both he and Marilee had remained single and continued to share a home. People thought that much togetherness between brother and sister was strange. Or worse. She tried not to let people who entertained dirty thoughts like that bother her.

The bell above the entrance jangled again. She didn't turn this time but looked into the mirrored wall behind Linda's workstation and saw Wes Hamer come in with his son, Scott.

Linda called out to them. "Hey, Wes, Scott, how're y'all?"

Wes returned her greeting, but it was Marilee with whom he was making eye contact in the mirror. He sauntered over, leaned close over her shoulder, and took a whiff of the cocoa. "Damn, that smells good. I'll take one of those, too, Linda. It's a hot cocoa kind of day."

"Hello, Wes. Scott," Marilee said.

Scott acknowledged her with a mumbled "Miss Ritt."

Wes sat down on the stool beside her. His knee nudged hers as he slid his legs beneath the counter. "Mind if I join you?"

"Not at all."

"You ought not to be cussin', Wes Hamer," Linda said. "You being a role model for kids and all."

"What did I say?"

"You said 'damn.'"

"When did you get to be so prissy? I remember a time or two you letting fly with a cussword."

She snorted, but she was grinning. Wes had that effect on women.

"You want some cocoa too, hon?" Linda asked Scott, who was standing behind his father, hunched inside his coat, hands in his pockets, shifting his weight from one foot to the other. "Sure. Thanks. That'd be great."

"No whipped cream on his," Wes said. "He won't win any points with football scouts if he's got a gut on him."

"I don't think he's in danger of getting a gut anytime soon," Linda said. But she left off the whipped cream. Wes had that effect on people, too.

He turned on his stool so that he was facing Marilee. "How's Scott coming with American lit?"

"Very well. He made eighty-two on the test over Hawthorne."

"Eighty-two, huh? Not bad. Not great. But not bad," he said, addressing Scott over his shoulder. "Go on back there and speak to those young ladies. They've been all aflutter ever since you walked in. Make sure William knows you're here."

Scott ambled off, taking his cocoa with him.

"Girls won't stay away from that boy," Wes said as he watched Scott make his way down the aisle toward the video section.

"You cain't be surprised," Linda said. "He's cute as the dickens."

"They all seem to think so. Calling the house at all hours and hanging up if he doesn't answer. Drives Dora nuts."

"What do you think about his popularity with the ladies?" Marilee asked.

Wes's gaze swung back to her, and he winked. "The apple doesn't fall far from the tree."

She looked down into her cup and nervously searched for something to say. "Scott is doing well on the extra assignments, too. His writing has improved dramatically."

"With you tutoring him, how could he keep from learning something?"

Several weeks into the fall term, Wes had approached her about tutoring Scott on Saturday mornings and Sunday evenings. For her services, he offered to pay her a modest stipend, which she'd tried to reject. He'd insisted. In the end, Marilee had accepted the offered fee and consented to help Scott with his studies, not only because she knew the importance of his scoring high on his college entrance exams but because few could say no to Wes Hamer and make it stick.

"I hope you think you're getting your money's worth," she said to him now.

"If ever I don't think so, you'll be the first to know, Marilee." He grinned at her, his eyes twinkling.

"Hey, Wes?" William called to him from the end of the aisle of baby care products. "I've got a free minute. You want to come on back?"

Wes held Marilee's gaze for several more seconds, then asked

Linda to add the two cups of cocoa to his account and left them to join William and Scott in the pharmacy section.

"That's curious," Marilee said, wondering what business the Hamers had with her brother.

But Linda was busy filling the order of another customer and didn't hear her.

Lilly was still puzzling over how Ben Tierney knew she had a cabin on Cleary Peak when he asked testily, "Have you got a better idea?"

Being buffeted by the strong wind, she had to think about it for only a moment. "No. We should go to the cabin."

"First, let's check out your car."

They made it to her car without mishap, although he was wobbly on his feet. She got in on the driver's side. He pushed her suitcase aside and climbed into the backseat because the right half of the dashboard had been jammed into the front passenger seat. Once he had pulled the door closed, he removed his gloves and rested his forehead against the heel of his right hand.

"Are you going to faint again?" Lilly asked.

"No. We don't have time for it." He lowered his hand and peered at her over the back of the seat, giving her a critical once-over. "You're underdressed."

"Tell me," she said through chattering teeth.

"What have you got in your suitcase? Anything useful?"

"Nothing warmer than what I've got on."

Apparently wanting to judge that for himself, he opened the suitcase on the seat beside him. He rifled through her garments, heedlessly sorting through lingerie, nightgowns, socks, slacks, tops. "Thermal underwear?"

"No."

He tossed her a wool sweater. "Put this on over what you're wearing."

She removed her coat long enough to pull on the sweater.

"Let me see your boots."

"My—"

"Boots," he repeated impatiently. She pulled up her pants leg and extended her leg far enough for him to see her foot. He frowned. Taking several pairs of socks from the suitcase, he tossed them over the seat at her. "Put those in your pocket. Take this, too. You can put it on once we get to the cabin." He passed her a thin silk turtleneck that she'd originally bought to wear under ski clothes.

Then, startling her, he reached over the seat and took a strand of her hair. "Wet." He dropped the strand quickly, but Lilly was glad he was thinking about her damp hair and not the fistful of panties he was holding in his other hand. "Have you got a cap? A hat of any kind?"

"I didn't plan on being outdoors much during this trip."

"You've got to have something on your head."

He tossed the undies back into the suitcase and pulled the stadium blanket from his shoulders. "Lean toward me."

She came up on her knees and faced the backseat. He fashioned a hood for her out of the blanket, placing it over her head and folding it across her chest. He buttoned her coat up over it, then patted it into place. "There. Before you get out of the car, pull this loose fabric up over your nose and mouth. Is there anything in the trunk except a spare tire?"

The familiar way in which he'd touched her left her surprised and slow to process thought. Her mind raced to catch up with what he'd asked her. "Uh, a . . . I think there's a first-aid kit that came with the car."

"Good."

"And some food I was taking from the cabin."

"Even better." He gave the car's interior a cursory glance. "Flashlight, anything in the glove box?"

"Only the instruction manual for the car."

"Just as well. I doubt we could have gotten anything out of it, bashed in as it is." He made a swipe at the fresh blood trickling down his cheek, then pulled on his gloves. "Let's go."

"Wait. My handbag. I'll need it."

She looked around for her purse and discovered that it had been slung down to the passenger-side floorboard when the car crashed into the tree. It was difficult, but she managed to reach between the dash and the seat and wrest her bag from beneath the wreckage.

"Loop the shoulder strap around your neck to keep your arms free. Better balance."

She did as he suggested, then reached for the door latch. There, she paused and looked at him apprehensively. "Maybe we should just stay put until we can call for help."

"We could, but nobody's coming up this road tonight, and I doubt we'd survive till morning."

"Then I guess we don't have a choice, do we?"

"Not really, no."

Again she reached for the door latch, but this time it was he who stopped her by laying a hand on her shoulder. "I didn't mean to sound so curt."

"I understand the need for haste."

"We've got to get to shelter before it gets worse out here."

She bobbed her head in agreement. Their gazes held for a second or two, then he removed his hand from her shoulder, opened the back door, and got out. Lilly joined him at the rear of the car, where he was surveying the contents of the open trunk. He found the first-aid kit and told her to put it in her pocket. "Some of those canned goods, too. And the crackers."

He was likewise filling the many pockets of his coat with cans, which must have weighed him down, especially after he retrieved his backpack from where they'd left it lying in the road.

"Ready?" he asked, squinting at her through the blowing frozen precipitation.

"As much as I'll ever be."

Using his chin, he motioned for her to precede him. They'd trudged only a few yards when they determined that trying to walk uphill on the road's icy surface would be futile. For every step forward they took, they slipped back three. Tierney nudged her toward the road's shoulder. It was narrow, often forcing them to walk single file, hugging the embankment and dodging outcropping boulders. However, the uneven ground actually worked to their advantage. They found purchase on rocks and vegetation beneath the ice and sleet.

The grade was steep. On a fair day with ideal weather conditions, the uphill hike would have been a strenuous workout for even the most physically fit. Most of the time, they were walking directly into the wind, which forced them to keep their heads bent against it, sometimes walking blind through a maelstrom of ice pellets that felt like shards of glass when they struck the exposed skin of their faces.

They stopped frequently to catch their breath. Once Tierney stopped suddenly, turned away from her, and vomited, leading her to believe that he had a concussion. At the very least. She noticed that he had begun to favor his left leg and wondered if he also had a fracture.

Finally, walking became such an effort for him she insisted that he place one arm across her shoulders. He did so reluctantly, but out of necessity. With each footstep he leaned more heavily upon her. She slogged on.

They reached a state of total exhaustion and continued only because they had to. The distance she had covered in three minutes by car took almost an hour on foot. They were stumbling over each other by the time they reached the cabin's porch steps.

Lilly propped him against a support post on the porch while she unlocked the door, then assisted him inside. She paused only long enough to shut the door and dump her handbag on the floor before collapsing onto one of the sofas. Tierney slid his backpack off and sprawled on the sofa facing hers, separated by the coffee table.

For several minutes they remained where they'd landed, their breath soughing loudly in the darkness. Because she had turned off the heat before leaving, the room was cold. But compared with outside, it felt balmy.

Lilly didn't think she would have the energy ever to move again, but eventually she stirred and sat up. She reached for the lamp on the end table and switched it on. "Thank goodness," she said, blinking against the sudden light. "I was afraid the electricity may have been shut off by now."

She unloaded the cans of food from her pockets and set them on the coffee table, then fished out her cell phone and punched in a number.

Suddenly alert, Tierney sprang up and asked, "Who are you calling?"

"Dutch."

CHAPTER

5

LILLY'S PREDICTION ABOUT THE CHAOS IN TOWN HAD BEEN COR-
rect.

Dutch had been back for only a couple of hours, and already
he was wishing for the peace of his mountain cabin. *Formerly* his
cabin, he thought bitterly.

Rush hour in downtown Atlanta had never been as congested as
Main Street in Cleary this evening. It was bumper to bumper in both
lanes, a ribbon of red taillights on one side, a ribbon of white headlights on the other. Everyone on one side of town seemed bent on
getting to the other side, and vice versa.

The sheriff's office was dealing with the outlying areas of the
county, leaving the township itself up to Dutch and his department.
Now would have been a good time for a burglar to burgle, because
no one was at home where they should be, and every police officer
was busy trying to control the pandemonium generated by the approaching storm.

The signal light at Moultrie and Main was busted again. On any
other day it would be no big deal. Drivers would take turns, politely
waving one another through the intersection and joking about the inconvenience. But today, when patience was wearing thin, the mal-
functioning traffic light had caused a gridlock that was making
motorists fractious.

The officers not on the streets directing traffic were monitoring
the crowds in the market, trying to prevent fistfights over the scant
merchandise left on the shelves. There had been one altercation already over the last tin of sardines.

With sleet pellets larger than grains of rock salt, the rapid accumulation would soon become nasty. As the weather system moved over the mountain and swept down the eastern face of it into the valley, picking up moisture, conditions were going to get even more unmanageable. Until the storm was over, and all the ice and snow had melted, Dutch could count on little or no rest.

Glancing up toward the crest of Cleary Peak, he saw that it was completely engulfed in cloud. He'd come down just in time and was relieved to know that Lilly had been right behind him and was well on her way south to Atlanta by now. If she made good time, she could probably outrun the storm, arriving home before it caught up with her.

He still thought of her constantly, of where she was, of what she was doing. It was a habit that no goddamn decree of divorcement could break. Remembering how she'd looked at him before he left the cabin created a weight in his chest as heavy as an anvil. She'd been afraid of him. Which was nobody's fault but his own. He'd given her reason to fear him.

"Hey, Chief!" Wes Hamer was shouting at him from the sidewalk just outside Ritt's Drug Store. "Get over here. I'm a taxpaying citizen, and I've got a gripe."

Dutch pulled his Bronco out of the line of cars inching along Main Street and into the handicapped parking space in front of the drugstore. He lowered his window, letting in a blast of frigid air.

Wes came toward him with the shoulder-rolling amble of a former football player. Both his knees and one hip were afflicted with osteoarthritis, but that wasn't something Wes advertised. He would do damn near anything to keep from owning up to a weakness of any sort.

"You got a complaint, Coach?" Dutch deadpanned.

"You're the number one peace officer around here. Can't you clear the streets of these morons?"

"I'd start with you."

Wes guffawed but immediately sensed Dutch's dour mood and leaned in closer. "Hey, buddy, why the long face?"

"I said good-bye to Lilly for the last time. Couple hours ago. Up at the cabin. She's gone for good, Wes."

Wes turned away. "Scott, go warm up the car. I'll be right there." Scott, who'd been standing beneath the awning outside Ritt's store, caught the set of car keys Wes tossed to him, raised his other hand in a farewell wave to Dutch, then sauntered off down the sidewalk.

"Has he heard anything from Clemson yet?" Dutch asked.

"We can talk about that later. Let's talk about your wife."

"Ex-wife. Emphasis on the *ex*, which she made perfectly clear this afternoon."

"I thought you were going to talk to her."

"I did."

"No go?"

"No go. She's got her divorce and she's happy about it. She wants nothing to do with me. It's over." He rubbed his brow with his gloved hand.

"Are you gonna cry, or what? Jesus, Dutch, don't make me ashamed to call you my best friend."

Dutch turned and looked at him. "Fuck you."

Unfazed, Wes continued. "The way you're mewling around." He shook his head over Dutch's pathetic behavior. "Lilly didn't know a good thing when she had it. So screw her. My opinion of her has always been—"

"I don't want to hear your opinion of her."

"She thinks her shit don't stink."

"I said I didn't want to hear it, all right?"

Wes held up both hands as though in surrender. "All right. But it isn't like she holds me in high esteem."

"She thinks you're an asshole."

"Like I'm gonna lose sleep over what Ms. Lilly Martin Burton thinks of me." Smiling crookedly, he clapped his hand on Dutch's shoulder. "You're taking this breakup way too hard. You lost your wife, not your manhood. Look around," he said, gesturing expansively. "There are women everywhere."

"I've had women," Dutch muttered.

Wes tilted his head. "Yeah? All along or lately?"

Both, Dutch thought. He'd lined up plenty of justifications for his first affair. He was under continual pressure at work. Lilly was preoccupied establishing her career. Their lovemaking had become predictable and uninspired. Blah, blah, blah.

Lilly had shot down his excuses like ducks in a shooting gallery. He had acknowledged his weaknesses and pledged never to stray again.

But the first affair was followed by a second. And then another, and soon he'd run out of even lame excuses. Now he realized that it wasn't his *last* affair that had spelled the beginning of the end of his marriage. It had been the *first*. He should have known that a woman like Lilly wouldn't tolerate unfaithfulness.

Wes was looking at him expectantly, waiting for an answer. "There for a time, you know, after Amy, when I was in a bad way, I looked for relief anywhere I could find it, with any woman who would say yes, and there were plenty of them. None of them could replace Lilly, though."

"Bullshit. You just haven't shopped long enough. Are you getting laid now on a regular basis?"

"Wes—"

"Okay, okay, don't ask, don't tell. But what woman would look twice at you these days? If you don't mind my saying so, you look like crap."

"That's what I feel like."

"Right, and it shows. In your face, the way you walk. Your butt's dragging, my friend. You look about as much fun as a case of recurring herpes. That approach isn't going to attract the kind of woman you need right now."

"What kind is that?"

"The anti-Lilly. Stay away from brunettes with brown eyes."

"Hazel. Her eyes are really green with brown flecks."

With a look, Wes scorned the detailed correction. "Get yourself a bleached blonde. Short, not tall. Big titties and a butt you can hold on to. A gal that's none too bright, without an opinion of her own except regarding your cock, which she thinks is a fucking magic wand." Wes was pleased with his description of the perfect female; his entire face was involved in his grin.

"Tell you what," he said, "come over to the house later. We'll kill a bottle of Jack while considering your options. I've got a dirty video or two we can watch. That'll change your outlook, or you aren't human. Wha'd'ya say?"

"I'm not supposed to be drinking, remember?"

"Rules don't apply during an ice and snow storm."

"Who said?"

"I did."

It was nearly impossible to resist Wes at his most affable, but Dutch gave it an earnest try. He pushed the Bronco's gearshift into reverse. "I'll have both hands full tonight, and then some."

"Come over," Wes said, wagging a stern finger at Dutch as he backed away. "I'll be looking for you."

Dutch pulled back into traffic and pointed his Bronco toward the single-story brick building one block off Main Street that housed the police department.

Before finally being booted out of the Atlanta PD, Dutch had been required to see the department's psychiatrist twice a week. He'd told Dutch during one of their sessions that he was borderline paranoid. But what was that old joke? Just because you're paranoid doesn't mean everybody still isn't out to get you.

He was beginning to think that everybody in the whole damn world had it in for him today.

When he entered headquarters and saw Mr. and Mrs. Ernie Gunn sitting in the waiting area, that cinched it. He must have a bull's-eye painted on his back. Lilly, Millicent Gunn's folks, the people of Cleary, even the weather had conspired to make this the worst day of his life.

Okay. *One* of the worst.

Mrs. Gunn, a rawboned sparrow of a woman on her best day, looked like she hadn't slept or had a meal since her daughter's disappearance a week ago. Her small head poked from the collar of her quilted coat like that of a turtle from its shell. As Dutch walked in, she looked at him with naked despair.

He wasn't a stranger to that feeling. He empathized, all right. He just didn't want to cope with Mrs. Gunn's desperation tonight, when he was having a hell of a time battling his own.

Mr. Gunn was a rotund man who looked even larger in his redand-black checked wool coat, the kind Dutch associated with lumberjacks. Gunn did, in fact, work with wood. His carpenter's hands, roughened by decades of manual labor and chapped by the cold, looked like sugar-cured hams.

He was threading his hat between his scarred fingers, staring vacantly at the stained brown felt. At an elbow nudge from his wife, he looked up and followed her hollow-eyed gaze toward Dutch.

He stood. "Dutch."

"Ernie. Mrs. Gunn." Dutch nodded at them in turn. "It's getting bad out there. You ought to be at home."

"We just came by to ask was there anything new."

Dutch knew the reason for this ambush. He'd received several telephone messages from them today but hadn't responded. He wished one of his men had warned him that they were in the office so he could have delayed his return until they gave up and went home. But he was here, and so were they. He might just as well get the meeting over with.

"Come on back. We'll talk in my office. Did somebody offer you coffee? It's thick as road tar, but it's usually hot."

"No thanks," Ernie Gunn said, speaking for both of them.

Once they were seated across the desk from him in his private of-

fice, Dutch frowned with regret. "Unfortunately I don't have anything new to report. I had to call off the search today for obvious
reasons," he said, motioning toward the window.

"Before this storm hit, we towed Millicent's car to the county
pound. We'll be gathering all the trace evidence we can from it, but
there are no obvious signs of a struggle."

"Like what?"

Dutch squirmed in his seat and shot a glance at Mrs. Gunn before answering her husband. "Broken fingernails, clumps of hair,
blood."

Mrs. Gunn's head wobbled on her skinny neck.

"That's actually good news," Dutch said. "My men and I are
still trying to reconstruct Millicent's movements her last evening at
work. Talking to everybody who saw her in and out of the store. But
we had to suspend the canvassing this afternoon, again on account
of the storm.

"I haven't heard anything more from Special Agent Wise, either," he said, heading off what he figured would be their next question. "He was called back to Charlotte a few days ago, you know.
He had another case there that needed his attention. Before he left,
though, he told me he was still actively working on Millicent's disappearance and wanted to use the computers there in the bureau office
to check out some things."

"Did he say what?"

Dutch hated admitting to them that Wise—in fact all those FBI
sons of bitches—was stingy with information. They were especially
tight-lipped around cops they considered to be inferior, incompetent
burnouts. Like yours truly, for instance.

"I believe you gave Wise access to Millicent's journal," he said.

"That's right." Mr. Gunn turned to his wife and clasped her
hand for encouragement. "Maybe Mr. Wise will come across something in it that'll lead them to her."

Dutch pounced on that point. "That's a very real possibility.
Millicent might have left of her own accord." He held up his hand to
stave off their protests. "I know that's the first thing I asked you
when you reported her missing. You dismissed it out of hand. But
hear me out."

He divided his best serious-cop look between them. "It's entirely
possible that Millicent needed some time away. Maybe she's not connected to the other missing women at all." He knew the chances of
that were highly remote, but it was something to say that would give
them hope.

"But her car," Mrs. Gunn said in a voice so reedy Dutch could barely hear her. "It was still in the parking lot behind the store. How could she have left without her car?"

"Maybe a friend took her somewhere," Dutch said. "Because of the widespread panic her disappearance has caused, that friend is afraid to come forward now and 'fess up, afraid that he or she will get into trouble along with Millicent for scaring us out of our wits."

Mr. Gunn frowned doubtfully. "We've had our problems with Millicent, same as all parents with teenagers, but I don't think she'd pull a stunt like this to spite us."

Mrs. Gunn said, "She knows we love her, knows how worried we'd be if she just up and ran off." Her voice faltered on the last few words, and she crammed a soggy Kleenex against her lips to contain a sob.

Her misery was painful to witness. Dutch focused on his desk blotter, giving her a moment to compose herself. "Mrs. Gunn, I'm sure that deep down she knows how much you love her," he said kindly. "But I understand Millicent wasn't too keen on that hospital you sent her to last year. You checked her in against her will, isn't that right?"

"She wouldn't go voluntarily," Mr. Gunn said. "We had to do it, or she was gonna die."

"I understand," Dutch said. "And probably, on some level, Millicent understands that, too. But could she be holding a grudge over it?"

The girl had been diagnosed with anorexia, and she was bulimic. To her parents' credit, when her condition became life-threatening, they had borrowed against nearly everything they owned in order to send her to a hospital in Raleigh for treatment and psychiatric counseling.

She was there for three months before being pronounced cured and sent home. The scuttlebutt around town was that she had reverted to her bingeing and purging habits as soon as she was released, afraid any weight gain would keep her off the high school cheerleading squad. Having been a cheerleader since sixth grade, she didn't want to miss out her senior year.

"She was doing good," her father said. "Getting better, healthier every day." He gave Dutch a hard look. "Besides, you know as well as I do that she didn't run away. She was *took*. A blue ribbon was tied to her steering wheel."

"You're not supposed to talk about that," Dutch reminded him.

A blue ribbon had been left at the scene of each woman's supposed abduction, but that fact had been withheld from the media. Because of the ribbon, the unknown kidnapper had been nicknamed Blue.

The cell phone on Dutch's belt vibrated, but he let it go without answering. He was addressing a serious issue here. If word had leaked out about the blue ribbon, you could bet the feebs would think the leak had sprung from Dutch's department. Maybe it had. Of course it had. Nevertheless, he would do all he could to contain it and try to avoid blame.

"Damn near everybody already knows about it, Dutch," Mr. Gunn argued. "You cain't keep something like that a secret, especially since the sumbitch has left that ribbon five times now."

"If everybody knows about it, then more than likely Millicent does. She could have put the ribbon there as a decoy to make us all think—"

"The hell you say," Ernie Gunn retorted angrily. "She wouldn't be so cruel as to scare us like that. No sir, Blue's got Millicent. You know he does. You gotta get out there and find her before he..." His voice cracked. Tears formed in his eyes.

Mrs. Gunn stifled another sob. But it was she who spoke next. Her expression had turned bitter. "You coming from the police department in Atlanta and all, we thought you'd catch this man before he had a chance to get our Millicent or some other girl."

"I worked homicide, not missing persons," Dutch said tightly.

He'd been nothing but sympathetic to these people, doing everything he could to find their daughter, but he was still underappreciated. They were expecting a miracle from him because he'd been a cop in a metropolitan area.

The way he was feeling at that moment, he wondered why in hell he'd taken this job. When the city council—led by Chairman Wes Hamer—offered it to him, he should have told them that he would become their chief of police only after they'd caught their serial kidnapper.

But he had needed the employment. More important, he'd needed to get out of Atlanta, where he'd been humiliated personally by Lilly and professionally by the department. His divorce had become final the same month he'd been fired. Admittedly, there had been a correlation.

When he was at his lowest point, Wes had come to Atlanta to extend him the offer. He'd boosted Dutch's flagging ego by saying that his hometown was in dire need of a badass cop with his experience.

It was the brand of bullshit at which Wes excelled. It was a half-time, locker room pep talk, the kind he delivered to fire up his team. Even recognizing it as such, Dutch had liked hearing it, and before he quite knew how it had come about, they were sealing their deal with a handshake.

He was known and respected here. He knew the people, knew the town and the area like the back of his hand. Moving back to Cleary was like slipping into a comfortable pair of old shoes. But there was a definite drawback. He had walked into a mess left by his predecessor, who'd known nothing about crime solving beyond writing a citation for an expired parking meter.

His first day on the job, the four unsolved missing persons cases had been dumped into Dutch's lap. Now, he had a fifth woman missing. He had a limited budget, a staff that was minimally trained and experienced, and the condescending interference of the FBI, which had become involved because it appeared this was a kidnap situation, and that was a federal offense.

Now, two and a half years after the first girl had vanished off a popular hiking trail, there was still no suspect. It wasn't Dutch's fault, but it had become his baby, and it was turning ugly.

He was in no mood for criticism, even coming from people who were going through a living hell. "I've still got a list of Millicent's acquaintances to talk to," he said. "Soon as the weather clears, I swear to you that I and every man on the force will be out there searching for her." He stood up, signaling an end to the discussion. "Would you like me to get somebody to drive you home in a patrol car? The streets are becoming treacherous."

"No thank you." With admirable dignity, Mr. Gunn assisted his wife from her chair and ushered her toward the front of the building.

"Hard as it is, try to keep a positive outlook," Dutch said as he followed them down the short hallway.

Mr. Gunn merely nodded, put on his hat, and escorted his wife through the door into the wailing wind.

"Chief, we got a—"

"In a minute," Dutch said, holding up his hand to interrupt the officer manning the incoming phone lines, all of which were blinking red. He pulled his cell phone from his belt and checked to see who had called.

Lilly. And she'd left a message. Hastily he punched in the keys to access his voice mail.

"Dutch, I don't know if...get...or not. I...accident coming down the mountain...Ben Tierney...hurt. We're...the cabin. He needs med...attention. If...possibly can...help. As soon...possible."

CHAPTER

6

LILLY HAD KEPT THE VOICE MAIL MESSAGE BRIEF AND TO THE point, in case her cell phone lost its tenuous signal. By the time she stopped talking, the phone was dead again.

"I don't know how much of that went through," she said to Tierney. "Maybe Dutch will get enough of it to figure out the rest." She had pulled the stadium blanket off her head, but it was bunched around her shoulders. The wool was wet, unmelted sleet still clinging to it. She was cold, wet, and uncomfortable.

Of course she couldn't complain of her discomfort. It was mild compared with Tierney's. He was sitting upright but swaying as though at any moment he would topple over. Fresh blood had soaked the black watch cap. Frost clung to his eyebrows and eyelashes, making him look ghostly.

She motioned toward his eyes. "You've got—"

"Frost? You've got it, too. It'll go away in a minute."

She brushed the ice crystals from her eyes and nostrils. "I've never been exposed to the elements like this. Never. Nothing more extreme than getting caught in the rain without an umbrella."

She got up and crossed the room to the wall thermostat. After setting the gauge, she heard the reassuring whir of moving air coming from the vent in the ceiling. "It'll get warm in here soon." As she moved back toward the sofa, she said, "I can't feel my toes or fingers."

He put his middle finger between his teeth and used them to pull off his glove, then motioned her toward the sofa on which he sat. "Sit down and take off your boots."

She sat down next to him and removed her gloves, then worked her feet out of her wet boots. "You knew these weren't going to keep my feet dry."

"It was a safe guess."

Her socks were wet, as were the legs of her slacks from the knees down. Her outfit had been chosen for fashion, not for protection against blizzard conditions.

He patted the top of his thigh. "Put your leg up here."

Lilly hesitated but then settled her leg across his thighs. He removed her thin sock. She didn't recognize her own foot. It was as white as bone, bloodless. He pressed it tightly between his hands and began to chafe it vigorously.

"This will hurt," he warned.

"It does."

"Got to get the circulation going again."

"Have you ever written about surviving a blizzard?"

"Not from firsthand experience. I realize now just how smug and uninformed that article was. Better?"

"My toes are stinging."

"That's good. Blood is returning to them. See? Turning pink already. Give me the other foot."

"What about yours?"

"They can wait. My boots are waterproof."

Lilly switched legs. He peeled off her sock, closed his hands around her foot, then began to massage feeling back into it. But not quite so briskly as before. He lightly pinched each toe. The pad of his thumb followed the curve of her arch, forward toward the ball of her foot, back toward her heel.

Lilly watched his hands. He watched his hands. Neither spoke.

Finally, he sandwiched her foot warmly between his palms. He turned his head, bringing them face-to-face, so close she could see individual eyelashes left wet by melting frost. "Better?" he said.

"Much. Thank you."

"You're welcome."

He made no move to release her foot, leaving it to her to withdraw it from his hands. She lowered her leg off his thighs. Taking a dry pair of socks from her coat pocket allowed her to move away from him without it being awkward.

She watched him from the corner of her eye as he bent down and untied the laces of his hiking boots. But even when they'd been loosed, he remained bent forward. He propped his elbow on his knee and rested his head in his hand.

"Are you going to be sick again?" she asked.

"I don't think so. Just a wave of dizziness. It'll pass."

"You probably have a concussion."

"No probably about it."

"I'm so sorry."

Her apologetic tone brought his head up. "Why should you be sorry? If it hadn't been for me, you wouldn't have crashed your car."

"I couldn't see beyond my hood. Suddenly you were just there, right in front of me, and—"

"It was as much my fault as yours. I saw your headlights coming around the curve. I didn't want to miss my last hope of getting a ride into town, so I started running full out. Gained too much momentum coming down the incline. Next thing I know, I'm not *at* the road, I'm *in* the road."

"It was stupid of me to brake so hard."

"Reflex," he said with a dismissive shrug. "Anyway, don't blame yourself. Maybe I was put in your path for a reason."

"You probably saved my life. If I'd been alone, I would have stayed in the car and been frozen by morning."

"Then it's lucky I came along."

"What were you doing up here on the peak on foot?"

He bent down and began tugging off his right boot. "Sightseeing."

"Today?"

"I was hiking along the summit."

"With a storm bearing down?"

"The mountains have a different kind of allure during the winter months." He took off his second boot and tossed it aside, then began to massage his toes. "When I got ready to head back into town, my car wouldn't start. Dead battery, I guess. Anyway, rather than follow the road and all those switchbacks, I decided to take a shortcut through the woods."

"In the dark?"

"In hindsight, it wasn't the smartest of decisions. But I would have been okay if the storm hadn't moved in so quickly."

"I miscalculated, too. Stupidly I fell asleep and..." She stopped when she noticed that he was blinking rapidly as though to ward off vertigo. "Are you about to pass out?"

"Maybe. This damn dizziness."

She stood up and placed her hands on his shoulders. "Lean back, lay your head down."

"If I pass out, wake me up. I shouldn't go to sleep with a concussion."

"I promise to keep you awake. Lie back."

Still he resisted. "I'll get blood on your couch."

"I hardly think that matters, Mr. Tierney. Besides, it's not my couch anymore."

He relented and let her press him back until his head was resting on the cushion.

"Okay now?"

"Better, thanks."

She went to the other sofa and, being chilled in spite of her coat, wrapped herself in the knitted throw.

Although Tierney kept his eyes closed, he said, "Not your couch anymore? I'd heard this place was on the market. It sold?"

"The closing was yesterday."

"Who bought it? Someone in town?"

"No, a retired couple from Jacksonville, Florida, who want to spend their summers here."

He opened his eyes and looked around the main room. The cabin had every modern convenience, but it had been built and decorated to look rustic, in keeping with the mountain setting. The furnishings were oversize and homey, designed for comfort rather than show.

"They bought themselves a great second home."

"Yes, they did." She glanced around the room, gauging the sturdiness of its construction. "We'll be all right here, won't we? For the duration of the storm, I mean."

"What's your water source?"

"A reservoir on a plateau about midway between here and town."

"Hopefully the pipes aren't frozen yet."

She got up and rounded the bar that separated the main room from the kitchen. "We have water," she announced as it sputtered from the faucet.

"Got anything to collect it in?"

"Kitchen utensils were included in the sale of the cabin."

"Start filling every pan and pot available. We need to collect all the drinking water we can before the pipes freeze. Lucky you had that food with you. We won't starve."

She found a roasting pan she had used one Thanksgiving and put it in the sink beneath the faucet. As she came back into the main room, she motioned toward the hearth. "There's firewood stacked on the porch."

"Yeah, but I noticed when we came in that most of it is wet, and the logs haven't been split."

"Very observant of you."

"I have a knack for taking in details quickly."

"So I've noticed."

"When?"

"When?" she repeated.

"When did you notice my knack for taking in details? Tonight, or during that day last summer?"

"Both, I suppose. At least on a subconscious level." She wondered what details about her his keen blue eyes had taken in quickly, both tonight and last June.

"Why did you call him?"

His blunt question seemed out of context. But it wasn't really. She glanced toward her cell phone, which she'd laid on the coffee table, within easy reach should it ring.

Before giving her time to answer, he said, "I heard you got divorced."

"We did."

"So why did you call him tonight?"

"Dutch is Cleary's chief of police now."

"I heard that, too."

"He'll be handling emergencies caused by the storm. He has the authority to get help to us if he can."

He mulled that over for several seconds, then glanced toward the door. "Nobody's coming up here tonight. You realize that?"

She nodded. "I think that for tonight we're on our own." In reaction to her sudden nervousness, she shoved her hands deep into her coat pockets. "Oh, the first-aid kit," she exclaimed. "I'd almost forgotten it."

She pulled it from her pocket. It was a small white plastic box with a red cross on the lid, something a conscientious mom would pop into her tote bag before an excursion to the playground. She opened it and checked the contents.

"There's not much here, I'm afraid. But that head wound should at least be cleaned with one of these disinfectant pads." She looked at him dubiously. "Do you want to remove your cap yourself, or do you trust me to do it? Either way, Mr. Tierney, I'm afraid it's going to be painful."

"Lilly?"

"Hmm?"

"Why have I suddenly become *Mr.* Tierney?"

She shrugged uneasily. "It seems, I don't know, more appropriate somehow. Under the circumstances."

"The circumstances being that we're stranded together for an indefinite period of time and dependent on each other for our survival?"

"Which is rather awkward."

"Why awkward?"

She frowned at him for being obtuse. "Because, except for that day on the river, you and I are strangers."

When he stood up, he swayed noticeably. But he was steady enough on his feet as he walked toward her slowly. "If you think we're strangers, then you're not remembering the day we met the same way I remember it."

She took a step back and shook her head, either to clear it of memories of a sun-sparkled day or to stave him off. She wasn't sure which. "Look, Tierney—"

"Praise be." He flashed the engaging smile she remembered with unsettling detail. "I'm back to being Tierney."

"Tierney?" Special Agent in Charge Kent Begley repeated the name.

"That's right, sir. T-i-e-r-n-e-y. First name Ben," replied Special Agent Charlie Wise.

Everyone in the FBI office in Charlotte called Charlie Wise by his nickname, Hoot. Someone—no one could remember specifically who—had linked his last name to a hoot owl. The moniker was doubly apropos because he wore tortoiseshell eyeglasses with large, round lenses, making him resemble an owl.

Begley was peering through those lenses now, directly into Hoot's unblinking eyes, giving him one of the incisive stares that his subordinates called nutcrackers. Behind Begley's back, of course.

Begley was a staunch born-again believer, always having at hand the large Bible with his name engraved in gold lettering on the black leather binding. It had the worn look of being read frequently. He quoted from it often.

One of the notches on Begley's rigid moral yardstick was the usage of foul or suggestive language. He had no tolerance for it and didn't allow it from the men and women serving under him. He used it himself only when he felt it was absolutely necessary to getting his point across—which was about every ten seconds.

Hoot was a confident, capable, and unflappable agent. He quailed less than most beneath Begley's nutcrackers. No one knew his accuracy on the firing range, but indisputably he was a quick draw on a computer. He excelled at research, and there his talent was unsurpassed. If Hoot couldn't uproot needed data, the data didn't exist.

He met his boss's hard stare with aplomb. "I've been looking at Ben Tierney for several days now, sir, and some interesting facts have emerged."

"I'm listening."

Begley motioned him into the chair facing his desk, but since he was still giving Hoot the look that said the agent better not be wasting his time, Hoot began talking even before he sat down.

"Over the past couple of years, Ben Tierney has been drifting in and out of the area, specifically Cleary, every few months. He stays a few weeks, sometimes a month, then moves on."

"Lots of weekenders up there. Vacationers," Begley said.

"I'm aware of that, sir."

"So what makes him special? Do his visits to Cleary coincide with the disappearances?"

"Yes, sir, they do. He stays in a lodge about two miles from the center of town. Private cabins with kitchenettes, decks overlooking a waterfall, and private lake."

Begley nodded. He knew the type of place Hoot described. There were hundreds of them in that area of the state, where tourism was a main source of revenue for the small mountain communities. Outdoor activities like fishing, hiking, camping, and kayaking were huge draws.

"According to the lodge's manager, Mr. Tierney always reserves the largest cabin. Number eight. Two bedrooms, living area with a fireplace. And this I think is significant. He does his own cleaning. No matter how long he stays, he picks up clean linens at the registration desk twice a week and declines the daily housekeeping service."

"Hardly a smoking gun, Hoot."

"But odd."

Begley left his desk and moved to the easel holding the corkboard that Hoot had brought into the office in advance of their meeting. On it were tacked photographs of the five women missing from the Cleary area, along with compiled data on each: DOB, driver's license and Social Security numbers, date of disappearance, physical description, family members and close friends, interests and hobbies, religious affiliations, level of education, bank accounts or other sources of funds—none of which had been tapped—location of where she was last seen, and anything else that might help locate the woman or point to the unknown subject who had abducted her, who in this case had been nicknamed Blue.

"Does this Tierney fit the profile of a serial sex offender?"

Although it hadn't been established that sexual offenses had been committed against the missing women, it was assumed that was the reason for their abductions. "Yes, sir. He's white. More or less a loner. Married once, briefly. Currently divorced."

"Ex-wife?"

"Remarried."

"What do you know about the marriage and divorce?"

"Perkins is working on that angle for me. He's digging."

"Go on."

"He's forty-one. He has a U.S. passport and a Virginia driver's license. Six feet three inches tall. Weight, one eighty-five. At least that's what he weighed when he renewed his license two years ago. Hair, brown. Eyes, blue. No facial hair, tattoos, or visible scars.

"The manager of the lodge says he's polite and undemanding, and he tips the housekeeper even though she doesn't clean for him. He has one major credit card. Uses it for nearly everything and pays the total balance each month. No outstanding debts. No hassles with the IRS. He drives a late-model Jeep Cherokee. Registration and insurance are current."

"Sounds like a solid citizen, a prince among men."

Despite his remark, Begley knew that one's appearance and demeanor could camouflage a criminal, psychotic, or sociopathic mind. During his long career, he'd run across some very twisted folks.

There was the woman who was widowed six times before anyone thought to investigate the bizarre coincidence. Her excuse for killing her husbands, each in a distinctive and inventive way, was that she just adored arranging funerals. She was as plump as a partridge and as pretty as a peach. No one would have thought her capable of killing a housefly.

Then there was the guy who played Santa Claus at the neighborhood mall every Christmas. Jolly and kind, beloved by all who knew him, he would sit children on his knee and listen to what they wanted for Christmas, pass out candy canes, remind them not to be naughty, and then select one to violate sexually before dismembering the body and placing the various parts in Christmas stockings, which he hung from his mantel. Ho, ho, ho.

Nothing surprised Begley anymore, especially not a woman snatcher who was polite, tipped generously, and paid his bills on time.

"What about friends?" Begley asked. "Anyone ever join him in that cabin he rents?"

"No one. 'He keeps to hisself,' to quote Mr. Gus Elmer, the owner of the lodge."

Begley stared at a picture of Laureen Elliott, the third woman to disappear. She had a bad perm and a sweet smile. Her car had been found at a barbecue restaurant between the clinic where she worked as a nurse and her home. She didn't pick up her phone-in order of ribs.

"Where does Ben Tierney call home?"

"He gets his mail at a condo he owns in Virginia, just outside D.C.," Hoot replied. "But he's rarely there. Travels extensively."

Begley came around. "Do we know why?"

Hoot shuffled the stack of printed materials he'd brought in with him and came up with a popular magazine for outdoor sports and activities. "Page thirty-seven."

Begley reached for the magazine and thumbed to the page, finding there a story about rafting the Colorado River.

"He's a freelance writer," Hoot explained. "Goes on thrill-seeking adventures and vacations, writes about them, sells the articles to magazines that cater to particular interests. Mountain climbing, hiking, hang gliding, scuba diving, dogsledding. You name it, he's done it."

Accompanying the article was a color photograph of two men standing on the rocky shoal of a river, white water in the background. One of the men was bearded, stocky, and a lot shorter than six feet three. He was identified beneath the photo as the guide for the trip.

The other smiling rafter fit Tierney's description. Wide, white smile in a lean, tanned face. Windblown hair. Calves as hard as baseballs. Sculpted arms. Washboard abs. Michelangelo's *David* in a pair of cargo shorts.

Begley scowled down at Hoot. "Are you fucking kidding me? He's the kind of man women throw their panties at."

"Ted Bundy was a reputed ladies' man, sir."

Begley snorted, conceding the point. "What about women?"

"Relationships?"

"Or whatever."

"His neighbors in Virginia barely know him because he's seldom there, but unanimously they said they'd never seen a woman at his place."

"A good-looking bachelor like him?" Begley asked.

Hoot shrugged. "He could be gay, I guess, but there's no indication he is."

"He could have a ladylove stashed away somewhere else," Begley ventured.

"If he does, we've found no evidence of one. No long-term relationship. Or short term for that matter. But, as I said, he travels a lot. Maybe he, you know, catches, uh, romance when and where he can."

Begley ruminated on that. Serial rapists or women killers rarely cultivated or maintained healthy, lasting relationships. Indeed, they typically had an intense dislike for women. Depending on the psyche of the offender, the hostility could be latent and well concealed, or openly expressed. Either way, it was usually manifested in violent acts against the opposite sex.

"Okay, you've aroused my interest," Begley said, "but I hope you have better than this."

Hoot shuffled through more paper. Finding the sheet he was looking for, he said, "This is a quote from Millicent Gunn's diary. 'Saw B.T. again today. Second time in past three days. He's so freaking cool. Always very nice to me.' The *very* is underlined, sir.

" 'I think he likes me. Takes time to talk to me even though I'm fat.' That entry was dated three days before her disappearance. Her parents claim none of her friends are named B.T. They don't know anyone who goes by that name or has those initials."

"Fat?"

"Actually, Miss Gunn is anorexic and bulimic."

Begley nodded, having read on her stat sheet about her hospitalization last year. "Where did she see this B.T. twice in three days?"

"That's what put me onto Ben Tierney. I went digging to see who B.T. might be. The first logical place to look was the high school. I came up empty. All the B.T.s were girls.

"Second logical place would be where Millicent works. She clerks part-time in her uncle's store. In addition to hardware and gardening equipment, he sells..." Hoot paused and pushed up his eyeglasses. "Sporting goods, clothing, and equipment."

Begley turned back to the corkboard, studying the photographs of the five apparent victims as he thoughtfully tugged on his lower lip. He focused on the first. "Was he in Cleary at the time Torrie Lambert disappeared off that hiking trail?"

"I don't know," Hoot admitted. "So far I have no record of his being there on the actual day she disappeared. But he definitely was in town soon thereafter. The lodge's registry bears that out."

"Maybe after Torrie Lambert he thought the pickins in the area were good, so he came back, and has kept coming back ever since."

"My thinking exactly, sir."

"He travels. Have you researched similar missing persons cases near any of his destinations?"

"Perkins is working on that, too."

"ViCAP, NCIC?" Begley asked, referring to the information networks widely used by law enforcement agencies.

"Nothing." After a short pause, Hoot continued. "But we don't yet know all the places he's been. We're having to review his credit card statements to see where his travels have taken him over the last several years, then cross-checking our unsolved cases in those specific areas. It's tedious and time-consuming."

"Was he in the vicinity of Cleary when Millicent Gunn disappeared?"

"He checked into the lodge a week before her parents reported her missing."

"What do the boys in the RA out there think about him?"

"I haven't shared this information with them, sir."

Begley came around. "Then let me rephrase. What do they think about you working this case?"

There was a resident agency nearer to Cleary than Charlotte. Hoot had been transferred from it to the field office in Charlotte thirteen months ago, but his investigation into Torrie Lambert's disappearance and assumed kidnapping had begun in the RA that covered that jurisdiction. "It's been my case from the start, sir. The agents in that office recognize it as such and frankly are glad to let me have it. I'd like to see it through, sir."

Twenty seconds of silence ticked by as Begley continued to stare at the photographs on the corkboard. Suddenly he made an abrupt about-face. "Hoot, I think it's worth our time to make a trip up there to talk to Mr. Tierney."

Hoot was stunned. "You and me? Sir."

"I haven't done fieldwork in a long time." Begley glanced around the walls of his office as though they'd suddenly become constricting. "It'll be good for me."

Having made the decision, he began immediately to plan their course of action. "I don't want it to get around Cleary that we're looking at Ben Tierney. How did you explain your interest to that... What's his name, the owner of the lodge?"

"Gus Elmer. I told him that Tierney is a contender for a humanitarian award at his alma mater and that all aspects of his life are being reviewed."

"And he bought that?"

"He's got three teeth, sir."

Begley nodded absently, his mind already racing ahead. "For as long as possible, let's keep the local PD in the dark, too. I don't want to put them on alert and give them a chance to fuck it up if this guy's Blue. What's the asshole's name?"

"Tierney."

"Not that asshole," he said impatiently, "the police chief."

"Burton. Dutch Burton."

"Right. Isn't there a story there?"

"He was formerly with Atlanta PD," Hoot explained. "Outstanding homicide detective. Commendations. Flawless record. Then he went round the bend, started drinking heavily."

"How come?"

"Family problems, I believe."

"Whatever, he got his ass fired. I remember now." Begley had been gathering up personal items, including his cell phone, the framed photograph of his wife of thirty years and their three children, and his Bible. He yanked his overcoat from the coat tree and pulled it on.

"Bring all that with you." He indicated the case files stacked in Hoot's lap. "I'll read them on the way while you drive."

Hoot stood up and cast a wary glance out the window, where darkness was closing in over the city. "You mean you want...We're going tonight?"

"We're going right fucking now."

"But, sir, the forecast."

He got the undiluted, full-out nutcracker treatment.

He didn't cringe, but he cleared his throat before continuing. "They're predicting record freezing temperatures, ice and snow and blizzard conditions, especially in that part of the state. We'd be driving straight into it."

Begley pointed to the corkboard. "Do you want to venture a guess as to what happened to those ladies, Hoot? What sort of sicko torture do you think this jerk-off puts them through before he kills them?

"I know, I know, we don't know with absolute certainty that they're dead, because no bodies have turned up yet. I'd like to think we'll find them alive and intact, but I've had thirty-plus years of dealing with this kind of shit.

"Let's face it, Hoot, the odds are good that we're going to locate bones, and that'll be all that's left of those ladies who had futures, dreams, and people who loved them. Now, can you look at the faces in those pictures and still whine about a little bad weather? Hmm?"

"No, sir."

Begley turned and strode out the door, saying as he went, "I didn't think so."

Tierney had pulled the watch cap from his head in one swift motion. Lilly had been standing by with a towel. That had been fifteen minutes ago, and his scalp wound was still bleeding. The towel was almost saturated. "Scalp wounds always bleed a lot," he said when she expressed concern. "All those capillaries up there."

"Here's a fresh towel." As she passed it to him, she reached for the bloody one.

He withheld it. "You don't have to touch that. I'll take it into the bathroom. I assume it's through there?" He indicated the door leading into the bedroom.

"To your right."

"I'm going to wash the blood out of my hair. Maybe the cold water will help stanch the bleeding." As unsteady as a drunk, he walked toward the bedroom, where he braced himself against the doorjamb and turned back. "Keep filling up every available container with water. Pipes will freeze soon. We'll need drinking water."

He disappeared into the room, and the light in there came on. He'd left a smear of blood on the doorjamb, she noticed.

When he'd said, "Praise be. I'm back to being Tierney," he'd smiled in the relaxed, easy fashion that she remembered from last summer. It had dispelled her rash of awkwardness, which seemed rather silly and juvenile now.

She didn't know much about him, but he wasn't a total stranger. She'd spent an entire day with him. They'd talked. They'd laughed. Since then she'd read his articles and had learned that he was a well-respected writer who was published often.

So why had she acted like such a dolt?

Well, for one thing, this was a bizarre situation. Misadventures such as this happened to other people. One heard about remarkable survival experiences in the media. They did not happen to Lilly Martin.

Yet here she was, scrounging through a kitchen that no longer belonged to her, searching for containers to fill with life-sustaining water for her and a man she barely knew, with whom she could be marooned in very close quarters for several days.

And, she had to admit that, if Tierney weren't quite so attractive, so vitally masculine, she probably wouldn't be this jittery about being isolated with him. If they hadn't shared that day on the river last summer, being confined in close quarters might actually be less awkward.

"Water still running?"

She jumped slightly when he spoke from close behind her. "Yes, luckily." She turned away from the sink, where she was filling another cook pan with water. Tierney was holding a towel against the back of his head. His hair was wet. "How is it?"

"It hurt while the water was running over it, partially because the water is so cold. But I think the cold actually numbed it." He removed the towel. It was stained with fresh blood, but the amount had decreased substantially. "Helped the bleeding, too. Mind taking a look?"

"I was about to insist."

He straddled one of the bar stools, facing its back. She set the first-aid kit on the bar, then moved behind him and, after a moment's hesitation, gently parted his hair just below the crown of his head.

"Well?" he asked.

The gash was wide, long, and deep. To her inexpert eyes, it looked bad. She exhaled through her lips.

He gave a short laugh. "That bad?"

"You've seen overripe watermelons whose rinds have split?"

"Ouch."

"There's a lot of swelling around it."

"Yeah, I felt that as I was washing it."

"I'd say you could use a dozen stitches, at least." He'd draped the blood-spotted towel around his neck. She took a corner of it and gingerly dabbed at the wound. "The good news is, it's not pumping blood any longer. Just leaking it."

There were only four disinfectant pads in the kit, each sealed in its own envelope. Lilly tore open one of them and withdrew a square of gauze that was soaked with an antibacterial solution. It wasn't much larger than a saltine cracker. However, if the smell indicated the strength of the solution, it was going to sting. The thought of applying it to the raw wound caused her stomach to somersault.

"Brace yourself," she said, unsure whether she was cautioning Tierney or herself.

He gripped the back of the stool and propped his chin on the backs of his hands. "Ready."

But the instant she touched the gauze to the open flesh, he flinched. His breath hissed on a quick intake. In the hope of distracting him, she began talking. "I'm surprised you weren't carrying a

first-aid kit in your backpack. Being the seasoned hiker you are."
He'd dropped the backpack on the floor when they arrived at the
cabin and hadn't touched it since except to push it beneath an end
table out of their way.

"Gross oversight. I won't be without one next time."

"Anything else in your backpack?" she asked.

"Like what?"

"Something useful?"

"No, I was traveling light today. Energy bar. Bottle of water.
Both consumed."

"Then why did you bring it from the car?"

"Sorry?"

"Your backpack. If there's nothing useful in it, why did you
bring it along?"

"God forbid you think I'm a sissy," he said, "but are you about
finished? That's burning like hellfire."

She blew gently on the wound, then leaned away from him and
surveyed it. "I covered all of it with the antiseptic. It looks very angry."

"It feels angry." He picked up the first-aid kit and inspected the
meager contents. "I'll toss you for the aspirin tablets."

"They're yours."

"Thanks. Do you have one of those little sewing kits? Like a
matchbook. For emergencies like a button falling off."

Her stomach clenched. "Please don't ask me to do that."

"What?"

"Sew up the wound."

"You wouldn't?"

"I don't have a sewing kit."

"Lucky you. Manicure scissors?"

"Those I have."

While he swallowed the two aspirin tablets, she took her makeup
bag from her purse and produced a small pair of scissors.

"Good," he said. "By the way, that pan is full."

She exchanged the cook pan beneath the faucet with a plastic
pitcher. He peeled the wrapper off a Band-Aid. "We'll cut strips of
the sticky part. Lay them like cross ties across the gash. It's not
stitches, but maybe that'll help close it."

His fingers wouldn't fit into the holes of the tiny scissors. "Here,
let me." She took the Band-Aid and scissors from him, cut strips of
the adhesive, and applied them to the wound as he instructed. "It's
barely bleeding at all now," she said when she was finished.

"Cover it with one of those bandages."

As gently as possible she patted one of the sterile gauze bandages from the kit into place over the wound. "It's going to pull your hair when we take it off."

"I'll live." Then in an undertone, he added, "I hope."

CHAPTER

7

Startled by his grim expression, she asked, "Why do you say that? Do you have injuries I don't know about?"

"Maybe. The whole left side of my body is bruised and sore. Ribs feel like someone's tried to pry them apart with a crowbar, but I don't think I have any broken bones."

"That's good, isn't it?"

"Yeah, but something on the inside may be busted. Kidney, liver, spleen."

"Wouldn't you know if you were bleeding internally?"

"You'd think. But I've heard that people can die of internal hemorrhage before it's discovered. If my belly starts to balloon, that'll be a good indicator that it's filling up with blood."

"Have you noticed any distention, tenderness?"

"No."

She pulled her lower lip through her teeth. "If there's a chance you're bleeding, should you have taken the aspirin?"

"The way my head feels, it was worth the risk." He eased himself off the bar stool, went to the kitchen sink, and removed the pitcher that had been filling. "Assuming I live, we're going to need drinking water for an indefinite period of time. What other containers have you got?"

Together they searched the cabin and began filling anything that would hold water. "Too bad you only have a shower," he said. "We could use a bathtub."

Once they'd filled all the pots and pans, even the mop bucket, they began thinking of other matters. "What's the source of your heat, electricity?" he asked.

"Propane. There's an underground tank."

"When was it last filled?"

"As far as I know, last winter. Because I was selling the place, I didn't order it to be refilled this past fall. To my knowledge Dutch didn't either."

"So it could run out."

"I suppose. Depending on how much Dutch used it when I wasn't here."

"How long since you were here?"

"Until this week, it had been months."

"Did you stay up here this week?"

"Yes."

"Did Dutch?"

Suddenly the emphasis of their conversation had shifted away from the amount of propane remaining in the tank.

"That's an inappropriate question, Tierney."

"Meaning he did."

"In fact he didn't," she said testily.

He held her gaze for several beats, then turned away and walked to the thermostat on the wall. "I'm going to set the temperature lower so the propane will last longer. Okay?"

"Fine."

"If the tank empties, we'll have to rely strictly on the fireplace. I hope you've got more wood than what's on the porch."

She disliked his implication that she was still sleeping with her ex-husband, but cooped up together as they were, there was no room for anger. She let the matter drop. "More firewood is stored in a shed," she replied, motioning in the general direction. "There's a path to it through—"

"I know where it is."

"The shed? You do?" The small structure had been built of weathered wood and positioned so it wouldn't be visible from either the road or the cabin. It blended seamlessly into the environment and was virtually invisible. Or so she had thought.

"How did you know about this cabin, Tierney?"

"You told me about it last summer."

She remembered specifically what she had told him because, since then, she'd replayed their conversations in her head a thousand times. "I told you I had a cabin in the area. I didn't say where it was."

"No, you didn't."

"So, tonight, how did you know?"

He gave her a long look, then said, "I've hiked all over this mountain. One day I came upon the cabin, and the shed, without realizing I was on private property. I suppose I was trespassing, but not on purpose. I saw the For Sale sign and, because I liked the look of the place, contacted the realtor. I learned that it belonged to you and your husband, but because of a pending divorce, you were selling." He raised his arms at his sides. "That's how I came to know the location of your cabin."

He gave her a look that practically dared her to question him further. Then he said, "Now, how much wood is in the shed? A cord?"

Although she wasn't quite ready to relinquish the matter of his knowing so much about her, she didn't see any advantage to pursuing it and creating ill will. "No way near a cord," she replied.

"Well, hopefully we'll be rescued before we have to start breaking up the furniture and burning it."

"How long do you think that might be? Until we're rescued, I mean."

He sat down on the sofa, where a towel now covered the bloodstain on the back cushion, and laid his head against it. "Probably not tomorrow. Possibly the day after. Depending on the storm and the amount of ice accumulation, it could be longer."

She recalled the winter before last, when an ice storm had closed the mountain road for days. People in remote areas were stranded without electricity because of downed lines. In some cases, it had taken weeks for the service to be restored and the communities returned to normal. The storm raging outside now was predicted to be much worse and longer lasting than that one.

Lilly sat down on the opposite sofa and pulled the throw over her legs and feet, very glad that Tierney had thought of the extra socks. She'd hung the wet ones over the back of one of the barstools to dry. The legs of her trousers were still damp, but she could live with that so long as her feet were dry and reasonably warm.

"What did you set the thermostat on?" she asked.

"Sixty."

"Hmm."

"I realize it's not exactly toasty," he said. "You should put on that other turtleneck for extra insulation. Keep in your body heat."

She nodded but made no move to get up. "What do you think the outdoor temperature is?"

"Windchill is subzero," he replied without hesitation.

"Then I'm not going to complain about sixty." She glanced at the fireplace. "A fire would be nice though."

"It would. But I honestly think—"

"No, no, you're right about conserving the fuel. I was just wishing out loud. I love the ambience of a fireplace."

"Me too."

"Makes any room seem cozier."

"Yeah."

After a moment, she asked, "Are you hungry?"

"My stomach's still queasy. But if you're hungry, don't be polite. Eat something."

"I'm not really hungry either."

"Don't think you have to sit up with me," he said. "I can keep myself awake. If you're tired or sleepy—"

"I'm really not."

No way would she go to sleep and risk his slipping into unconsciousness and possibly a coma. He needed to stay awake for a few more hours before it would be safe for him to sleep. Besides, her nap that afternoon had been long enough to keep her from being sleepy now.

She'd been talking to fill the silence. Now that they'd stopped, the only sounds were those of the wind, tree limbs knocking against the eaves, and the sleet pattering on the roof. Their eyes drifted around the room, which had been stripped of everything except the furniture. There was little to look at, so eventually they looked at each other. When their gazes connected, the emptiness of the room closed in around them, creating a taut intimacy.

Lilly was the first to look away. She noticed her cell phone lying on the coffee table between them. "If Dutch got my message, he'll be working out a way to get someone up here."

"I shouldn't have said what I did. About the two of you staying here together."

With a gesture she indicated that an apology was unnecessary.

"I'd just like to know how involved you still are with him, Lilly."

She thought of contesting his need to know but then decided to lay the issue to rest once and for all. Apparently he was going to continue bringing it up until she did. "I called Dutch tonight because he's the chief of police, not because of any lingering personal involvement. Our marriage is over, but he wouldn't leave me to freeze to death any more than I would turn my back on him in a life-or-death situation. If it's at all possible, he'll rescue us."

"He'd rush to your rescue," Tierney said. "I doubt he'd rush to mine."

"Why do you think that?"

"He doesn't like me."

"Again, what makes you think so?"

"It's nothing he's done, really. More what he hasn't. I've bumped into him on occasion. He's never gone out of his way to introduce himself."

"Maybe it just hasn't been convenient."

"No, I think there's more to it than that."

"Like what?"

"For one thing, I'm an outsider, immediately distrusted because my great-great-great-grandparents didn't hail from these mountains."

She smiled, acknowledging that he'd accurately described the prevailing regional attitude. "The people around here can be clannish."

"I'm a visitor, but I've been coming here often enough that a lot of people at least know my name and speak when they see me. Welcome me back. That kind of thing. But whenever I go to the soda fountain at Ritt's for my morning coffee, I still sit alone at the counter. I've never been invited to join the good ol' boys' club that fills up the booths every morning. Dutch Burton, Wes Hamer, a few others, all who grew up here. That's a closed clique. Not that I want to be included, but they're not even friendly enough to say hello."

"Then accept my apology for them."

"Trust me, it's not that important. But I wondered," he began, then hesitated.

"What?"

"I wondered if . . . if the reason for him avoiding me was that you might have mentioned me to him."

She ducked her head. "No. That is, not until yesterday."

He said nothing in response to that, so after a long moment, it was left to her to fill the ponderous silence. "I was surprised to see you in town. Haven't you run out of things around here to write about?"

"It's not subject matter that's bringing me back, Lilly."

The bait he'd thrown out was dangerous but enticing and impossible to resist. She raised her head and looked across at him. He said, "I sold an article about our day on the river."

"I know. I read it."

"Yeah?" he asked, obviously pleased.

She nodded. "That water sports magazine and mine have the same publisher, so I receive complimentary copies. I was thumbing through an issue and spotted your byline." Actually, she'd been perusing that and similar magazines for months, wondering if he'd written and sold an article about the kayaking excursion.

"It was great writing, Tierney."

"Thanks."

"Truthfully. Your descriptions were vivid. They captured the excitement we experienced. Catchy title, too. 'The Tempestuous French Broad.' "

He grinned. "I thought that would grab those not in the know. You had to read the article to learn that's the name of the river."

"It was a good piece."

"It was a good day," he came back in a low and stirring voice.

Early June, last summer. They'd been two of a dozen people who'd signed up for a daylong white-water kayaking excursion. They'd met on the bus that transported the group several miles upriver, where they put in for the wild ride through several Class Three and Class Four rapids.

Equally skilled, they'd fallen into a natural comradery, especially after discovering that their careers were, as Tierney had put it, "kissing cousins." He was a freelance writer who sold articles to magazines; she was a magazine editor.

When the group put ashore for lunch, they separated from the others and sat together on a large boulder that was cantilevered over the rushing water below.

"You're editor in chief?" he exclaimed when she told him the position she held.

"Going on three years now."

"I'm impressed. That's a slick publication."

"It started out as a magazine for the southern woman. We now have national distribution, and the numbers are increasing with each issue."

Smart contained features on home decorating, fashion, food, and travel. Its target reader was the woman who combined homemaking with a career, who wanted it all and made it happen. An article might be about how to convert carry-out dinners into gourmet delights simply by adding a few spices from the kitchen pantry and serving the meal on good china, or a preview of shoe trends for the upcoming season.

"We certainly don't exclude stay-at-home moms from our readership," she'd explained, "but our focus is on the woman who wants to succeed in the office, plan the perfect family vacation, and host fabulous dinner parties she can throw together at a moment's notice."

"Is that possible?"

"You'll find out how in the July issue."

Laughing, he had toasted her success with his water bottle. The sun was warm and the conversation relaxed. They developed an easy I-like-the-looks-and-sound-of-you rapport. As much fun as they'd had in the river before lunch, they were a bit reluctant to resume when the guide announced an end to the lunch break.

Throughout the afternoon, they chatted when they could, although they were forced to concentrate on the challenge of the sport. But they were constantly aware of each other. They communicated with hand signals and smiles. Their admiration for each other's skill allowed for good-natured teasing when one or the other went belly-up.

He shared his sunblock cream when she discovered she'd come away without any. But he also shared it with two college girls who flirted with him shamelessly and strove all day to attract his attention.

When they put in at the area where they'd left their cars that morning, Lilly went her way, he went his. But after stowing his gear in his Cherokee, he jogged over to her. "Where are you staying?"

"Cleary. I'm there most weekends during the summer. I have a cabin."

"Nice."

"Yes, it is."

The college girls pulled their open Jeep even with them. "See ya later, Tierney," the driver said.

"Uh, yeah, sure."

"You remember the name of the place?" the other asked from the passenger seat.

He tapped his forehead. "Committed to memory."

Ignoring Lilly but grinning conspiratorially at him, they drove away, raising a cloud of dust.

As he waved them off, he shook his head. "Party girls, begging for trouble." Then he turned back to Lilly and smiled. "It hurts my manly pride to admit it, but you bested me with your rodeo moves coming through that last Class Four."

She gave a mock curtsy. "Thank you very much. Coming from someone as skilled as you, that's a real compliment."

"The least I can do is buy you a congratulatory drink. Can we meet somewhere?"

She nodded toward the wake of dust created by the girls' Jeep. "I thought you had plans."

"I do," he said. "I plan to see you."

Her smile faltered. She got busy searching for her car keys. "Thank you, Tierney, but I have to decline."

"Oh. What about tomorrow night?"

"I'm sorry, I can't." She took a deep breath and looked up at him. "My husband and I have a dinner engagement."

His smile didn't falter, it collapsed. "You're married." He said it as a statement, not a question.

She nodded.

He glanced down at her empty ring finger. His expression, a combination of bewilderment and disappointment, spoke volumes.

And then for the longest time they simply stared at each other bleakly, saying nothing, communicating only with their eyes while the fading sun coming through the trees cast dappled shadows over their unhappy faces.

Eventually, she extended her right hand. "It was wonderful meeting you, Tierney."

He shook her hand. "Same here."

"I'll watch for your articles," she said as she got into her car.

"Lilly—"

"Good-bye. Be safe." She closed her car door quickly and drove away before he could say anything more.

That was the last time they'd had any contact until yesterday, when she spotted him across Main Street in downtown Cleary. Dutch bumped into her as she came to a sudden halt on the sidewalk. "What are you looking at?"

Tierney was just about to climb into his Cherokee when he happened to glance her way. He did a double take. They made eye contact, and it held.

"Ben Tierney," she said, replying absently to Dutch's question. Or perhaps she was just speaking aloud a name that for the past eight months had never been far from her mind.

Dutch followed her gaze across opposing lanes of traffic and the median in between. Tierney was still standing there, half in, half out of his car, looking at her as though waiting for a signal as to what he should do.

"You know that guy?" Dutch asked.

"I met him last summer. Remember the day I kayaked the French Broad? He was in the group."

Dutch pushed open the door to the attorney's office where they had an appointment to sign the closing papers on the sale of the cabin. "We're late," he said and ushered her inside.

When they left the office a half hour later, she found herself looking up and down Main Street for the black Cherokee. She would have liked to say hello at least, but there was no sign of Tierney or his car. But now, when he was sitting four feet from her, she found it difficult to look at him and was at a loss over what to say.

Feeling his gaze on her, she looked across at him. He said, "After that day on the river, I called your office in Atlanta several times."

"Your articles wouldn't be for my readership."

"I wasn't calling to peddle an article."

She averted her head and looked into the empty fireplace. She'd swept the ash out of it that morning, which seemed now like a very long time ago. Softly she said, "I knew why you were calling. That's why I couldn't take your calls. For the same reason I couldn't meet you for a drink after our kayaking trip. I was married."

He stood up, went around the coffee table, and joined her on the sofa, sitting close and forcing her to look at him. "You're not married now."

William Ritt smiled up at his sister as she cleared away his empty plate. "Thank you, Marilee. The stew was excellent."

"I'm glad you enjoyed it."

"I've been thinking about running a daily special on the lunch menu. Something different for each day of the week. Wednesday meat loaf. Friday crab cakes. Would you agree to sharing your stew recipe with Linda?"

"It's Mother's recipe."

"Oh. Well, she's past caring if you share it, isn't she?"

To anyone else's ears the words would have sounded harsh, but Marilee knew the reason for William's insensitivity and couldn't fault him for it. Their parents were deceased, but neither was missed. One had been completely indifferent, the other unconscionably selfish. To them, treating their offspring with love and affection had been an alien concept.

Their father had been a stern and taciturn man. A mechanic by trade, he would get up before dawn every morning and make the trip down the mountain into town to the automotive shop where he worked. He returned home in time for dinner, which he ate methodically. He grumbled answers to direct questions but otherwise had nothing to say that wasn't a criticism or a reprimand. After dinner he took a bath, then retired to his bedroom, closing the door behind him, shutting out his family.

Marilee had never seen him derive pleasure from anything except the vegetable garden he cultivated each summer. It was his pride and joy. She was seven years old when her father caught her pet rabbit nibbling at a cabbage plant. He'd wrung its neck right in front of her and made her mother fry it for their supper. Marilee considered it poetic justice when he dropped dead of a heart attack while hoeing a row of onions.

Their mother had been a complainer and a hypochondriac who referred to her husband as an uncouth hillbilly behind his back. For forty years she made sure everyone knew that she'd married far beneath her. Her misery was the focus of her life, to the exclusion of all else.

When failing health made her practically bedridden, Marilee took a semester's leave of absence from Cleary High School to tend to her. One morning when Marilee tried to awaken her, she discovered that her mother had died in her sleep. Later, while the minister consoled her with platitudes, Marilee's only thought was that a woman as embittered and self-absorbed as her mother hadn't deserved such a peaceful departure.

The two children of these emotionally disabled people had learned early in life to be self-sufficient. Their family home had been on the far side of Cleary Peak, away from town, isolated from neighborhoods where children played together. Their parents had been lacking in social skills, so neither she nor William had been taught them. The ways and means of how people interacted had been awkwardly acquired in public school.

William was a good student who'd applied himself to scholastics. His efforts were rewarded with excellent report cards and prizes for achievement. He tried to make friends with the same kind of determination, but his overzealous attempts usually had the opposite result.

Marilee had found the nurturing that was missing from her own life in the pages of books. William, being several years older, was the first to learn to read. She prevailed upon him to teach her, and by the time she was five years old she was reading literature that would challenge some adults.

With the exception of the years they were at college, she and William had lived in the same house all their lives. After their mother died, he decided it was time they move into town. It would never have occurred to him that Marilee might have plans of her own. Nor did it occur to her to live independently of him. Actually, she'd been thrilled at the prospect of leaving the ugly, sad dwelling on the mountain that evoked so many unhappy memories.

They bought a small, neat house on a quiet street. She made it into a comfortable home, full of color and light and potted plants, which had been missing in the house of her upbringing.

But after the last curtain was hung and the last room arranged, she'd looked around and realized that nothing except her surroundings had changed. Her life hadn't taken an exciting, new direction. Her rut was prettier and better furnished, but it was still a rut.

As for the family homestead on the mountain, she would have sold it, or let it rot until the wilderness claimed it. But William had other ideas.

"The storm is going to suspend your work on the house for a while," she remarked now as she wiped the dining table with a damp cloth, sweeping cornbread crumbs off the edge into the palm of her hand.

From behind his newspaper he said, "True. It may be days before anyone is able to navigate the main road. The back road up to our place will take even longer to clear."

The back road to which he referred snaked up the west side of the mountain, which was always the colder, the darker, and the last to show signs of spring. "As soon as the road reopens, I'd like you to take me up there," she said. "I want to see what you've done with the place."

"It's coming along. I hope to have it finished, not by this summer but next."

His idea was to refurbish the house and rent it to vacationers. There were dozens of listing agents in the area that kept rental properties occupied for months during the summer and fall. He'd been doing most of the work himself, hiring contractors only when absolutely necessary. He spent virtually all his free time working on the renovation. The house would have to be razed before it held any appeal for Marilee. But William was excited about the project, so she supported it.

"I heard the old Smithson place was leasing for fifteen hundred a week last summer," he said. "Can you believe that? And that house was practically falling down when they started the renovation. Ours will be much more desirable."

"What were you doing with Wes and Scott Hamer this afternoon in the back of the store?"

He tipped down the corner of the newspaper and looked at her sharply. "Come again?"

"This afternoon, in the back of the store, you—"

"I heard that part. What do you mean what was I doing with them?"

"No need to take umbrage, William. I merely asked—"

"I'm not taking umbrage. It's just a strange question, that's all. Completely off the subject *and* inappropriate. Next you'll be asking me what prescriptions my customers take when you know I can't disclose personal information like that."

In truth, he was a busybody who loved to gossip, often about his customers and their medical conditions.

"Was your business with Wes and Scott something personal?"

He sighed, laying the newspaper aside, as though she'd spoiled it for him. "Personal but not confidential. Wes had called earlier, said Dora had a headache, and asked what over-the-counter analgesic I could recommend. He came by to pick it up."

He left the table and went to the counter to refill his coffee cup. Looking at her above the rim as he took a sip, he asked, "What made you ask? Did you imagine that Wes came in just to flirt with you?"

"He wasn't flirting with me."

William looked at her snidely.

"He wasn't," she insisted. "We were just chatting."

"Honestly, Marilee, I can't believe you'd be flattered by Wes's attention," he said with what sounded like pity. "He flirts with everything that has ovaries."

"Don't be crude."

"Crude?" He sputtered coffee around a short laugh. "You haven't heard crude until you've heard the way Wes talks about women. Out of their hearing, of course. He uses gutter language that you probably don't even know, and brags about his sexual conquests. The way he talks, you'd think he was still in high school. He boasts about his affairs with the same cocky attitude that he used to carry the game ball through the halls after a big victory."

Marilee realized that most of William's deprecation was caused by jealousy. He would have loved to have been as macho as Wes. Truth be known, he hadn't outgrown his adolescent envy of his popular classmate. Being valedictorian didn't have near the cachet of being captain of the football team. Not where they lived anyway.

But she also knew that what he said about Wes, while possibly exaggerated, was basically true. She was on the high school faculty with Wes Hamer. He did strut down the corridors of the school as though he owned them. He seemed to think that proprietorship was his due as athletic director. He gloried in the title and all the celebrity and privileges it implied.

"Did you know that he has seduced his own students?"

"That's gossip," Marilee argued softly. "Started, I believe, by the wishful-thinking girls themselves."

William shook his head as though saddened by her naïveté. "You're so innocent about the ways of the world, Marilee. Delude yourself about Wes Hamer if you must. But as your older brother, who's looking out for your best interest, I recommend that you find yourself another hero."

Taking his coffee and newspaper with him, he went into the living room. Not unlike their father, William had a routine. He expected dinner to be ready each evening when he got home from the drugstore. Following dinner, he read the newspaper while she cleaned up the kitchen and did any other housekeeping chores that needed doing. By the time she was ready to settle down in the living room to grade homework papers, he was retiring to his bedroom to watch TV until he went to bed.

They shared a house but rarely a room.

Without fail, she asked him about his day, but he seldom asked about hers, as though her work was insignificant.

He expressed his thoughts, feelings, and opinions freely, but when she shared hers, they were dismissed or disparaged.

He could go out in the evening without having to account for his time or tell her where he was going. If she went out, she had to notify him ahead of time, tell him where she was going and when he could expect her return.

After the second local woman's disappearance, he'd become particularly vigilant about her comings and goings. Cynically, she wondered if he was truly that concerned for her safety or if he just enjoyed exercising authority over her.

She performed the mundane duties of a wife but didn't have the status of one. She was an old maid, doing for her brother because she didn't have another man to do for. No doubt that was how people regarded her, with pitying shakes of their heads and a murmured "Bless her heart."

William had a life. So did she. His.

Until recently, when everything had been sweetly, marvelously changed.

CHAPTER
8

Tension around the Hamers' kitchen dining table was as thick as the blood-rare T-bone Wes was knifing into.

He cut off a chunk of the meat, dunked it in the puddle of ketchup on his plate, and put it in his mouth. "You told me those application forms had already been mailed," he said, talking around the bite. "I go into your room this evening, and there they are, the lot of them, scattered across your desk like birdcage liners. So on top of shirking your responsibility, you lied to me. More than once."

Scott was slouched in his chair, his eyes downcast. With the tines of his fork, he was making disinterested stabs at his serving of mashed potatoes. "I was studying for semester exams, Dad. Then we spent that week at Grandpa's house over Christmas. Ever since school started again, I've been busy."

Wes washed down the steak with a swallow of beer. "Busy with everything except your future."

"No."

"Wes."

He shot a look at his wife. "Keep out of this, Dora. This is between Scott and me."

"I'll start filling out the forms tonight." Scott pushed back his chair and laid his napkin beside his plate.

"*I'll* start on them tonight." Wes jabbed his knife toward Scott's plate. "You finish your supper."

"I'm not hungry."

"Eat it anyway. You need the protein."

Scott replaced his napkin in his lap and, with attitude, forked the steak and sawed his knife through it.

"During the holidays, I let you get by with eating junk," Wes said. "From now until spring training is over, I'm going to monitor your diet. No more desserts."

"I made an apple pie for tonight," Dora said.

The sympathetic glance she cast Scott irritated Wes more than the idea of the pie. "Half of what's wrong with him is *you*. You've spoiled him, Dora. If you had your way, he wouldn't even go to college. You'd keep him here and baby him for the rest of his life."

They finished their meal in silence. Scott kept his head down, shoveling food into his mouth until his plate was clean, then asked to be excused.

"Tell you what," Wes said, giving his son a magnanimous wink, "let your dinner settle, then I don't think one slice of pie will hurt you."

"Thanks." Scott tossed down his napkin and stamped from the kitchen. Seconds later they heard the door to his bedroom slam shut and loud music come on.

"I'll go talk to him."

Wes caught Dora's arm as she tried to stand up. "Leave him alone," he said, guiding her back into her chair. "Let him sulk. He'll get over it."

"Here, lately, he sulks a lot."

"What teenager doesn't have mood swings?"

"But Scott didn't have them until recently. He hasn't been himself. Something's wrong."

With exaggerated politeness, Wes said, "I'll take my pie now, please."

She kept her back to him as she sliced the pie that had been cooling on the counter. "He loves you, Wes. He works hard to please you, but you rarely give him credit for anything. He would respond better to praise than to criticism."

He groaned. "Can't we get through one conversation without you slinging some Oprah-inspired bullshit on me?"

She served him his pie. "Want ice cream?"

"Don't I always?"

She brought the carton to the table and spooned a scoop onto his pie, then returned the carton to the freezer and began to stack the dishes. "You're going to drive Scott away. Is that what you want?"

"What I want is to eat my dessert in peace."

When she turned to him, he was surprised to see a flicker of Dora the coed, whom he'd first seen sashaying across campus in a tennis skirt, racquet bag slung over her shoulder, T-shirt damp with sweat, fresh from a match that he learned later she'd handily won.

That afternoon her eyes were flashing with anger because she'd seen him toss a candy wrapper onto the carefully cultivated lawn in front of the athletic dorm where he and several buddies were lounging on the wide verandah.

"Dumb, dirty jock." She said it like he'd crapped in a water fountain or something. Then she walked over to the wrapper, picked it up, and carried it with her to the nearest trash can. She continued on her way without ever looking back.

His cronies, including Dutch Burton, whistled and catcalled after her, making lewd remarks and propositions when she bent over to pick up the wrapper. But Wes stared after her thoughtfully. He'd liked her pert tits and firm ass, sure. They'd heated up his loins. But he'd been blown away by her "and the horse you rode in on" attitude.

Most coeds swooned when he walked into a room. Girls notched their bedposts same as guys, and sleeping with a star athlete ranked high. At that time, he and Dutch were the football team standouts. He quarterbacked. Dutch carried and caught. Girls withheld nothing from them, and usually they were given even more than they asked for. It was easy to get laid or blown, to the point where easy had lost its allure. He'd liked this girl for showing him some sass.

He wondered what had happened to Dora's sassiness. Since they'd married, it had all but disappeared, although there was a trace of it in her expression now.

"Is apple pie more important to you than your son?"

"For chrissake, Dora, I only meant—"

"One day you'll push him too hard. He'll leave us, and we'll never seen him again."

"You know what your problem is?" he asked angrily. "You don't have enough to do, that's what. You sit around all day, watching those male-bashing talk shows on TV and applying every flaw they discuss to *me*. Then you dream up these crazy scenarios that are never going to happen to our family. My daddy was hard on me, and I turned out all right."

"Do you love him?"

"Who?"

"Your daddy."

"I respect him."

"You *fear* him. You're scared shitless of that mean old man."

Wes tossed down his spoon and stood up suddenly, his chair

scraping loudly against the floor. They faced off across the table for several tense moments. Then he smiled. "Gee, Dora, I love it when you talk dirty."

Giving him her back, she faced the sink and turned on the faucets.

Wes moved up behind her, reached around her, and turned them off. "The dishes can wait." Placing his hands on her hips, he drew her back against him. "You've given me a hard-on that can't."

"Take it somewhere else, Wes."

He snickered with contempt and dropped his hands. "I do."

"I know." She turned the water taps back on.

Dutch knocked several times on the Hamers' back door. Through the window he could see into the kitchen, where all the lights were on, but there was no sign of anyone.

Stamping his feet with impatience and cold, he knocked once more, then opened the door and shouted, "Wes, it's me, Dutch."

He stepped inside, frigid air sweeping in along with him. He closed the door, crossed the kitchen, and peered into the living room. "Wes?" he called in a voice that he hoped could be heard above the bass thrum of rock music issuing from somewhere toward the back of the house, presumably Scott's bedroom.

The door connecting the kitchen to the garage came open behind him. He turned in time to see Wes clump through it. Seeing Dutch standing in his kitchen, Wes laughed. "So you came after all. Figured you would once you'd had time to think about those X-rated videos. I've been putting antifreeze in Dora's car. Cold as it is—" Then his smile dimmed. "Something the matter?"

"Lilly had an accident."

"Jesus. Is she hurt?"

"I don't think so. I'm not sure."

Wes wrapped his hand around Dutch's biceps, guided him into the living room, and pushed him down onto the sofa. Dutch removed his hat and gloves. His boots had tracked a sludge of melting ice and mud onto the rug, but neither noticed. Wes poured a shot of Jack Daniel's into a glass and carried it over to him.

"Take a slug of that, then tell me what's happened."

Dutch tossed back the shot of whiskey, grimaced, then sucked in a deep breath as a chaser. "She left a message on my cell phone. I was talking to the Gunns and didn't answer the call. Goddammit! Anyhow, there was some kind of accident as she was coming down the mountain. Hell, man, when I left the cabin I thought she was right behind me. I should never have left ahead of her. The road was already getting icy. I guess she spun out, something, I don't know. Anyway, she said she'd made it back to the cabin, and that Ben Tierney—"

"Tierney? The—" Wes pantomimed typing.

"Yeah, that guy. That adventure writer or whatever the hell he is. Lilly said he's hurt."

"Did their cars collide, you think?"

"All she said, all I could understand because the cell reception was for shit, was that they were in the cabin, that Tierney was hurt, and to send help."

"What's happened?" Dora appeared, wearing a high-necked robe belted tightly around her waist. Her expression always reminded Dutch of a tightrope walker who's just realized she's made a misstep.

Wes gave her an abbreviated account of the situation. She expressed her concern, then asked, "Did Lilly tell you anything about Mr. Tierney's injury or how bad it is?"

Dutch shook his head. He extended his empty glass to Wes, who refilled it. This time Dutch took a more prudent sip. "I don't know if he's got a scratch, or if he's in critical condition and barely clinging to life. Frankly, I don't care. It's Lilly I'm worried about. I've got to get up there. Tonight."

"Tonight?" Dora echoed.

Wes took a glance out the living room window. "That stuff is still coming down, Dutch. Thicker than before."

"No need to tell me. I've been driving in it." Every outdoor surface was now coated with ice. There was no sign of letup in the precipitation, and the temperature continued to drop.

"How do you propose getting up there, Dutch? You can't drive on that road up to your place. Even your four-wheel is useless on solid ice."

"I know," he said with anger and chagrin. "I already tried it."

"Are you crazy?"

"Yeah, I am. Was, anyway. When I heard that message on my phone, I reacted without thinking. Got in my truck, started up the road, but..." He ended by draining the second drink. "I spun out, barely managed to regain control."

"I'll get coffee." Dora retreated into the kitchen.

"You could've killed yourself," Wes said. "Doing a damn fool thing like that."

Dutch came off the sofa and began to pace. "Then what am I supposed to do, Wes? Sit here with my thumb up my ass till the roads are clear? That could take days. I can't just wait it out. What if Lilly is hurt, too? It would be like her not to tell me."

"I understand your concern. But it's not like you're responsible for her anymore."

Dutch rounded on him, balled his hands into fists, and came very close to decking his friend. Although technically Wes spoke the truth, he didn't want to hear it. He especially didn't want to hear it from Wes. Superior in every way Wes. Wes, who'd never known a day of defeat or suffered a moment of self-doubt in his whole life. Wes kept everything well under control.

"I'm the chief of police. If for no other reason than that, Lilly is my responsibility."

Wes patted the air between them. "Okay, okay, settle down. Getting riled at me won't solve anything."

Dutch accepted one of the mugs of coffee that Dora carried in on a tray. He took several sips, which he needed after two belts of neat whiskey. The sour mash had been like nectar to his system. The aroma, the taste, the warmth it had spread through his belly, the pleasurable buzz, the tingle in his bloodstream, had made him realize just how much he'd missed his hourly shots of it.

He said, "Cal Hawkins still has the sanding truck monopoly, doesn't he?"

"The city renewed his contract last year," Wes replied. "But only because the worthless son of a bitch owns the rig."

"I've had men trying to chase him down. I went to his house myself. It's dark and locked up. Nobody answers his phone. If he's not out sanding the roads, where the hell is he?"

"A bar would be my guess," Wes replied. "That's why he likes his job so well. Only has to work a few days a year. The rest of them, he's free to drink himself into a stupor."

"We've already checked the bars."

"Where they serve taxed liquor out of bottles with labels?" Scoffing, Wes arched his eyebrow. "That's not where you'll find Cal." He went to the entryway closet, got his coat, hat, and gloves. "You drive. I'll tell you where to go."

"Thanks for the coffee, Dora," Dutch said as he walked past her.

"Please be careful."

All Wes said to her was "Don't wait up."

As they stepped out into the worst winter storm in recent history, Wes walloped Dutch between the shoulder blades. "Don't worry, my man. By hook or crook, we'll rescue your lady."

*   *   *

The windows of Scott's bedroom overlooked the backyard. He watched his dad and Dutch Burton practically skate out to the black Bronco with the light bar across the roof and a stenciled seal on the doors. Dutch had kept the motor running while he was inside. The exhaust formed a dancing white ghost behind the truck. As they backed out of the driveway, the wheels spun, seeking traction.

Scott was still staring after the diminishing taillights when his mom knocked on his bedroom door. "Scott?"

"Come in." He turned down the volume on his sound system.

"Would you like your pie now?"

"Can I save it for breakfast? I ate too much steak. I saw Dad leaving with Mr. Burton."

She told him what had happened. "I guess Lilly didn't start down in time and got trapped by the weather. At least she had a good reason for being up there. For the life of me, I can't imagine what Mr. Tierney was doing on the peak today."

"He's a hiker."

"But shouldn't he have known better than to go hiking with a storm moving in?"

Scott wondered about that, too. He was an experienced hiker as well and had read Tierney's articles on the regional trails. He'd grown up exploring and camping in the mountain forests, first with the Boy Scouts, then alone. As much as he enjoyed exploring Cleary Peak, which could be hostile terrain even on a good day, he certainly wouldn't have wanted to be on it this afternoon when the weather turned bad.

"Even if they find Cal Hawkins, I don't think anybody can drive up Mountain Laurel Road tonight," he remarked.

"Neither do I, but they wouldn't have listened to me. If anyone is more stubborn than your father, it's Dutch Burton. Can I get you anything? A cup of hot chocolate?"

"No thanks, Mom. I'm going to work awhile on those applications like I promised Dad. Then I'm turning in."

"Okay. Good night. Sleep tight."

"Don't forget to lock up and set the alarm before you go to bed," he told her on her way out.

She smiled at him. "I won't forget. Wes has reminded me often enough to keep the doors and windows locked, especially since Millicent disappeared. But I don't worry about a break-in."

Why would you? thought Scott. A loaded pistol was kept in the nightstand drawer beside her bed. He wasn't supposed to know about it, but he did. He'd discovered it when he was in sixth grade and had sneaked into his parents' bedroom looking for rubbers with which to impress his friends. He'd been much more awed by the revolver in the drawer than he had been by the tube of spermicidal lubricant.

"It doesn't look like Millicent or the others were taken by force," she continued. "Whoever the culprit is, he's someone the women know, or at least recognize and consider harmless. They seem to go with him willingly."

"Well, anyway, be careful, Mom."

She blew him a kiss. "I promise."

Once the door was shut, Scott turned the volume back up on his sound system and set the built-in sleep timer to turn it off twenty minutes later. Then he bundled up in outerwear for his covert excursion.

His bedroom window opened soundlessly because he kept all the sliding parts oiled. In a flash, he was outside, closing the window again. He didn't want his mom to feel a cold draft and come to investigate its source.

The frigid air stung his eyes and made his nose drip. He hunched his shoulders against the blowing precipitation and dug his gloved hands into his coat pockets. Keeping to the unlighted areas of the yard, he set off on foot.

Sometimes, particularly following one of his old man's lectures on how he was goofing off, when in fact he'd busted his balls to do everything he'd been told, he simply had to escape his house.

Of course nothing he did was ever enough to suit his dad. No blue ribbon was blue enough, no silver trophy shiny enough for Wes Hamer's kid. If he won an Olympic gold medal, his dad would want to know why he hadn't won two.

Seeing a pair of headlights approaching and fearing it might be Dutch Burton's Bronco, he dodged behind a hedge and waited for the vehicle to pass. Going no more than ten miles an hour, it seemed to take forever to reach Scott, whose legs were growing stiff with cold.

But his caution was unnecessary. It wasn't the Bronco that crept past. He began walking again, the collar of his coat flipped up against his cheeks, his cap pulled down low so he wouldn't be recognized by anyone who happened to be watching the storm from his front window.

People in this town loved to talk. If someone spotted him out tonight and later mentioned it to his dad, he would be in a world of hurt. What if he slipped on the ice and damaged something? His old man would stroke out. But only after killing him first.

Lost in that thought—or perhaps fearing it so badly he made it happen—he slipped on the icy sidewalk. His feet went airborne and he came down hard, landing flat on his butt. His tailbone felt like it had been jammed up against the ceiling of his skull. The fall jarred his teeth, causing him to bite his tongue.

He gave himself several moments to recover from the impact before he even tried to stand. After a few somewhat comical attempts to regain his footing on the slippery surface, he succeeded. He hobbled over to a picket fence and leaned against it.

"Jesus," he whispered shakily as he imagined what his dad would have done if he'd limped home dragging a shattered ankle or broken tibia.

See, Dad, it was like this. I sneaked out of the house. While walking the streets of town, I fell down on the ice. You should have heard the sound that bone made when it snapped. Like a couple of two-by-fours being clapped together. Sigh. Guess I won't be going out for the Crimson Tide of Alabama after all. They'll have to win the NCAA football championship without me.

As he moved along the sidewalk, staying close to the fence, he shuddered to think of the H-bomb effect a mistake like that would have on his life. He would be paying for it until the day they buried him, when his dad would be leaning over his open casket saying, *What the fuck were you thinking, Scott?* There would be no end to Wes's ranting and raving. Only an end to his grand ambitions for Scott.

He glanced back at the icy patch that had caused him to fall. He'd come within a hairsbreadth of disaster. It was damn lucky that he hadn't broken his neck.

Or was it un*lucky?*

Without any forewarning, the thought popped out of Scott's subconscious and stopped him dead in his tracks. Where had such a mutinous thought come from? he wondered.

It was the kind of thought that, just for thinking it, you got struck down by lightning. He'd done some things lately that would be considered worthy of damnation by any moral code or religion on the planet. But he hadn't really feared a fiery eternity until now, and all because he had entertained, if only for a millisecond, that traitorous thought. But who can be condemned for what he's thinking? And who's to know?

It was several moments before Scott continued on his way.

With extreme caution.

CHAPTER

9

HAVING JUST BEEN REMINDED BY TIERNEY THAT SHE WAS NO longer married, Lilly tossed aside the afghan and scrambled off the sofa. She expected him to try to keep her beside him, but his injuries prevented him from moving that quickly. He managed only to stand up unsteadily. "Lilly—"

"No, listen, Tierney." Although he hadn't touched her, she put out her hand to stop him from trying. "Our present circumstances are unnerving enough without—"

"Unnerving? You're unnerved? Don't you feel safe with me?"

"Safe? Yes, of course. Who said anything about *safe*? It's just..."

"What?" Eyebrows arched in silent inquiry, he let the question hang there.

"We were getting personal. For the time we're here, we should avoid that. Let's leave everything personal alone and concentrate on practical matters." He seemed on the verge of arguing, but she added a please that softened her tone of voice.

He agreed, reluctantly. "All right, let's be practical. Are you up for a project?"

"Like what?"

"Scavenger hunt."

He suggested they search the rooms to see if she had overlooked anything when she had cleared out the cabin earlier. He said he would start in the kitchen. Turning away from her, he hobbled off in that direction.

"Tierney?"

He came back around. Before she lost her nerve or talked herself out of it, she asked, "Did you meet up with them later?"

He frowned quizzically. "Who?"

"The two college girls. The ones in the Jeep, begging for trouble. After I turned down your invitation to meet for a drink, did you hook up with them?"

He gave her a long, measured look, then turned and continued toward the kitchen. "See what you can find in the bedroom and bath."

The bedroom yielded only three straight pins she found stuck in a crack in a bureau drawer. She presented them to Tierney. "That's it, other than two dead cockroaches under the bed. I left them there."

"We may need them for protein," he said, only half in jest. He produced two candles that were faded and warped but would come in handy if the electricity went out. "They were way in the back of the drawer of the end table."

He was leaning heavily against the kitchen bar, his hand planted firmly on the granite surface. His eyes were closed. "You should lie down," she said.

"No, I'm fine," he mumbled absently as he opened his eyes.

"You're about to keel over."

"Just another wave of dizziness." Leaving the bar, he walked over to one of the windows flanking the front door and pushed aside the drape. "I've been thinking."

Lilly waited to hear his thought, but already she had a bad feeling about it.

"If snow comes behind this sleet and freezing rain, which is likely at this altitude, our situation is going to become more dangerous. I'm worried that the propane tank will empty, which means we'll need fuel." He turned back into the room. "While it's fractionally safer than it will be later, I should go to the shed and bring back what firewood I can."

She looked beyond his shoulder toward the window, then back at him. "You can't go out there! You can barely stand up without losing your balance. You have a brain concussion."

"Which won't matter much if we freeze to death."

"Well forget about it. You can't go. I won't let you."

Her vehemence made him smile. "I'm not asking permission, Lilly."

"I'll go." Yet even as she heard herself volunteering, she quailed at the thought of setting foot outside the security and relative warmth of the cabin.

He looked her up and down. "You couldn't carry enough to

make any difference. I may not be able to bring back much, but it would be more than you could handle. Besides, your boots are wet. You could get frostbite. I'm the one who has to go."

They argued about it for another five minutes, but all the while, regardless of her arguments against the idea, he was preparing to do it. "Is there anything in the shed I could use, like a sled? Something to stack the wood on and drag along?"

She ran a quick mental inventory, then shook her head. "Unfortunately Dutch and I removed everything except some basic tools. As you go in, on your right, there's a large wooden chest we used as a toolbox. You may find something useful in it. There's an ax, I know. Larger than the hatchet on the porch. You said the logs needed to be split, so if you can carry the ax, too, you should bring it back."

"Once I get past the porch steps, I angle off that way, correct?" He indicated the general direction.

"Correct."

"Anything between here and there I should be aware of? Tree stump, sinkhole, boulder?"

She tried to envision any potential obstacles on the path. "I don't believe so. It's a fairly straight shot. But once you get across the clearing and into the woods..."

"Yeah," he said grimly. "It'll be rougher."

"How will you see?"

He removed a tiny flashlight from his coat pocket.

It didn't look all that reliable. "What if the battery runs out? You could get lost."

"I have a sixth sense about direction. If I can see well enough to get myself there, I'll be able to find my way back. But if the cabin lights should go out while I'm not here—I'm expecting that at any time. Ice is hell on power lines." She nodded agreement. "If you lose power, light one of the candles and put it in a window."

"I don't have any matches."

He withdrew a matchbook from another coat pocket and handed it to her. "Keep the matches and candles together so you'll know where they are if you need them."

Suddenly she was struck by the lunacy of what he was about to do. "Tierney, please rethink this. We can break up the furniture and burn it. The shelves in the bookcases, the coffee table, cabinet doors. Before we run out of fuel we'll be rescued. And the propane may last longer than we expect."

"I'm not willing to risk it. Besides, no sense in trashing the cabin unless we're absolutely forced. I'll be all right. I've trekked through worse."

"During a blizzard?"

He didn't respond to that as he reached for his cap. When he picked it up, he frowned with distaste. "It's stiff with dried blood. Mind if I borrow your stadium blanket?"

She helped him fashion a hood as he had for her earlier, and then he was ready. Trying one last argument, she said, "People with concussions aren't supposed to exert themselves. You could black out, your sixth sense of direction could fail you, you could lose your way and either walk off a cliff or get lost and freeze to death."

"We who are about to die..." He saluted her.

"Don't joke."

"I wish I was." He worked his scarf up over the lower half of his face and reached for the doorknob. But after taking hold of it, he hesitated, turned back, and pulled the scarf down past his mouth. "If I don't make it back, I'm going to hate like hell that I never kissed you."

His eyes were as blue as flame, and as entrancing. They held her gaze as he worked the scarf back up over his nose. When he opened the door, the blast of icy air was like a slap in the face, and about that short-lived. He pulled the door securely shut as soon as he'd slipped through.

Rushing to the window, Lilly shoved back the drapery, lending him light through the panes. He turned and gave her a thumbs-up for thinking of it. She went to the other window and did the same, then cupped her hands around her eyes and watched him through the frosted glass. With each step, he carefully planted his boot and made certain he had solid footing beneath him before putting his full weight on it.

The windows shed an apron of light over the area immediately in front of the cabin, but it didn't extend far, and Tierney eventually walked out of it. Impatiently Lilly wiped away the fog created by her breath on the cold glass. She saw the feeble beam of the flashlight bobbing erratically in the swirling precipitation.

Soon she couldn't see even that.

They found Cal Hawkins in the kind of place that Wes had described.

It was deep in the woods where a dirt road ended at a wall of solid rock two hundred feet high. Tucked beneath the face of the mountain, the windowless, single-story structure had all the architectural detail of a cracker box.

In the center of its flat facade was a dented metal door. A bare yellow lightbulb had been screwed into an electrical socket directly above it. There were three pickup trucks parked in front of the building. Judging from the depth of the sleet on the windshields, they'd been there awhile.

Dutch had finessed his Bronco over two miles of dark, narrow, treacherous road to get there, so he was in a truculent mood when he and Wes went inside. Lighting was dim. The room was foggy with smoke and stank like wet wool and b.o. They stepped over splats of tobacco juice on the floor as they made their way to the particle board bar along the far wall.

Without ceremony, Dutch said, "Cal Hawkins."

The bartender nodded his head of stringy, greasy hair toward a corner. Hawkins was seated at one of the rickety tables, his head lying on it, his arms dangling lifelessly at his sides. He was snoring.

"Been that way 'bout an hour," the bartender volunteered as he absently scratched his armpit through his dirty flannel shirt. "Whach' y'all want him for?"

"What's he been drinking?" Dutch asked.

"Somethin' they brung in."

He hitched a thumb in the direction of the only other occupied table, where a trio of sullen, bearded men was playing cards beneath the stuffed head of a snarling black bear mounted on the wall.

"The bear's got the highest IQ of that lot," Wes whispered to Dutch. "I hope your gun isn't just for show. You can bet theirs aren't."

Dutch had already spied the shotguns propped against each chair. "Cover my back."

"Three against one? Thanks for nothing."

Dutch approached the table where Hawkins was sleeping it off. His slack lips had drooled a puddle of saliva onto the table. Dutch hauled back his foot and literally kicked the chair out from under the man.

Hawkins landed hard. "Fuckin' hell!" He came off the floor with his hands balled into fists. But catching the glint of Dutch's badge, he backed down and blinked at them in confusion. Then he grinned. "Hey, Dutch. When I was a kid, I used to watch you play ball."

"I ought to throw your sorry ass in jail," Dutch snarled. "But if you're sober enough to be stupid, you're sober enough to be working, and I need you."

Hawkins wiped saliva off his chin with the back of his hand. "What for?"

"What do you think?" Dutch thrust his face closer, only to recoil from the other man's breath. "You've got a contract with the city to sand roads during ice storms. Well, guess what, genius? We're in the throes of one. And where are you? Out here in the middle of freaking nowhere, stinking drunk. I've wasted several hours I didn't have tracking you down."

He yanked what he assumed to be Hawkins's coat off the back of a chair and threw it at him. Hawkins caught the coat against his chest. Dutch was glad to see that his reflexes weren't completely pickled.

"You're getting out of here right now. We'll follow you to the garage, where your truck has already been loaded and is waiting for you. Have you got the keys?"

Hawkins dug into the pocket of his oily blue jeans and produced a set of keys, which he extended toward Dutch. "Why don't you just take 'em and—"

"I would, except nobody else has experience with the truck's mechanisms, and you're the only one who's insured to drive it. I don't need the liability, and neither does the township of Cleary. You're going, Hawkins. And don't think you can lose me between here and town. I'm going to stay so close I could bite your butt through your tailpipe. Let's go."

"Won't do no good," Hawkins protested as Dutch gave him a hard shove toward the door. "I'll go with you, Chief, but fast as this stuff is coming down, anything I put down tonight will be a waste of good sand. It'll cost the town double, 'cause it'll just have to be did again, soon's the storm blows outta here."

"That's my problem. Your problem is to keep me from beating you senseless once you've done what I need you to do."

Lilly had been anxiously watching for Tierney's return and gave a glad cry when she saw him trudging out of the darkness. He was dragging something along behind him. When he got closer she saw it was a tarpaulin stacked with firewood.

He left it at the foot of the steps and stumbled up them. She opened the cabin door, caught him by the sleeve of his coat, and hauled him inside. He collapsed against the doorjamb and pushed back his makeshift hood. His eyebrows and eyelashes were again covered with frost. Instinctually she brushed it off them.

"Glass of water, please."

She rushed into the kitchen and filled a glass from the pitcher. The trickle from the faucet had stopped, she noticed. They'd done well to fill the containers while they could.

Tierney had slid down the wall and was sitting propped against it on the floor, his legs stretched out in front of him. He had removed his gloves and was clenching and flexing his fingers, trying to restore circulation. She knelt beside him. He gratefully took the glass of water from her and drank it all.

"Are you all right? Besides the obvious."

He nodded but didn't answer.

Ordinarily the walk to the shed would have taken about sixty seconds. According to her wristwatch, he'd been gone for thirty-eight minutes, minutes during which she had repeatedly castigated herself for letting him go.

"I'm glad you're back," she said with all the sincerity at her disposal.

"I'm going again."

"*What?*"

With a groan, he worked himself up the wall until he was standing. More or less. Actually, he was swaying, as though saved from toppling only because the soles of his boots were nailed to the floor.

"Tierney, you can't."

"One more load could make a difference. I don't think it'll take as long this time," he said as he pulled on his gloves again. "Now that I know where everything is. A lot of the time was spent feeling my way around inside the shed." He stared into near space for a moment before shaking his head slightly as though to clear it.

"You're not up to this."

"I'm okay." He replaced the makeshift hood and scarf.

"I wish I could talk you out of going."

He smiled grimly. "I wish you could, too."

Then he pulled the scarf over his nose and went out. She watched through the window as he transferred the logs on the tarp to the stack of firewood beneath the overhang. She continued to watch until he disappeared once again into the darkness. Turning back into the room, she decided on a better way to pass the time than fretting.

Sooner than she expected, she heard his boots clomping up the steps. When she opened the door, he was dragging the tarp stacked with firewood up onto the porch. It was a chore, requiring all his strength because the logs were large. "Did you remember the ax?"

"Wasn't there." His voice was muffled behind his scarf.

"I saw it there only a few days ago."

"It wasn't there." He said it tersely and with enough emphasis to silence her.

Note to self, she thought. *Tierney doesn't like anyone to challenge his word.*

Or his mandates, it seemed. He glanced at the fire burning in the grate and frowned.

"Too late now to argue about it," she said.

He stacked a pile of logs inside the door so they could begin to dry out, then spread the tarp over the replenished woodpile on the porch and stamped into the room. Lilly pushed him toward the fireplace. "You may as well enjoy it."

He pulled the blanket from his head, went to the hearth, and dropped to his knees in front of it like a penitent before an altar. He pulled off his gloves and extended his hands toward the blaze. "I smelled smoke from the chimney as I was coming back. How'd you manage?"

"I found a few drier logs near the porch wall."

"Well, thanks."

"You're welcome."

"I also smell coffee."

"I'd left an unopened can in the freezer of the fridge," she explained, moving into the kitchen. "I splurged on our drinking water, I know, but I only made two cups. There's no cream or sugar."

"Never use them anyway."

He had removed his coat, scarf, and boots and was standing with his back to the flames when she brought him the steaming mug. "Will it make you nauseous?"

"I'll take my chances." He closed both hands around the mug and raised it to his lips, then halted. "Where's yours?"

"It's for you. You earned it."

He took several sips, savoring the taste and the warmth, making small sounds of pleasure. "I may marry you."

She gave a nervous laugh and sat down in the corner of the sofa nearest the fire, tucking her stocking feet under her hips. She hugged the throw to her chest as though for protection. Against what, she wasn't quite sure. Tierney's eyes maybe, which seemed always to follow her, to see into her, to know more about her even than she knew about herself.

He sat down on the hearth and extended his feet toward the fire.

To fill the silence, she asked, "How's your head?"

"Reeling."

"Still hurt?"

"Some."

"I don't see any fresh blood in your hair, but after you've rested awhile, I'd better check the wound again."

He nodded but didn't say anything. Eventually she got up and took the empty coffee mug from him, then went into the kitchen to refill it. When she brought it back, he shook his head. "That's yours."

"I made it for you."

"I insist you have some, too."

She took a few sips, murmured thanks, then passed the mug back to him. As she did, his fingertips brushed hers. "This feels good, Lilly. Thanks again."

"Thank you for going after the firewood."

"You're welcome."

She took up her former post in the corner of the sofa. No sooner was she settled than he began a new conversation with a flat statement. "I know about your daughter." Her astonishment must have shown, because he gave a small shrug, adding, "I picked up tidbits of information here and there."

"From whom?"

"The people in Cleary. There's been a lot of talk about you, especially since Dutch moved back to become police chief. You two remain a hot topic of gossip at Ritt's soda fountain."

"Do you spend a lot of time there?"

"When in Rome. It's the place to be."

"Oh, it's the hub of the city, all right," she said sarcastically. "I expected my split with Dutch to cause a flurry of rumor and speculation. Gossips thrive on marriages, pregnancies, affairs, divorces."

"Deaths," he said softly.

"Yes." Sighing, she looked over at him. "What do they say about Amy's death?"

"That it was tragic."

"Well, that much isn't rumor. She was only three when she died. Did you know that?" He nodded. "Four years ago. It's hard for me to believe that I've been without her for longer than I had her."

"Brain tumor?"

"Right again. A real bastard of one. Sneaky and deadly. For the longest time, it didn't manifest itself. No paralysis, or partial blindness, or slurred speech. No warning of any kind of what was in store. Amy appeared to be a perfectly healthy little girl. That was the good news. It was also the bad news. Because by the time we did begin to realize that something was wrong, the tumor had invaded an entire hemisphere of her brain."

She picked at the fringe on the throw. "We were told at the outset that it was inoperable and incurable. The doctors said even with aggressive chemotherapy and radiation treatments her life could be extended for a few weeks, perhaps a month or two, but not spared.

"Dutch and I elected not to put her through the grueling treatments. We took her home and had six relatively normal weeks with her. Then the damn thing had a growth spurt. Symptoms appeared and progressed quickly until one morning she couldn't swallow her orange juice. By lunch, other systems had begun to shut down. She would have had supper in the hospital, except that by then she had lapsed into coma. Early the following morning, she stopped breathing, then her heart beat one last time, and she was gone."

Her gaze slid over to him and then toward the flames. "We donated her body for medical research. We thought it might do some good, maybe prevent other children from suffering the same rotten fate. Besides, I couldn't bear the thought of sealing her inside a coffin. She was afraid of the dark, you see. Wouldn't sleep without her night-light on. It was a little translucent angel, wings spread like a Christmas herald. I still have it and burn it every night myself. Anyway, I couldn't fathom putting her into the ground."

"We don't have to talk about it, Lilly."

"No, I'm all right," she said, blotting tears off her cheeks.

"I shouldn't have brought it up."

"I'm glad you did. It's actually good for me to talk about her, about *Amy*. My grief counselor emphasized how healthy it is for me to talk about it and to refer to Amy by name." She met his steady gaze. "Curiously, after she died, few people would talk to me about her. Without quite looking me in the eye, they made euphemistic references to my 'loss,' my 'sorrow,' my 'period of bereavement,' but no one spoke Amy's name out loud. I guess they thought they were sparing me sadness by avoiding the subject, when actually I needed to talk about her."

"What about Dutch?"

"What about him?"

"How did he deal with it?"

"What do the gossips say?"

"That he developed a fondness for whiskey."

She snuffled a humorless laugh. "The gossips of Cleary are nothing if not accurate. Yes, he began drinking excessively. It began affecting his work. He started making blunders, which were dangerous to himself and his partners. He became unreliable. He had his hand slapped a few times, then was formally reprimanded, then demoted, which caused him to slip into a deeper funk, which caused him to drink more. It became a vicious downward spiral. Ultimately he was fired.

"Just today he said that if it hadn't been for Amy, our marriage would have lasted forever. Perhaps he's right. Death did part us. *Her* death. I'm afraid we became a cliché, the couple whose marriage couldn't withstand the tragedy of losing a child. We were never the same. Not as a couple and not as individuals."

She looked from the embers to Tierney. "Did I omit anything? Do the die-hard busybodies know the terms of our divorce settlement?"

"They're working on it. In any case, they're glad to have Dutch back among them."

"What do they say about me?"

He gave a dismissive shrug.

"Come on, Tierney. I've got a thick skin. I can take it."

"They say that you insisted on the divorce. Demanded it."

"Making me a coldhearted bitch if ever there was one."

"I haven't heard it put quite that way."

"But close, I'm sure. I would expect the Clearyans to side with their hometown boy." She stared into the fire again, speaking her thoughts aloud as they came to her. "Divorcing Dutch wasn't a decision I made out of anger or spite. It was for my own survival. His failure to recover from Amy's death was preventing *my* recovery."

She willed Tierney to understand what no one else seemed able to grasp. "I had become his crutch. It was easier for him to lean on me than to get professional help and heal himself. He became a liability I could no longer carry and still move forward with my own life. It wasn't a healthy relationship for either of us. We're better off without one another. Although Dutch still refuses to accept that the marriage is over."

"Understandable."

She reacted as though he'd jabbed her with the red-hot tip of the fireplace poker. "Excuse me?"

"Can you blame him for being confused?"

"Why would he be confused?"

"Any man would be. You divorced him. No, you demanded a divorce. Yet tonight, when you got in trouble, he was the first person you called."

"I explained why I called him."

"But it still amounts to sending an ex-husband mixed signals."

She had made clear her reason for calling Dutch for help. Why should she care whether Tierney believed her? She told herself she didn't, but actually his criticism stung. She glanced down at her wristwatch without really registering the time. "It's getting late."

"You're angry."

"No, I'm tired." She pulled her handbag off the coffee table and onto her lap, then began rifling through it.

"I spoke out of turn."

She stopped what she was doing and looked at him. "Yes, Tierney. You did."

Rather than being conciliatory and apologetic, which she expected, he spoke tightly. "Well, too damn bad, Lilly. Want to know why I've stayed on this hearth instead of joining you on the sofa? Want to know why I did nothing to comfort you, didn't come up there and hold you, while you cried over Amy? Only because I'm as confused as Dutch seems to be over how you feel about him."

She opened her mouth to speak but found no words. Lowering her gaze, she fiddled with the clasp of her handbag. "I don't want Dutch back in my life," she said slowly. "Not in any capacity. But I suppose my feelings are ambiguous. I wish him well. He was a football hero, you know. Usually scored the touchdown that cinched the win. That's what I wish for him now."

"A touchdown?"

"A big score. This job in Cleary has given him a fresh start. He has an opportunity to reestablish himself as a good cop. More than anything I want him to succeed here."

"More than anything," Tierney repeated thoughtfully. "That's a strong statement."

"And I mean it."

"Then I suppose you would help him any way you could to ensure his success."

"Absolutely. Unfortunately, there's really nothing I can do."

"You may be surprised."

With that cryptic statement, he got up, muttered something about needing to be excused, and walked through the bedroom, presumably heading for the bathroom.

Lilly watched him go, feeling out of sorts and a bit let down, as though her therapist had cut her appointment short, leaving her with more to say. She was glad that Tierney already knew about Amy, put-

ting them past the difficult part. It was a clumsy topic to introduce
into conversation with someone you were just getting to know. You
didn't just announce it, although she was often tempted to in order to
avoid the inevitable *Do you have children?* Which led to the necessary
explanation, followed by the mandatory *Oh, I'm so sorry, I didn't
know.* Which made the other party feel awkward and embarrassed.

At least she and Tierney had skipped that uncomfortable exchange. She'd also appreciated his not blathering a lot of platitudes
or asking a lot of questions about how she'd felt about it when how
she'd felt about it should have been obvious. He was an exception-
ally good listener.

But his preoccupation with Dutch and her present relationship
with him was beginning to grate. Dutch was no longer a factor in her
life. But apparently Tierney wasn't convinced of that.

And if he'd wanted to know how she would react if he took her
in his arms and held her, why hadn't he done so and found out, instead of using Dutch as an excuse not to?

"You've been plowing through that purse for five minutes." He
was back. She hadn't realized he was standing at the end of the sofa,
watching her, until he spoke. "What are you looking for?"

"My medication."

"Medication?"

"For asthma. I picked it up at Ritt's yesterday. He, by the way,"
she said sourly, "is the worst offender when it comes to gossip. While
I was there yesterday to pick up a prescription refill, William Ritt
asked a dozen leading questions about Dutch and me, our divorce,
the sale of this place. He even asked how much we got for it. Can you
believe that?

"Maybe he was just being friendly, but I can't help thinking...
that...uh..." Distracted by the search through her handbag, she let
her voice trail off. Impatiently, she upended the handbag and
dumped everything in it onto the coffee table.

There was the makeup bag where she'd found the manicure scissors earlier, her wallet and checkbook, a pack of tissues, a roll of
breath mints, cell phone charger, security pass for her office building
in Atlanta, key ring, sunglasses, hand soap.

Everything was there except what she needed.

Dismayed, she looked up at Tierney. "It's not here."

CHAPTER

10

DUTCH RODE SHOTGUN IN CAL HAWKINS'S SANDING TRUCK, primarily because he didn't trust Hawkins to make an honest effort to get up the mountain road. Second, he wanted to be the first to reach the cabin, first through the door, Lilly's knight in shining armor.

It had been a harrowing trip back to town from the dive in which he and Wes had found Hawkins. Bridges were perilous, the roads weren't much better. When they arrived at the garage, Dutch had poured several cups of black coffee into Hawkins. He had bitched and whined nonstop until Dutch threatened to stuff a gag in his mouth if he didn't shut up, then literally boosted him into his rig.

The cab of the truck was a pigsty. Trash and food wrappers left over from last winter littered the floor. The vinyl seat covers had open wounds that exposed stained stuffing. Dangling from the rearview mirror, along with a pair of oversize fuzzy dice and a hologram of a naked girl being intimate with a vibrator, there was a deodorizer shaped like a pine tree. It was doing a lousy job of masking the various odors.

The sanding truck had been in the fleet of heavy equipment that old Mr. Hawkins had rented to municipalities, public utility companies, and construction crews. It had been a successful business until he died and Cal Junior inherited it. This sanding truck was all that remained of the legacy.

Cal Junior had used his late father's assets as collateral against loans that he failed to pay back. Everything had been repossessed except this rig. Dutch was unsympathetic to Cal's financial woes and didn't care if a collection agency claimed the sanding truck tomorrow, so long as it got him up to the peak tonight.

He glanced into the exterior side mirror and saw the headlights of his Bronco following at a safe distance. One of his officers, Samuel Bull, was at the wheel. He had the advantage of driving on the mix of sand and salt that Hawkins was putting down. Nevertheless, the road's surface was still hazardous. Occasionally Dutch saw the Bronco drifting toward the ditch or across the center stripe.

Wes was riding with Bull. Before they left the garage, Dutch had told him he didn't have to come along. "Go home. This is my problem, not yours."

"I'll stick around to lend moral support," he'd said and climbed into the Bronco.

Dutch would need moral support only if this attempt to reach Lilly failed. Apparently Wes thought failure was inevitable. So did Bull. So did Hawkins. Doubt rang loud and clear behind everything they said, and he detected pity in the looks they cast him.

I *must appear desperate to them,* he thought. Desperation was an unfit state of mind for a chief of police. For a *man.* It certainly didn't inspire the confidence of others. About the only thing he could inspire in Cal Hawkins was fear.

When they were about fifty yards from the turnoff onto Mountain Laurel Road, he said, "If I feel like you're holding back on purpose, I'll jail you."

"On what charge?"

"Pissing me off."

"You can't do that."

"I advise you not to test it. You give this heap everything it's got, do you understand me?"

"Yeah, but—"

"No excuses."

Hawkins wet his lips and gripped the steering wheel tighter, mumbling, "Can't see worth a goddamn." But he downshifted as he approached the intersection.

It was tricky because it was a sharp turn, and coming out of it the road went into a steep incline. To keep from spinning out, Hawkins would have to take the turn slowly but have enough acceleration to handle the incline.

Dutch clicked on the two-way radio in his hand. "Hang back, Bull. Don't get too close."

"No need to worry about that, buddy," Wes replied through the speaker. "My instructions to him exactly."

"Nice and easy," Hawkins said under his breath, talking either to himself or to the truck.

"Not too easy," Dutch said. "You've got to get up that incline."

"I'm the one experienced at driving this thing."

"So drive it. But you'd sure as hell better drive it right." Surreptitiously he took a deep breath and held it.

Hawkins went into the turn cautiously. The rig made it without mishap.

Dutch exhaled. "Now give it some gas."

"Don't tell me my job," Hawkins snapped. "Shit, this road's darker than Egypt."

The state highway, which became Main Street in Cleary proper, was lined with streetlights all the way to the city limit signs at either end of town. But once off the beaten path, the roads were unlighted, and the contrast was dramatic. The truck's headlights illuminated nothing except the dizzy dance of windblown, frozen precipitation.

It spooked Hawkins. He let off the accelerator.

"No!" Because Dutch had driven this road a thousand times, he knew that this was the point where acceleration was necessary in order to make it up the first incline. "Give it some juice!"

"I can't see nothing," Hawkins screeched. He put the truck in neutral and let it idle while he swiped his coat sleeve across his face. Despite the frigid temperature, his forehead was beaded with sweat that smelled as acrid as the moonshine that had produced it.

"Put this truck in gear," Dutch said, straining each word through clenched teeth.

"In a minute. Let my eyes adjust. All that stuff swirling around is making me woozy."

"Not in a minute. Now."

Hawkins frowned at him. "You got a death wish or somethin'?"

"No, *you* must. Because I'm going to kill you if this truck isn't rolling in five seconds."

"I don't think a chief of police is supposed to be threatening private citizens like that."

"One."

"What's going on up there?" Wes's voice squawked through the two-way radio.

"Two." Dutch depressed the button on his receiver and spoke into it. "Cal's considering the best way to approach the incline." He clicked off. "Three."

"Dutch, you sure about this?" Wes sounded worried. "Maybe you should reconsider."

"Four."

"Bull can barely keep this Bronco on the road, and that's with driving on sand. We can barely see beyond the hood and—"

"Five." Dutch drew his pistol from the holster.

"Shit!" Cal ground the gear stick into first.

"It's okay, Wes," Dutch said into the radio with what he thought was remarkable calm. "Here we go."

Cal let out on the clutch and pressed the accelerator. The truck rolled forward a few feet.

"You're gonna have to give it some punch or it'll never make it," Dutch said.

"We got a heavy load, don't forget."

"So compensate."

Hawkins nodded and shifted into second. But the moment he accelerated, the rear tires began to spin uselessly. "Ain't gonna make it."

"Don't let up on it."

"Ain't gonna—"

"Keep trying! Give it more!"

Hawkins muttered something about Jesus, Mary, and Joseph, then did as Dutch ordered. The wheels spun but then found traction, and the truck lurched forward.

"See?" Dutch said with more relief than he was willing to show.

"Yeah, but we gotta make that first hairpin."

"You can do it."

"I can also drive us both straight into Hell, 'cause I can't see shit. I don't fancy tumbling ass over elbows down the hillside in this thing."

Dutch ignored him. Beneath his clothes, he was sweating even more profusely than Hawkins. He concentrated on the glare of the headlights just beyond the hood. In fairness to Hawkins, he didn't dispute the danger of driving a truck this size up an icy mountain road when visibility was limited to a few feet. The heavy precipitation had already covered the sand that the rig had just applied. He noticed that Bull had driven the Bronco no further than the turnoff. The two inside it—his best friend and one of his subordinates—were probably discussing his blind stupidity. He couldn't let their opinions worry him.

Grumbling and groaning, the truck labored up the twenty-degree incline. It was slow going, but Dutch kept telling himself that every inch it won moved him closer to Lilly. And Ben Tierney.

Of all the men she could be stranded with, why did it have to be that guy? The thought of her being alone in the cabin with any man was enough to make him crazy. But she was up there with a man she'd been gawking at just yesterday.

Dutch had seen other women, old and young alike, sizing up Ben Tierney, going all atwitter over his hard body and chiseled jaw. And you could bet that he damn well knew he caused a stir among the ladies.

He must fancy himself some sort of superstud. Thrill seeking, exploring, getting his picture in magazines. It all added up to a free pass into the sack with any woman he chose.

Kayaking, my ass.

Pushing his bitter thoughts aside, he said, "Heads up, Hawkins. We're getting close to that first switchback."

"Yep."

"Another ten yards maybe."

"We ain't got a snowball's chance of making it."

"If you know what's good for you, we will."

For several seconds Dutch believed they were actually going to. Maybe he was willing it to happen so hard he saw it happening. But positive thinking couldn't override the laws of physics. In order to make the switchback turn safely, Cal had to downshift. When he did, the truck didn't have enough speed to propel it up the incline. It stalled and seemed to remain motionless for eternity and a day. Dutch held his breath. Then the rig began to slide backward.

Hawkins squealed like a woman.

"Give it some gas, you idiot!"

Hawkins complied, but it seemed to Dutch that his efforts weren't as aggressive as what were called for to combat the inexorable pull of gravity. In any case, nothing Hawkins did was successful, except the gradual application of brakes that eventually stopped their downhill skid and prevented them from going off the road.

When the truck finally came to a halt, Hawkins expelled a long breath. "Fuck me. That was a close one."

"Try again."

He turned his head so fast it caused his neck vertebrae to pop like bursting corn kernels. "Are you *nuts*?"

"Put it back in gear and try again."

Hawkins shook his head like a wet dog. "No way, uh-uh. You can take out your pistol again and shoot me right between the eyes, but at least that'd be a quick death. Better than having my guts squashed by tons of truck and sand. No thank you, sir. You can wait till this stuff clears out, or get yourself another driver, or drive it your own self. I don't give a fuck, except I ain't doin' it."

Dutch tried staring him into submission, but Cal Hawkins's bloodshot eyes glared back at him. His stubbled jaw was thrust pugnaciously forward. They were both surprised when someone knocked on the passenger window.

Wes peered in at them. "Y'all okay in there?"

"We're fine," Dutch replied through the glass.

"Like hell we are," Hawkins yelled.

Wes stepped onto the running board, pulled open the door, and immediately sensed Hawkins's fear. "What's going on?"

Hawkins pointed a shaking finger at Dutch. "He pulled a gun on me, told me he was gonna kill me if I didn't get him up this mountain. He's crazy as a shithouse rat."

Wes shifted his disbelieving gaze to Dutch, who said in a tired voice, "I wasn't going to shoot him. I just wanted to scare him into giving it his best effort."

Wes regarded him closely for a moment, then addressed Hawkins in a quiet, confidential voice. "His wife's up there in their cabin with another man."

Hawkins assimilated that, then looked at Dutch, seeing him in a new light. "Aw, man. That sucks."

What sucked was being pitied by the likes of Cal Hawkins.

Wes said, "Cal, think you can back your rig down to the main road?"

Hawkins, inspired by sympathy into a more agreeable mood, said he would give it a shot. With them guiding him, he got the sanding truck back onto the highway and turned in the direction of town. Dutch ordered Bull to ride with Hawkins, warning his officer to keep a sharp eye on him and not let him do anything that would sabotage the rig's future use.

"Wouldn't put it past him to wreck it on purpose so he'd get out of trying again tomorrow." Following in the Bronco, Dutch ground his teeth. "That gutless, drunken son of a bitch."

"The demise of Cal Hawkins Jr. would signify no great loss. I give you that," said Wes. "But Jesus, Dutch, weren't you a bit over the line to draw a gun on him?"

"Did you have to tell him that Lilly was with another man? It'll be all over town by daybreak. No telling what they'll be saying she and Ben Tierney are doing together up there to keep warm and while away the hours. You know how the minds of these people work."

"I see how yours is working."

Dutch shot him an angry glance.

"Besides," Wes continued, "I didn't mention Ben Tierney by name. For all Hawkins knows, she's holed up with some old coot."

"Hardly."

"Look, I told him because that's a situation he can relate to. Driving up this mountain during a blizzard to rescue a stranded citizen? He can't understand a sense of duty like that. But going after your woman who's with another man, now that would justify any rash action. Even threatening someone with a gun."

They said no more until they reached the garage. Dutch told Bull to return to headquarters and see if his help was needed anywhere. If not, he could go home.

"Will do, sir." Looking down at the floor, the officer said awkwardly, "I'm sorry about, you know, not being able to get to your wife."

"See you tomorrow," Dutch said curtly.

The officer headed for his squad car. Hawkins was already scrambling into his pickup when Dutch caught up with him. "I'll be looking for you first thing tomorrow morning. You'd better be easy to find."

"I'll be at my house. You know where it's at?"

"I'll pick you up at dawn. When I get there, if you're drunk or hungover, you'll wish I'd gone ahead and shot you."

They followed Hawkins's pickup out of the garage. Not surprisingly, one of its taillights was missing. "I should write him a citation for that," Dutch grumbled when Hawkins split off at an intersection.

When they reached the Hamers' house, Wes said, "Drop me at the end of the driveway. No need to pull in."

Dutch brought the Bronco to a stop. Neither man spoke for several moments. Wes stared glumly through the windshield and finally said, "No sign of it letting up, is there?"

Dutch cursed the maelstrom of snow and sleet. "I'm getting up there tomorrow if I have to sprout wings and fly."

"That's exactly what you may have to do," Wes said. "Where are you off to now?"

"I'm going to drive around town a bit. Check things out."

"Why don't you park it for the night, Dutch? Get some sleep."

"Couldn't if I tried. I'm running on adrenaline and caffeine now."

Wes studied him for a moment before saying, "I recommended you for this job."

Dutch turned and gave his friend a hard look. "Having second thoughts?"

"None. But I don't think I'm out of order by reminding you how much your future is riding on succeeding here."

"Look, if you think I'm botching the job—"

"I didn't say that."

"Then what?"

"I'm saying your reputation is on the line, and so is mine."

"And you always have your ass well covered, don't you, Wes?"

"You're goddamn right I do," he fired back.

Dutch snorted. "You always had big, bad linemen blocking you, and if they didn't, you gave them hell. I was out there being hammered by linebackers with necks thicker than my waist. You didn't give a shit that I got creamed, so long as you were protected."

Realizing how juvenile he must sound, harking back to their football days, he bit back any further comments. What Wes had said was the sad, ugly truth. He knew it. It just irked him to hear it.

"Dutch," Wes said in a carefully measured tone, "we're not playing tiddlywinks here. Or even football. Our little town has got itself a psycho, some weirdo, snatching up women. Five of them now. God only knows what he's doing to them. People are scared, on edge, wondering how many are going to fall victim before he's caught."

"What's your point?"

"My point is that I haven't seen you get worked up over our town crisis nearly the way you got worked up over Lilly being stuck in a nice, cozy cabin on a snowy eve. Sure, you're worried about her. Okay. Some concern is justified. But for chrissake give it some perspective."

"Don't preach to me, Mr. Chairman of the city council." Dutch's soft-spoken voice was in contrast to the rage pulsing through him. "You're hardly a moral yardstick, Wes." To hammer his point home, he added with emphasis, "Especially where the welfare of women is concerned."

CHAPTER

11

"YOU HAVE ASTHMA?"

"Chronic asthma. Nonallergic asthma." Lilly ran her hand around the inside of her empty handbag, knowing it was futile. The small pouch in which she kept her medication wasn't in there. Anxiously she pushed her fingers through her hair, then cupped her mouth and chin with her hand. "Where is it?"

"You're not having an asthma attack."

"Because I take medication to prevent them. An inhaler and a pill."

"Without them—"

"I could have an attack. Which would be bad since I don't have my bronchodilator."

"Broncho—"

"Dilator, dilator," she said impatiently. "An inhaler to use during an attack."

"I've seen people use those."

"Without it I can't breathe." She stood up and paced a tight circle. "Where is that bag? It's about this big," she said, holding her palms six inches apart. "Green silk, crystal beads on it. One of my staff gave it to me last Christmas. She'd noticed the one I had was worn out."

"Maybe you left—"

Even before he finished, she was shaking her head and interrupting. "It's always in my purse, Tierney. Always. It was there this afternoon."

"You're sure?"

"Positive. Breathing cold air can bring on an attack, so I used one of my inhalers right before I left the cabin." Growing more frantic by the moment, she wrung her hands. "It was in my bag this afternoon, but it's not there now, so what happened to it?"

"Calm down."

She rounded on him, angry over his inability to understand her panic. He didn't know what it was like to gasp for breath and fear that soon he'd be unable to do even that. "Don't tell me to calm down. You don't know—"

"Right." He took her by the shoulders and gave her a slight shake. "I don't know anything about asthma except that hysteria can't be good for it. You're working yourself into a tizzy. Now calm down."

She resented his stern tone of voice, but of course he was right. She nodded at him and wiggled herself out of his grip. "All right, I'm calm."

"Let's backtrack. You used the inhaler as you were leaving the cabin, correct?"

"As I was walking out the door for the final time. I know I replaced it in my handbag. I remember fumbling with the clasp because I had my gloves on. But even if I had accidentally left it behind, it would be in this room. We've been over every square inch of this cabin. It's not here or one of us would have seen it."

"Your handbag was slung onto the floorboard when your car struck the tree, remember?"

No, she hadn't remembered that until now. "Of course." She groaned. "The pouch must have fallen out then. It would have been on top of everything else because I'd just put it back in."

"Then that's the only logical explanation. When you pulled your purse from under the dash, did you check to see if the medicine bag was inside?"

"No. It didn't occur to me to check for anything that might have spilled out. My mind was on our predicament."

"Under normal circumstances, when would you next need the medication?"

"Bedtime. Unless I had an episode, in which case I would need one of my inhalers immediately."

Tierney digested that. "Then we'll just have to do everything we can to prevent an attack. What precipitates them? Besides breathing cold air. And, by the way, how in hell did you walk uphill, practically carrying me, without suffering an attack?"

"My medications work well to prevent them. If I use common

sense and take my meds, I can do just about anything I want. Kayak in white water, for instance," she added with a weak smile.

"But that walk up here nearly did me in, Lilly. How did you do it?"

"Maybe I was imbued with superhuman strength after all." To let him in on the inside joke, she explained. "When you were lying in the road, and I was rushing to get the blanket and so forth, I wondered why I wasn't experiencing the adrenaline rush people are supposed to get during a crisis situation."

"Maybe you did and just didn't realize it."

"Evidently. Anyway, attacks are brought on by overexertion, certainly. Irritants like dust, mold, and air pollution. I'm pretty safe from all that up here, especially in the winter. But then there's stress," she continued. "It can cause an attack.

"After Amy died, I had frequent attacks from crying so much. They decreased over time, of course, but I should avoid becoming overwrought." She gave him a smile that she hoped looked courageous. "I'm sure I'll be fine. It probably won't matter if I skip a few doses."

He looked at her thoughtfully, then glanced at the door. "I'll go back to the car and get it."

"No!" She grabbed his sleeve and held on for dear life. Worse than not having her medication within reach would be not having it and suffering an attack while she was alone.

Soon after Amy's death, she'd been seized by an attack during the night. The sound of her own wheezing had awakened her, and she began coughing up the most vile mucus. Her air passages were almost completely blocked by the time she inhaled the life-saving drug.

It had been a particularly scary episode because she had been alone. Dutch hadn't come home that night. Nor had he called to tell her that he would be late. Having run out of flimsy excuses, he found it easier not to phone at all than to phone with a lying explanation.

She had eventually given up waiting for him and gone to bed. She remembered thinking later that it would have served him right if she hadn't used her inhaler in time, or if it hadn't been sufficient to clear her air passages, if he'd come home to find that she'd suffocated while he was with another woman.

Realizing she was still holding Tierney's sleeve in a desperate clutch, she let go. "You couldn't make it to the car and back without collapsing," she said. "You'd be out there lost, frozen, or unconscious, and I'd still be here without my meds. We'd be worse off, not better."

He took a deep breath, let it out slowly. "I'm afraid you're right. I'll put off going until there's no other choice."

"If it comes to that, don't go without telling me." She was ashamed of the emotion welling up inside her, but it was vitally important to her that he understand this. "I've lived with asthma all my life, but a severe attack is still a terrifying experience. I'm comfortable with being alone as long as my emergency inhaler is within reach. But it's not. I don't want to wake up gasping for air and find myself here alone, Tierney. Promise me."

"I promise," he vowed softly.

A log in the fireplace shifted, sending a shower of sparks up the chimney. Lilly turned away from him and knelt on the hearth to stir the embers beneath the iron grate.

"Lilly?"

"Hmm?" When Tierney didn't respond, she turned her head. "What?"

"How would you feel about sleeping together?"

Marilee Ritt had a relaxing evening.

Although it hadn't been officially announced, she knew there would be no school tomorrow. Even if the buses could run their routes, which they couldn't, it would cost the school district dearly to heat the buildings in temperatures this extreme.

Nevertheless, the superintendent took perverse pleasure in notifying everyone of the cancellation at the last possible moment, usually in the morning about an hour before the bell was due to ring. It was his little power play not to let everyone sleep in.

Rather than grade papers, which was what she usually did with her evenings, Marilee watched one of the videos she had brought home from the drugstore. The female protagonist was a vacuous character. The male was a cad with no redeeming qualities. The film's only merits were the chemistry between the equally attractive actors and a good theme song performed by Sting. So what if there were holes in the plot and the dialogue was sappy? It wasn't Dostoevsky, but it was fun escapism, and she had enjoyed it.

As she made her way through the house, she switched off lights and checked to see that all the doors were locked. Glancing down the bedroom hall, she noticed that no light was coming from beneath William's door. She guessed he'd been in bed for hours. He was early to retire, early to rise.

She went into her bedroom and closed the door, but she didn't turn on the lamp. A streetlight halfway down the block cast enough of a glow through the window shade for her to see her way around. She removed the decorative throw pillows from her bed and folded back the down comforter.

Then she went into the bathroom and began to undress. She took her time, removing each garment slowly, then carefully setting it aside before removing another. Her skin broke out in gooseflesh, but still she didn't rush.

When she was naked, she removed the elastic band that held her ponytail and shook her hair free, combing her fingers through the wheat-colored strands, about which she was secretly vain. She liked feeling it loose and soft against her bare shoulders.

Her nightgown was hanging on a hook on the back of the door. She slipped it on. It was unseasonably skimpy, but she loved lacy, silky nightwear and wore it year-round. Shivering, she padded into the bedroom.

She was climbing onto her bed when he caught her around the waist with one arm and clamped his other hand over her mouth. She tried to scream and arched her back in an effort to break away from him.

"Shh!" he hissed, directly into her ear. "Be still or I'll have to hurt you."

Marilee stopped struggling.

"That's more like it," he said. "Is your brother asleep?"

"Hm-mmm?"

He squeezed her waist tighter, drawing her up hard against his chest. His breath was warm and humid against her ear and neck. "I asked if your brother is asleep?"

She hesitated a moment, then nodded.

"Okay. That's good. Do as I say, and I won't hurt you. Understand?"

Her heart was knocking against her ribs, but she gave another nod of assent.

"If I take my hand away from your mouth, will you scream?" She shook her head, perhaps too quickly to be sincere. He growled, "If you do—"

She shook her head more adamantly.

Gradually, he removed his hand from her mouth. She whimpered, "What are you going to do to me?"

Then he showed her.

CHAPTER

12

THE INTRUDER ROUGHLY GRABBED HER HAND, PULLED IT around to her back, and pressed her palm against his exposed penis. Marilee gasped in shock. He folded her fingers around his erection and moved her hand up and down.

She could see their reflection in the cheval glass across the room. It was an old-fashioned piece that had come to her through her mother and maternal grandmother. Wide oval mirror, cream-colored wood with pink roses painted on it.

But there was nothing quaint about the reflection caught in it now. It was carnal. Raw. Erotic. In the semidarkness she saw herself in her short, skimpy nightgown. He was in shadow. All she could make out of him was a watch cap and a pair of eyes meeting hers in the mirror.

Nudging the furrow between her buttocks, he whispered, "Lower your gown."

She shook her head, slowly at first, then more decisively. "No."

Before she could react, he yanked the straps of her nightgown off her shoulders. It fell as far as her waist, leaving her breasts exposed. At once he had both arms around her, mashing her breasts against her chest.

Marilee moaned.

"Shh," he hissed sharply.

She clamped her teeth over her lower lip.

He slid one hand down the center of her body and tried to work it between her thighs. "Open them."

"Please—"

"Open them."

She moved her feet apart a few inches.

"Wider." She hesitated, then did as he ordered. He pushed his fingers into her. She met his eyes in the mirror; they seemed to be alight. "Get on your knees and put your face to the mattress."

Planting her knees on the edge of the bed, she bent forward until her cheek was resting on the mattress. His hands were hot as he caressed her, separated her, exposed her. The tip of his penis probed and teased before he thrust into her.

Convulsively her hands gripped the sheet beneath her as tightly as her body clenched around him. He groaned and pressed deeper. "Say it, what am I doing to you?"

She mumbled a reply into the mattress.

"Louder."

She repeated the word and rocked back against him.

"You're going to come, aren't you?" His strokes became shorter, faster.

On a serrated sigh, she moaned "Yes."

The orgasm left her damp and weak and deliriously happy. It was just beginning to wane when she felt his climax. As he held her hips between his hands, his entire body strained and pulsed. She came again, her orgasm smaller this time but no less satisfying.

After catching her breath, she crawled forward onto the bed, then rolled over and reached for him. "That was exciting." He knew all her fantasies because she had told them to him. They didn't always act them out, but she loved when they did.

He took her breasts in his hands and rubbed his thumbs across her hard nipples. "You like to be scared."

"I must, or I wouldn't have you sneaking in here." They shared a long and languid kiss. When they finally broke apart, she touched his face lovingly. "Did you catch my act in the bathroom?"

"Couldn't you feel me watching?"

"Honestly, yes. The instant I came into the room, I knew you were here. I wanted to draw out the striptease longer. Maybe, you know, touch myself."

"I'd like that."

"Another time. It was too cold tonight. In fact, because of the weather, I didn't expect you."

He kissed his way down the center of her torso, then knelt between her open thighs. As he pressed his face into her, he groaned, "I can't stay away from this."

*   *   *

Outside Marilee's bedroom, William listened at the door for a few more minutes, then, smiling smugly, barely suppressing a chuckle, silently crept back down the dark hallway to his own room.

Tierney's question took Lilly off guard. She stared at him, too shocked to respond.

"Maybe I should have led up to it gracefully, rather than just springing it on you like that," he said. "I'm usually more subtle."

More subtle when inviting a woman to sleep with him. And how often was that, she wondered, although she was reasonably sure it was often. She was equally sure that few who were invited turned him down.

Her carefree laugh was totally false. "Should I be flattered or offended? Why don't you think a more subtle approach would work with me?"

"None of the rules apply to you, Lilly."

"Why not?"

"You're too smart and too beautiful."

"I'm not beautiful. Attractive, perhaps, but not beautiful."

"You are. I thought so the minute you stepped aboard that bus."

She had been several minutes late and the last to board the bus, she recalled. She'd stood facing the others, looking for a seat. Tierney had been sitting in the third row, next to the window. The aisle seat beside him was vacant. They'd made eye contact. She returned his smile but didn't accept his silent invitation to sit beside him. Instead she moved past and took the aisle seat in the row behind him.

The doors closed and the bus pulled out. Their guide for the excursion stood up in the aisle to welcome them all. He gave a ten-minute spiel about safety and what they could expect during their day on the French Broad River. His jokes were lame, but she laughed politely, as did Tierney.

When the guide finished his cheerful speech and sat down behind the driver, others in the group began chatting among themselves. Tierney turned to her.

I'm Ben Tierney.

Lilly Martin.

Pleased to meet you, Lilly Martin.

"You looked great that day," he said.

She knew she should stop this conversation here. It was violating the ground rules she'd laid down about keeping their minds on practical matters and leaving anything personal out of the situation. But the woman in her wanted to hear what he had to say.

She frowned at him dubiously. "In my kayaking getup?"

"Black spandex has never looked so good."

"Untrue, but thanks anyway."

"You introduced yourself by your maiden name. I didn't learn until my next trip to Cleary that the Lilly Martin I'd met on the river was in fact Mrs. Burton, estranged wife of Dutch, newly hired chief of police."

"I used my maiden name professionally. Once I'd filed for divorce, I started using it all the time. Who told you that Dutch and I were married?"

"An old man named Gus Elmer. Do you know him?"

She shook her head.

"He's the owner of the lodge where I stay when I'm in the area. Colorful character. Always eager to talk to his guests. Without making it too obvious, I asked him if he knew of a Lilly Martin who had a cabin in the vicinity."

"And got an earful."

He smiled crookedly. "If Gus had any qualms against gossip, bourbon cleared his conscience. By the time the bottle was empty, I knew the basic facts about you, including Amy's death. That explained a lot."

"About?"

He gave careful consideration to his answer. "That day on the river, I noticed that every time you laughed, you seemed to catch yourself in the act, and you would stop. Suddenly. Your smile would vanish. The sparkle would go out of your eyes.

"At the time, it threw me. I wondered why you'd trip a switch to stop having fun. It was like you didn't have a right to enjoy yourself, like it was wrong for you to be having a good time."

"That's it exactly, Tierney."

"Enjoying yourself makes you feel guilty, because Amy is dead and you're alive."

"According to my grief counselor, yes."

His perception of her was uncanny. He seemed to know the contents of every secret chamber of her heart. Apparently he'd been able to read her mind even on the day they met. It felt good to talk freely about Amy, but his insight was disconcerting.

He eased himself onto the hearth beside her. "Tonight, when you told me in your own words about Amy's death, I recognized the sadness in you that I'd noticed that day on the river."

"I'm sorry."

"Why apologize?"

"Sorrow makes people uncomfortable."

"Maybe other people. Not me."

She looked at him curiously. "Why is that?"

"I admire how you've tried to conquer it."

"Not always successfully."

"But the important thing is that you didn't give in to it." He didn't add, *Like your husband,* but that was what he was implying.

"Be that as it may, no one wants to be around a sad sack," she said.

"I'm still here."

"You can't escape. We're stranded, remember?"

"I'm not complaining. In fact, I have a confession. I'm glad you and I are here alone, cut off from the rest of the world." His voice dropped to a lower pitch. "This conversation began with a question."

"No, I won't sleep with you."

"Hear me out, Lilly. We could conserve heat, even generate it, by undressing and snuggling under a pile of blankets. Our combined body heat would help keep us warm."

"Hmm, I see. You're suggesting it strictly out of necessity."

"Not strictly. About seventy-five percent."

"It's the other twenty-five that concerns me."

He reached out and claimed a strand of her hair, but unlike when he touched it in the car, he didn't immediately let it go. He rubbed it between his fingers. "I've wanted you from day one. Why waste time on subtlety when I'm absolutely sure you knew it from the start? I want you under me.

"But—and this is important—nothing will happen until I know you want it, too. It stops at snuggling for warmth." He spread his fingers and watched the strands of her hair sift through them, then met her eyes again. "I swear."

Looking into his eyes, hearing the sincerity in his husky voice, she trusted him to keep his word. Well, sort of. That had been an awfully arousing profession of desire.

What she didn't trust was the situation. She tried to imagine herself and Tierney lying together, even partially unclothed, hugging one another for warmth without any sexual exploration or experimentation. Who did he think he was kidding? Himself, perhaps, but not her.

Not that the sky would fall if they submitted to their attraction. Her sensual impulses were certainly green-lighting the idea. But she'd known him for all of...what? Counting that day on the river, she'd spent a total of perhaps fifteen hours with him. Even in this age of sexual permissiveness and self-gratification without regard for consequences, that was a little too accelerated for her.

All she really knew about him was that he was a good listener and could write an entertaining and concise magazine article. Was she ready to be physically intimate with a man about whom so little was known? Women of the younger generation would call her old-fashioned, prudish, and cowardly. She preferred thinking of herself as intelligently cautious.

"No, Tierney. My answer remains no."

"All right." He gave her a crooked half smile. "Honestly, if the roles were reversed, I wouldn't trust me either." He stood up. "On to plan B. We shut the vents in the bedroom and bath, close off those rooms entirely, and confine ourselves in here, where we have a small reserve of heat.

"I could bring the mattress off the bed and put it near the fireplace for you. I'll sleep on one of the sofas, a safe yard and a half away from you. But if you don't want even that much togetherness, I'll certainly understand."

She came to her feet and dusted off the seat of her trousers. "Plan B makes perfect sense."

"Glad you agree. I'll get right on it." He headed for the bedroom.

"Tierney?"

He stopped and turned back.

"Thank you for accepting my decision without further argument. You're being awfully nice about it."

He looked at her for several beats, then closed the distance between them in two long strides. "I'm not that nice."

CHAPTER
13

"Ever read the Book of Jeremiah, Hoot?"

"Jeremiah? No, sir. Not straight through. Selected verses only."

SAC Begley closed his Bible. He'd been reading it for the last ten miles, which had taken Special Agent Wise almost two hours to navigate. "The Lord had a good man in Jeremiah."

"Yes, sir."

"Commissioned by Jehovah God to tell people things they didn't want to hear and would just as soon not have known."

Hoot's knowledge of Old Testament prophets was hazy, so he agreed with Begley's assessment with a noncommittal grunt.

"He's killing them, you know."

Trying desperately to keep the car on the road and stay on track with Begley at the same time, Hoot wondered if the antecedent to the pronoun "he" was the prophet, the Lord, or the unknown subject who was preying on the community of Cleary. He figured the unsub.

"You're probably right, sir. Although, if he's confining his activity to this area—and so far we haven't linked this case to any in other parts of the country—one would think some remains would have been discovered by now."

"Hell, but look at this 'area.'" Begley rubbed his sleeve against the frosted passenger window to improve his view of the frozen landscape. "There are hundreds of square miles of solid forest out there. It's rough, mountainous terrain. Rocky riverbeds. Caves. He's even got wildlife on his side. For all we know he's feeding those girls to bears."

That triggered Hoot's acid reflux. The last cup of coffee he'd drunk tasted sour in the back of his throat. "Let's hope not, sir."

"It's a sparsely populated region. The son of a bitch that bombed Atlanta's Olympic Park hid out here for years before they found him. No, Hoot, if I was killing young women, I'd choose country like this for my hunting grounds." Pointing up ahead, he asked, "That it?"

"Yes, sir."

Hoot had never been so happy to see a destination in his life. He'd been driving all night over roads that were more suited for a luge. At one interchange not too far out of Charlotte, a highway patrol car was blocking an entrance ramp. The officer got out and motioned for Hoot to back up. On Begley's orders, Hoot stayed put.

The patrolman approached them, shouting angrily, "Don't you see me motioning you? You can't come this way. The highway's closed."

Hoot lowered his window. Begley leaned across him and flashed the patrolman his ID, explained that they were in hot pursuit of a felon, argued with the officer, pulled rank, and ultimately threatened to push his goddamn patrol car out of the fucking way if he didn't fucking move it immediately. The officer moved his car.

Hoot had managed to get them over the ramp without spinning out, but the muscles in his neck and back had been tied in knots ever since. Begley seemed impervious to their peril. Either that or he trusted Hoot's driving skills more than Hoot did.

Begley had allowed only two stops for snacks and coffee, which they took with them. At their last stop, Hoot had barely had time to zip up after using the urinal before Begley was knocking on the door and telling him to hurry it along.

Dawn had reduced the darkness only marginally. Cloud cover was thick and low. Fog and blowing snow limited visibility to a few feet. Hoot's eyes were tired from straining to see beyond the hood ornament. His speed had maxed out at fifteen miles an hour. Driving any faster would have been suicidal. The freezing rain and sleet that had fallen yesterday were now being exacerbated by a heavy snowfall, the likes of which Hoot had seen only rarely in his thirty-seven years.

Before they interviewed Ben Tierney, he would have liked a shower, a shave, a pot of black coffee, and a hot, hearty breakfast. But as they approached the burg of Cleary, Begley instructed him to drive directly to the lodge on the outskirts of town.

The Whistler Falls Lodge was a collection of cabins on a small lake formed by the waterfall just above it. Deep snowdrifts had accumulated along the fence that encircled a playground. Smoke was coming from the chimney of the office. Except for that sign of human occupation, the place seemed a deserted snowscape.

Hoot carefully steered the sedan off the highway, onto what he hoped was the driveway. It was indistinguishable under the deep snow.

"Which one's his?" Begley asked.

"Number eight." Hoot inclined his head in that direction. "The one nearest the lake."

"And he's still registered?"

"He was as of yesterday evening. But his Cherokee isn't here," Hoot observed with disappointment. Only one cabin had a vehicle parked in front of it, and it was partially buried in snow. There were no tire tracks. "Should we check in with the manager?"

"What for?" Begley asked. Hoot looked over at him. "I can see from here that the door to cabin number eight is standing ajar, Special Agent Wise. I bet if we knock on it, it'll open right up," he said with a disingenuous smile.

"But, sir, if this is our guy, we don't want him to get off because his civil rights were violated."

"If this is our guy, I'll violate his head with a bullet before I let him get off on some procedural bullshit."

Hoot parked in front of cabin number eight. When he got out of the car, it felt good to stand up and stretch, even though he sank to his ankles in snow. The wind sucked the breath out of his lungs, and his eyeballs seemed to freeze instantly, but getting to arch his back was worth these discomforts.

Begley seemed not to notice either the blinding snow or the bitterly cold wind. He plowed his way up the steps to the wraparound porch of the cabin. He tried the door, and when he found it locked, he nonchalantly slid a credit card into it. Seconds later, he and Hoot were inside.

It was warmer than outdoors but still cold enough for their breath to vaporize. The ashes in the fireplace were gray and cold. The kitchenette adjoining the main room was clean. No food had been left out. Dishes had been washed and left in the drainer. They'd been there long enough to dry.

Begley put his hands on his hips and pivoted slowly, taking in the details of the main room. "Doesn't look like he's been here for a while. He didn't drive a Cherokee out of here this morning or we'd have seen some tracks even with the way that snow's coming down.

Do you have any thoughts on where Mr. Tierney spent the night, Hoot?"

"None, sir."

"No girlfriend around here?"

"Not that I know of."

"Relatives?"

"No. I'm sure of that. He was an only child. Parents are deceased."

"Then where the hell did he pass the night?"

Hoot had no answer to that.

He followed Begley into the front bedroom. After taking a cursory look around, Begley pointed toward the double bed. "Mrs. Begley would consider that a sloppily made bed. She'd say that's the way a man makes up a bed if he makes it up at all."

"Yes, sir."

Hoot was a man, but he never left a bed unmade, and he always checked to see that the bottom edges of the bedspread were even. Nor did he leave dishes in the drainer; he dried them himself and put them away in their proper places. He also alphabetized his CDs, according to recording artist, not title, and had his sock drawer arranged by color, from the lightest to the darkest, moving left to right.

But he would cut out his tongue before contradicting Mrs. Begley.

Unlike the cabin's main room, the bedroom where Tierney slept looked lived in. A pair of muddy cowboy boots had been kicked into the corner. There was an open duffel bag in the center of the floor with articles of clothing spilling out. Magazines were scattered across the desk beneath the window. Hoot fought his compulsion to straighten them as he ran a quick survey of the glossy covers.

"Pornography?" Begley asked.

"Adventure, sports, outdoors, fitness. The kind he writes articles for."

"Well, shit," Begley said, sounding disappointed. "That room out there would indicate that Tierney is a neat freak."

"Which fits the profile of the unsub we're looking for," said Hoot, realizing as he did that he was indicting his own obsessive-compulsive tendencies.

"Right. But this. Goddammit," Begley said. "This looks like my oldest boy's bedroom. So which is Tierney? A fucking psycho, or just exactly what he looks like? A normal guy who likes the outdoors and doesn't use fiddle books to get his rocks off?"

The question was rhetorical. Which was good, since hearing pornography referred to as "fiddle books" had left Hoot speechless.

The closet door was standing open. Begley peered inside. "Casual, but it's quality stuff," he remarked after checking several labels.

"His credit card statements will attest to that," Hoot said. "He doesn't shop at discount stores."

Begley turned on his heel and quickly left the room. He stamped across the living area and opened the door to the second bedroom. He'd taken no more than two steps into the room when he was brought up short. "Here we go. Hoot!"

Hoot rushed to join him just inside the doorway. "Oh, man," he said under his breath.

Pictures of the five missing women had been taped to the wall above a table, which Hoot realized was the dining table that should have been in the kitchenette. He hadn't missed it there until he saw it here.

On the table was a personal computer and an evidence treasure trove of printed material. Newspaper accounts of the missing women had been clipped from the *Cleary Call*, as well as from newspapers as far away as Raleigh and Nashville. Passages had been marked with colored felt-tip pens.

Yellow legal tablets contained pages of scribbled notes, some scratched through, some underlined or otherwise noted as worth reviewing or remembering. There were five file folders, one for each of the young women. They contained sheets of handwritten notes, newspaper clippings, photos that had been published on missing persons posters or in the media.

And every time there was a mention of the unidentified culprit, it had been highlighted with a blue marker.

Begley pointed down to such a passage. "Blue."

"I noticed that, sir."

"His signature color."

"So it would seem."

"Ever since he took Torrie Lambert."

"Yes, sir."

"The computer—"

"Will no doubt have a user password."

"Think you can crack that, Hoot?"

"I'll certainly try, sir."

"Awright, hold it right there, 'less you want yore heads blowed clean off." The voice had the resonance of a cement mixer. "Raise yore hands and turn round real slow-like."

Begley and Hoot did as asked and found themselves looking down the twin bores of a double-barreled shotgun.

Hoot said, "Hello, Mr. Elmer. Remember me? Charlie Wise?"

He was standing in the center of the room, shotgun raised to chest level. When Hoot called him by name, he squinted for better focus. His face was as red and wrinkled as a persimmon that had been in the sun too long. He was wearing a ratty, moth-eaten watch cap, from which trailed strands of stringy hair that were the same dingy white as his bushy beard. Tobacco juice stains rimmed his lips, which broke into a smile that revealed toothless gums, save for three brown stumps.

"Lord a'mighty. I could've kilt you." He lowered the shotgun. "Did you come to give Mr. Tierney his award?"

Hoot had to think a moment before remembering the cover story he'd fabricated to explain his interest in Ben Tierney. "Uh, no. This is Special Agent in Charge Begley. We're—"

"Gus? You in there?"

"Aw, hell," Gus Elmer said. "I done called the *po*-lice. Thought somebody was in here stealing Mr. Tierney's stuff while he weren't here."

Under his breath, Begley muttered a stream of profanity.

The old man turned to wave in the police officer who poked his head inside the main door. Pistol in hand, he gave the FBI agents a curious once-over. "These the burglars?"

"We're not burglars." Hoot could tell by Begley's voice that he'd had enough of this nonsense and was about to regain control of a situation that had rapidly unraveled. He pushed Hoot forward and soundly closed the door to the bedroom behind them to prevent the other two from seeing what they'd discovered.

"We're FBI agents," Begley continued, "and I'd like for you to reholster your weapon before you shoot somebody, namely me."

The policeman was young, under thirty by several years unless Hoot missed his guess. SAC Begley's nutcracker and authoritative tone flustered him. Only after his pistol was put away did he remember to ask to see their identification. They complied.

Satisfied that they were who they purported to be, he smartly introduced himself. "Harris. Cleary PD." He touched the brim of his uniform hat, which was dusted with melting snow. His uniform pants were stuffed into tall rubber boots. His shearling-lined leather bomber jacket looked a size or two too small, preventing his arms from hanging naturally at his sides. They stuck out several degrees from his body.

Gus Elmer scratched his beard as he gawked at Hoot. "You're an FBI agent? No foolin'?"

"No foolin'," Begley replied, answering for him.

"So what're y'all doin' here? Wha'd'ya want with Mr. Tierney?"

"To talk."

" 'Bout what? Is he wanted for somethin'? What's he did?"

"I'd like to know that myself," said Harris. "Are you serving an arrest warrant?"

"Nothing like that. We just have a few questions for him."

"Huh. Questions." Harris chewed on that for a moment, giving each of them a dubious appraisal. "Have you got a warrant to search these rooms?"

So, Hoot thought, Harris wasn't as inexperienced as he'd appeared.

Ignoring the question, Begley asked, "Your chief's name is Burton, correct?"

"Yes, sir. Dutch Burton."

"Where can I find him?"

"Right now?"

It was such a stupid question, Begley didn't deign to answer it. He didn't recognize a timetable other than *right now*.

When Harris realized his gaffe, he stammered, "Well, uh, I just heard dispatch say the chief was going to round up Cal Hawkins—he has the town's only sanding truck—then take him over to the drugstore for some coffee."

"Hoot, do you know where the drugstore is?" Begley asked. Hoot nodded. Begley turned back to Harris. "Tell Chief Burton that we'd like to join him there in half an hour. Got it?"

"I'll tell him, but he's anxious to—"

"Nothing is as important as this. You tell him I said that."

"Yes, sir," Harris replied. "About that warrant?"

"Later." Begley rapidly crooked his finger at the young officer, who clumped over to him. Unlike his jacket, his boots seemed a size too large. Begley drew close to him and spoke in an urgent undertone. "If you communicate my message to Chief Burton over your police radio, tell him only that it's imperative we meet this morning. Don't mention any names. Do you understand? This is a top-priority, extremely delicate matter. Discretion is vital. Can I count on your confidentiality?"

"Absolutely, sir. I understand." He touched the brim of his hat again and rushed out.

When Hoot had been reassigned to the bureau office in Charlotte, he'd welcomed the opportunity to serve under its famed director. Up till now, he'd worked with Begley from the sidelines. This was Hoot's first chance to watch him in action and observe the skills for which he'd become a living legend with other agents and criminals alike. Colleagues learned from him. Lawbreakers learned from him too, but to their detriment.

Although he never discussed his days of service in the Middle East, the story was that Begley had talked himself and three other men out of being executed for conducting intelligence operations against Saddam Hussein's regime. Although that was exactly what they were doing, Begley convinced their captors that they had the wrong guys, that it was a case of mistaken identity, and that there would be hell to pay if they were harmed, mistreated in any way, or murdered.

Five days after their capture, the quartet of dusty, thirsty men walked into the lobby of the Hilton Hotel in downtown Baghdad to the amazement of colleagues, diplomats, and media personnel, who'd given them up for dead.

The story had been elaborated with each retelling, but Hoot didn't doubt the essence of it. Begley was as straight as an arrow, but he had the soul and mind of a con man. His reputation for manipulation was well deserved.

He had revealed nothing of consequence to young Harris but had appealed to his ego by including him in their "top-priority, extremely delicate matter" and thereby made him forget that they didn't have a search warrant and that, basically, they'd been caught red-handed breaking and entering.

Begley also had emphasized that Harris contact his chief without further delay, which effectively got rid of him, freeing them to question Gus Elmer without an audience.

"I'd love some coffee, wouldn't you, Hoot?" he said suddenly. "Mr. Elmer, may we impose upon your hospitality?"

The old man squinted at Begley with misapprehension. "Huh?"

"Have you got any coffee?" Hoot said, interpreting.

"Oh, sure, sure. In the office. And a good fire going, too. Watch yore step. These steps is as slick as snot on a doorknob."

A few minutes later they were seated in ladder-back rocking chairs in front of a crackling fire. Snow was melting inside Hoot's shoes, making his feet cold, wet, and uncomfortable. He placed them as near the fire as possible.

The coffee mugs Gus Elmer gave them were as chipped and stained as his three teeth, but the brew was scalding, strong, and delicious. Or maybe it just tasted good because Hoot had been craving it so badly.

For all his willingness to assist in an FBI investigation, Gus Elmer didn't provide them with much more information than Hoot had already obtained from him. Ben Tierney was a quiet, personable guest whose credit card charges always cleared. About the only thing odd about him was that he refused to let the lodge's housekeeper clean the cabin while he was occupying it. That peculiarity had been explained by what they'd discovered in the second bedroom.

"But if that's his only quirk, I ain't complainin'," Gus told them. "Ax me, he's the ideal guest. Always leaves the cabin in good condition, turns out the lights, puts his garbage in the cans so the bears and coons cain't get to it. And on the day he checks out, he's out by noon. Yessir, he follows the rules, all right."

"That's an impressive stag, Mr. Elmer," Begley remarked, pointing to the stuffed head mounted on the rock wall above the fireplace. "Was that your kill?"

It was a tactic Begley was famous for. During an interrogation, he would periodically toss out an unrelated comment. He said it served to keep answers spontaneous. By suddenly switching subjects, he kept the person he was questioning from anticipating what he was going to ask next and mentally formulating an answer. It was a means of getting an unfiltered response to a pertinent question.

"Has Mr. Tierney ever talked to you about women?"

Elmer, who'd been admiring his hunting trophy, whipped his head around and looked at Begley quizzically. "Women?"

"Wives, ex-wives, girlfriends, lovers?" Lowering his voice, he added, "Did he ever make reference to his sex life?"

The old man chuckled. "Not that I recall, and I think I'd recall that. I axed him once if his missus would be joining him, and he told me no, on account of he was divorced."

"Do you think he's straight?"

The old man's mouth dropped open, affording them an unappetizing view into the toothless maw. "You tellin' me he's a *queer*? *Him*?"

"We have no reason to think he's homosexual," Begley replied. "But it seems a little strange that a single, good-looking guy like him never mentioned the fairer sex to you."

Again, Hoot was impressed. Begley was probing Gus Elmer's memory without appearing to. He'd counted on Elmer being a homophobe. A man like him wouldn't want his regular lodger, with whom he'd become friendly, to be anything other than a man's man, hetero to the marrow. So if Tierney had ever introduced a woman's name into a conversation, the old man would now be racking his brain to remember it.

While he was concentrating, his grubby little finger plunged into the tuft of hair sprouting from his ear and began mining it for wax. "Now that I think on it, he did say to me the other mornin' somethin' 'bout that last girl who's gone missing."

"Mind if I pour myself another cup?" Without waiting for an answer, Begley got up and went to the coffeemaker on a table across the room.

"He came here to the office to pick up an issue of the *Call* and was reading the front page. I said, 'Ax me, seems like this town's cursed with some kinda nutcase.' He said he sympathized with the girl's folks. What they're goin' through and all."

Begley returned to his rocking chair, blowing on his coffee to cool it. "This is excellent coffee, Mr. Elmer. Special Agent Wise, make a note of the brand, please."

"Of course."

"I'd like to take some back to Charlotte with me for Mrs. Begley. That's all Mr. Tierney said about the girl?" he asked Elmer.

"Uh, let's see," the old man said, trying to keep up. "Uh, no. He remarked he'd seen her just a day or so before she disappeared."

"Did he say where?" Hoot asked.

"In the store where he buys his gear. Said he'd stopped in there to get a new pair of socks and she rung 'em up for him."

"What time was that?"

"That he was in the store? Didn't say. He folded the newspaper, picked up a map, and said he was going hiking up on the peak. I warned him not to let a bear get him. He laughed and said he'd try not to let that happen, and anyway weren't they hibernating this time o' year? Bought a couple o' them granola bars outta the machine yonder and left."

"Has he ever talked about any of the other missing women?"

"Naw. Cain't say as I recall—" Suddenly Elmer stopped. He gave Begley a shrewd look, then shifted his rheumy gaze to Hoot, who tried to keep his expression impassive. When Elmer looked back at Begley, he swallowed hard. Hoot could only hope he'd spat out most of his tobacco first. "Y'all thinkin' Mr. Tierney's the one snatching those women?"

"Not at all. We just want to talk to him so we can cross him off our list of possibilities."

Begley had shown more emotion when talking about the Book of Jeremiah, but Gus Elmer wasn't fooled by his nonchalance. He shook his head, sweeping his chest with his dingy beard. "He's the last person I'd've thought would've did any meanness like that."

Hoot leaned forward, asking, "Have you ever heard him make any derogatory remarks about women?"

"Derog...de...what?"

"Negative or unflattering comments."

"Oh. 'Bout women, you say?"

"Either about women in general or about a particular woman?" Hoot asked.

"Naw, I done told you, the only time he said anything 'bout—" He paused, reached for an empty Dr Pepper can, and spat into it. "Hold on. Just a minute now. I just thought on somethin'." He closed his eyes. "Yeah, yeah, it's comin' back to me. It was last fall. I remember, 'cause we was sitting together on the deck out yonder admiring the foliage. He axed did I want to share a drink, and I said sure. Just to take the chill off the evenin' air, you understand. And somehow we got off on Dutch Burton."

"The chief of police?" Hoot asked, showing surprise.

"Yep, yep. Dutch hadn't been chief long, only a month or so, and me and Mr. Tierney was talkin' 'bout how he'd bit off an awful big bite what with the missing women and all."

"What did he say about that specifically?"

"Nothing. Just that." He spat into the can again, wiped his mouth with the back of his hand, and grinned at them. "Ax me, he was more interested in Dutch's wife. Ex-wife now."

Begley glanced at Hoot as though to make sure he was paying attention. "What about her?"

"Seems Mr. Tierney had met her back during the summer." Gus Elmer's grin widened with what appeared to be relief. "Matter of fact, I can say for sure he ain't no fag. Ax me, he seemed right taken with Dutch's former missus."

Begley stopped his idle rocking. "Taken with her?"

The old man gave a phlegmy laugh. "Moony eyed, smitten, horny, whatever you want to call it."

CHAPTER
14

LILLY WOKE UP COLD. IT TOOK A MOMENT FOR HER TO REMEMber where she was and why. Fully clothed, she lay beneath a triple layer of blankets with her knees pulled up nearly to her chest. The bone-chilling cold had penetrated all the layers.

She lay facing the fireplace, but it was no longer giving off heat. The embers that had been smoldering when Tierney turned out the lights had long since turned to ash. She tipped the blanket down, away from her face, and exhaled through her mouth. Her breath formed a cloud.

The propane tank must have emptied during the night. The fireplace would be their only source of heat now. She should get up and stack the firewood in the grate, get the kindling going. Moving around would help her warm up. But she couldn't bring herself to leave this cocoon of relative warmth.

The room was still dark, with only dull, gray light limning the edges of the drapes. The wind was as strong as it had been the night before. Every now and then an ice-encrusted tree limb would knock heavily against the roof. If ever there was a perfect day for snuggling, this was it.

Perhaps she should have accepted Tierney's proposal. If she had, she might not be shivering with cold now.

But no, she'd made the right decision. That much togetherness would have changed the tenor of their isolation and complicated the situation tenfold. It had been complicated enough by a mere kiss.

Mere kiss? Hardly.

It had been breathtaking but brief. Tierney had released her immediately. Turning his back to her, he'd continued their conversation as though the kiss had never happened. He said that it was probably safe for him to sleep, since it had been several hours since he'd suffered the concussion.

Trying to appear as blasé as he, she had agreed.

He urged her again to eat something, but she said she wasn't hungry, and he said he wasn't hungry either.

He'd offered her first use of the bathroom. While she was in there, he'd dragged the mattress off the bed and into the living room. She'd chided him for not waiting on her to help him, and he'd said she had no business struggling with a mattress when the exertion could bring on an asthma attack. She'd reminded him that he had a brain concussion and shouldn't be exerting himself either. But it was done, so the argument ended there.

By the time he came out of the bathroom, she was huddled beneath her share of the blankets. He switched off the lights and stretched out on one of the sofas. He asked if she was warm enough and offered her one of his blankets, but she declined it, saying she was fine, thanks.

He was restless. It took him a while to settle. She asked him if his head was hurting, and he said it wasn't too bad. She asked if he wanted her to check it for him, apply more antiseptic and new bandage strips, and he said no thanks, he had checked it while he was in the bathroom. She wondered how he'd managed to see the back of his head when there was only one mirror, but she didn't pursue it.

He mentioned that although he was bruised as hell, he hadn't noticed any signs of internal bleeding, and she'd responded with an inane understatement like "That's good." His unintelligible grunt of agreement had signaled an end to their dialogue.

It took her at least an hour to fall asleep, and she was fairly certain that he was still awake when she finally drifted off. During that time between lights out and when she'd fallen asleep, she'd lain stiff and silent and . . . what? Expectant?

After the kiss, the tension between them had been thick enough to cut with a knife. Their conversation became stilted. They avoided making eye contact. They were overly polite toward one another.

Ignoring the kiss had made it all the more meaningful. If they'd joked about it, said something like "Whew, at least that's out of the way. Now that our curiosity has been satisfied, we can relax and get on with the business of surviving," the kiss would have been more easily dismissed.

Instead, they'd pretended it hadn't happened. Neither knew how the other felt about it. Consequently, because each was afraid of bungling, of doing or saying something that would upset a tenuous balance, it went unacknowledged.

And yet, after all their clumsy parrying and phony indifference to the kiss, she halfway expected him to mutter something like "This is bullshit," leave the sofa, and join her on the mattress beneath the blankets. Because it hadn't been a mere kiss. It had been a prelude.

"I'm not that nice," he'd said.

A heartbeat later he was holding her face between his strong hands, which she had been admiring all evening, and pressing his mouth upon hers. He hadn't hesitated or asked permission. Apologetic or tentative? Not in the least. From the moment their lips touched, his were hungry and demanding.

He flipped open her coat and reached inside. His arms went around her, and dipping his knees slightly, he drew her up and into him. He splayed his hand over the small of her back and held her flush against him in a way that said, without equivocation, *I want you.*

A warm, fluid tide of desire spread through her belly and thighs. It had felt great to experience again that rush of sensation that no potable or drug could replicate. There was no other buzz like it, nothing to compare with the intoxicating tingle of sexual excitement.

It had been years. Certainly not since Amy had died, when neither she nor Dutch had had the emotional resources to make good sex. They'd tried, but it became so difficult to pretend enthusiasm for it, she hadn't even attempted to fake orgasms.

Her lack of response was a further blow to his self-esteem, which was already foundering. He'd sought to restore his ego by having a series of affairs. Those she could almost forgive. He'd gone to other women for what she was no longer able to give.

What she couldn't forgive were the affairs he'd had before Amy was even conceived.

It had taken her a long time to understand why Dutch had slept with other women during those early years of the marriage, when their sex life was still so active and good. But she had come to realize that he required constant reassurance. In bed, certainly. Even more so out of it. She also came to realize how exhausting it was to provide that reassurance on a nonstop basis. No amount of bolstering was ever sufficient.

They had met at a black-tie fund-raising event for the Atlanta PD's favorite charity. Riding a wave of recent publicity for solving a multiple homicide case, Dutch was the department's poster boy and had been asked to speak at the banquet.

At the podium, he was handsome, charming, and eloquent. He was a dazzling package: former college football star turned crime-solving hero. His speech had prompted the glitterati in attendance to be generous with their contributions and also had prompted Lilly to approach him afterward and introduce herself. By the end of the evening, they'd made a dinner date.

Within six months they were married, and for a year life couldn't have been better. They both worked hard in pursuit of their careers, but they also played hard and loved hard. They bought the cabin and retreated to it on weekends; sometimes they never left the bedroom.

During those times, he'd brought his self-confidence into their bed. It showed in the way he made love. He was a sensitive and generous partner, an ardent and considerate lover, a supportive husband.

Then the quarrels began, arising out of his resentment of her earning capacity, which far exceeded his. She argued that it didn't matter who made the most money, that he'd chosen a public service career, where the toughest jobs went underpaid and mostly unappreciated.

She was speaking the truth. He heard only rationalizations for his perceived failure. He feared he would never reach the same level of achievement in the police department that she would at the magazine.

Over time his obsession with failure became a self-fulfilling prophecy. Simultaneously, Lilly's star was rising. Her success continued to chip away at his pride. He sought to repair it with women who regarded him as the dashing hero he wanted desperately to be.

Each time Lilly confronted him with his cheating, he expressed deep remorse, claimed his affairs were nothing more than meaningless flings. But they weren't meaningless to Lilly, who eventually threatened to leave him. Dutch declared that if she left him he would die, swore to her that he would remain faithful, told her he loved her, and begged her to forgive him. She did—because she was pregnant with Amy.

The promise of a child reinforced the marriage. But only until Amy was born. During Lilly's postpartum months, Dutch began seeing a policewoman. When Lilly accused him of what she knew for fact, he denied it and blamed her suspicion on fatigue, depression, lactation, and unstable hormones. His ridicule had offended her more than his transparent lies.

In the midst of this marital battleground, Amy created a neutral zone in which they could coexist. She generated enough love to make things seem almost normal. Their shared joy over the child helped them forget past disagreements. They avoided the issues that caused friction. They weren't exactly happy, but they were stable.

Then Amy died. The weakened underpinnings of the marriage rapidly crumpled under the weight of their grief. Their relationship became increasingly bad until Lilly didn't think it could get any worse.

And then it did.

Now, recalling the incident that, for her, had been the deathblow to the marriage, Lilly shuddered and instinctively pulled her knees closer to her chest, burrowing her head deeper into the pillow.

However, after a few seconds she reminded herself that her marriage was history. She didn't even have to think about it anymore. Yesterday had marked her emancipation from Dutch. No longer shackled to him legally or emotionally, she could look strictly forward.

The timing of Ben Tierney's reentry into her life was strangely ironic. He had reappeared on the day she was officially free. Last night, he hadn't only roused slumbering erotic sensors but awakened them with a clamor and a clang. His kiss had made her ears ring.

She had been attracted the moment he smiled at her from his seat on that creaky, rusty bus. Over the course of that day on the river, she'd grown to like everything about him. His looks, certainly. What wasn't to like? But she also liked *him,* his intelligence, the ease with which he could converse on any subject.

Others in the group that day had also been attracted to him. The college girls had made no secret of their infatuation. But even the blowhard, who at first had seemed resentful of Tierney's superior kayaking skill, was asking him for pointers by the end of the day. With no apparent effort, Tierney drew people. No one was a stranger to him.

Yet *he* remained a stranger.

He befriended people by inviting them to talk about themselves, but he revealed nothing of himself. Was it that paradox that made him mysterious and seductive?

It startled her even to think the word *seductive,* because of its sinister overtones. But she couldn't think of a better word to describe Tierney's magnetism. On the two occasions she'd been with him she had responded to that indefinable quality to a degree that was disquieting.

Since their first hello they'd been moving toward last night's kiss. Separately but unquestionably. So when he kissed her, it had seemed like an inevitability that had simply been postponed for a few months.

The kiss had been worth the wait. She had vivid recollections of his thumbs pressing against her cheekbones as he tilted her face up to his, of his breath against her lips, of his tongue sliding evocatively into her mouth. Thinking about it now caused a purl of desire deep within her.

Making as little noise as possible, she turned to look at him and smiled. He was too long for the sofa. The armrest caught him mid-calf. He'd rolled a pillow into a neck support to keep the back of his head elevated.

He was covered with blankets up to his chin, which overnight had become shadowed with stubble. He'd had years of exposure to wind and sun, but he wore their damage remarkably well. She liked the lines that radiated from the corners of his eyes. His lips were slightly chapped. She remembered that from the kiss, how they'd felt rubbing against hers.

She wouldn't have minded a longer kiss. Or a second one. Her refusal to sleep with him hadn't necessarily excluded kissing, but apparently he had taken it as such.

Either that or he hadn't liked it as much as she. No. Impossible. Even if she hadn't felt the unmistakable pressure in his groin, his low growl of self-denial when he released her was enough to convince her that he'd been into it as much as, if not more than, she. He'd seemed almost angry when he broke the kiss, released her, and turned away.

So why hadn't he continued? Or at least asked if it was all right if he did? She'd made it clear that she no longer had any romantic inclinations toward Dutch. He should assume she wasn't involved with someone else, but—

Her train of thought derailed.

She wasn't involved with anyone else, but what about Tierney?

He didn't wear a wedding ring. He'd never mentioned a wife or significant other, but she had never specifically asked. It meant nothing that he'd asked her for a date the day they met. Married men dated other women all the time.

Last night he'd made no reference to a wife or girlfriend who would be worried about him when he didn't return home, but that didn't mean there wasn't one who was frantically pacing the floor and wondering where he was and with whom, just as she'd wondered about Dutch too many nights to count.

How naïve of her to assume there wasn't a woman in his life. A man who looked like him? *Come on, Lilly, get real.*

Her gaze drifted from him to his backpack, which was still on the floor beneath the end table where he'd pushed it last night, claiming it contained nothing useful.

It might, however, contain something informative.

"Scott."

"Hmm?"

"Get up."

"Hmm?"

"I said get up."

Scott rolled onto his back and pried open his eyes. Wes was standing in the doorway of his bedroom, frowning down at him. Scott propped himself on his elbows and looked through the window at total whiteout. He couldn't even see the backyard fence. "They didn't cancel school?"

"Sure they did. But if you think you're going to lay on your lazy butt all day, you've got another think coming. Get up. I'll be waiting for you in the kitchen. You've got three minutes."

Wes left the door open, signaling that there would be no going back to sleep for Scott. With a curse, he fell back onto the pillow. He wasn't even allowed a snow day. Every other person in town would get to blow off today, but no, not him, not the coach's son.

He wanted to pull the covers over his head. He could probably sleep away the whole day if he was left alone. But if he wasn't in the kitchen in three minutes, there would be hell to pay. A few extra z's weren't worth the hassle.

With a scorching *shit!* he threw off the covers.

His old man had actually been timing him. When he entered the kitchen, Wes glanced at the wall clock, then gave him a look that let him know he hadn't made it under the deadline. His mom came to his rescue.

"Good morning, sweetheart. Bacon and eggs or waffles?"

"Whichever's easier." He sat down at the table and poured himself a glass of orange juice, yawning widely.

"What time did you turn in last night?" his dad asked.

"I'm not sure. You weren't home yet."

"I was with Dutch."

"All that time?"

"Hours."

"Did you make it up the mountain?"

By the time Wes had finished giving them an account of the previous night's events, Dora had served Scott a plate with bacon, two fried eggs, and two waffles. He thanked her with a smile.

"We had a real adventure," Wes said. "Especially driving out to that dive where we picked up Cal Hawkins. We were lucky to escape without being shot or buttfucked by a trio of hillbillies."

"Wes!"

He laughed at his wife's horror. "Relax, Dora. Scott knows such things go on, don't you, son?"

Embarrassed for his mother, Scott kept his head down and continued eating. His dad thought it was cute to use vulgar language around him, like he was including him in the society of men who were allowed such privileges. It was bogus, of course, because in every other respect, he was treated like a two-year-old. He was only a few months away from his nineteenth birthday, but he was told what to eat, when to go to bed, and when to get up.

He was the oldest student in the senior class. His dad had made him repeat sixth grade, not because he'd failed any courses, not because he was socially immature or in any way maladjusted, but because Wes had wanted to give him an extra year to grow and develop before he went into middle school sports.

Being detained had been humiliating, but Wes had made the decision before discussing it with either Scott or his mom, and he'd stuck to his decision despite their protests.

"College scouts start looking at players as early as seventh or eighth grade," he'd said. "Another year of growth will give you an advantage. Coming from a small school like ours, you'll need every leg up you can get."

Wes was still making all his decisions for him. Legally, Scott was a man. He could go to war and die for his country, but he couldn't stand up to his father.

As though reading his mind, Wes said, "Finish filling out those application forms today. You've got no excuse not to."

"Everybody's invited to Gary's house to hang out." Gary was one of his classmates. Scott didn't particularly like him, but he had a rec room with a pool table. Spending a snow day shooting stick had more appeal than filling out college application forms.

"Finish the forms first," his dad said. "This time I'll be checking to see if they're done. After lunch, I'll drive you over to the gym so you won't miss a workout."

"I can drive myself."

Wes shook his head. "You spin out on the ice, hit something, have your leg broken. No, I'll drive you."

His mom said, "I don't think it would hurt to miss one workout."

"Then that shows just how little you know about it, doesn't it, Dora?"

The phone rang.

"I'll get it," Scott said.

"*I'll* get it." Wes snatched the phone from his hand. "You start on those forms."

Scott carried his plate to the sink and offered to help his mom load the dishwasher. She shook her head. "Better do as Wes said. The sooner you finish, the sooner you can join your friends."

Wes hung up. "That was William Ritt."

The hair on the back of Scott's neck stood on end.

"He said I should get over to the drugstore right away."

"What for?" Scott asked.

Dora glanced out the window. "Is he open today?"

"Oh, he's open and doing business. You won't believe who just arrived for a meeting with Dutch." He held Scott and Dora in suspense for several seconds before saying in a stage whisper, "The FBI."

"What do they want with Dutch?" Dora asked.

Scott could guess, but he waited for his dad to tell them.

"I'd bet good money it's about Millicent." Wes retrieved his coat and pulled it on. "Since I'm chairman of the city council, Ritt thought I should know about this development." He opened the back door, saying as he went out, "Maybe they've got a lead."

Scott watched him go, staring at the closed door long after he'd left.

CHAPTER

15

Ordinarily, Linda Wexler reported to work at Ritt's Drug Store at six sharp to start brewing coffee and making preparations to open at seven for the diehards who were there every morning hungry for grits and fried ham.

This morning, she wasn't going to make it. She phoned just before daybreak to tell William that her property looked like Siberia. "And it's still coming down something fierce. Until the sanding truck makes it out to these back roads, I'm stranded."

William reported this to Marilee, who tried to dissuade him from leaving the house and opening the drugstore. "Who's going to venture out this morning? At least wait a few hours, until the roads have been sanded."

But he was stubbornly committed to opening on time. "I've already shoveled the driveway. Besides, my customers count on me."

The attached carport had sheltered their cars. She watched through the kitchen window as William got into his, cranked the motor, and gave her a thumbs-up through the windshield when it kicked on. He backed out carefully and drove away.

Although Marilee had tried to talk him out of going, she welcomed being alone in the house. To have an entire day to herself made her feel incredibly lighthearted and free. She returned to her bedroom, removed her robe, and climbed back into her warm bed to indulge in the erotic memories she and her lover had created last night.

He never got to stay all night, of course, but he never left immediately after making love either. For a brief but enchanted while, they would lie together and engage in licentious dalliance. Their heads close, whispering, using the language of poetry or the gutter, they plotted fantasies that would scandalize even the most adventurous lovers. More often than not, they wound up acting out their verbal foreplay.

She denied him nothing. He'd been given unrestricted access to her body. Before him, her sexuality had been an uncharted wasteland. Their first time together, without shame or reservation, she had invited him not only to explore but to exploit it.

The buildup to that first time had been gradual. They'd been acquainted for years, but their perceptions of each other suddenly changed. Simultaneously, it seemed, they began to view one another in a different light. Each was unsure if this new awareness was reciprocated, so they gravitated toward one another cautiously, until the sexual interest was tacitly acknowledged.

Once it was, they began inventing reasons to cross paths. Their conversations were spiced with suggestiveness, although to anyone else they sounded innocent and proper. Should their eyes happen to meet, even in a crowded, public place, they telegraphed an unspoken desire which, each confessed later, had made them flushed and weak.

Then one evening they got what they had independently wished for—time alone. William had gone up the mountain to work on the old homestead, so there was no reason for Marilee to rush home after school. She'd stayed in her classroom, electing to grade papers at her desk rather than tote them home only to carry them back the following day.

He'd noticed her car in the faculty parking lot and went into the building on the pretext of looking for someone else.

He appeared at the open door of her classroom, startling her because she'd thought she was alone in the building. They ran their altogether polite and proper drill. He asked if she'd seen the individual he was supposedly looking for, and she said no she hadn't, but each knew that the exercise was all pretense.

He lingered. She picked up her stapler and studied it as though it were a new and incomprehensible invention, then set it back down in the same spot. He took off his jacket and folded it over his arm. She fingered her pearl earring. They exchanged chitchat.

Soon they ran out of things to say that didn't sound banal. Still, he didn't leave. He stayed, gazing at her with longing, waiting for a signal from her to act on the physical yearning each felt in the other's presence.

In effect, he abdicated the initiative to her. He wasn't free to take a lover. Marilee knew this, accepted it, disregarded it. For once in her life, she was going to be selfish and seize what she wanted without taking into consideration anyone else's opinion. To hell with the consequences.

The boldest thing she'd ever done was ask if he would accompany her into the storeroom and heft a box of books to bring back to the classroom. "My fifth-period class starts reading *Ivanhoe* next week," she told him as they made the short walk, their footfalls echoing off the metal wall lockers along the deserted corridor. "The copies are stored in here."

She unlocked the storeroom door and went in ahead of him. She yanked on the string that dangled from the ceiling light, turning it on, then reached around him to shut and lock the door. Facing him, she stood with her arms at her sides and waited. She'd brought them this far. The next move was his.

He held out for perhaps three seconds before pulling her against him and kissing her with unleashed ardor. He squeezed her ass. He fondled her breasts. He pulled the elastic band from her hair, then grasped handfuls of it and twisted it around his fingers.

Marilee had only read fictional accounts of passion that fiery and could scarcely believe that she was the object of it.

He groped beneath her sweater, but she did better than that. She pulled it over her head and removed her brassiere, revealing her breasts to a man for the first time. Reaching beneath her skirt, she peeled off her panty hose and underpants, then invitingly propped her hips against a stack of boxes.

"Anything you've imagined or fantasized, do with me," she whispered. "I want you to look your fill. Touch me to your heart's content."

He slid his hands up her thighs. Already she was wet. As his fingers moved inside her, she threw back her head. "Anything you want. Anything."

His eyes were glazed with lust, but as he opened his fly and put on a condom, he had the presence of mind to ask if she was a virgin. She told him about her only experience. Her last year in college. A philosophy study partner. It had happened only once, with no more preliminary than a dry kiss.

"The front seat of a car makes for a very unsatisfying fuck."

Miss Marilee Ritt was the last person on earth he would have expected to use that word. Hearing it from her prim lips aroused him beyond his ability to contain himself. It also swiped his conscience clear of any misgivings. He took her fast and furiously, climaxing before she did.

Pulling out of her, he said, "You didn't come, did you?"

"It's all right."

"Like hell it is."

He used his fingers.

Afterward, she was so shaky she had trouble dressing. He helped her. There was laughter over his clumsiness with her garments, sighs when he paused to caress a part of her body, playful remonstrations over his deliciously lewd comments. He helped her into her panties, then stroked her through the damp fabric until she came again, clinging to his shoulders, gasping for breath against his chest.

The air in the storeroom had become close and musky. As they left, Marilee wondered if the next faculty member to unlock that door would notice the scent of sex. She hoped so. The wicked thought made her smile.

The clandestine aspect of the storeroom had added excitement to that first encounter, but from a practical standpoint they couldn't continue to use it. Not only was there a high risk of discovery, but romantically speaking, it left a lot to be desired.

"There are French doors on the north side of my bedroom," she told him. "I'll leave them unlocked for you every night. Come to me whenever you can."

He questioned the plan, but she dismissed his fears that William would discover them. "He goes to bed early and doesn't leave his room until the next morning."

The first night he sneaked into her house, they agreed that making love lying down, in a bed, completely naked, was worth any risk. In words that made her blush, he praised every inch of her body. She amazed him with her unabashed curiosity over his.

"My beautiful lover," she whispered now, repeating what she had said to him last night when she took his penis between her lips. He loved that. Loved it when she closed her mouth around just the tip, which was as smooth and firm as a plum.

The telephone rang, shattering the lovely recollection.

Rolling onto her side, she looked at the caller ID box beside the phone. William, calling from the drugstore. If she didn't answer, she could always claim she'd been in the shower. But if he truly needed her help, could she ever forgive herself for not answering because she wanted to daydream about her secret lover? Guilt won out.

"What is it, William?"

Marilee sounded groggy but also piqued. Had she returned to bed after he left the house? William wondered. Probably. She hadn't gotten that much sleep last night. Ah well, such was the price of passion. Served her right if she didn't get to lallygag around all day as she'd obviously planned to do after last night.

Actually she was to be admired for her stamina. It was a marvel to him that his sister could crawl after one of their marathons of fornication. Her lover's staying power was equally remarkable.

Often he was tempted to ambush one or both of them with his knowledge of their illicit affair. He practically licked his chops in anticipation of the moment when he revealed that he knew about the fervent rutting in his sister's boudoir. They would gape at him in horror, realizing that their futures depended upon his whim.

It would be such a triumphant moment. Of course, half the fun was knowing that such a moment was inevitable, so he could wait. He would know when the time was right, and when it was, he would spring the trap. In the meantime, let them fuck themselves into complacency.

It was difficult to keep the smile out of his voice. "Marilee, I need you to come to the store right away."

"Why? What's wrong?"

"Nothing's *wrong*. I've got customers. Important customers," he said in an undertone. "Two FBI agents. They were waiting in their car when I got here. They're meeting with Dutch to discuss the Gunn girl's disappearance. I should offer them breakfast, and as you know, Linda can't get here."

"I don't know how to use that stove."

"How hard can it be? You'll figure it out. Don't dawdle. I need you here now. I called Wes—"

"Why Wes?"

"As head of the city council, I thought he should know about this. Anyway, he's already on his way. How soon can you get here?"

"Give me ten minutes."

William hung up, with a smirk and a snuffle of self-satisfaction.

The bell above the door jingled when Dutch walked into the drugstore. The merry sound set his teeth on edge.

With a death grip on Cal Hawkins's elbow, Dutch half-dragged him to the lunch counter and unceremoniously plunked him onto a stool, hoping the sudden motion would jar the cretin awake.

"Get him some coffee, please," he said to William Ritt, whose cheerful smile was as annoying as that stupid bell above his door. "Make it black and strong. Same for me."

"Coming up." Ritt motioned toward the burbling coffeemaker.

Unsurprisingly, Hawkins had not been up and raring to go when Dutch arrived at his ramshackle house. Hawkins didn't answer the knock, so Dutch let himself in. The place was so full of junk it was a fire hazard. It stank of backed-up plumbing and sour milk. He'd found Hawkins sleeping fully dressed in a bed that a mangy dog wouldn't be caught dead in. He hauled him off it and propelled him through the house and out to his waiting Bronco.

During the drive downtown, he'd reiterated to Hawkins how vital it was that he pull himself together and get his sanding truck up the mountain. Even though Hawkins had responded to everything he'd said with a nod and a grunt, Dutch wasn't convinced he was completely conscious.

And, as if dealing with Hawkins wasn't bad enough, he had to make nice with the freaking FBI. It was his least favorite thing to do anytime, but it was going to be especially irksome after the night he'd had.

After dropping Wes at his house, he hadn't gone straight to headquarters. It had been very late when he got there, and by way of greeting, the dispatcher had handed him dozens of call memos.

All were complaints he could do nothing about until the weather improved, like the frozen fountain in front of the bank building, a missing milk cow, and a tree branch that had broken off from the weight of the ice and snow. It had fallen onto the owner's outdoor hot tub and cracked the cover.

And this was his problem, why?

Then there was a call from Mrs. Kramer, who had more money than God from Coca-Cola stock a wise great-grandfather had bought cheap. But you would never meet a meaner and more miserly old bat. She'd called to report a prowler in her front yard. Dutch reread the message as written down by his dispatcher. "Does this say Scott H.?"

"Yeah. The Hamer kid. She says he was strolling past her house like it was an evening in May. Up to no good, if you ask her."

"Well, I didn't ask," Dutch had said, "and anyway she's delusional. I was at the Hamers' house. Scott was holed up in his room with the stereo blaring. Besides, Wes wouldn't let him go out on a night like this."

The dispatcher raised his bulky shoulders in a shrug and didn't take his eyes off the John Wayne shoot-'em-up he was watching on a black-and-white TV. "What do you expect from a crackpot whose hobby is digging in trash cans?" Mrs. Kramer was known to pull on Rubbermaid gloves and scavenge through trash cans under cover of darkness. Go figure.

Dutch balled up the memo and shot it into the overflowing wastebasket. He put the other memos in his shirt pocket to deal with later, but only after Lilly was safely down from Cleary Peak. That was all he was interested in this morning—getting Cal Hawkins to drive his sanding truck up the mountain to rescue her.

True, it was still snowing like a son of a bitch. True, beneath the snow was a layer of ice an inch thick. Those were the objections that Hawkins was sober enough to raise, and they were valid. But it wouldn't be as difficult as last night, when they'd had darkness working against them. At least that was what Dutch argued.

Catching his reflection in the mirror along the soda fountain's back wall, he saw what the FBI agents would see—a loser, a burnout. He'd catnapped in his desk chair until dawn, his sleep frequently interrupted by disturbing thoughts of Lilly and what she might be doing at any given moment. What Ben Tierney was doing. What they were doing *together*.

Before leaving headquarters, he had washed up and shaved in the men's restroom, using a dull razor, bar soap, and tepid water in a shallow basin. Had he known sooner that he was going to come under FBI scrutiny, he would have gone home to shower and put on a fresh uniform.

No help for it now.

"How's that coffee coming?" he asked Ritt.

"Another minute or two. I'll bring it over when it's ready."

Having exhausted reasons to delay the meeting, Dutch turned toward the booth where the two agents were waiting like vultures over a dying animal. The older one made a point of checking his wristwatch.

Asshole, Dutch thought. Did they think he was at their beck and call? Apparently so, gauging by the way they had mandated this meeting, giving him virtually no warning.

He'd just pulled up out front of Hawkins's place when he got a call from Harris. The young policeman had sounded out of breath and was sputtering with excitement, but Dutch finally interpreted the message: meet the feebs at the drugstore. "In half an hour, he said."

"Who said? That Special Agent Wise?"

"No," Harris replied. "Older guy. Introduced himself as the SAC."

Fuckin' fabulous. "Where'd you run into them?"

"Uh, I don't think I'm supposed to say. He told me not to mention names over the radio."

"What's he want to see me for?"

"That's something else I'm not supposed to say over the radio."

Dutch swore beneath his breath. What had happened to Harris, for chrissake? Had he been bewitched? "Well, if they're at the drugstore when I get there, fine. But I'm not going to hang around waiting on them."

"I don't think you want to cross this guy, sir."

Dutch hated having his authority challenged, especially by the officers on his force. "I don't think he wants to cross me either."

"No, sir," Harris said. "But the SAC told me it was important that you meet this morning. And the way he said it, it was like... well, like he'd be good and pissed if you didn't show. Just my opinion, sir."

Now that Dutch had seen the SAC for himself, he shared Harris's opinion. One glance and Dutch sized him up as a no-nonsense ballbreaker. He'd had plenty of experience with tight asses like him in the APD. He disliked the feeb instantly.

Without hurry, he ambled over to the booth and slid in across from them. "Morning."

Wise made the introductions. "Police Chief Dutch Burton, this is SAC Kent Begley."

Begley was brittle and brusque, even in the way he said, "Burton," as they shook hands across the Formica. That alone revealed what he thought of Dutch. Begley had dismissed his importance even before they had exchanged a how-do-you-do. In the SAC's mind, this was a formality, protocol he had to go through before elbowing out the dumb local cop.

The federal sons of bitches claimed not to feel that way about local law enforcement outfits. The company line was that they had the utmost respect for anyone wearing a badge. Bullshit. You might find an exception to the rule if you looked hard enough among the rank and file, but generally speaking, they thought they were the know-all, be-all. Period. End of story.

"We apologize for the short notice," Wise said.

Wise had been introduced to Dutch shortly after he moved back to Cleary and assumed the job of chief. As they shook hands the first time, Wise had said he was relieved that someone with know-how would now be working on the missing persons cases. But Dutch had seen through the good manners. Wise had only been humoring him and playing politics.

Ritt delivered three cups of coffee. Begley ignored his. Wise opened a packet of sweetener. Dutch took a sip from his cup before asking, "What's the urgency?"

"You mean besides five missing women?" Begley said.

He was like an industrial-strength abrasive scouring Dutch's raw nerve endings. Dutch wanted to hit him. Instead he locked gazes with the senior agent, and each telegraphed his disdain for the other.

Wise coughed lightly behind his fist and pushed up his slipping eyeglasses. "Sir, I'm certain Chief Burton didn't mean to diminish the importance of finding the missing persons."

"This weather has temporarily suspended my investigation."

"Which amounts to what?" Begley asked.

Ever the diplomat, Wise quickly amended Begley's question. "Perhaps you could bring us up to date on your investigation, Chief Burton."

Dutch was hanging on to his patience by a thread, but the sooner he answered their questions, the sooner he could get on his way. "Since I first learned of Millicent Gunn's disappearance, I've had every spare man I could recruit—from my department, the state police, county sheriff's office, and a goodly number of volunteers—combing the area.

"But the terrain around here makes it slow going, especially since I ordered them not to leave a twig unturned. Yesterday, when the storm moved in, I was forced to call off the search. We're hamstrung as long as this weather keeps up. And I don't have to tell you what it'll do to evidence."

As he gestured toward the front of the building, he saw Wes Hamer and Marilee Ritt approaching the entrance from opposite directions, reaching the door at the same time. Wes held it open for her, then quickly followed her in. They were chuckling over the snow that clung to their clothing. Standing just inside the door, they stamped their feet to shake the snow off their boots.

Wes removed his hat and gloves. Marilee pulled a cap from her head, and he laughed when static electricity made her hair stand on end. The tip of her nose was red, but Dutch was struck by how pretty and animated she looked this morning.

William called to her, and she hurriedly joined him behind the soda fountain. Wes glanced toward the booth where Dutch sat with the FBI agents. He didn't seem surprised to see him there with them. Ritt, in his self-cast role as town busybody, had probably called Wes to inform him of the meeting.

Last night he and Wes had exchanged some harsh words and parted angry at each other. After Dutch's crack about Wes and women, Wes had shoved open the passenger door of the Bronco and stepped out. "You can't afford to piss me off, Dutch. Not when I'm about the only friend and ally you've got left." He'd slammed the door before stamping off into the maelstrom of snow.

Now they acknowledged each other with a curt nod, then Dutch returned his attention to Wise and Begley.

"I spoke with Mr. and Mrs. Gunn last evening," he continued. He didn't tell them that Millicent's parents had sought him out, not the other way around. He was glad he had even this to report. It made him appear on top of the case, proactive.

"I updated them on our canvass of the people that Millicent had contact with on the day she disappeared, first at the high school, later at work. We had compiled a comprehensive list but couldn't get around to interviewing everyone before this storm hit. I have a small department and limited personnel. I operate on a shoestring budget." Because his excuses had begun to sound like whining, he stopped and took another sip of coffee.

He glanced toward the soda fountain. Hawkins sat with his shoulders hunched, holding his coffee cup between his hands as though both were required to keep it steady. Wes was holding court for Ritt and Marilee. He was talking softly, but he had their rapt attention. Dutch wondered what he was saying that was so bloody captivating.

Shifting his attention back to business, he addressed Wise. "Did you learn anything from reading Millicent's diary?"

Let them share the hot seat, he thought. They were on this case, same as he was. With all the resources at their disposal, they hadn't solved it either.

"An entry or two snagged my curiosity," Wise replied. He added another packet of sweetener to his coffee and idly stirred it. "Chances are they're insignificant insofar as her disappearance goes."

"Insignificant?" Dutch scoffed. "If it was insignificant, you wouldn't be here. SAC Begley sure as hell wouldn't be. What got your curiosity up?"

Wise glanced at Begley. Begley continued to stare at Dutch without speaking. Wise cleared his throat and looked at Dutch again, peering at him through his large lenses. "Do you know a man named Ben Tierney?"

Tierney woke up with a start.

He'd been in a deep and dreamless sleep one second. The next he was wide awake, sensors tingling as though he'd been shocked with a cattle prod.

Instinctively he pushed off the blankets and made to sit up. A battery of pains assaulted him, causing him to gasp, his eyes to tear. He was assailed by dizziness. He remained still, taking light, shallow breaths, until the pain receded to a tolerable level and he regained some equilibrium, then cautiously lowered his feet to the floor and sat up.

Lilly was already up, probably in the bathroom.

Although the room was dark, he knew it must be after dawn. He tried the lamp on the end table, and it came on. The cabin still had electricity. However, it was so cold he was shivering. Apparently the propane had run out during the night. First order of the day was to build a fire.

Ordinarily, he would have acted on that immediately. This morning, however, merely sitting upright had seemed an insurmountable task. His muscles were sore, his joints stiff from sleeping all night in one position—the only position the sofa allowed. Even the expansion of his rib cage when he breathed was painful.

Lifting his coat and sweater, he examined his torso. The entire left side was the color of eggplant. Gingerly, he felt along each rib. He didn't think any were broken, but he wouldn't swear to it. It couldn't hurt any worse if they were. Luckily he didn't have a punctured organ, or if he did, it was leaking slowly. In any case, he hadn't bled to death during the night.

His head wound had left spots of blood on the pillowcase, but it wasn't a substantial amount. No more shooting pains through his skull, just a dull headache and the recurring dizziness, which he could control if he didn't move too suddenly.

Fortunately he wasn't as nauseous as he'd been last night. In fact, he was hungry, which he took as a positive sign. The thought of coffee made his mouth water. He would ration enough of their water reserve to brew them one cup each.

He glanced toward the closed door of the bedroom. Lilly was taking her time in the bathroom, and it had to be even colder in there than it was here. What was she doing that could possibly take this long? A delicate question, and not one you posed to a woman.

Hell of a thing, being trapped in this cabin with her. Hell of a thing.

Easing himself off the sofa, he hobbled to the window. The wind was still blowing, though not as hard as the night before. That was the only improvement. Snow was falling in such abundance it had begun to build up against vertical surfaces. The ground cover was at least knee-deep, he guessed. They wouldn't be getting off the mountain today. He'd hated like hell making those trips to the shed, but it was a good thing he had. They would need the extra firewood.

He let the drape fall back over the window, crossed to the bedroom door, and knocked softly. "Lilly?" He put his ear to the wood and listened but detected no movement or sound.

Something isn't right.

He didn't just sense it, he knew it. He knew it as positively as he knew that his feet were cold and that his head had begun to hurt again, probably because of his rising blood pressure.

He knocked on the door again, louder this time. "Lilly?" He pushed the door open and looked in. She wasn't in the bedroom. The bathroom door was closed. Quickly he went to it and knocked so hard it hurt his cold knuckles. "Lilly?" When he didn't get an immediate answer, he opened the door.

The bathroom was empty.

Alarmed, he spun around but came to a staggering halt when he saw her standing behind the bedroom door, where she must have been hiding when he came in.

Fuck!

The contents of his backpack lay scattered on the floor at her feet. And in her hands, aimed directly at him, was his own pistol.

CHAPTER

16

HE TOOK A STEP TOWARD HER.

"Stay there or I'll shoot you."

He indicated the items on the floor. "I can explain all that. But not while you're pointing a gun at me." He advanced another step.

"Stop, or I will shoot you."

"Lilly, put down the gun," he said with infuriating calmness. "You're not going to shoot me. At least not intentionally."

"I swear to God I will."

Her trembling hands were wrapped around the gun the way Dutch had taught her. Over her objections, he had insisted she learn how to fire a pistol. He said he'd made enemies of criminals who might come looking for him once they were released from their incarceration, for which he was largely responsible. He'd taken her to the firing range and coached her until he was satisfied that she could protect herself in a crisis situation.

The lessons had been more for his peace of mind than for hers. She couldn't conceive of ever having to put them to the test. She certainly never thought they would be tested on Ben Tierney.

"Who are you?" she asked.

"You know who I am."

"I only thought I did," she said gruffly.

"Every male above the age of twelve carries some kind of firearm in this part of the country."

"True. A pistol in a hiker's backpack isn't cause for alarm."

"Then explain why you're pointing it at me."

"You know why, Tierney. You're not stupid. But I believe I have been."

So much of what he'd said and done over the past eighteen hours had struck her as curious but in no way frightening. Combined with what she had discovered in his backpack, that perception had dramatically changed.

"Lilly, put down the—"

"Don't move!" She thrust the pistol forward another inch when he took a hesitant step. "I know how to fire this, and I will."

Her voice lacked enough steam to sound convincing. Because she was trapped without any hope of rescue with a man she now suspected of kidnapping five women, probably murdering them, and because she had missed two doses of medication, her breathing had become increasingly labored.

It didn't escape his notice. "You're in trouble."

"No, *you* are."

"You've started to wheeze."

"I'm all right."

"Not for long."

"I'll be fine."

"You said that becoming emotionally overwrought can bring on an attack. Fear will do that."

"I'm the one with the pistol, why would I be afraid?"

"You don't need to be afraid of me."

She made a scoffing sound and willed herself to resist his piercing blue gaze. "Do you expect me to take your word for that?"

"I would not harm you. I swear it."

"Sorry, Tierney. You'll have to do better than that. What were you doing on the mountain yesterday?"

"I told you, I—"

"Don't insult my intelligence. It was a lousy day for sightseeing. Who goes sightseeing on a mountaintop when an ice storm is forecast? Certainly not someone with your experience of the outdoors."

"I admit it was careless."

"Careless? You? Out of character. Try again."

His lips formed a hard, thin line, reminding her that he resented his word being challenged. "The storm rolled in faster than I expected. My car wouldn't start. I had no choice but to walk down."

"That much I believe."

"I was taking a shortcut to avoid the switchbacks on the road. I got lost—"

"Lost?" She pounced on the word. "You, with the sixth sense for direction, got lost?"

Trapped in the lie, he faltered, then tried another tack. "You've been caught up in the mania."

"Mania?"

"Over the disappearances. Every woman in Cleary is afraid that she may be the next to vanish. It's a communitywide preoccupation. You've been here for a week. The panic has rubbed off on you. You regard every man with suspicion."

"Not every man, Tierney. Only one. The one who doesn't have a logical explanation for wandering around in the woods during a blizzard. The one who knew the location and layout of my cabin without my telling him. The one who refused to open his backpack last night, for reasons which are now obvious."

"I promise to explain all that," he said tightly, "but not while you're holding me at gunpoint."

"You can explain it all to Dutch."

The features of his face turned hard and pronounced, as though the skin had suddenly been stretched tightly over the bones.

She withdrew her cell phone from the pocket of her coat. It was still showing no service.

"You're making a mistake, Lilly."

The words and the low, measured tone in which he spoke them chilled her blood.

"To let your imagination run wild will be a costly error."

She couldn't listen, couldn't be swayed. He had been lying to her ever since that first disarming smile on the bus. He'd only been playing a role, one that must have worked well for him before. Everything he had done and said was a lie. *He* was a lie.

"I beg you to give me the benefit of doubt."

"All right, Tierney," she said. "I'll give you the benefit of doubt if you can explain these."

Lying at her feet were the handcuffs she'd found in one of the backpack's zippered compartments along with the pistol. She kicked them forward. They slid across the hardwood floor and came to rest against his stocking feet. He stared down at them for a long moment before raising his head and looking at her, his gaze implacable.

"That's what I thought." Keeping the pistol in her right hand, she used her left to punch in Dutch's cell number. The phone was still dead as a stone, but she pretended that the call went through to his voice mail. "Dutch, I'm in grave danger from Tierney. Come soon."

"You're so wrong, Lilly."

She slid the phone back into her coat pocket and gripped the pistol between both hands. "I don't think so."

"Listen to me. Please."

"I'm through listening. Pick up the handcuffs."

"How can you possibly think I'm Blue? Because of a pair of handcuffs and a ribbon?"

She'd heard Dutch refer to the unknown suspect as Blue. Hearing it fall so casually from Tierney's lips caused her heart to thud against her ribs. But that wasn't what struck terror in her.

It must have shown in her expression. "Come on, Lilly," he said softly. "You can't be surprised I know the cops' nickname for the culprit. It's a small town. Everyone in Cleary knows."

"Not that," she said, wheezing loudly. "I hadn't even mentioned the ribbon."

Special Agent Wise's question was out of context, or so it seemed to Dutch. For a moment he was flummoxed. "Ben Tierney?" They'd been talking about his investigation into Millicent Gunn's disappearance when, out of nowhere, Wise asked if he knew Ben Tierney.

He divided a puzzled look between Wise and Begley, but he might just as well have been looking into the eyes of two dolls. Theirs were that planar and opaque. "What's Ben Tierney got to do with the price of tea in China?"

"Do you know him?" Wise asked.

"Face with a name, that's it." Then, suddenly, he was seized by a chill that had nothing to do with the outdoor temperature. He felt that unease he used to feel when entering a building where a suspect was believed to be holed up. You knew something bad was bound to go down, you just didn't know what form it would take, or how bad it would be. You didn't know what to be afraid of but knew enough to be afraid. "What about Ben Tierney?"

Wise looked down into his coffee and carefully balanced the spoon on the rim of the saucer.

His avoidance was more telling than anything he might have said. Dutch's heart clenched. "Look, if he's involved in this—"

"How well does your ex-wife know him?"

Dutch's gaze swung to Begley, who'd fired the question at him. Blood rushed to his head. "What the hell are you talking about?"

"We understand that they're acquainted."

"Who led you to understand that?"

"How well are they acquainted? What's the nature of their relationship?"

"There's no relationship," Dutch said angrily. "She met him once. Why?"

"Just curious. We're checking out several angles to—"

Dutch banged his fist on the table hard enough to rattle cutlery and dishes. Wise's spoon fell off the saucer and clattered onto the table. "Cut the bullshit and tell me what you know about this guy. You're big, bad FBI agents, but I'm a cop, goddammit, and as such I'm entitled to your respect, as well as any information you have pertaining to my investigation. Now what about Ben Tierney?"

"Calm down," Begley commanded. "And just so you know, I don't condone foul language and taking the Lord's name in vain. Don't do it in my presence again."

Dutch slid from the booth, reached for his coat and gloves, and put them on with jerky, angry motions. Then he leaned down and thrust his face close to Begley's. "First of all, fuck you. Second, get this, you sanctimonious prick. If you've got an interest in Ben Tierney related to the disappearance of these women, I need to know it, because as we speak, my wife is marooned in our mountain cabin with him."

For once they showed reactions, which ranged from surprise to a degree of alarm that caused Dutch to fall back a step. "Christ almighty. Are you telling me that Ben Tierney is Blue?"

Casting a cautious glance toward the rapt group at the soda fountain, Wise said in an undertone, "We've recovered some circumstantial evidence that warrants further investigation."

The agent was beating around the familiar bush Dutch himself had beaten around many times while he was a homicide detective. It was what you said when you knew a suspect was guilty as sin and needed only one scrap of hard evidence to nail his ass.

He pointed his finger at Begley. "I don't need further investigation to know that the bastard spent the night with my wife last night. If he's touched a single hair on her head, you'd better hope to God you get to him before I do."

Turning his back on them, he strode to the lunch counter, grabbed Cal Hawkins by the collar, and plucked him off the bar stool. "Showtime."

"If that motherfucker's jealous temper blows my case, I'll wring his frigging neck."

This from the FBI agent who'd told Dutch less than sixty seconds ago that he didn't condone foul language.

As he and the younger agent approached the soda fountain counter, their expressions were so resolute, their bearings so intimidating, Marilee felt like backing away from them. The older one barked, "Any of you know where he's going?"

"Up the mountain to rescue Lilly." Wes stood up and extended his right hand. "Wes Hamer, chairman of the city council, head coach of the high school football team."

He shook hands with them in turn as they introduced themselves. Wes waved away the small leather wallets they proffered. "No IDs necessary. We know you're legit. I've seen you around town a time or two," he said to Wise. Motioning toward her and William, who were behind the counter, he said, "William Ritt, and his sister, Marilee Ritt."

"Can I get you anything?" William asked. "More coffee? Some breakfast?"

"No thanks." Marilee could tell that the one named Begley had grown impatient with the pleasantries. "I understood that Burton and his wife were divorced, that she even goes by Lilly Martin now."

"He's had a hard time accepting it," William said.

"They lost a child, a daughter, a few years ago," Wes explained. "People react differently to tragedies like that."

Begley looked over at his partner as though instructing him to make mental notes. Marilee figured he already was.

"What do you know about her being marooned with Ben Tierney?" Begley asked. "Did they plan on meeting up there?"

"I don't know for sure, but I seriously doubt it was a rendezvous." Wes told them about the cabin previously belonging to the Burtons and its recent sale. "They were up there yesterday afternoon clearing out the last of their stuff. Dutch left for town ahead of her. Apparently on her way down the mountain road, there was some sort of accident involving Tierney. She left a cryptic message on Dutch's cell phone, said that Tierney was hurt but that they were in the cabin, and asked that Dutch send help ASAP."

"Hurt how?"

"She didn't say, or how badly. There's been no further communication. The cabin's phone line had already been disconnected, and the cell service in these mountains is for shit—sorry, Mr. Begley. On good days our cell service around here is crummy at best. In bad weather, you can forget it."

Wes took Begley's silence as a signal to continue. "Dutch called on me last night to help him find Cal Hawkins. The guy he just hauled out of here? He has the town's only sanding truck." He recounted the aborted attempt to drive up the mountain road. "Finally even Dutch had to concede it was impossible. He's damned and de-termined to try again this morning. That's where he's off to now."

Wise said, "I don't hold out much hope for success this morning either."

"Try telling him that."

"I'd like to get to that cabin myself," Begley said, pulling on his overcoat. "Last thing we need is Burton charging up there half-cocked."

"Do you really think Ben Tierney is Blue?"

"Where'd you hear that?" The look Begley fixed on William, who had ill-advisedly asked the question, would have halted a charg-ing rhino. It stopped the storekeeper from stating the obvious, that he would have to be deaf not to have overheard their conversation with Dutch.

Nervously he wet his lips, saying instead, "It just makes a weird kind of sense."

"Oh? How's that, Mr. Ritt?"

"Well, everyone else in town is well known. Mr. Tierney is a stranger. We know very little about him."

"What *do* you know about him?" Special Agent Wise asked.

"Only what I've observed whenever he comes into the store."

"How often is that?"

"When he's in town, he comes in frequently. He always..." William cast a wary glance around at his listeners. "It's probably not important."

"What, Mr. Ritt?" Impatiently Begley slapped his gloves against the palm of his other hand. "Let us decide if what you've observed is important or not."

"Well, it's just that, whenever he's in the store, he attracts atten-tion."

"Attention?" Begley shot Wise another look. "From whom?"

"Women," William replied simply. "He attracts them like a mag-net." Looking over at Wes, he added, "I've overheard you and Dutch and your friends talking about him. Someone called him a peacock."

"Guilty," Wes said, raising his right hand. "I think the guy knows that women swoon over that rugged outdoorsy type."

All eyes turned toward Marilee, who felt herself go rosy with embarrassment. "I've only seen Mr. Tierney on a few occasions, but I've read some of his articles. They're quite good, actually, if you're interested in that kind of thing."

Apparently Begley wasn't. He turned back to William. "Does he ever engage women in conversation?"

"All the time."

"What do they talk about?"

"I don't make a practice of eavesdropping on my customers."

All evidence to the contrary, Marilee thought. He'd just admitted that he listened in on Wes and Dutch's conversation.

Begley looked skeptical of William's claim, too, but he let it pass without comment. "What does Tierney buy when he comes in? If you can tell me without it violating professional privilege," he added, tongue in cheek.

William actually smiled at him. "Not at all, since he's never had a prescription filled. He buys lip balm, sunscreen, toothpaste, disposable razors. Nothing out of the ordinary, if that's what you're asking."

"It is."

"Nothing out of the ordinary. The only curious thing is that he usually makes only one purchase at a time. One day it's Band-Aids, the next it's a tin of Advil, the next a paperback book."

"Like he's creating reasons to come in here?" Begley probed.

"Now that I think on it, yes. And it seems that he's always in the store when I'm swamped with customers. Mid to late afternoon. A lot of people stop here before going home."

"Millicent Gunn?"

"Sure. A lot of the high school kids come to the soda fountain after school. As long as they behave themselves, I let them—"

"Have Ben Tierney and Millicent Gunn ever been in the store at the same time?"

William was about to answer when the importance of the question registered with him and his lips snapped shut. He looked at each of them in turn, then seemed to wilt as he slowly nodded his head. "Week before last. Only a couple of days before she disappeared."

"Did they talk?" Wise asked.

William gave another nod.

Begley turned to Wes. "Where do we find this sanding truck?"

"If you want to follow me, I'll take you."

Begley didn't wait for Wes to lead the way. Turning, he strode swiftly toward the door, pulling on his gloves as he went.

"Is he always that abrupt?" William asked Wise, who was wading through his layers of clothing to get to his wallet.

"No. He was up all night, so his reactions this morning are a little slower than usual. What do we owe you?"

William motioned for him to keep his money. "On the house."

"Thank you."

"My pleasure."

Wise nodded at William, tipped an imaginary hat to Marilee, then left to join Begley.

Wes was about to follow when she called him back and passed him the pair of leather gloves he'd left lying on the counter. "You'll need these."

He took them from her and playfully tapped the end of her nose with them. "Thanks. See y'all later."

As she watched Wes leave, Marilee caught William's knowing smirk reflected in the mirror. She ignored it, saying, "I guess no one wanted breakfast after all."

"I'm going to fry a couple of eggs." He turned on the griddle. "Would you like some?"

"No thanks. You shouldn't have mentioned Blue."

"What?"

"The code name. I'm sure you noticed Begley's reaction. No one outside the authorities is supposed to know about the blue ribbon. You told me. Wes had told you. Who told Wes?"

William dropped a pat of butter onto the griddle, and it began to sizzle as it melted. "He got it straight from the horse's mouth."

"Dutch?"

"Of course Dutch."

"He's the chief of police," she exclaimed. "He should know better than to tell Wes about evidence that's supposed to be a secret."

"They're best friends. Bosom buddies." He cracked two eggs onto the griddle. "They don't keep secrets from each other. Besides, what's the harm?"

"It could jeopardize his investigation."

"I fail to see how."

"If you and I know, how many other people know?"

He reached for the saltshaker and shook it over his eggs. "What difference does it make now that they've identified Blue?"

"None, I suppose."

"However," he said, flipping the eggs, "there's a good lesson to be learned, Marilee."

"What's that?"

"Nobody in this town can keep a secret." He smiled at her, but she had an uneasy sense that it wasn't as benign a smile as he pretended.

CHAPTER

17

LILLY NUDGED HER TOE AGAINST THE CURL OF BLUE VELVET RIB-bon on the floor. She'd found it in a zippered compartment of Tierney's backpack while she was looking for evidence of another woman in his life. When she lifted her gaze to him, words were unnecessary.

"I found it," he said.

"Found it?"

"Yesterday."

"Where?"

He raised his chin in the direction of Cleary Peak's crest.

"Just lying on the ground in the forest? A length of blue ribbon?"

"It was caught in some brush," he said. "Fluttering in the wind. That's how it caught my attention."

Her distrust must have been apparent.

"Look, I know why you freaked out when you saw it," he said. "I know what it implies."

"*How* do you know?"

"Everyone knows about the ribbon, Lilly."

She shook her head. "Only the police and the culprit."

"No," Tierney said evenly, "everyone. Dutch's police force isn't an airtight organization. Somebody let it leak that a blue velvet ribbon had been left at the presumed spot of each abduction."

That was what Dutch had told her, but in confidence. "They intentionally withheld that information."

"Not very well. I've overheard it being discussed in the drugstore," he said. "Once while I was picking up my dry cleaning, the owner told the lady customer in front of me to beware of Blue, and she knew what he was talking about. Everyone knows."

He nodded down at the strand of ribbon. "I don't know if that's the kind of ribbon Blue is leaving behind, but it's a damned odd thing to come across in the wilderness. So I removed it from the brush, tucked it into my backpack, and was taking it back to town with me to turn over to the authorities."

"You didn't mention this last night."

"It wasn't relevant."

"Those missing women have been the talk of Cleary for more than two years. If I had found something that was possibly an important piece of evidence, I think I would have mentioned it."

"It slipped my mind."

"I asked if there was anything useful in your backpack. You said no. Why didn't you mention the ribbon then? Why didn't you say, 'No I don't have anything useful, but take a look at what I found fluttering from a bush today'?"

"And if I had? Think about it, Lilly. If I had shown you the ribbon last night, would that have precluded me from being Blue?"

She didn't have an answer for that. She didn't have answers for a lot of things. She wanted desperately to believe that he was exactly what he appeared to be: a charming, talented, intelligent, fun, sensitive man. None of those qualities, however, disqualified him from committing crimes against women. Indeed, those personality traits would work to his advantage.

He still hadn't explained the handcuffs. Outside of S & M sex and law enforcement, what purpose did they serve? It made her ill to speculate. "Millicent Gunn was reported missing a week ago."

"I've been following the story."

"Is she still alive, Tierney?"

"I don't know. How would I?"

"If you took her—"

"I didn't."

"I believe you did. I believe that's why you had a length of blue ribbon and a pair of handcuffs in your backpack."

"Incidentally, why were you searching through my backpack?"

Ignoring that, she said, "Up on the crest yesterday afternoon, you were doing something you wanted done before the storm. Disposing of the body, perhaps? Digging Millicent's grave?"

Again, the skin seemed to stretch tightly across his features. "After sleeping a couple feet away from me last night, you actually believe that only hours before I was digging a grave?"

Not wanting to think about her misjudgment and vulnerability last night, she tightened her grip on the pistol. "Pick up the handcuffs."

He hesitated, then bent down and picked them up.

"Put the bracelet around your right wrist first."

"You're making a dreadful mistake."

"If I am, you'll spend an uncomfortable afternoon, and it'll piss you off. If I'm right, and you are Blue, I'll be saving my life. Given the choice, I'd rather piss you off." She raised the pistol a fraction. "Lock the bracelet around your right wrist. Now."

Ponderous seconds ticked by. Finally, he did as she asked. "In case the cabin catches on fire, or you start to suffocate from an asthma attack, do you have the key handy?"

"In my pocket. But I won't be releasing you until help arrives."

"Which could take days. Can you survive that long without your medication?"

"That's for me to worry about."

"I worry about it, too, goddammit." His voice had turned harsh, husky. "I care what happens to you, Lilly. I thought my kiss would have conveyed that."

Her heart tripped over a few beats, but she ignored the flutter. "Get on the box springs and put your right arm through the ironwork of the headboard." Supported by a frame of sturdy wood, the decorative wrought iron had spaces wide enough for him to reach through.

"When I kissed you—"

"I'm not going to talk about that."

"Why not?"

"Get on the box spring, Tierney."

"You were as shaken by that kiss as I was."

"I'm warning you, if you don't—"

"Because it satisfied our curiosity and then some. I'd fantasized kissing you, but it—"

"Get on the box spring."

"It was a million times better than my fantasies of it."

"This is your last warning."

"I am not handcuffing myself to that headboard!" he shouted angrily.

"And I'm not asking again."

"You lay there last night for a long time before going to sleep, didn't you? I knew you were awake. You knew I was. We were thinking about the same thing. About that kiss and wishing—"

"*Shut up* or I'm going to shoot you!"

"—that we hadn't stopped there."

She pulled the trigger. The bullet smacked into the wall, coming close enough for him to have felt the movement of air against his cheek. He looked more shocked than afraid.

"I'm good," she told him. "The next shot counts."

"You wouldn't kill me."

"If I take out your kneecap, you'll wish I had. Get on the bed," she said, enunciating each word.

Regarding her with renewed respect, he backed up until his calves made contact with the box spring. He sat down and scooted backward on his butt. She knew his grimaces of pain must be genuine, but she didn't let them weaken her resolve. When he reached the headboard, he hooked his right hand through the iron fretwork.

"Now lock the other ring around your left wrist."

"Lilly, I beg you not to make me do this."

She said nothing, just stared at him down the short barrel of the pistol until he relented and fastened the bracelet around his left wrist. "Pull down on them hard, so I can see that they're locked."

He gave several hard tugs, rattling metal against metal. He was secured.

Lilly's arms dropped to her sides as though they weighed a thousand pounds. She slumped against the wall behind her and slid down it until her bottom reached the floor. She rested her head against her raised knees. Until this moment, she hadn't realized how terribly cold she was. Or perhaps she was shaking with fear.

She was afraid her assumption that he was Blue was right. And equally afraid it was wrong. By keeping Tierney handcuffed to the headboard, she could be dooming herself to death by suffocation.

No. She refused to contemplate anything except survival. Dying was not an option. Death had cheated her daughter out of a long life. She'd be damned before it cheated her, too.

After a few moments, she pushed herself to her feet. Without even a glance toward Tierney, she went into the living room.

"You need to bring in more firewood while you still have the strength," he called to her.

She refused to engage in conversation with him, but that had been exactly what she was thinking. The leather of her boots was damp and cold, but she worked her feet into them regardless of the discomfort.

Tierney's watch cap was crisp with dried blood, but it was handier than dealing with the bulky stadium blanket for head covering.

She pulled the cap down over her ears and as low as her eyebrows. She also used his scarf to wrap around her throat and the lower half of her face. Her cashmere-lined gloves were inadequate against such brutally cold temperatures, but they were better than nothing.

When she was ready, she approached the door.

Watching her from the bedroom, he said, "For godsake, Lilly, let me do this for you. You can hold me at gunpoint the whole time. I don't care. Just let me do it."

"No."

"That cold air—"

"Be quiet."

"Christ," he swore. "Don't leave the porch. Move the logs inside before you start splitting them."

Sound advice. He had excellent survival skills. Was he as good at getting women to trust him? she wondered. Evidently so. Five had trusted him. Actually six, counting herself.

The interior of the cabin was cold, but nothing compared with outside. The cold air slashed her exposed cheekbones. She had to keep her eyes narrowed to slits. The tarpaulin Tierney had placed over the stack of firewood was covered with several inches of snow that had been blown beneath the overhang.

She reached beneath it and dragged a log off the top of the stack. It was so heavy it slipped from her hands and banged against the floor of the porch, narrowly missing her toe. Awkwardly, she picked it up and cradled it in her arms while she opened the door. She carried it inside, shutting the door with her foot.

She placed the log on the hearth, then paused, inhaling deeply through her mouth in an attempt to fill her lungs, trying to convince herself that breathing was easy.

"Lilly, are you all right?"

She tried to tune him out and concentrate on forcing air through her constricting bronchial tubes.

"Lilly?"

His alarm sounded sincere. The handcuffs rattled against the wrought iron as he pulled against it. She moved away from the hearth and stepped into his line of sight. "Stop yelling at me. I'm okay."

"Like hell you are."

"I'm fine except for being trapped with a serial criminal. What do you do to them while they're handcuffed, Tierney? Do you torture and rape them before you kill them?"

"If that's what I do, why haven't I tortured, raped, and killed you?"

"Because I called Dutch and left the message that I was here with you." She was struck by sudden enlightenment. "Now I understand why you flinched every time I mentioned his name, why you were so preoccupied with him, why you hounded me with questions about our current relationship."

"Because I wanted to know if you were still in love with him."

That was exactly what she had concluded. He had duped her into thinking that jealousy was behind his persistent questions about Dutch, the ex-husband. That she'd fallen for the ploy made her as angry at herself as at him. "I won't waste any more breath talking to you."

He gave the handcuffs several vicious yanks. Fortunately, they held.

She went back outside. For almost an hour she labored, carrying in one log at a time. Each seemed heavier than the one before it. The chore became increasingly difficult. The rest periods between trips grew longer.

Luckily some of the logs were small enough to catch when she ignited kindling beneath them, and the warmth from the fireplace was welcome. The hatchet, as feared, wasn't up to the task of splitting the larger logs.

She debated walking to the shed to get the ax Tierney had overlooked but decided against it, fearing she wouldn't make it back. Instead, she used the hatchet to hack away at the wood until she had enough chunks to last for several hours.

What was uncertain was whether *she* would last that long.

"Lilly?"

For half an hour she'd been sitting on the mattress with her back against the sofa, resting and trying to ease her breathing.

"Lilly, answer me."

She laid her head back against the end of the sofa and closed her eyes. "What?"

"How are you doing?"

She was tempted not to answer, but he'd been calling her name intermittently for the last five minutes. Evidently he wasn't going to give up until she responded.

Throwing off the afghan, she stood up and padded to the open bedroom door. "What do you want?"

"Jesus, Lilly." His face registered shock, confirming her suspicion that she must look like a zombie. She'd seen herself in the throes of an asthma attack before. It wasn't pretty.

"Are you warm enough?" she asked ungraciously.

"You're starved for oxygen."

She was about to turn away when he said quickly, "I could use a blanket over my legs."

She retrieved one from the mattress. The woven wool had retained the heat from the fireplace. Standing at the foot of the bed, she unfurled it above him and let it settle over his outstretched legs.

"Thanks."

"You're welcome." She noticed that his wrists were raw from pulling against the handcuffs. "That won't do any good. You're only going to hurt yourself."

He glanced at the abraded skin. "I finally came to that conclusion." He flexed his fingers a few times. "My hands get numb for lack of circulation. I didn't plan very well when I locked myself to the headboard. I should have placed my hands lower. Waist level. Then I wouldn't be in such an awkward and uncomfortable position."

"That was lousy planning."

"I don't suppose you would consider unlocking the cuffs long enough—"

"No."

"I didn't think so." He shifted his position, wincing with pain, but she didn't give in to the pity he was trying to invoke.

"Are you hungry?" she asked.

"My stomach's been growling."

"I'll bring you something."

"Coffee?"

"Okay."

"It'll have to count for a ration of water."

Always the Boy Scout. Ever prepared.

Five minutes later she returned to the bedroom with a mug of fresh coffee and a plate of crackers spread with peanut butter, staples they had brought with them from her car.

She said, "I left the pistol, along with the key to the handcuffs, in the living room." She moved aside so he could look past her to the end table. "If you're thinking about burning me with the coffee, or pinning me down with your legs, or overpowering me in any way, it won't do you any good. You still couldn't get to the gun or the key."

"Very clever."

Setting the coffee and the plate on the floor, she unwound the scarf from around her neck and tossed it far out of reach.

He frowned at her. "Have I just been insulted?"

"You could use it as a weapon."

"Strangling you wouldn't be very smart, would it? You'd be dead, and I'd be helplessly handcuffed."

"I'm taking no chances."

"Why were you wearing my scarf?"

"Can you handle the mug?"

"I'll try. Can't promise not to dribble. Why were you wearing my scarf?"

"For warmth, Tierney. No other reason. I don't want to go steady."

She placed the mug between his hands. He folded his fingers around it, then lowered his head to it and took a sip. "I guess it's a good thing my hands aren't at waist level after all. I couldn't eat or drink if they were."

"I wouldn't let you starve or die of thirst."

"You're a kind jailer, Lilly. Not into cruel and unusual punishment. Although." He waited until he was sure he had her full attention before saying, "It'll be pretty damn cruel if you die on me."

"I don't plan to."

"See that you don't."

His voice had meaning behind it. So did the way he was looking at her. She resisted both. "Ready for your crackers?"

"I'll finish my coffee first."

She backed away and sat down in the rocking chair a safe distance from the bed, keeping her head averted.

"Did Dutch talk to you often about the missing persons cases?"

Surprised by the question, she looked at him sharply.

"He must have been the one who told you about the blue ribbon, the nickname Blue."

"I never asked him to discuss his cases, but I listened when he did."

"What else did he tell you about the Cleary disappearances?"

She responded with a cool, steady stare.

"Come on, Lilly. If you're convinced I'm Blue, you won't be divulging anything I don't know. Did Dutch know the significance of the blue velvet ribbon?"

"Its significance to Blue, you mean?"

He nodded.

"He had a theory about it."

"What was it?"

She was hesitant to discuss what she knew about the cases with Tierney. But if she did, she might learn something. "The first to disappear, Torrie Lambert, is the only one who isn't a local resident."

"She and her parents were vacationing in Cleary," he said. "They went on a guided hike to enjoy the autumn foliage. She and her mother quarreled. In typical fifteen-year-old fashion, the girl stalked off to pout alone. She was never seen again."

"That's right."

"Stop looking at me like that, Lilly. I came to Cleary shortly after the girl disappeared. The story was front-page news for weeks. I read the accounts like everybody else. Anyone could tell you what I just did. What's Dutch's take on the ribbon?"

"That's all they found of her," Lilly said. "The other hikers in the group, including her parents, thought she would eventually catch up with them. When she didn't, they became concerned. By nightfall they panicked. After twenty-four hours they concluded that this was more than just an adolescent snit, that she was no longer missing by choice. Either she had been injured and couldn't make it back, or she was hopelessly lost, or she'd been taken."

"Rescue teams searched for weeks, but winter came early that year," he said, picking up the story. "The girl—"

"Stop calling her 'the girl,' " she said testily. "Her name is Torrie Lambert."

"Torrie Lambert vanished as though the ground had opened up and swallowed her. Not a trace of her has been found."

"Except for a blue velvet ribbon," Lilly said. "It was discovered in some underbrush. Across the state line in Tennessee."

"That's what led the authorities to believe that she'd been kidnapped. To get to the spot where the ribbon was found, she would have had to walk ten miles over some of the most rugged terrain east of the Mississippi," he said.

"Her mother identified the ribbon as the one Torrie had been wearing in her hair that day." She stared into near space for a moment, then said quietly, "Mrs. Lambert must have gone through pure hell when she saw that ribbon. Torrie has very long hair, almost to her waist. Lovely hair. That morning, she wore it in a single braid and had plaited the ribbon into it."

Shifting her gaze back to Tierney, she said, "So, whatever else you did to her, you took the time to unbind her hair and remove the ribbon."

"Blue did."

"I wonder," she continued as though he hadn't contradicted her. "Were you careless, or did you leave the ribbon behind deliberately?"

"Why would it deliberately be left behind?"

"To throw off the search parties. Mislead them. If so, it worked.

After the ribbon was found, trained track dogs were brought in. They quickly lost the scent." She ruminated for a moment. "I question why you didn't take the ribbon as a trophy." .

"Blue had his trophy. He had Torrie Lambert."

His tone made Lilly shiver. "So the ribbon is only a symbol of success."

Tierney took a last quick sip of coffee. "I'm done. Thanks."

She took the mug from his hands and passed him two of the crackers, one for each hand. He demolished the first in one bite. When he bent his head to eat the second, she noticed the bandage. "Does the head wound hurt?"

"It's tolerable."

"It doesn't appear to be bleeding." She extended him another cracker. But instead of taking it, he snatched her wrist, tightly closing his fingers around it. "I'll survive, Lilly. I'm more worried about your survival."

She tried to pull her hand free, but he held on. "Let go of my hand."

"Unlock the cuffs."

"No." She struggled futilely.

"I'll go to your car and get your medication."

"Flee, you mean."

"Flee?" He gave a short laugh. "You've been outside. You know what it's like. How far do you think I'd get if I wanted to *flee*? I want to save your life."

"I'll live."

"Your face is gray. I could hear every breath you took when you were in the living room. You're struggling."

"I'm struggling with *you*."

This time when she tugged on her hand, he released it. She took several wheezing breaths. "Do you want this?" she asked, extending the last cracker toward him.

"Please."

Rather than holding it within reach of his hands, she held it a few inches from his mouth. "Don't bite me."

Frowning as though she had again insulted him, he inclined his head forward and caught the cracker between his teeth, being careful not to touch her fingers. She snatched her hand back. He worked the cracker into his mouth. She picked up the empty plate and mug and headed for the living room.

"If you won't let me go, at least move me in there, where I'll be able to keep an eye on you."

"No."

"If I'm in there, you'll be able to watch me closer."

"I said no."

"Lilly."

"No!"

"You never did tell me Dutch's theory about the ribbon. What does it represent to Blue?"

After a moment's hesitation, she said, "Dutch says he's using it as a symbol of his success to taunt the authorities."

"I agree. And that's probably the only time Dutch and I will ever agree on anything. The man's a fool for a lot of reasons, one being that he left you alone on this mountain yesterday with an ice storm moving in. What was he thinking?"

"It wasn't entirely his fault. I encouraged him to leave ahead of me."

"Why?"

"I'm not going to talk to you about Dutch and me."

He looked at her for a long moment, then said, "I respect you for that. Honestly, I do. I wouldn't want you talking to him about us, either."

"There is no *us,* Tierney."

"That's not true. Not at all. And you know it. Before you decided that I'm a deviate, we were well on our way to becoming an *us.*"

"Don't read too much into one kiss."

"Ordinarily I wouldn't," he said. "But that kiss wasn't ordinary."

She knew she should separate herself from him without delay. Close her ears. Avoid looking into his eyes. Yet they held her in place as though they'd cast a spell over her.

"Deny it all you want, Lilly, but you know that what I'm saying is the truth. It didn't start for us last night. It's been going on from the moment you stepped aboard that bus. Every second of every day since then, I've wanted to put my hands on you."

She dismissed the quickening in her lower body. "Is that how you do it?"

"What?"

"Do you sweet-talk those women into going with you without a whimper?"

"You think this is sweet talk?"

"Yes."

"A line to woo you?"

"Yes."

"So you'll unlock the cuffs and I'll be free to ravage you?"

"Something like that."

"Then explain why I stopped with one kiss last night."

His eyes searched hers while he waited for an answer that never came.

Eventually he said, "I stopped because I wouldn't take advantage of the situation. We were in dangerous circumstances. Cut off from the rest of the human race. We'd been talking about Amy. You were emotionally fragile, vulnerable, in need of comfort and tenderness.

"We were also hungry for each other. If we had continued kissing, I knew where it would lead. I also knew that, later, you might either regret it or question my motives. I didn't want you to have any misgivings afterward, Lilly. That's the only reason I didn't join you on the mattress."

He sounded earnest. God, did he ever. "That was quite a sacrifice. Saint Tierney."

"No." His eyes speared into hers like twin pinpoints of light. "If you had asked me to fuck you, I would have in a heartbeat."

Her sudden intake of air caused her lungs to wheeze. "You're very good, Tierney." Her voice was a mere croak, not entirely from asthma. "Sweet one minute, erotic the next. You say all the right things."

"Unlock the cuffs, Lilly," he whispered.

"Go to hell."

Last night her survival had depended on trusting him.

Today it depended on mistrust.

CHAPTER
18

W HAT THE HELL, WES?"
       "Before you blow a gasket, stop and think about this."
       Wes joined Dutch where he was standing in front of an
electric space heater. It did minimal good inside the cavernous
garage, but the glowing red coils gave the impression that, by standing near it, he was staving off the penetrating cold. It was only an
impression. The cement floor conducted the cold up through the
thick soles of Dutch's boots and woolen socks, straight into his feet
and legs.

He stamped his feet to keep the blood circulating. He also
stamped with impatience. Cal Hawkins had been in the men's room
since they arrived. The last time Dutch had checked on him, he was
still heaving into a nasty toilet.

"They were going to follow you anyway," Wes said of the two
FBI agents who had trailed him to the garage in their own car.
They'd remained inside the sedan with the motor running. The
tailpipe was emitting a cloud of exhaust, which to Dutch looked like
the breath of a beast on his tail.

"This Begley character wants to get to Tierney just like you do,"
Wes continued. "So instead of tearing up the mountainside on your
own, why not let them shoulder some of the responsibility?"

As much as Dutch hated to admit it, Wes made sense. If something bad happened up there—for instance, if Tierney sustained a fatal gunshot wound while trying to escape—there would be inquiries,
and review boards, and paperwork out the wazoo. Why not let the
feebs bite off a chunk of that?

"If this doesn't work," Wes said, nodding toward Hawkins, who had emerged from the restroom looking like a walking cadaver, "the feds have choppers, trained rescue teams, high-tech tracking equipment, all that."

"But if I use them, I answer to them," Dutch argued. "That galls. Big time. Besides, when I get to Tierney—"

"I hear you, and I'm with you one hundred percent on that issue, buddy," Wes said in a low voice. "Especially if he's our woman snatcher. All I'm saying is—"

"Use the FBI up to a point."

Wes slapped him on the back and gave him the grin he used to give him in the huddle when they'd agreed on the play that would leave the other team bumfuzzled and beaten. "Let's get this show on the road." But as they walked toward the sanding truck, he frowned. "Is he all right, you think?"

Hawkins was in the driver's seat, but his arms were draped over the steering wheel, hugging it like a life preserver. "He'd better be. If he fucks this up, I'm going to kill him, and then I'm going to keep him in jail for the rest of his natural life." Dutch opened the passenger door and climbed in.

"I'm right behind you if you need me," Wes told him.

When Wes closed the passenger door, Hawkins flinched. "No need to slam it," he grumbled.

"Start her up, Hawkins," Dutch said.

He cranked the ignition key. "I'll start her, but it ain't gonna do no good. I've said it a thousand times, and I'll say it again. This is nucking futs."

Dutch eyed him suspiciously. "Do I smell liquor on your breath?"

"Last night's. Recycled," he replied as he checked his side mirrors.

Dutch looked into the mirror on the passenger door and watched Special Agent Wise back up the sedan. Then Wes backed his car into the street, leaving Hawkins a clear route.

No more than ten seconds out of the garage, the windshield became blanketed in snow. Hawkins's glance toward Dutch said, *I told you so.* Muttering to himself, he turned on the windshield wipers and shifted gears. With a great deal of reluctance—or so it seemed to Dutch—the rig chugged forward.

The plow attached to the truck's front grille cleaved a temporary path for the cars following them. Hawkins also laid down the mix of sand and salt. It helped, but each time Dutch looked into the side mirror, Wise and Wes were searching for traction. So he stopped looking.

He had set his cell phone to vibrate rather than ring. Knowing it hadn't, he checked it anyway to see if he had a voice mail. He didn't. He dialed Lilly's cell number, hoping that on a fluke he would find a signal. He got the expected No Service indicator.

She would call if she could, he told himself. Her cell phone was as useless as his. Otherwise she would contact him.

He leaned into the windshield and craned his neck to look toward the crest of Cleary Peak. He could see no farther than a few feet above the roof of the truck. It was total whiteout beyond the point where individual snowflakes were distinguishable as they kamikazed into the windshield.

If it was this bad down here, it would be far worse at the top of the mountain. Not wanting to spook his driver, he didn't say that out loud, but Hawkins read his mind.

"Higher we go, the worse it's gonna get," he said.

"We'll take it a foot at a time."

"More like an inch." After a moment, he said, "What I'm wonderin'..."

Dutch looked over at him. "What?"

"Does your old lady want to be rescued?"

"What do you think, Hoot?"

"About what, sir? Specifically." Hoot was focused on the center of the car's hood, trying to keep it in the middle of the chute that the sanding truck had opened for them.

"Dutch Burton. What's your read on him?"

"Extremely sensitive to criticism. Even when it's only implied, he immediately gets his back up."

"The common reaction of one who perpetually fails and/or has low self-esteem. What else, Hoot?"

"He wants to get his former wife away from Ben Tierney, more from rank jealousy than a conviction that Tierney is Blue. He's reacting like a man, not an officer of the law."

Begley beamed at him as though he were a prodigy who'd given the correct answer to a trick question. "What did Perkins unearth about the lady?"

While waiting for Chief Burton to arrive at Ritt's store, Hoot had used the pay phone to call the Charlotte office. He had his laptop with him, of course, but the computers in the office had faster and better access to more extensive information networks. He'd asked Perkins to see what he could find on Burton's ex and had warned his counterpart that Begley was in a hurry to get the information.

Perkins had said, "Damn. Okay. Give me ten." He'd called back in under five.

"She's editor in chief of a magazine called *Smart*," Hoot told Begley now.

"You're shitting me," he exclaimed.

"No, sir."

"Mrs. Begley swears by that magazine. I've seen her spend a weekend with an issue. She redecorated our living room to match one she saw in it. Are you married, Hoot?"

The sudden question gave him a start. "Sir? Oh. No, sir."

"Why not?"

He wasn't opposed to the idea. In fact, he favored it. The problem was finding a woman who wouldn't become bored with him and his ordered life. That had been the pattern with him and women. There would be a few dates, some of them overnighters, before he and the woman drifted apart for lack of enthusiasm.

Recently he'd begun exchanging e-mail with a woman he'd met on the Internet. She lived in Lexington and was pleasant to "talk" to. She didn't know he worked for the FBI. Women were often more infatuated with the macho image of the bureau than with him. All Karen—that was her name—knew of his work was that it involved computers. Miraculously, she was still interested.

Their last chat had lasted an hour and thirty-eight minutes. She actually had him sitting at his computer in his immaculate home office laughing out loud over an anecdote involving her one and only attempt to save money by coloring her own hair. She assured him that the disastrous result had been remedied in a salon and had been worth every penny spent on it. It had got him to thinking that maybe he needed a little zaniness in his life.

More than once she had mentioned to him how pretty Kentucky was in the spring. If that lead-in resulted in an invitation for him to come and see the splendor of a Kentucky spring for himself, he would seriously consider going. He got nervous thinking about meeting her face-to-face, but it was a good kind of nervousness.

Hoping that Begley couldn't see the flush he felt in his cheeks, he said stiffly, "My focus the last few years has been the pursuit of my career, sir."

"Fine, well, and good, Hoot. But that's your job, not your life. Work on that."

"Yes, sir."

"Mrs. Begley keeps me sane and happy. Don't know what I'd do without her. I'd like you to meet her sometime."

"Thank you, sir. It would be an honor."

"Lilly Martin. It's safe to assume that she's a savvy lady?"

Hoot's brain tried to shift tracks with the agility of Begley's. "Yes, sir. She holds dual degrees in art and journalism. Started out as a gofer at another magazine and came up through the ranks to her current position. Perkins passed along some websites we can look at later. He said photos show her to be quite attractive."

He cast a glance at Begley before continuing. "And there was something else, sir. About Ben Tierney. Perkins said that on one of his credit card statements there was a charge to a catalog that sells paramilitary gear. He purchased a transponder and a pair of handcuffs."

"Jesus Christ. How long ago?"

"The charge was on his August statement."

Begley thoughtfully tugged on his lower lip. "Mr. Elmer told us that Tierney had met Lilly Martin last summer."

"And that he was attracted to her."

"What we don't know is whether or not the attraction was mutual," Begley said. "Maybe they've been seeing each other since last summer. As the ex, Dutch Burton wouldn't necessarily know about it."

"Correct."

"On the other hand...," Begley began.

"If Ms. Martin was *not* attracted to Tierney, and if he is Blue..."

"Yeah." Begley sighed. "He wouldn't like being rebuffed." He lapsed into a glum silence for several minutes, then thumped his fist against his thigh with aggravation. "Son of a bitch! This just doesn't gel, Hoot. According to Ritt, and Wes Hamer agreed, women are naturally attracted to Tierney. So tell me why he would kidnap them. Huh, Hoot? Any ideas?"

Although Begley was impatiently waiting for an answer, Hoot carefully thought it through first. "When I was in law school—"

"Speaking of that," Begley interrupted. "I learned only a short while ago that you had a law degree. Why didn't you become a lawyer?"

"I wanted to be an FBI agent," he said without hesitation. "For as long as I can remember, that's all I ever wanted to be." His ambition had been ridiculed by the tough guys in school. Even his parents had suggested that he have an alternative in mind should his first choice of career not pan out. He hadn't let the skepticism of others dissuade him.

"The problem was, well, sir, I didn't serve in the military. I had no police training. To look at me, you wouldn't immediately think that I would be a suitable candidate for the best criminal investigation agency in the world. I don't fit the image most people have of a federal agent. I was afraid the bureau wouldn't accept me unless and until I distinguished myself in some other way. I figured a law degree would help, and obviously it did."

He glanced at Begley, who had been handpicked by the bureau because of his outstanding military service record, leadership qualities, and—most important—his set of brass balls. Their qualifications were so disparate it was laughable.

Begley was assessing him thoughtfully, although not harshly. Hoot thought that maybe, hopefully, he had passed muster in Begley's estimation. That was no small thing. In fact, it was huge. It was the big bang of approval ratings.

"You asked me why Tierney takes women, sir. I was about to give you a correlation that may apply. From my first semester in law school, a classmate and I were in a dead heat to be top of our class. He looked like a young John Kennedy. Athletic. Charismatic. Dated a *Sports Illustrated* swimsuit model. In addition to all those attributes, he was brilliant. Positively brilliant.

"But he cheated. Rampantly. In just about every class, through every year of law school, he cribbed on every assignment and test. He wound up with a grade point a fraction higher than mine and graduated in the number one spot."

"He was never caught?"

"No, sir."

"That must have been difficult for you to stomach."

"Not really, sir. He probably would have outscored me anyway. The point is, he didn't need to cheat."

"So why did he?"

"Law school didn't present a challenge. Cheating and getting away with it did."

Up ahead, Wes Hamer's taillights blinked on once, twice, three times. Hoot took that as a signal that he would need to brake soon. He let up on the accelerator. Beyond Hamer the sanding truck's brake lights came on, and with them, the right turn signal. Gently Hoot applied his brakes so he could slow down gradually.

Begley seemed oblivious to anything beyond the windshield. He was ruminating on Tierney's motivation. "So here we have another overachiever who's run out of challenges. He's taking them to see if he can. But why these women? Why not—"

Suddenly he unbuckled his seat belt and turned toward the back-seat, making Hoot awfully nervous. Reaching between the seats, Begley picked up the five file jackets containing the countless bureau forms and investigative information that Hoot had compiled for each missing persons case. Facing forward again, Begley stacked the files in his lap. Hoot breathed easier when he was buckled back into his seat.

"Last night, as I was wading through these files, I kept thinking I was reading the same story time and again," Begley said. "I just now figured out why."

"I'm not following, sir." Hoot took the sedan into a careful turn. By following Hamer at a safe distance, he was able to roll to a stop, coming short of ramming into Hamer's rear end when he braked. Ahead of Hamer, the sanding truck was laboring to get traction on the incline that rose sharply just beyond the turn.

Begley slapped his palm on the top file. The abrupt noise startled Hoot enough to make him jump. "These women had something in common, Hoot."

"No one working the cases has found a common thread among the victims, sir. Not a place of employment, body type, back-ground—"

"Neediness."

Not sure he'd heard correctly, Hoot risked turning his head to look at Begley. "Sir?"

"They were all needy in one way or another. Millicent, we know, was anorexic, which is symptomatic of emotional and self-image problems, right?"

"That's my understanding."

Begley took them in descending order. "Before her was Carolyn Maddox. Single mother, working long hours to support her diabetic child. Laureen Elliott." He opened her file and scanned the contents. "Ahh. Five feet three inches tall, two hundred forty pounds. She was overweight. I'll bet if we investigate her, we'll learn that her weight had been a lifetime problem, that she'd been on every fad diet ever invented.

"She was a nurse. Working in the medical profession, she was constantly reminded of the health risks associated with obesity. Maybe pressure had been placed on her to lose weight or lose her job."

"I see where you're going with this, sir."

"Betsy Calhoun's husband died of pancreatic cancer six months prior to her disappearance. They'd been married twenty-seven years. She was a homemaker. What does all that indicate to you, Hoot?"

"Uh..."

"Depression."

"Of course."

"Betsy Calhoun was married immediately after high school. She never worked outside the home. Her husband handled all their personal business. She probably never even signed a check until after he died. Suddenly she's having to fend for herself, and besides that, she's lost the love of her life, her reason for living."

Begley was so wound up that Hoot didn't have the heart to point out this was all conjecture. Conjecture based on sound logic, but still conjecture that wasn't substantiated and would never hold up in a courtroom.

"This is key, Hoot," Begley continued. "He hasn't taken a woman who's secure in her career, who's in a solid romantic relationship, physically fit, or emotionally stable. Before they disappeared, all these women were dodging the slings and arrows, so to speak.

"One's depressed, one's obese, one's working her fingers to the bone trying to make ends meet and keep her kid semihealthy, and one binges on junk food and makes herself puke. Then," he said with a dramatic flair, "enter our perp. Gentle and understanding, compassionate and kind, and looking like fucking Prince Charming to boot."

Warming to the theory, Hoot said, "He befriends them, wins their confidence and trust."

"Gives them his broad shoulders to cry on and holds them in his strong, tanned arms."

"His m.o. is to help needy women."

"Not just help, Hoot, *rescue*. Deliver. Looking the way he does, being the rugged adventurer he is, he could get all the sex he wants, whenever he feels the urge. That may be a component, a fringe benefit, but what gets his pole up is being their savior."

Then a thought occurred to Hoot that toppled the whole hypothesis. "We forgot Torrie Lambert. The first. She was a beautiful girl. Straight A student. Popular with her classmates. No major hang-ups or problems.

"Besides," Hoot continued, "Blue didn't seek her out. He stumbled across her when she left the group of hikers. He didn't know she was going to be wandering alone in the woods that day. She was taken because she was available, not because she was needy."

Frowning, Begley opened her file and began flipping through the contents. "What about the men in that group of hikers?"

"Present and accounted for the whole time she was missing. They were questioned at length. No one left the group except Torrie."

"Why did she?"

"In interviews, Mrs. Lambert, Torrie's mother, admitted that they'd had a row that morning. Nothing serious. Typical teenage angst and attitude. I would guess she resented being on vacation with her parents."

"That's precisely where Mrs. Begley and I are with our fifteen-year-old. We're an embarrassment. She's mortified if we acknowledge her in public." He brooded on that a moment before continuing. "So Blue happens upon Torrie, who's in a pissy, fifteen-year-old mood. He chats with her, sympathizes, takes her side against her mother, says he remembers what a pain in the ass parents can be..."

"And she's his."

"In a New York minute," Begley said with finality. "Eventually she'll start to feel uneasy with him and try to return to her parents. He asks her, why would you want to go back to them when I'm the friend you need? Creeped out by now, she tries to get away. He loses his temper. She dies under his hands.

"Maybe it wasn't his intention to kill her," Begley continued. "Maybe things got out of hand and he didn't realize until too late that she was no longer breathing. But all the same, whether he raped her or not, he got off on it."

He closed his eyes as though following the actions and thought processes of the perpetrator. "Later, when he isn't captured, and no one's even looking at him as a suspect, he realizes how easy it was. Now he's got a taste for it. Dominance is the ultimate ego trip. The quintessential rush is taking someone's fate into your own hands, controlling her destiny.

"While he's off ice climbing or some damn fool thing, he realizes it's just not as thrilling as it used to be. The adrenaline isn't pumping as it once did. He starts thinking about the high he derived from killing that girl, and suddenly he's got a hard-on to do it again.

"He decides to return to Cleary and see what kind of aid he might render to some other needy female, see if he can recapture that particular exhilaration. He comes back here because the risk of capture is slim to none. He thinks the cops are hillbillies, not nearly as smart as he is. There are lots of places to hide, acres of wilderness in which to stash corpses. He likes it here. It's the perfect place for his latest thrill-seeking pastime."

By the time Begley concluded the imaginary scenario, he sounded angry. His eyes sprang open. "Why aren't we moving?" Wiping the foggy windshield with his coat sleeve, he asked, "What the fuck's taking so long?"

Inside the cab of the sanding truck, Dutch was rapidly losing patience. "You can do better than this, Cal."

"I could if you'd stop yelling at me." Hawkins sounded close to tears. "You're making me nervous. How do you expect me to drive when you're cussing me out with every breath? Forget what I said about your old lady, about if she wanted to be rescued. Didn't mean to make you mad. I was just asking."

"Lilly is my business."

Hawkins mumbled something under his breath that sounded like "Not anymore, she ain't," but Dutch didn't address it because, factually, Hawkins was right. Besides, they were approaching the road's second hairpin curve, the one that they'd been unsuccessful navigating last night. He wanted Hawkins to give the switchback his undivided attention.

He downshifted, and as he did, Dutch noticed that the man's hands were shaking. Maybe he should have allowed Hawkins one pull on a bottle of whiskey. From his own heavy drinking days, he knew that sometimes even a small hit could make all the difference between having the shakes and a steadier hand. But it was too late now. Hawkins went into the turn.

Or tried.

The front wheels followed the command of the steering wheel. They turned to the right. The truck didn't. It continued going straight, heading unerringly for the drop-off, which Dutch knew was at least eighty feet.

"Turn it!"

"I'm trying!"

As the treetops loomed large in the windshield, Hawkins screamed and reflexively stamped the clutch and brake pedals, then let go of the steering wheel and crossed his forearms in front of his face.

Dutch was helpless to stop the momentum of the skid. The plow on the grille struck the guardrail, which crumpled and gave way to several tons of momentum. The front wheels went over the edge and seemed to hang there for several seconds before the rig tipped downward.

Dutch remembered the movie *Duel,* where during the climactic scene, an eighteen-wheeler went off a highway and plunged down a mountainside. The sequence had been filmed in slow motion. That was what this was like for him—watching and experiencing their inexorable descent in agonizingly slow motion.

Vision was a blur. Everything ran together. But the sounds had a stark clarity. The windshield shattering. Boulders knocking against the underside of the chassis. Breaking branches. Tearing metal. Hawkins's terrified screams. His own animalistic roar of disbelief and defeat.

Actually, the trees probably saved their lives by slowing them down. Had the slope not been so heavily forested, their plunge would have been swifter and therefore deadly. After what seemed like an eternity, the rig came up against an immovable object with brain-rattling force. Inertia propelled them forward, although they went no further. The truck surrendered and came to a shuddering standstill.

Miraculously, Dutch's brain hadn't been instantly liquified by the impact. He was sentient, and was surprised to realize that he was alive and basically unhurt. Apparently Hawkins had also survived. Dutch could hear him mewling pitiably.

Dutch unbuckled his seat belt and, putting his shoulder to the passenger-side door, shoved it open. He rolled out, landing several feet below, in snow that came almost to his waist after he struggled to his feet.

He tried to get his bearings but was blinded by the wind-driven snow that seemed to be aimed at his eyes. He couldn't even see what had stopped the truck's descent. All he could make out was a forest of black tree trunks against a field of white.

However, he didn't have to see it.

He heard it.

He felt the vibration of it in the ground, in the trunk of the tree he had propped himself against for balance, in his balls.

He didn't bother to shout a warning to Hawkins or try to pull him from the wreckage to safety. He didn't attempt to run and save himself. Defeat had robbed him of initiative, immobilized him.

The futility of his life culminated in this single moment. He would just as soon die here and now because his hope of reaching Lilly had been crushed.

Wes watched in disbelief as the sanding rig disappeared over the ridge.

He leaped from his car and stood in the wedge of the open door, as though being outside would give him a clearer understanding of how this had happened.

He could hear the rig plowing its way down the slope. A tremendous crash was followed by what sounded like a metallic sigh, the truck's death rattle. Following that was an eerie silence that was even more horrific. The hush was so absolute, Wes could hear snowflakes striking his clothing.

The quiet was broken by Begley and Wise, who approached as quickly as the slippery incline of the road would allow. Their vehicle had been far enough behind Wes's that they hadn't had his vantage point. Begley reached him first, huffing and emitting plumes of vapor from his mouth. "What happened?"

"They went over."

"Holy shit."

Begley didn't even chide Hoot for his whispered expletive. Because at that moment the three of them heard another sound, one which they couldn't identify but which they knew portended a continuation of the disaster.

They traded mystified looks.

Later they determined that what they'd heard was the splintering of wood. Trees that three grown men couldn't reach around had been snapped as easily as toothpicks. At the time, they couldn't see it happening because of the whiteout.

Speaking for all of them, Wes said, "What the hell is that?"

Then they saw it, dropping out of the low clouds, snow, and fog, destined for earth like a landing spacecraft with its red warning lights still flashing. The power line tower struck the ground with such force that even the deep snow didn't cushion it. Later, Wes swore to those to whom he gave an account of the bizarre event that the repercussion caused his car to bounce off all four tires.

He and the two FBI agents stood in speechless awe for several moments, unable to absorb what they'd just witnessed, unable to believe that they'd survived. Had the tower fallen thirty yards closer, it would have crashed on top of them.

Dutch's fate was unknown. Wes could only hope that he and Hawkins had survived. But the other casualty was Mountain Laurel Road. It was now blocked by tons of steel and forest debris that formed a barricade two stories high and almost that wide. No one could go up that road now.

It was equally impassable to anyone hoping to come down.

CHAPTER

19

LILLY ADDED A STICK OF FIREWOOD TO THOSE SMOLDERING ON the grate. She'd been stingy with them, adding one at a time, and only when necessary to keep the fire alive.

Despite her frugality, the wood supply she'd carried in earlier had dwindled to a few chunks, which she'd hacked off the larger logs. If the wood continued to burn at this rate, she might have enough for another two hours.

What she would do when it ran out, she didn't know. Even inside the cabin, without a fire she would probably freeze during the coming night. She desperately needed the fire to survive. But—and here was the irony—the exertion of carrying in more firewood would likely kill her.

"Lilly?"

She rolled her lips inward and squeezed her eyes shut, wishing she could close off her ears as effectively. His voice was too persuasive, his arguments too reasonable. If she let them sway her, she could become victim number six.

Arguing with him was exhausting. They went round and round, getting nowhere. She wasn't going to release him; he had an arsenal of arguments for why she should. And then there was her wheezing. Talking exacerbated it, so she had stopped answering him altogether.

"Lilly, say something. If you're still conscious, I know you can hear me."

His tone had developed an angry edge, sharpened by her refusal to respond. She left her place near the fireplace and went to the living room window, glancing into the open bedroom door as she walked past. "Why don't you be quiet?"

She pushed aside the drapery and looked out, hoping to see that the snowfall had abated. Far from it. It was so thick she could see only a few yards beyond the porch overhang. The mountain peak had become an alien landscape, white and soundless and separate.

"Has it slowed down any?"

Shaking her head, she turned from the window and hugged her elbows for warmth. Moving away from the fireplace for even a brief time had allowed the cold to penetrate through her layers of clothing. She had put on every pair of socks she had with her, but her feet remained cold. She would have blown on her hands for warmth, but she couldn't spare the breath.

Tierney hadn't complained of being cold. His strenuous efforts to escape the handcuffs were keeping him warm. Apparently he had decided that escape was worth having raw, bleeding wrists after all. He hadn't even tried to cover the sounds. She'd heard the continual clank of metal against metal, the thumping of the headboard against the wall, and curses of sheer frustration when the cuffs refused to give.

"How's the firewood situation?" he asked.

"Okay for now."

"For now. What about later? An hour from now?"

She stepped into the open doorway. "I'll worry about it when I need to."

"When you need to, it will be too late for worry."

He had vocalized her worst fear, so she didn't waste breath on a contradiction. "Would you like...another blanket...over your legs?" She was forced to pause between phrases to gasp for breath.

"When did you take the last dose of your medication?"

"My pill?" she wheezed. "Yesterday morning."

"You don't sound so sure."

God, could he read her mind?

Truth was, she couldn't remember taking her pill yesterday morning. Thinking back over the day, she couldn't isolate a memory of taking her medication.

She'd had several errands in town. She had gone to the local moving company to purchase some packing boxes. After that, she remembered stopping at an ATM to withdraw cash for her trip back to Atlanta.

Her final stop before returning to the cabin had been at the pharmacy. She had taken her last pill the night before. Luckily, when she started visiting Cleary on a regular basis, she'd had a local doctor write her a prescription for theophylline, the drug she took to help prevent asthma attacks. The extra prescription was a safeguard, so she would never be caught without.

Yesterday William Ritt had filled the prescription for her. From there her memory got hazy. She couldn't remember if she had taken the tablet when she stopped at the soda fountain to buy a vanilla Coke from Linda Wexler, or if she had waited to take it once she reached the cabin.

Surely she hadn't forgotten to take it. She never failed to take her medication. It was part of her daily routine. However, yesterday had been an unusual day, and not only in terms of her schedule. Dutch had placed her on an emotional seesaw.

He was waiting for her when she returned to the cabin. He was sitting on the edge of the sofa, staring into near space, shoulders hunched, looking forlorn. His greeting had been "How could you do this to me?"

In view of the events that had followed, taking her medication might have slipped her mind.

"Lilly, are you sure you took it yesterday?"

She refocused on Tierney. "Of course I'm sure," she lied.

"But it's been over twenty-four hours."

Or thirty-six.

"It's worn off," he said. "You're in distress."

"Well, that happens . . . when you discover . . . you're trapped with a . . . serial killer."

"You know I'm not a killer. Unlock the handcuffs. I'll go get your medication."

She shook her head.

"You're running out of time."

"We could be rescued—"

"Nobody's coming up that mountain road until at least tomorrow. Probably not even then. And if you're counting on some Rambo-type helicopter rescue, think again. Not even the bravest pilot is going to take one up in this storm and risk being slapped down by these winds or crashing into a mountain he can't see."

"Somehow . . ."

"It is not going to happen," he said with mounting asperity. "You may be willing to gamble with your life, but I'm not. Get the key."

"They could come . . . on foot."

"No one's that crazy."

"Except you."

That silenced him, but only for several seconds. "Right. Except me. I'd take any risk to keep you alive. I don't want you to die, Lilly."

"I don't...much like...the idea...myself."

"Let me go."

"Can't."

His lips flattened with anger. "Let me tell you what you can't do. You can't afford to keep me chained to this goddamn bed. Every second spent arguing about it uses time and breath that you don't have. Now get the key and unlock these—"

"No!"

"—fucking handcuffs!"

The lights went out.

Dora Hamer approached the closed door to Scott's bedroom. It seemed ominously silent in the house without his stereo system vibrating the walls. She knocked twice. "Scott, are you okay?"

He opened the door as though he'd been expecting her. "Fine, except for the electricity going out."

"I think it went out all over town. I don't see any lights in our neighbors' windows. Are you warm enough in here?"

"I put on an extra sweater."

"That may help for a while, but it's not going to take long for the house to get cold. Until the power comes back on, we'll have to rely on the fireplace for heat. Would you bring in some more wood from the garage, please?"

"Sure, Mom."

"And get the lantern you and your dad take on camping trips. Do we have fuel for it?"

"I think so. I'll check."

He disappeared down the hall. Dora followed him part of the way before hastily retracing her footsteps back into his bedroom. The college application forms were scattered across his desk. She didn't take the time to read them, but a glance showed her that he'd been working on them as Wes had mandated.

Quickly she moved to the nearest window and checked to see that the alarm system detector was intact. Two magnets, one on the window frame, the other on the jamb, formed a connection which, if broken, would trigger the alarm whenever it was set. The components were aligned as they should be. The same was true of the second window she checked.

Not wanting to be caught snooping, she paused to listen. She could hear Scott stacking logs in the open space in the rock wall of the living room fireplace. She heard him dusting off his hands as he headed back to the garage for another armload.

She went to the third window. Two magnets were making the required connection, all right. But the one on the window jamb was an ordinary magnet, a kid's toy. It had been used to replace the missing connector and positioned so that no connection would be broken if the window was opened.

"Mom?"

When he called to her, Dora jumped as though she were the guilty party. She hurried from his bedroom, hoping she looked more composed than she felt when she joined him in the living room.

"Should I stack some wood up here on the hearth?" he asked.

"Good idea. It'll save you the trouble of going for more later."

"Okay. Want me to light the lantern?"

"Let's reserve it for nighttime."

"The kerosene can is practically full. I'll leave it and the lantern in the kitchen."

"Fine. I've got candles to use until dark. And there are plenty of batteries for flashlights."

She followed him as far as the kitchen, where he disappeared through the door to the garage. She wanted to go after him, place her arms around him, and hug him close. Wes accused her of babying him. Well, so what? Scott *was* her baby. If she lived to see him become a very old man, he would still be her baby and she would want to protect him.

Something was going on with him, and whatever it was, it terrified her. "Worried sick" wasn't merely a figure of speech. After the discovery she'd made in his bedroom, she was nauseated with worry.

He had rigged the alarm detector on his bedroom window not to go off when he sneaked out. What other explanation could there be for his tampering with it? How long had this been going on? Was she blind, deaf, and dumb not to have known that he was leaving the house?

It was by accident that she had come even to suspect it. She'd been delivering fresh laundry to his room this morning when she noticed his boots on the floor beside his bed.

They were waterproof, fleece lined, perfect footwear for a snowstorm. But Scott hadn't been wearing them yesterday when he and Wes came home for dinner. Ostensibly, Scott hadn't left the house since then.

But there were his boots, standing in small puddles of water formed on his bedroom floor as the snow melted off them. It had been on the tip of her tongue to ask him when he had gone out, but she'd stopped herself.

She'd decided she should be armed with some kind of backup evidence before accusing him of sneaking out. The power outage had provided her with an opportunity to investigate.

However, now that she could confront him with the disabled alarm system, she was reluctant—or too cowardly—to do so. He was certainly old enough to come and go as he pleased. Wes imposed a curfew on him, but if Scott wanted to leave the house, there was little Wes could do to stop him short of physically restraining him.

So why didn't he defy Wes and simply walk out the door? Why was he sneaking out? It was symptomatic of other changes in him. Her sweet, considerate, and easygoing Scott had turned sullen, even prone to outbursts of temper. He was withdrawn, hostile, and unpredictable.

Because of the unrelenting pressure Wes placed on him, performance anxiety must be partially responsible. But knowing her son as she did, Dora feared that these personality changes were being caused by something even more consequential than Wes's badgering. Scott was no longer himself, and she wanted to know why.

Mentally she traced back over the past year, trying to determine when she began noticing these changes.

Last spring.

About the time—

Everything inside Dora went terribly still.

Scott began to change about the time he and Millicent Gunn stopped seeing each other.

When the telephone rang, she nearly jumped out of her skin.

"I'll get it," Scott said. "It's probably Gary." He had just come in from the garage. Setting the Coleman lantern on the kitchen table, he reached for the phone. It was the old-fashioned kind of wall phone, without caller ID or anything else that required electricity to be operable.

"Oh, hi, Dad." Scott listened for several seconds, then said, "How come? Okay, she's right here." He passed the phone to Dora. "He's calling from the hospital."

Begley wasn't feeling too kindly toward Dutch Burton. In fact, he would have liked to plant his size eleven foot in Burton's anus. He settled for speaking candidly. "Your face looks like raw hamburger."

"They're only superficial cuts." The police chief was sitting on the end of the examination table, his posture that of a fifty-pound potato sack that was only three quarters full. "The doc picked out the glass slivers. I'm waiting for the nurse to come back with some antiseptic stuff to put on them. It may not be pretty, but I'll be okay."

"Better than Hawkins. He's got a broken arm, which is a clean break. They popped his dislocated shoulder back in. But his ankle-bones are going to take some work. Both are splintered all to hell."

"Wish it was his skull," Burton muttered.

"Mr. Hawkins was intoxicated," Hoot said from where he stood just inside the privacy curtain that divided the treatment areas in the community hospital's ER. From the other side of the yellow fabric, they could hear Cal Hawkins moaning. "His blood-alcohol ratio was well over the legal limit."

"Then he lied to me," Burton said defensively. "I asked him if he'd been drinking, but he said—"

Begley cut him off. "I think you hear only what you want to hear."

Burton glared at him.

"Reconstructing his ankles is going to require delicate surgery," Hoot said. "They can't do it here. Because of the weather, it could be several days before he can be transported to a hospital that has an or-thopedic surgical team. In the meantime, he's in misery."

"Look," Burton said angrily, "it's not my fault the guy's a drunk."

"He couldn't have driven up that road stone fucking sober," Beg-ley roared. "Thanks to you, the whole damn countryside is without electricity. You're lucky this hospital's got an emergency generator or you'd be sitting here in the cold and dark, looking like a freak show with hunks of glass sticking out of your face."

Hawkins's rig had collided with one of the tower's four supports. In ordinary circumstances, it probably could have withstood the damage. But with the weight of the ice and snow making it top-heavy, it had toppled, taking dozens of ageless trees and a network of power lines with it. Worse, it had fallen across the mountain road, blocking access to the peak.

Dutch Burton had let his emotions outweigh his judgment. Unac-ceptable behavior for any man, but unforgivable for a public servant. His jealousy-inspired determination to get up the mountain road to-day had been irrational and dangerous, and had resulted in numer-ous casualties: Hawkins was probably crippled for life; the sanding truck was out of commission during one of the worst storms in decades; and the power outage extended into several surrounding counties.

All that was catastrophic.

But what really chapped Begley was that Burton's idiocy had eliminated any possibility of going after Tierney. He couldn't even attempt it again until the mess on that road was cleared, which could take weeks, or until the weather broke enough for a chopper to take him to the summit. Either way, valuable time had been squandered. Wasted time was not just one of Begley's pet peeves; he considered it a sin.

His consolation was that he wasn't the only one hamstrung by the situation. Ben Tierney couldn't go anywhere, either.

"Excuse me? Chief?" Harris, the young cop they'd met earlier at the lodge, poked his head around the privacy curtain.

"What is it?"

"Dispatch called my radio. Mr. and Mrs. Gunn are at headquarters."

"Shit," Burton hissed. "They're all I need. Tell whoever's there to tell them that I'm in the hospital, to go home, and I'll get over to see them as soon as I can."

"He already tried that," Harris said. "Didn't budge them. Because it's not you they want to talk to. It's . . ." He nodded in Begley's general direction. "They want to know is it true that Ben Tierney is Blue."

Begley saw red. He managed to keep his volume at a reasonable level, but his voice vibrated with fury. "I hope you're joking."

"No, sir."

Begley advanced on the young cop. "Who told them? Who told them we were interested in Tierney? If it was you, Officer Harris, I'll pin your badge to your scrotum and weld it shut."

"Wasn't me, sir. I swear. It was Gus Elmer. The old man out at the lodge?"

"We told him not to mention our investigation to anyone," Hoot said.

"I don't think he meant to," Harris said. "He didn't talk to the Gunns directly. He called his cousin to check on her, see how she was faring the storm on account of her stove has a faulty flue? And he sort of let it slip."

"*Let it slip?*"

Begley's bellow roused Hawkins from his drug-induced stupor, and he groaned loudly. Harris took a cautious step back. "His cousin does Mrs. Gunn's ironing," he explained, sounding apologetic. "I guess she felt she owed it to them to, you know, to tell . . ." He stammered, then fell silent beneath Begley's stare.

"Who else does Mr. Elmer's cousin do ironing for?" His sarcasm escaped Harris. While the cop was pondering his answer, he turned to Dutch Burton. "I'd like to use your office for this interview with the Gunns."

"Fine, but I'm coming, too."

"What about your face?"

"I've got some cream I can put on it."

They trooped out. Begley glanced at Cal Hawkins as he passed his bed. Hooked up to IVs, he'd lapsed into unconsciousness. Despite defending him to Burton, he didn't have any sympathy for the man.

Once they were in their car and under way, Hoot said, "I thought you planned on talking to the Gunns anyway, sir."

"I was going to call on them as soon as we left the hospital."

"They why did you get so upset in there?"

"I hoped to scare them into believing how important it is that we keep a lid on this investigation. We need to have Tierney in custody before too many locals learn that we're even looking at him."

"You see how fast gossip travels."

"That's what worries me, Hoot. If we don't pick Tierney up soon, I'm afraid a band of Bubbas, led by the chief of police himself, will assume he's Blue and take matters into their own hands. Righteous indignation beats the law of the land every goddamn time in situations like this.

"These good ol' boys, out to protect their womenfolk, may revert to the unwritten law of the hills. If they got to Tierney before we did, he'd be lucky if his rights were read to him as he lay drowning in his own blood. And wouldn't that be a party and a half? The media would have a field day. They'd harken back to Ruby Ridge and Waco. The gun control fanatics would be all over it. We'd be left with one hell of a clusterfuck."

"And many unanswered questions."

"Precisely. Like where to find the five bodies."

They drove in silence for a moment, then Hoot said, "You said you're afraid they'll go after Tierney, assuming he's Blue. What if he *isn't*?"

Begley frowned. "That's another thing I'm afraid of."

CHAPTER
20

To retain heat inside the cabin, all the draperies had been kept drawn. When the lights went out, the bedroom was plunged into darkness.

"That was inevitable," Tierney said.

Lilly gave her eyes a few seconds to adjust, then went to the windows and pushed back one of the drapes. The premature gloaming outside provided Tierney with a fresh argument.

"It'll be full darkness by midafternoon," he said. "Which means there are only a couple hours of daylight left. It'll take me at least that long to get to the car and back if I leave now."

Lilly placed the heels of her hands against her temples. "I can't ... argue ... anymore."

"So don't. Just unlock the handcuffs."

"You'll kill me."

"I'm trying to *save* your life."

She shook her head, laboring to inhale. "I can ... identify ... you ... as Blue."

"You can't identify me as anything if you suffocate."

"A note."

"Oh, I see. You'd leave a note, telling them that I'm Blue. You'd place it where they'd be certain to find it."

She nodded.

"If that happened, I'd say that you became delusional from oxygen deprivation, that you were also convinced elephants were dancing inside the walls. They'd believe me. As for that"—he nodded at the blue ribbon, now curled on the seat of the rocking chair—"I'd tell them what I told you—I found it and was taking it back to town with me to turn over to the authorities."

She motioned toward his hands.

"Yeah, explaining the cuffs would be tricky, but I'd have a day or two to think of something plausible. And just possibly I would be able to work my hands free before anyone got up here."

"I don't think so," she said, nodding toward his bloody wrists. "Even if...I was dead...they'd have you." Ending her argument there, she turned to leave the room.

"What's the worst that could happen?"

She stopped but didn't turn around.

He pressed on. "If you release me, what's the worst that could happen, Lilly? Say I *am* Blue. Say I kill you so you can't finger me to the authorities. You're going to die anyway. In a matter of hours, if that long. So how could my murdering you be any worse?"

She turned to face him. "Save another...victim..."

"Ah, I see what you're saying. You don't want to unleash me onto an unsuspecting public, leaving me free to victimize more women, do to them whatever I've done to the others. Is that it?"

She nodded.

"Okay. That's reasonable. Very altruistic, too. You're placing the lives of others above your own." He thought on it for a moment, then said, "Once I'm back with your medication, once I've carried in enough firewood to last for another day, I'll let you handcuff me again. I'll remain handcuffed until we're rescued."

She tried to laugh but didn't have adequate breath. "I'm...not that...gullible...not that...oxygen deprived...yet."

"You don't trust me to keep my word?"

"No."

"You can, Lilly. I swear it. You can trust me."

"Give me one...one reason." In spite of her determination not to cry, tears filled her eyes.

"Don't cry," he whispered roughly.

Drawn by his fierce gaze, by the memory of their kiss, she took a step closer. "Give me...one reason why...I should trust you, Tierney."

He was about to speak when her cell phone rang.

For a second or two she didn't grasp what the sound was or where it was coming from, only stood there gaping at Tierney, who appeared equally stunned by the unexpected noise.

When she realized the jangle was her cell phone, she frantically fished it from her coat pocket and flipped it open. "Dutch? Dutch!" Her voice was a mere croak. But it didn't matter. The phone was dead, the LED dark. The connection had been momentary. A tease. Fate taunting her.

With a sob, she sank to her knees, clutching the silent phone to her chest.

"Lilly, don't cry."

"Leave me alone."

"You must not cry. That'll only make it worse."

Her sobbing brought on a coughing fit. The spasms racked her whole body, contracted every muscle, squeezed precious air from her lungs. While she struggled to breathe, her mind registered Tierney's elaborate swearing and his redoubled efforts to break the lock on the handcuffs.

It took several minutes for her to bring the coughing under control, but finally it subsided into loud wheezing.

"Lilly."

She raised her head and wiped the tears from her eyes. Tierney had kicked the blanket off his legs and was straining against the cuffs like an animal caught in a trap, willing to tear off his hands in order to reach her.

"It's true that I've given you very few reasons to trust me," he said. "And many reasons for you not to. But I believe you know, you *know*, that I'm not someone you have to be afraid of. Rely on your instincts. Trust them, even if you don't trust me." He continued looking at her for several beats before adding, "Don't die on me."

She analyzed each feature of his face, looking for a telltale sign of villainy. If he were a sly abductor of women, wouldn't she be able to tell? Wouldn't she sense a disguised malevolence?

She looked, looked hard, but could find no trace of duplicity. If it was indeed there, he'd mastered the art of hiding it. He seemed sincere, trustworthy enough to make her doubt herself.

But his victims hadn't detected his guile, either. They had trusted him.

Her expression must have conveyed her determination not to be duped, because he said angrily, "All right, ignore your instincts and plain common sense. Forget our day on the river. Never mind the kiss last night. Discount all that, but play the odds."

"Odds?"

"Stay alive, and you'll have a chance of capturing Blue. Die, and you'll have none."

I don't know what to do, her mind screamed, but the only sound issuing from her throat was a terrible gurgling noise.

"Even a slim chance is better than none, Lilly."

His argument was sound. But as soon as she released him, he would probably kill her. Her slim chance of incriminating him would die with her.

Taking advantage of her hesitation, he said, "I've saved the most obvious argument for last. The pistol. You still have it, and you know how to use it. What could I do to you as long as you're holding me at gunpoint?"

She gave that rationale a few seconds' thought. He was right. When all the arguments and second-guessing were pared away, it came down to her playing the odds. Slowly, she came to her feet. Warding off the light-headedness caused by oxygen deprivation, she turned and walked into the living room.

"Lilly! Goddammit!"

She returned just as quickly as she'd left, carrying the pistol in one hand, the key to the handcuffs in the other.

His shoulders slumped with relief. "Thank God."

She set the pistol on the chair, far out of his reach. As she approached the bed, she extended the key toward him. "You...do...it."

As soon as he had a grip on the key, she backed away hastily and reclaimed the pistol, aiming it at him.

There was just enough play in the cuffs for him to angle one hand down and the other up. With amazing dexterity, he fit the key into the tiny hole and turned it. The bracelet on his left wrist came free. In a matter of seconds he had the other bracelet off.

Then, in one fluid motion, he vaulted off the bed and yanked the pistol out of Lilly's hands. It happened before she could blink, insufficient time for her brain to process that she should pull the trigger. She wheeled around and tried to run from him, but he hooked his arm around her waist, bringing her up short and trapping her right arm against her side. He lifted her off the floor and held her against his chest.

"Stop it!" he ordered when she began screaming.

"I knew," she wheezed hysterically. "I knew. You're *him.*" She thrust her free elbow against his rib cage and sank her nails into the back of his hand.

"Son of a bitch!" Ungracefully hauling her into the living room, he pushed her onto the sofa, then raised his hand to his mouth and sucked at the blood flowing from the deep scratches.

Lilly perched on the edge of the sofa only long enough to gasp several breaths, then launched herself at him again, flailing at his head. But the shortage of oxygen had affected her coordination. Her arms felt heavy and rubbery. She tried to connect her fists with his head, but the attempts were futile. Most of her blows fell short, went wide, or landed with negligible impact.

When he took her by the shoulders and pushed her back onto the sofa, she was helpless to do anything except fall heavily into the back cushions. He crammed the pistol into the waistband of his jeans and swiped his bleeding hand against his leg. The angry-looking scratches immediately leaked as much blood as he had wiped away.

His breathlessness was almost as bad as hers. He was noisily inhaling great drafts of air and rapidly blinking as though to stave off dizziness. His upper torso was angled forward from the waist. The blow she'd given his sore ribs had made standing upright impossible.

Good, she thought. *I hope you're suffering terrible pain.* She would have gloated out loud, but she didn't have enough breath.

But she looked up at him defiantly. If he was going to kill her now, she wanted to be looking him in the eye. She wanted him to take her defiance into hell with him and remember it for eternity.

He seemed on the verge of saying something but, without a word, went to the door and opened it. Within seconds he was back with an armload of firewood, which he dumped onto the hearth. He knelt down and stirred the coals to reignite the logs already on the grate.

This mystified her. "You aren't...going to...kill me?"

"No," he said brusquely as he came to his feet. He motioned at the logs he'd just carried in. "As they dry out, add them to the fire. They'll last you a couple of hours."

Only then did she realize his intention. He didn't need to kill her. All he had to do was abandon her, leave her in the throes of a fatal asthma attack, and let the bothersome matter of Lilly Martin resolve itself. Why chalk up another murder on his roster of crimes when he didn't need to?

To cover the ones he'd already committed, he had the presence of mind to retrieve the evidence against him from the bedroom. He replaced the handcuffs and ribbon in his backpack. As he zipped them into separate compartments, he avoided looking at her. Was he feeling a twinge of guilt?

Because by not killing her, he was condemning her to her worst fear. While she'd been debating whether or not to release him, one scenario she hadn't considered was that he would abandon her to live through her nightmare before succumbing to it. Her heart constricted. "You promised—"

"I know what I promised," he said, cruelly cutting her off.

He pulled on his coat and worked the watch cap down over his head. He draped the stadium blanket over the cap and folded the ends of it across his chest before zipping it inside his coat. He wound the wool scarf around his neck and the lower half of his face, then pulled on his gloves. Last, he picked up his backpack and slung it over his shoulder. Every motion caused him to grimace and gasp in pain. Nevertheless he moved with haste, purpose.

As he walked toward the door, she was tempted to call him back, beg him to shoot her now. It would be a swift and painless death, not the prolonged and terrifying one facing her. She was more frightened of the fear and dread of dying than she was of death itself.

But she had too much pride to beg him for anything, nor would her survival instinct concede a voluntary death. So she watched him walk away, leaving her to struggle for each breath until she could struggle no longer, leaving her to die alone.

When he reached the door, he paused with his hand on the knob and turned only his head. Above the scarf, his eyes connected with hers, but only for an instant, no longer.

He opened the door. A swirl of snow engulfed him. Then it vanished as quickly as he.

Lilly's cell phone rang twice before the connection was lost, which was more tormenting to Dutch than if it hadn't rung at all. The aborted call increased his frustration, which was already strained to the breaking point.

The anteroom of police department headquarters was more crowded than he remembered it being since he was hired as chief. The feebs were there. Agent Wise was solemnly—did that guy ever crack a smile?—introducing Begley to Millicent Gunn's parents. Mrs. Gunn looked scrawnier today than she had yesterday.

Wes, for reasons unbeknownst to Dutch, had been there when they arrived and was drinking coffee and chatting with the officer manning the desk. He was head of the city council, but since when was a police investigation any business of his?

Harris had followed them from the hospital in his squad car. He was starstruck by Wise and Begley, trailing them like a puppy, stumbling over his own big feet in his eagerness to assist. Why wasn't he out on patrol, where he was supposed to be? And why wasn't he, Dutch, ordering Harris back to his unit and onto the streets, where he could be of some use, instead of in here, further crowding the place, getting in everybody's way?

For some reason, Dutch didn't have the wherewithal to correct the young officer. It didn't seem worth the effort it would take to issue an order and put any level of authority behind it. He felt oddly detached from what was going on around him, and he wondered not only at what point he had lost control but when he had ceased to care.

When the FBI entered the picture in the form of big shot SAC Begley?

Or when Wes Hamer, his so-called best friend, started kissing Begley's ass as often as possible?

Or maybe when Cal Hawkins asked him the question he'd begun asking himself: *Does your old lady want to be rescued?*

He hadn't felt this defeated since his last screwup in Atlanta. It had been the coup de grâce, the mistake that was too serious for a disciplinary action like suspension or probation. Only being fired would suffice. When you pulled your service weapon on a nine-year-old kid, mistaking his aluminum baseball bat for a gun because you were shitfaced drunk, the APD had no choice but to fire you. Do not pass go. Do not collect your pension. You're outta there.

He felt equally defeated today. Betrayed by all: his wife, the weather, his best friend, his career, fate or the stars or God or whoever the hell was in charge of guiding his not-worth-a-crap destiny.

He needed a drink.

Officer Harris was leading the Gunns and the FBI agents down the short hallway toward Dutch's private office. Begley, bringing up the rear of this parade, turned back to address him. "Are you joining us, Chief Burton?"

"I'll be right there. Soon as I grab my messages."

Begley nodded, then continued on and entered Dutch's office through the door that Harris was holding open for him.

When they were out of earshot, Wes turned to Dutch and assessed the cuts on his face. "How're you doing?"

He snatched a wad of pink memo slips from his dispatcher. "Just great, thanks."

"Face hurt?"

"Like a son of a bitch."

"Didn't they have something to put on it?"

"It'll be okay."

"I could go over to the drugstore, pick up something from Ritt."

Dutch shrugged. "Whatever." He started toward the hallway, but Wes hooked his hand around his elbow.

"Are you sure you're all right, Dutch?"

He threw off Wes's hand. "Shit, no, I'm not all right!"

Realizing that his subordinate officer was all ears, he lowered his voice to a mumble. "In case you haven't noticed, it's been a lousy morning."

Wes sighed, ran his hand over his cropped hair. "Stupid question. I'm sorry. Look, Lilly is okay, Dutch. I'm sure of it."

"Yeah." Actually, he was more afraid that she was better than okay.

"Tell you what," Wes said. "I'll run over to the drugstore while you're talking with Millicent's folks. Pick up some salve for those cuts on your face, have Ritt or Marilee make some sandwiches to bring back."

Dutch looked into Wes's face and could see nothing disingenuous there. Just his old friend's handsome features and a sincere regard that, despite their friendship, Dutch was coming to mistrust. "That would be helpful. Thanks."

"You bet. Now get on back there. This is your show, don't forget."

Wes's parting words drilled their way through the bedrock of his defeatism. It *was* his show, but God. Everyone, including himself, seemed to have forgotten that. High time they were reminded.

As he headed down the hallway toward his office, he squared his shoulders and forced more confidence into his step. Harris was standing outside the door like a sentinel. Dutch hitched his thumb toward the front of the building. "Your squad car is getting cold."

Harris looked at him stupidly. "Sir?"

"This isn't a snow day, Harris," he barked. "See to your duties."

"Yes, sir." The young cop rushed down the hall.

Dutch entered his office in time to hear Mrs. Gunn telling Wise and Begley that they'd had no serious problems with Millicent other than her eating disorder, and that she'd been cured of it.

"I can't bear to think of her out there somewhere in this weather," she said.

"That's why we welcome this opportunity to talk to you, Mrs. Gunn."

Begley's tone of voice was that of a kindly father figure, and Dutch resented the way the Gunns responded to it. Give Begley a few days on the case, and they'd be questioning his methods and effectiveness just like they had his.

"You reckon Ben Tierney is the B.T. mentioned in her diary?" Mr. Gunn asked.

"We're not sure of that yet," Begley replied. "Agent Wise is looking into several possibilities. Mr. Tierney is only one of them. We must be very thorough before we draw any conclusions."

"But old Gus Elmer said that you'd sealed off this Tierney's rooms at the lodge. Did you find something in them? Something belonging to Millicent?"

Dutch saw the agents exchange a look of consternation. Wise was the one to address Mr. Gunn's question. "We sealed off his rooms to protect potential evidence in the event that Mr. Tierney has a connection to her disappearance. That's not to say we believe he does."

"But you haven't sealed off anybody else's rooms," Gunn argued. "How many other men around here have the initials B.T.?"

Begley dodged that by asking, "Did Millicent ever talk about him?"

"She'd mentioned him."

"In what context?"

"Down at my brother's store, where she works, they have this bulletin board. Somebody catches a big fish with a rod they bought there, or bags a deer with a rifle my brother sold, they bring him a picture of it, and he puts it on his bulletin board. Sorta like free advertising.

"So, naturally, Tierney's articles are tacked up there, too. He's by far their most famous customer. I think Millicent looks on him as a celebrity, him being in the magazines and all. She got excited every time he came into the store. Maybe she has a teenage crush on him."

"Did she ever see him outside the store?" Wise asked.

"Not that we know of. But now we're beginning to wonder. Pretty young girl like Millicent, with stars in her eyes over some older fellow..." Gunn cut a worried glance toward his wife, who was sniffing into a handkerchief. "You get my drift." He coughed behind his hand. "Have y'all connected him to any of the other women who're missing?"

"A colleague in the Charlotte office is working on that," Wise said.

"I apologize in advance for the bluntness of the questions I'm about to put to you," Begley said to the girl's parents. "Diplomacy takes time, and none of us wants to waste it, do we?"

"No, sir. Ask away. Enough time's been wasted already."

Dutch ignored the critical glance Ernie Gunn shot him.

"What caused Millicent's eating disorder?" Begley asked. "Was that ever determined?"

"Peer pressure, we think," Mr. Gunn said, speaking for both of them. "You know how girls are about their weight."

Begley smiled. "I've got a teenage daughter, a bit younger than Millicent, worries that she's too fat, and she weighs maybe one ten."

"Millicent got down to eighty-seven pounds," Mrs. Gunn said feebly. "That was her lowest. That's when we intervened."

At Begley's request, they gave him an account of her illness and alleged recovery.

"She's doing good," Mr. Gunn concluded. "Oh, sure, she might've dropped another couple pounds, but that's due to her cheerleading workouts. We're almost positive she isn't forcing herself to vomit. She's over that."

Dutch wasn't so sure, and he could tell that Wise and Begley weren't either.

"What about boyfriends?" Begley asked.

"She has them. Off and on. You know. Typical kids. She falls in and out of love as regular as she changes her hairdo," Mr. Gunn said.

"No steady boyfriend?"

"Not since Scott."

Dutch reacted with a start, which the agents noticed. They looked at him curiously, then turned back to the Gunns.

"Scott who?" Wise asked.

"Hamer," Mr. Gunn supplied. "Wes's boy. He and Millicent went steady all last year, although that's not what they call it these days. They were 'together,'" he said with a snort of disdain for the term.

"*Were?*" Wise said.

"They broke up right before school was out last spring."

"Do you know why?"

Mr. Gunn shrugged. "Got tired of each other, I reckon."

"No, honey," Mrs. Gunn chimed in. "Something happened that caused them to break up. I always thought so."

Begley leaned forward. "Like what, Mrs. Gunn?"

"I don't know. Millicent never told me. Hard as I tried to get her to talk about it, she wouldn't and still won't. Eventually I stopped asking because it made her upset, and she'd stop eating. I was more worried about her starving herself than I was about her boyfriend trouble."

If she had shouted that the two problems were related, it couldn't have been any more obvious to either Dutch or the FBI agents.

Wise was the first to break the ensuing silence. "I found nothing in her diary about Scott Hamer or their breakup."

"She only started keeping her diary since she left the hospital. It's part of her ongoing therapy," Mr. Gunn explained. "The psychologist said she should start writing stuff down. Positive things." His mouth became a hard, rigid line. "Guess she thinks Ben Tierney is a good thing."

"At this point we have no reason to think otherwise, Mr. Gunn," Begley cautioned, his tone more stern now than before.

"You think what you want, Mr. Begley." Gunn stood up and extended his hand to his wife to help her from her chair. "I'm putting my money on him. I've known everybody in Cleary and the three neighboring counties all my life. I can't think of anybody who could do such a thing as to cause five women to disappear. It's gotta be an outsider, but somebody who knows his way around these parts, and has the initials B.T. Mr. Ben Tierney fits the bill on all counts."

CHAPTER

21

THERE'S A KNACK TO IT," WILLIAM SAID. "NOT EVERYONE CAN do it."

"I think I can handle it. I mean, how hard can it be?"

William resented Wes Hamer's condescending tone. Just because he was the superstud football coach didn't mean he had a talent for giving injections. "I'll stop by your house on my way home and—"

"I can do it, Ritt."

William also hated to be called Ritt. Wes had been calling him Ritt ever since they were in grade school. He'd been a bully then, and he was still a bully. They were the same age, yet he addressed William with no more respect than he would talk to one of his students, and that rankled.

William had a good mind to take back the package of syringes and the small sack containing several days' supply of vials. But he didn't. Being Wes's supplier gave him definite leverage, which he enjoyed immensely.

"What's that?"

Marilee's sudden appearance in the stockroom startled them both. Wes was the first to recover. He pocketed the goods in his overcoat pocket and gave her one of his killer smiles. "Ready for me?"

William's sister responded to Wes's suggestive question with a simper. Just like every other woman who was exposed to his insinuating smile, she was instantly transformed into a twit.

"I came to remind you that I can't toast the bread because the power is out," she said to Wes. "Linda always makes pimiento cheese sandwiches on toasted bread."

"Everyone will understand."

"Sweet pickles or dill?"

"Half and half."

"Fritos or potato chips?"

"Half and half."

"Give me five more minutes."

She left them. Wes turned back to William and patted his coat pocket. "How much do I owe you for this?"

"I'll put it on your bill."

"Don't itemize it."

"As if I'd be that careless. Now, you said Dutch needs something for his face?"

Wes explained the cuts, and William gave him a tube of antiseptic salve, a free sample from the drug company. "This should keep them from becoming infected. If it doesn't work, I've got something stronger."

Wes read the label. "One of these days, you're gonna get busted for handing out prescription drugs without a doctor's authorization."

"Oh, I doubt that. Who's going to tell?" William asked guilelessly.

Wes laughed. "I guess you're right."

William motioned him out of the stockroom. As they walked through the shadowed store, Wes gave him an update on the morning's events. "It's a wonder both of them weren't squashed to death. We had to send a stretcher down by rope. Dutch strapped Hawkins to it. Never heard such screaming from a grown man as when we pulled him up. Poor bastard's not doing very well.

"Physically, Dutch is okay but fit to be tied because Lilly's still up there with Tierney. Then there are the FBI guys. Buttinskis in topcoats. In addition to his personal problems, Dutch is having to cope with them as well as Millicent's parents."

"What's the latest on the investigation?"

"I can tell you that." Marilee turned as they approached the counter of the soda fountain, where she was wrapping sandwiches. She nodded toward the battery-operated radio that was tuned to the local station. "It was just reported that the FBI has identified Blue to be Ben Tierney."

Tierney was weaker than he ever remembered being.

He was light-headed, partially from hunger, partially from the concussion. His injuries continued a relentless assault of sharp, stabbing pains or dull, throbbing aches. He clenched his jaws so tightly against the cold that he felt the pressure in the roots of his teeth.

There was no help for any of these adversities. In order to survive, he would be relying on sheer determination.

Unfortunately, self-will had no effect on the snowfall. It obscured the demarcation between earth and sky. It absorbed landmarks. He was trapped in a sphere of infinite white. Without a horizon for reference, he could easily become disoriented and hopelessly lost.

Nevertheless, he plowed on, wading through snow that, in places, came past his knees. Before leaving the vicinity of the cabin, he had made a brief stop at the toolshed to get a snow shovel he'd seen there. It helped somewhat to clear a path, but mostly he used his body to bulldoze through the drifts. The shovel became a walking stick to help support him when vertigo threatened to hurl him to the ground.

Even in the most extreme circumstances, habits die hard. Stubbornly, perhaps foolishly, he took a shortcut to avoid a switchback, knowing that eventually he would reach the road and would have saved himself several hundred yards. But in the forest were potential hazards he couldn't see. He was bushwhacked by boulders, fallen trees, and stumps, buried under two feet of snow. Roots became snares that caused him to stumble and fall.

Breaking an ankle or leg, falling into a crevasse he couldn't climb out of, or getting lost in this snow globe environment would mean death. If he paused to consider the life-threatening risks, he would stop, turn around, go back, so he willed himself to concentrate only on taking one step at a time, on pulling his foot from the well in the snow it had just created and planting it ahead of him to form another.

He didn't allow himself to dwell on the cold, either, although it was impossible to ignore. His clothing was a joke for its inadequacy. When he left the lodge yesterday morning, he'd been dressed for a cold day spent outdoors—coat, scarf, cap. But today the concept of cold had been taken to another dimension. The temperature, he guessed, was in the single digits. Factoring in the windchill, it was fifteen to twenty degrees below zero. He'd never been exposed to anything like it. Never. Not in all his travels.

His respiration and pulse rate soon reached dangerous levels. His heart felt like a balloon on the verge of bursting. Common sense dictated that he stop and rest. He didn't dare. If he stopped, even for a moment, he knew he would probably never move again.

Eventually his frozen body would be found. And along with it, his backpack. They would find the ribbon. The handcuffs.

Lilly would be discovered dead in the cabin.

A search of the entire area would ensue. One shocking discovery would lead to another. His abandoned car would yield the incriminating shovel in the trunk. Ultimately they would find the graves.

Tierney pushed on.

His eyelashes became encrusted by snowflakes that froze in place, causing temporary blindness that was annoying as well as dangerous. The condensation of his breath froze on the woolen scarf, making it stiff with ice crystals.

Beneath his clothing, he was sweating from the exertion. He could feel trickles of perspiration rolling down his torso where the injured ribs on his left side ached from Lilly's well-placed elbow jab.

Ordinarily his innate sense of direction was as reliable as a compass. But when he paused only long enough to check his wristwatch, he began to fear that his sixth sense had failed him. Even considering the terrain he'd had to walk over, surely he should have bypassed the first switchback and reached the road by now.

He looked around in the vain hope of getting his bearings, but in the maelstrom of snow, one tree looked exactly like another. Natural signposts like rock formations and rotten stumps were blanketed by the accumulation. The only thing marring the otherwise pristine snowscape was the track he'd made in it.

His conscious mind was telling him that his sense of direction was fallible, that he could have become confused and was moving in circles. But his gut instinct overrode it, insisting that he was still on course, that his only miscalculation was in how far he needed to go to bypass the switchback and reach the road.

He had relied on that instinct too many times to start mistrusting it now. Ducking his head against the wind, he plodded on, assuring himself that if he continued on his present path, just a little farther, he would soon find the road.

He did.

Not quite the way he expected.

He landed on it after a nine-foot plunge through thin air.

His right foot found it first. With the impetus of a pile driver, it tunneled through twenty inches of snow, striking the icy pavement below with enough force to cause him to scream.

After announcing to Begley, Hoot, and Burton that he considered Ben Tierney their culprit, Ernie Gunn had nothing more to say. Without another word, he resolutely escorted his wife to the door. Their departure created a vacuum in Chief Burton's cramped office.

Begley broke the uneasy silence. "We need to talk to that Hamer kid."

Hoot had predicted that would be Begley's next step. "It'll be interesting to feel his pulse about Millicent's disappearance."

"Hold on a minute," Burton said. " 'Feel his pulse'? Scott and the girl were sweethearts a year ago, so what?"

"So, we want to talk to him. You object?" Begley's nutcracker dared Burton to put up an argument.

"I'd like to notify Wes first."

"Why?" Hoot asked.

"This is a criminal investigation," Begley said. "Anybody is fair game, I don't care who his daddy is."

"Well, that's where we're different," Burton said belligerently. "We can't just show up on their doorstep and start asking questions about Scott's relationship with a missing girl."

Begley actually laughed. "Why the hell not?"

"Because," Burton replied tightly, "that's not the way we do things around here."

"Well, the way you do things around here hasn't found those women, has it?" Burton's lacerated face turned even redder, but Begley held up his hand to stave off whatever it was the police chief was going to say. "All right, all right. Simmer down. Never let it be said that the FBI violates local etiquette. Isn't Hamer bringing some sandwiches back for our lunch?"

"Yeah."

"When he gets here, tell him that we want to talk to Scott. Don't go into details, just say we've got some questions for him. We'll head over to their place after we've eaten."

Without so much as a nod, Burton stamped out.

"They're good friends," Hoot said after the chief of police was out of earshot.

"We'll have to keep that in mind."

Having said that, Begley requested some "quiet time." As Hoot was pulling the door closed, he saw the SAC reaching for his Bible.

In the anteroom, Hoot ignored Burton's jaundiced glance and asked the dispatcher for a working telephone line. He placed a call to Perkins in Charlotte but got his voice mail. In a succinct message, he told his associate about the power outage and the unreliable cellular service.

"If you can't reach me by phone here at the police station, call my pager and punch in three, three, three. That'll signal me to check my laptop for an e-mail."

As he was hanging up, Wes Hamer came in carrying a box full of wrapped sandwiches. But lunch was superseded by his news of what was being broadcast over local radio. Hoot said, "You can't be serious."

"As death and taxes," Wes said somberly. "Want me to drive over and tell them to cool it?"

"The horse is out of the barn," Dutch said, answering for Hoot. "Won't do any good to close the door now."

To Hoot's mind, Burton didn't appear to be too upset over the untimely broadcast of Tierney's name. In fact, he seemed secretly pleased. SAC Begley, by contrast, was going to go ballistic, and it was Hoot's misfortune to be the one who had to inform him of the fiasco.

He got as many details as he felt were necessary, then left the others with the sandwiches and went down the hall to the private office. He knocked lightly on the closed door. "Sir?"

"Come in, Hoot." Begley finished reading a passage of scripture, then closed his large Bible and waved Hoot inside. "Is lunch here? I'm starving."

Hoot closed the door. Wasting no words on a preamble, he gave Begley the news straight out.

The SAC banged his fist on the desk and surged to his feet. He spattered the walls with shouted obscenities. Hoot remained judiciously silent until the eruption had subsided to a slow boil. "Sir, the only good thing is that the station's listening audience is small, and only those who have battery-operated radios are tuned in today."

Hoot recounted the information he'd gotten from Dutch and Wes. "The two deejays—for lack of a better word—are local men. They retired from the forestry service a few years ago and, for something to do, began broadcasting a local news program, like a community bulletin board, each Saturday morning. It went over well and was expanded to seven days a week. They're on the air from six A.M. till six P.M., and most of their programming is chatter."

"They enjoy the sound of their own voices."

"Evidently. They play music, mostly country, and give weather reports and news, but basically they're glorified gossips. It's a very unsophisticated operation. They broadcast from a room in the Elks' lodge, but they have an emergency generator, so they've been able to stay on the air in spite of the power outage."

Begley rounded Dutch's desk, grinding his fist into his other palm. "If I ever find out who leaked the story to these loudmouths, I'm going to kick his ass so high, he'll be farting out his ears."

Hoot could think of no appropriate response to that, so he

waited several seconds before speaking. "I don't believe we'll ever know who the culprit was, sir. It could have been any number of people."

"Well, whoever it was, he shot our discretion all to hell."

"Yes, sir."

Begley's frown deepened. "Hoot, we've got to make damn certain we get to Tierney before anybody else does."

"I couldn't agree more."

"Grab a sandwich, then call the Charlotte office and order a chopper." Jabbing the space between them with his index finger, he said, "I want a helicopter and rescue team up here, and I mean A-fucking-Sap."

Hoot glanced out the window.

"I know, I know," Begley muttered irritably. "But I want a chopper here as soon as one can fly through this shit. Got it?"

"Got it, sir."

Begley headed for the door, then paused. "And, Hoot, keep all your communiqués with the Charlotte office private. The less the folks around here know about our plans, the better."

"Even the police?"

Begley opened the door and said out the side of his mouth, *"Especially* the police."

Pain sucked the air out of Tierney's lungs. Tears froze as soon as they formed in his eyes. Lying flat on his back, he cursed lavishly and loudly, in agony and outrage.

When the first searing pain receded, and it actually began to feel good just to lie there in the snow, he knew he was in serious danger of freezing to death. That was how it happened; it gave the victim a false sense of comfort.

It took a tremendous amount of willpower, but he forced himself to move his injured ankle. The pain that shot up through his leg made him gasp, but at least it yanked him out of the deceiving comfort into which he'd been lulled.

He sat up. His head reeled, so much that he clasped it between his hands in the hope of stopping it from spinning. He barely had time to pull the scarf away from his mouth before he retched into the snow. He threw up only sour bile, and the stomach spasms reminded him how much his ribs hurt.

He took several deep breaths, then, putting all his weight on his left leg, he stood up. He tested his right ankle by rotating it slowly. It hurt like bloody hell, but he didn't think it was broken. That was something. At this stage, anything short of outright disaster seemed like good fortune.

He set out again, now using the snow shovel as a crutch.

In his effort to keep moving, he lost all sense of time and distance. His ankle was a new focus. He could feel it swelling inside his boot. Actually, his tight boot would probably help keep the swelling to a minimum. Or would it cut off the blood supply and cause frostbite? Gangrene? Why couldn't he remember basic first aid? Or his zip code? Or his telephone number in Virginia?

Jesus, he was hungry. But he was also gripped by nausea that resulted in agonizing dry heaves.

He was cold to the bone, yet his skin felt feverish.

But the worst was the goddamn dizziness.

A fatal blood clot, jarred loose by his hard landing on the road, might even now be wending its way through his blood vessels to his brain or lungs or heart.

Random and bizarre thoughts such as that flitted through his mind like fireflies. They winked out before he could grasp and assimilate them. He was rational enough to recognize the onset of delirium.

Actually, his various pains were friends. Without them, he might have drifted into a state of euphoria, lain down, rested his cheek on a bosom of snow, and died. But the pains were persistent. Like spiked prods, they deviled him to continue. They kept him awake, on his feet, moving, alive. Meanwhile, his reason was shrieking for him to stop. Lie down. Sleep. Surrender.

CHAPTER

22

WHY? WHAT FOR? WHY ME?"

"Will you calm down?" Wes said, raising his voice above Scott's. "They're not coming here to accuse you of anything."

"How do you know?"

"Even if they do, you've got nothing to hide. Right? Right, son?"

"Right."

"So why are you freaking out?"

"I'm not."

In Dora's opinion, he was.

Scott was inordinately nervous about talking to the FBI agents. His eyes darted restlessly between her and Wes, making him appear guilty of something and contradicting his claim that he had nothing to hide. Wes's calculated nonchalance was equally troubling.

"All they're after is some background information on Millicent," Wes said. "Dutch said it's routine."

"They could get background information on Millicent from a hundred other sources," Dora said. "Why have they singled out Scott?"

"Because he was Millicent's steady boyfriend."

"That was last year."

"I know when it was, Dora."

"Don't take that tone with me, Wes. My point is that a lot happened to Millicent between last spring, when she and Scott broke up, and last week, when she disappeared. Why is her past relationship with him relevant?"

"It isn't, and that's what Scott will tell them." Turning to him,

Wes said, "They'll probably just want to know how long you and Millicent dated and why you broke up." Wes looked hard at Scott; Scott looked back at his father.

Dora looked at both of them and immediately sensed an unspoken communication. They were keeping something from her, and the omission was infuriating. "Scott, why *did* you break up with Millicent?"

"He's told us why," Wes said. "The new had worn off. He got tired of her."

"I don't think that's all there was to it." Looking directly into her son's face, she gentled her voice. "What happened between you?"

Scott rolled his shoulders as though trying to shrug off the question. "Just like Dad said, we, you know, just lost interest in each other." Dora silently communicated her doubt. "Jeez, don't you believe me?" Scott shouted. "Why would I lie about it?"

"Maybe for the same reason you sneaked out of your room last night."

He looked like he'd been hit between the eyes with a two-by-four. He opened his mouth, then shut it quickly, apparently realizing the futility of denial.

She turned to Wes. "This morning I discovered that the security alarm contact on his bedroom window had been disabled."

"I know."

It was now Dora's turn to feel as though she'd been struck. "You *know*? And you didn't tell me?"

"I know everything that goes on in this house," Wes said smoothly. "For instance, I know that he rigged the alarm when he was seeing Millicent. He often sneaked her into his bedroom after we'd gone to bed."

He must be telling the truth, she thought. Scott's cheeks were flaming.

"It doesn't surprise me that he sneaks out occasionally," Wes continued. "It's no big deal."

She looked at her husband with incredulity. "I disagree."

"He's almost nineteen, Dora. Kids that age keep late hours. Or don't you remember what it's like to be young?"

Enraged by his condescension, she closed her hands into fists. "It's not that he's keeping late hours, Wes. It's that he's doing it sneakily." She turned to Scott. "Where did you go last night?"

"Nowhere. I just...walked. *Breathed*. Because I can't stand to be cooped up in this house all the time."

"See?"

She ignored Wes. "Scott, are you doing drugs?"

"Jesus, Mom, no! Where'd you get that idea?"

"Drugs would explain your mood swings, your—"

"Will you relax, Dora?" Wes said, continuing in the patronizing tone she despised. "As usual, you're blowing this out of proportion."

She would not be swayed. "If it's not drugs, it's something else. What are you hiding from us, Scott?" She kept her voice soft and caring, nonjudgmental, nonthreatening. Going to him, she took his hand and squeezed it reassuringly. "Tell us what's going on. No matter how bad it is, your father and I will stand by you. What is it? Do you know what happened . . ."

She paused, unable to finish the dreaded question without taking a fortifying breath. "Was there more to your relationship with Millicent than met the eye? Have the authorities discovered something that—"

"Will you shut the hell up?" Wes took hold of her arm and yanked her around to face him. "Are you *crazy*? He's not involved in that. Or illegal drugs. Or anything else except being a typical eighteen-year-old."

"Let go of me." She pulled her arm free. "Something is wrong with my son, and I want to know what it is before the FBI get here and I learn it from them. What is going on?"

"Nothing."

"*Something,* Wes," she shouted. "Our son is not the same person he was last year. Don't tell me there's nothing wrong! I'm not blind and I'm not stupid, although you seem to think so. I have a right to know what's happening to my son."

He thrust his face close to hers. "You want to know?"

"Dad, no!"

"You want to know, Dora?"

"*Dad!*"

Wes stuck his hand in his coat pocket and withdrew a box of disposable syringes and several vials. She recoiled from his extended hand. "What *is* that?"

"Steroids."

She stared at him, agape, then turned to Scott. "You've been giving yourself steroid shots?"

His gaze flickered to Wes, then back to her. "Not me. Mr. Ritt."

In the silence of her stunned disbelief, someone knocked loudly on the front door.

"That will be our company." Wes calmly replaced the paraphernalia in his coat pocket, then removed his coat and hung it on the peg near the back door. "Scott, answer the door and invite them in. Don't be nervous. Dutch will be with them. Offer them a seat and tell them we'll be right there."

Scott remained where he was, looking at his mother with apology and shame.

"Did you hear me, Scott?" Wes's voice was soft but imperious.

Scott turned and went into the living room to answer the second knock.

Wes moved close to Dora. His breath was hot on her face. "You are to act like everything in this household is hunky-dory, do you understand? This is a private matter. It stays in our family."

She glared at him. "How could you do that to your own son? Those things are poison."

"An exaggeration, typical of you."

"Have you even considered the side effects, Wes?"

"They're a small price to pay for the difference they can make in his—"

"I don't give a damn about his athletic ability!" she exclaimed in a stage whisper, aware of the men in the next room. "I don't care how strong he is or how much stamina he has on a goddamn football field. I care about his *life*." She felt her control unraveling. Now wasn't the time to lose it. She took several breaths to calm herself, but with fury still humming inside her, she continued. "Can't you see how those things have changed him?"

"Okay, he's a little moody. That can be a side effect."

"So can aggression."

He shrugged indifferently. "More aggressiveness would be a benefit, not a drawback."

Even after all her husband's other absurd rationalizations, that statement appalled her. "You are a monster."

He snuffled a laugh. "What? I'd thought you'd be relieved, happy to learn that the changes you see in Scott are from the steroids and don't have anything to do with that manipulating bitch. And that's what she was, you know."

"*Was?* Why are you referring to Millicent in the past tense?"

Wes leaned in until he was towering over her. "Because as far as the Hamer family is concerned, she's history."

Now Dora wasn't only appalled, she was afraid. "What are you saying?"

"You want to know the scoop on why Scott and Millicent broke up? Here it is, and remember you asked for it. She was interfering with his training, calling him all the time, hanging around every practice until he was finished, giving him all the pussy he wanted. He wasn't thinking about anything else. I wasn't going to let that skinny cunt ruin all my plans for him. To get his head back into his game, I had to intervene. You want to know the big mystery behind their breakup? You're looking at him."

"What did you do?"

"Doesn't matter. The important thing is that I ended—for good—their hot little romance." He poked her hard in the sternum. "That's something else that stays in the family."

Then he turned and left her alone, amid everything familiar yet feeling like an alien in her own house, bewildered by how she had arrived at this place in her life.

She could hear Wes in the other room, being his gregarious self, welcoming into their home FBI agents who had come to question their son about Millicent Gunn's disappearance.

William and Marilee left the drugstore together. Without electricity there was no point to staying open. He couldn't operate his cash register, or the computer that stored all the data on his customers and their prescriptions. Not that it mattered, because no one had come into the store since Wes had left with the sandwiches bound for police headquarters.

Marilee took food from the soda fountain's refrigerator for them to eat at home later, knowing that it would ruin before the store reopened and Linda returned.

They decided to leave her car there and go home in William's. "No sense in both of us trying to navigate these roads," he said. As he locked up, he left a note on the front door, notifying any customer with an emergency that he could be found at home.

Once they were in his car and on their way, Marilee said through chattering teeth, "If anyone ever finds out that you keep a dispensary of prescription drugs in the house, you'll lose your license."

"I only keep them for emergencies, and only for customers that I know won't abuse the privilege. Besides, the drugs I give out can be bought over the counter everywhere except the United States." He took a corner slowly, then leaned closer to the windshield and peered through the fogged glass. "I wonder what that's about."

They were on the street where the Hamers lived. Parked in front of their house were a nondescript sedan and Dutch Burton's Bronco.

"Isn't that the car the FBI agents were driving?" Marilee asked.

"I believe it is. That Begley was one of the rudest people I've ever met."

"I don't think he was intentionally rude. He's just efficient and accustomed to exercising his authority."

"I'm efficient, and I have authority, but I don't talk down to people."

Managing a drugstore with only one employee was hardly comparable to directing an office of the FBI, but Marilee decided to keep that observation to herself. She didn't want to bicker with William, although he'd been baiting her at every turn today.

When they came even with the Hamers' house, he said, "I'm not surprised to see Dutch here, but what business would the FBI have with them?"

"Maybe they're talking to Wes about what he slipped into his coat pocket when I surprised the two of you in the stockroom." She tossed it out casually to see how her brother would react.

He gave her his rote reply. "Something for Dora's headaches."

"You're lying."

"While you, sister, never lie, either by word or by deed." Cutting his eyes to her, he added slyly, "Or do you?" He chuckled at her attempted impassivity. "Scratch the surface of even the most circumspect life, Marilee, and you'll find duplicity. Even yours."

She turned her head away from him and looked through the passenger window. "I only wish you were right, William. I would love to harbor a dark secret."

"Perhaps the Hamers have been harboring one that the FBI uncovered. My money is on Scott."

"Why Scott?"

"Surely by now these federal geniuses have linked him to Millicent."

"They were sweethearts for a time. So what?"

"Sweethearts," he said with a snicker. "What a quaint and outmoded term for their relationship. She was on birth control pills."

"Most girls are."

"How well I know. It's a good part of my business. But did you know that Millicent went off them?"

"When?"

"Early last spring. She complained that they were making her retain fluid, adding weight. When she and Scott broke up, it occurred to me that perhaps they'd had a little accident."

"You mean that she got pregnant?"

"That's exactly what I mean."

"Despite her anorexia?"

"It could happen."

"I'm sure you're wrong, William."

"From my observation point in the store, I see a lot and retain everything I see. One day Scott and Millicent were in a booth at the soda fountain, all over each other. Her hand was in his lap. Need I get more explicit?"

"No."

"I was about to tell them that if they couldn't control their impulses, they'd have to leave. They must have come to the same conclusion. They couldn't get out of there fast enough. He even forgot to pay the bill."

"And your point is...?"

"The next time they were in the store at the same time, no more than a week later, he wouldn't even look at her. Something happened in the interim. Something huge. My guess would be a late period."

Marilee shook her head decisively. "I still think you're wrong. If Millicent was pregnant, Scott would have accepted his responsibility. Even if he'd been disinclined, his parents would have seen to it."

William blurted a laugh. "Wes would not allow anything to jeopardize his plans for Scott's future. Nothing. Not even the wild sowing of his own seed. And we all know how extremely proud Wes is of his seed."

His last remark annoyed her, which she believed was the purpose behind it. "I'm confident that not Scott, certainly not Dora, not even Wes, would dismiss—"

"I didn't say they would dismiss an unwanted and inconvenient pregnancy. Wes would simply do whatever was necessary to make the problem disappear."

Uneasily Marilee conceded that William was right. Wes would.

"What the hell was going on in there?" Begley asked under his breath as he and Hoot carefully made their way down the icy front walkway of the Hamers' home.

"I couldn't tell you, sir."

Once they were inside the bureau's sedan and Hoot had the motor going, Begley said, "But you sensed something, right? I wasn't imagining those undercurrents?"

"Not at all. I felt like we were watching a play where everybody was carefully reciting his lines."

"Good analogy."

Begley took off his gloves and briskly rubbed his hands together as he watched Dutch and Wes say good-bye to each other at the Hamers' front door. The police chief then walked to his Bronco and climbed in.

Looking back at the front of the house, Begley mused out loud. "The mother seemed on the verge of disintegrating. Wes Hamer was too loud, too cooperative, and too jaunty by half. I didn't swallow a frigging thing he said. Burton was playing both ends against the middle, shielding his lifelong friend from us and not really giving a damn about Millicent Gunn because he's preoccupied with his ex-wife. And the kid was—"

"Lying."

"Through his teeth."

Hoot waited until the Bronco had pulled away, then steered the sedan behind it and followed at a safe distance.

Begley directed a heating vent toward him, although the air coming from it was still cold. "But what was he lying about, Hoot? What was everybody but us dancing around? That's what I can't quite figure."

"I don't know, sir, but I don't think Burton was clued in either."

"He appeared confounded, too, didn't he?"

After a moment of private reflection, Hoot said, "Even though he and Wes Hamer are supposedly best friends, I sense a friction between them. An underlying . . . rivalry."

Begley turned in his seat and fired an imaginary pistol at him. "Dead on, Hoot. I get that from them, too. They say the right things, go through the motions of being bosom buddies, but I don't know, there's something under the surface."

"Resentment," Hoot said. "For all practical purposes, Hamer, as city councilman, is Burton's boss. Burton hates answering to him."

"Maybe that's it, Hoot. Maybe that's it." He wiped the windshield with his sleeve. "Still not much visibility, is there?"

"No, sir." Begley heard the beep at the same time Hoot did. He checked the pager clipped to his belt. "Perkins."

Then for a time the only sounds in the car were the swish of the wipers, the purr of air coming through the vents, and the crunch of tires on snow. Finally Begley said, "The kid got particularly jittery when you asked him the cause of his breakup with Millicent. Both parents perked up and seemed awfully interested in the answer to that question, too."

"Especially Mrs. Hamer."

"Because I don't think she believes that 'got tired of each other' crock of crap any more than we do."

"What about Mr. Hamer?"

"I'm still mulling that over, Hoot. But my gut instinct is telling me that the coach knows a whopping lot more than he lets on."

"About their breakup?"

"About everything. Unless you're a movie star, a used-car sales-man, or a pimp, you've got no use for a smile like his."

Hoot pulled into the slot beside the Bronco outside police head-quarters. They tramped into the building seconds behind Dutch Burton. The interior smelled like scorched coffee, wet wool, and men who hadn't showered in a while, but at least it was warm.

The dispatcher said to Hoot, "You're supposed to call Perkins in Charlotte soon as you come in."

"Yes. May I use your phone again?"

The dispatcher motioned him toward an unoccupied desk.

Begley, forced to wait to hear what Hoot would learn, if any-thing, joined Burton, who was pouring himself a cup of coffee. "What do you make of our visit with the Hamers?"

"I don't *make* anything of it," Burton replied.

"No need to take umbrage."

Burton snorted into his coffee mug, took a sip, then asked, "What did you make of it?"

"Wes and Dora Hamer are a long way from Ward and June Cleaver, and there's something the matter with their kid."

"You deduced all that after only thirty minutes with them?"

"More like three."

"However long it took, it was a waste of time, as well as an inva-sion of their privacy. We've tagged our man. It's Ben Tierney."

"At this point, Mr. Tierney is wanted only for questioning. Nothing more."

"My ass," Burton said. "You were searching his rooms at Gus Elmer's place. Harris told me so. What did you find that gave you a hard-on for him?"

Begley refused to acknowledge the question.

"If that's the way you want to play it, fine," Burton said angrily. "I'll go out there and see for myself."

"Listen to me," Begley said, his voice low but vibrating with menace, "you tamper with anything out there, you even step foot in those rooms, and I'll personally see to it that you won't be able to buy yourself a job in law enforcement, and I'm talking goddamn game warden. I can do it."

"Why aren't you trying to get up there and apprehend Tierney?"

"Because a jealous hothead ruined all chance of that this morn-ing," Begley fired back.

Burton was so irate, the corners of his eyes were twitching. "Leave it to the fucking FBI to pester my best friend and his family about some pissant high school romance that has no bearing on the case while issuing empty threats to me. Meanwhile, the likely perp is—"

"Excuse me." Hoot practically wedged himself between them. "You'll both be pleased to learn that we've been guaranteed a helicopter and small tactical rescue team as soon as the weather clears, which, hopefully, will be tomorrow morning."

"I want Lilly rescued. I want Tierney *arrested,*" Burton declared. "You've got all the fancy equipment, but this is still my jurisdiction, and he's my prime suspect."

"Kidnapping is federal. We can—"

Begley raised his hand, stopping Hoot from saying more. "Understood, Chief Burton," he said, surprising even himself with his calm.

He wasn't backing down, he was simply trying to pacify a man on a ledge. It was only a matter of time before Dutch Burton self-destructed, either on purpose or accidentally. Either way, Begley didn't want him further provoked before Tierney was in custody and the former Mrs. Burton was safe.

"Between now and when the chopper arrives," he continued, "I suggest you get those cuts on your face treated by a medical professional, then go home and rest. You look done in. Whatever tomorrow holds in store, we'll all need to be sharp."

Burton looked angry enough to spit in his face, but he said nothing.

Begley pulled on his gloves and asked Hoot if he'd gotten what he needed from Perkins.

"Here, sir," he said, holding up a folder. "I took notes by hand."

"Good. I'm ready for a hot toddy and a crackling fire. I'd be willing to bet Gus Elmer can supply both." As he moved toward the door, he shot Burton a look that warned him against even trying to search Tierney's cabin at Whistler Falls Lodge. He would be watching.

A few minutes later, he and Hoot were back in the cold car, skidding along the deserted streets of Cleary. Begley said, "Dutch Burton is a calamity waiting to happen. My guess? He'll eat the barrel of his pistol one of these days."

Then he ran his hand over his face to wipe away the disturbing thought. "Give me the condensed version of your conversation with Perkins. Unless it's something rock solid, then I want details."

"Perkins has been searching for any linkage between Tierney and the other missing women."

"And?"

"Carolyn Maddox—"

"The young, single mother."

"Correct. She worked at two local motels prior to where she was working when she disappeared. As of now, it's unknown if Tierney ever stayed in those places. Perkins is still checking his credit card statements."

"He could have paid cash."

"In which case we would have to depend on the motel registries."

"Where he could have signed in as Tinkerbell."

Hoot nodded grimly.

"I don't suppose she ever worked at Mr. Elmer's lodge."

"No, sir. That was the first thing Perkins checked."

"Go on."

"Laureen Elliott, the nurse. Her only surviving relative is a brother, who lives with his wife in Birmingham. They're snowbound, too, but Perkins reached him on his cell phone. If his late sister knew anyone named Tierney, she never mentioned him."

"Tierney is a name you'd remember because it's not that common."

"My thought, too, sir."

"The widow?"

"Betsy Calhoun. Her daughter still lives here in Cleary. Perkins was unable to reach her."

"Do you have an address?"

"I'm headed there now. It's in the next block."

Begley smiled. "Excellent. And last?"

"Torrie Lambert, the teenager."

"Who was probably a random selection."

"More than likely. But I'd hate to assume that, and then have there be a previous connection we overlooked. Perkins is still trying to contact her mother."

"In the meantime..."

"What, sir?"

"Do we stay on Tierney to the exclusion of all others?"

"Scott Hamer, for instance?"

"Is it like Burton says, Hoot? Should we take the Hamers and everything they said at face value and end that line of thought entirely? Reasonably, Scott could have a motive for doing Millicent harm. Love affair gone awry, et cetera. It's even conceivable that he chanced upon Torrie Lambert in the woods that day. But what would a good-looking young man like him have to do with an obese nurse, a single mom with a sick kid, and a widow lady older than his mother?"

"Which brings us back to Tierney."

"To whom the same question applies. Say Tierney has a lech for teenage girls. Even Carolyn Maddox would fit if we fudged a couple of years. But the other two? *Goddammit!* Why can't we find a connecting thread?"

Begley appreciated Hoot for not trying to produce an answer just to fill the silence.

Eventually the senior agent sighed. "Until that commonality becomes obvious, give me an educated guess, Hoot. Is Tierney our man?"

Hoot stopped the car at the address he'd jotted down. The frame house was little more than a cottage, its small yard enclosed with a white picket fence, now half buried in snow. Smoke was curling out of the rock chimney covered in a dormant wisteria vine. A fat, yellow cat was sitting on a windowsill staring out at them through lace curtains.

The two men sat in silence as they looked at the house belonging to Betsy Calhoun's daughter. Begley was thinking that the house looked so innocent, so Norman Rockwellian, one couldn't imagine tragedy visiting the people who lived there. Yet Betsy Calhoun's daughter went to bed every night without knowing her mother's fate.

"That has to be pure hell." Begley didn't realize he'd spoken the thought aloud until he saw the vapor of his breath swirling in front of his face. "We gotta get the bastard, Hoot."

Hoot seemed to have followed his train of thought. "Absolutely, sir. We do."

"So, the Hamer family's jitters and evasions notwithstanding, does Ben Tierney still look good to you?"

"Yes, sir," he replied. "Tierney still looks good to me."

"Well, hell. He looks good to me too." Begley shoved open his car door, and as he stepped out, he glanced in the direction of the cloud-enshrouded peak and said another brief prayer for Lilly Martin.

CHAPTER

23

Each time Lilly exhaled, the tendrils of vaporizing breath became finer.

She was chilled to her bones but had neither the strength nor the initiative to get up and place another log on the coals. What would be the point?

She wasn't one of those people who dwelled on death and dying, fretting over it until the worry hastened the worrier's demise. However, after Amy died, she naturally had contemplated death, wondering what the passage was like from this life into the next, never questioning if there was a next. That sweet, vital nova of life and energy that her daughter had been couldn't simply have ceased to exist. Amy had merely moved from a dimension governed by physics into a realm of the spirit.

Believing that had helped Lilly survive her bereavement. Yet she had anguished over the nature of the journey between the two worlds. Had Amy glided into it peacefully on a carpet of light? Or had her passage been dark and terrifying?

That was when Lilly had come to think about her own death and ponder whether it would be serene or traumatic. But only in her nightmares had she died of suffocation while alone.

At least she would depart knowing that Blue would be caught. Before she became too weak, she used a paring knife to etch TIERNEY = BLUE into one of the kitchen cabinets, believing that would be more effective than a note written on one of her blank checks, which could easily be overlooked in the hubbub sure to arise during the discovery and removal of her body from the cabin.

Tierney.

Just thinking the name jerked a sob from her constricted chest. She was outraged over her own culpability. With self-scorn she thought of how easily she'd fallen for his rare combination of ruggedness and sensitivity that day on the river, of how she had pined these last months over the sacrificed opportunity to see him again.

From the start, he had seemed too good to be true.

Take note, Lilly: What seems that way, usually is.

She was a little old to be learning that valuable lesson, and unfortunately she wouldn't have an opportunity to apply it to her own life, but it was worth noting anyway, wasn't it? Maybe she should leave it etched into the cabinet as well, the way prisoners leave moral messages on the walls of their cells for future occupants.

But now she didn't have the strength even to hold the paring knife. Bouts of mucus-producing coughing had left her so weak she could no longer sit up. She was out of energy, to say nothing of time.

There was one advantage to dying. Imponderable questions were finally answered. For instance, she now knew with certainty that one wasn't propelled into the afterlife in a blaze of dazzling light. On the contrary. Death stole over one like a softly gathering dusk. The darkening was gradual, the shrinkage of vision almost imperceptible, until only a pinpoint of light and life remained.

And then that too was swallowed by the blackness that was absolute and all encompassing.

Desperately she looked for Amy in the impenetrable darkness, but she couldn't see her. She couldn't see anything. Her ears quickened, though, at the sound of a voice coming to her from far away.

It was her daddy. He was calling her home from where she was playing in the next block.

"Lilly! Lilly!"

I'm coming, Daddy.

She could envision him standing on their porch, hands cupped around his mouth, calling anxiously until she called back and told him that she was on her way home.

"Lilly!"

He sounded afraid. Frantic. Panicked.

Couldn't he hear her? Why couldn't he hear her? She was answering him.

I'm on my way home, Daddy. Can't you see me? Can't you hear me? I'm here!

"Lilly! Lilly!"

Tierney tilted her upper body over his forearm and thumped her hard on the back. A glob of mucus was expelled onto the blanket covering her lap. He struck her between the shoulder blades again, forcing out more mucus, which dribbled from her mouth. When he released her, she flopped back lifelessly onto the sofa, her head lolling to one side.

He tore off his gloves and slapped her cheeks, arguing with himself that her face was warm. It was his hand that was cold, not her gray skin.

"Lilly!"

He worked his hand inside her coat, beneath her sweater, and pressed his palm against her chest. When he felt her heartbeat, an involuntary cry issued from his raw, dry throat.

Rapidly he unzipped the coat pocket in which he'd placed her pouch of medications. It was a green silk bag with crystal beading decoration, just as she'd described. When he opened it, the bottle of pills fell onto the floor and rolled out of sight, but it was the inhalers he was after. He scanned the labels. They might just as well have been written in Greek.

One, he remembered her telling him, was used to prevent attacks. The other was to provide immediate relief to a patient suffering a severe attack. But he didn't know which was which.

He shoved one of the short nozzles past her bloodless lips, worked it between her teeth, and depressed the canister. "Lilly, breathe."

She lay perfectly still, unresponsive, gray as death.

He slid his arm under her shoulders and lifted her up again, shaking her viciously. "Lilly, breathe! Inhale. Please, please, please. Come on, take a breath."

And she did. The drug did as it was supposed to do, instantly relieving the muscle spasms that had closed her airways and, by doing so, reopened them.

She drew in a whistling breath. Another. As she exhaled the third, she opened her eyes and looked at him, then clasped her hands around his where they still held the inhaler inside her mouth. She depressed the canister again. Her inhalations were gurgling, wheezing, awful noises.

Tierney said, "Music to my ears."

Suddenly pushing the inhaler away, she coughed into her hands. "Here." From the other sofa, he snatched up the towel he'd used the night before to support his head and thrust it at her.

She coughed into it. The coughs racked her whole body. Tierney, kneeling in front of her, murmured encouragingly.

Finally, the coughing ceased. She lowered the soiled towel from her mouth. He took it from her. She seemed transfixed by the sight of him, and only then did he realize how scary he must appear.

He brushed frost off his eyelashes and eyebrows, and worked the stiff, icy scarf down beneath his chin. "I'm not a ghost. It's me."

"You came back?" Her voice was barely audible. "Why?"

"That was the plan all along. You thought I was abandoning you to die so I could escape."

She nodded.

"If I had promised you that I was coming back with your medication, would you have believed me?"

Slowly she shook her head no.

"Right. Trying to convince you would have wasted valuable time, so I had no choice except to leave with you thinking the worst of me. It wasn't easy to go."

Using the armrest of the sofa for leverage, he pushed himself off his knees and stood up, moving like a man decades older than himself. Inside his boots, his feet were numb. He couldn't feel the floor beneath them as he shuffled to the fireplace and arranged several sticks of wood on the grate. In order to get the dying coals to ignite, he bent down and gently blew on them. They caught, and soon hungry flames were licking at the logs.

He eased off his backpack, set it on the floor, and nudged it beneath the end table with the toe of his boot. He unwound the scarf from his neck and removed the stadium blanket and watch cap from his head. Along with his coat, he draped them over one of the stools at the bar so they could dry out. Tentatively he patted the back of his head, then inspected his fingers for fresh blood. Either his wound hadn't bled any more or the blood was frozen.

He sat down on the sofa opposite Lilly and unlaced his boots. He wavered on removing the one from his right foot, knowing that his ankle might swell so badly he wouldn't be able to get the boot on again. But if he didn't get more circulation to his foot, he could lose toes to frostbite.

Gritting his teeth against the pain, he worked his foot out of the wet boot and peeled off his sock. The ankle was slightly swollen, but not as bad as the pain had indicated it might be. He saw no signs of frostbite, but he roughly massaged his toes. It hurt like hell when blood started to flow into them again, but that meant the capillaries weren't frozen beyond repair.

While he was doing all this, Lilly had continued to sit wide-eyed and wordless, staring at him as though he were an apparition. Moving slowly so as not to spook her, he got up and went to kneel in front of the sofa again. He tried to speak her name, but it came out a hoarse croak. "Are you all right now?"

She merely bobbed her head once.

"Jesus, I forgot your pill." He found the small brown plastic prescription bottle beneath one of the armchairs. He got a glass of water from the kitchen and brought it to her. She used the second inhaler, then swallowed one of the pills. As she drank, he noticed that color was returning to her lips, reassuring him that she was getting adequate oxygen, although her respiration still sounded like an out-of-tune bagpipe.

"That inhaler is good stuff," he said. "I didn't know which one to use. I had a fifty-fifty shot. I guess I picked the right one."

She gave a small nod.

His gaze roved over her face. She was moving and breathing, and her color was returning, but he feared he might be having another hallucination, like many he had experienced on his return trek from the car.

Lilly had been at the center of all of them. In some, he returned to find her blue from cold and lack of oxygen, motionless, dead. In others she was radiant and warm, glowing with life, sexually needy, passionately taking him deep into herself.

In reality, she was neither lifeless nor lustful but dazed. "You must have passed out just before I came in," he explained. "I called your name several times, but you didn't respond, didn't even move. Your chest was perfectly still. Scared the shit out of me," he said, his voice turning gruff. "I thought I'd gotten here too late."

In less than a whisper, she said, "So did I." Then her face crumpled with emotion. As though a dam that had been tenuously holding back her tears suddenly gave way, they filled her eyes.

He reacted spontaneously. In a heartbeat, he was beside her on the sofa, his arm across her shaking shoulders. "It's okay now. I'm back, and you're alive."

She fell against his chest. He lifted her onto his lap, cradling her like a child, enfolding her in his arms and bending his head over hers. He felt her reflexively clutching handfuls of his sweater.

"Shh, shh." He rubbed his lips against her hair. "Don't cry, Lilly. You're not supposed to cry, remember? You don't want to bring on another attack by crying."

He tipped her head up and smoothed back her tangled hair.

Thank God her complexion no longer had the gray cast of death. Cupping her head between his hands, he ran his thumbs across her cheeks to wipe away the tears.

Looking directly into her eyes, he said, "Short of dying out there, nothing could have kept me from coming back."

His gaze lowered to her mouth. Her lips were soft, full, pink now, slightly parted, tremulous, damp from drinking water, possibly tears. At the base of her throat, the smooth skin throbbed with each beat of her heart.

Curbing the impulses dunning him, he stood up, lifting her with him, and carried her to the end of the sofa, where he lowered them both onto the mattress. He sat with his back against the armrest of the sofa, his feet stretched toward the fire, Lilly on his lap.

He guided her head back to his chest, where she rested her cheek. He reached for one of the blankets and pulled it over them, then hugged her close and propped his chin on the crown of her head.

To all this, she acquiesced. He didn't deceive himself into thinking she played the lamb because she trusted him. He'd seen the message she had scratched into the wood of the kitchen cabinet. She was allowing him to hold her only because the trauma she'd suffered had exhausted her.

Long after she fell asleep, he stared into the flames and savored the delight as well as the misery of having her this close, of the soft weight of her breast resting on his stomach. Occasionally her fingers curled into the wool weave of his sweater. He wanted to believe she was reassuring herself that he was still there, although it might have been simply a reflexive motion of agitation, subconscious unrest.

He tried not to think about how silkily her tongue had moved against his when he kissed her last night, or the twin delicacies that wet spandex had made of her breasts in the cold waters of the river that day last summer, or how badly he wanted to possess her, completely.

But of course in his effort not to think about those things, they were all he could think about. His skin hunger for her became so acute that he ultimately yielded to it and slipped one hand beneath her sweater.

Then he slept.

She came awake within the circle of his arms, sensing immediately that he was awake. She sat up but, embarrassed, kept her head averted.

"The fire needs stoking," was all he said.

With as much grace as possible, she climbed off him and sat back on her heels. He had to use the armrest to lever himself up. She noticed his grimace and remarked on it.

"I'm a bit banged up."

"You shouldn't have let me sleep so long," she said. "It couldn't have been comfortable for you."

"I slept, too, and woke up only a few minutes ago."

"How long did we sleep?"

He checked his wristwatch. "Four hours."

Four hours! Four hours? How had she been able to sleep that peacefully for that long in the arms of a man she believed was Blue? Her near-death experience must have radically muddled her thinking.

He looked her over from head to foot. "How are you feeling?"

"Much better. Better than I would have thought, considering the severity of the episode." She paused, then said softly, "I didn't thank you."

"Yes you did."

"No. I had an emotional breakdown and crying jag."

"I got the message."

"But I didn't put it into words, and I should. Thank you, Tierney."

"You're welcome." Seconds ticked by before he turned away and walked toward the bar stool where he'd left his coat.

"Your limp is worse."

"Yeah, I sprained my ankle on the way to the car. I was lucky not to have broken it."

"What happened?"

"I couldn't see where I was going and..." He made a gesture that said it didn't matter how he'd injured himself. "It'll be okay."

"Was that under the dash, as we thought?" she asked, indicating the silk pouch on the coffee table.

He related how he had finally reached the car after almost giving up hope. "It was completely covered with snow, ice underneath. Like to never have got the door open."

But he had. The toughest part, he said, was resisting the urge to rest. He knew if he did, he was in danger of falling asleep and freezing.

"Once inside the car, I allowed myself about thirty seconds to catch my breath, then got busy. I had to wedge my arm through the gap between your dashboard and the passenger seat, which was only a few inches wide."

He'd had to reach further than arm's length before he finally felt the silk bag. "I pinched some of the cloth between two fingers," he told her, demonstrating. "I was afraid I'd push it forward, out of reach. But I managed to drag it toward me until I could get a better grip on it."

"And then you had to make the trip back. With a concussion and a sprained ankle."

"The important thing is that I made it in time." He glanced at the fireplace. "We'll need more wood before the night's out."

"Are you going outside barefoot?"

He had pulled on his coat but was moving toward the door on bare feet. "I don't intend to stay out that long."

He stepped onto the porch and quickly shut the door behind him. Lilly was there to hold it open when he carried in an armload of logs. "Thanks." As he stacked the firewood on the hearth, he said, "I saw the message you left on the kitchen cabinet."

She didn't know how to respond, so she said nothing.

He stood up and faced her. "You're not the only one who thinks that. I got the motor of your car to start, turned on the radio in the hope of hearing a weather report."

She had an uneasy premonition of what was coming.

"The FBI is looking for me," he stated bluntly, then brushed past her on his way to the porch again. "Apparently one of your calls to Dutch got through after all." He slammed the door shut behind him.

Lilly sank onto the sofa. She was trembling but was unsure if the weakness came from relief or dismay. If he was Blue, this was good news. But if he wasn't, she had incriminated an innocent man.

In a flurry of blowing snow, he entered with another armload of firewood and kicked the door shut. "The forecast calls for the snow to end tonight. Temperatures will remain well below freezing, but conditions will improve."

He continued stacking the logs on the hearth. His tone was casual and unconcerned. "The roads will remain impassable for days, but with any luck, there's an outside chance you could be rescued tomorrow."

"Tierney—"

"We still have to get through tonight though," he said, brusquely interrupting. He turned to her, dusting off his hands. "That must be an awfully distressing prospect for you."

He motioned toward the backpack beneath the end table. "Pistol, handcuffs, you know where they are if you feel the need for them. Now that you've got your medication and a supply of firewood, you could fare on your own until help arrives."

"Are you leaving?" She was stunned by how fearful she was that he would go again.

He snuffled a bitter laugh. "I'm tempted, but no. Now that my name has been broadcast, every hillbilly with a deer rifle is going to be on the lookout for me. My hide would be the hunting trophy of the season, and in my present state I'd be easy prey.

"No, until I can get some food and rest, you're stuck with me. But I won't have you cringing every time I come near you. So if you want to handcuff me to the bed again, I'll go peacefully. Not exactly willingly, but I won't put up a fight."

She ducked her head and looked down at the floor, at her own stocking feet, then over at his bare toes, poking from under the wet hems of his jeans. It didn't take her long to make a decision. "That won't be necessary, Tierney."

"You're no longer scared of me?"

She looked at him and said simply, "If you were Blue, you wouldn't have come back."

"But don't you see, Lilly, I would have had to come back, for my own survival. I would have died out there, one way or the other."

"But you didn't have to revive me. Blue would have let me die."

"Where would be the thrill in that? Watching you die wouldn't be the same as taking your life. Not at all."

She studied him for a long moment, searching his eyes for answers to questions he adroitly dodged with more questions, or silence, or lies, or by playing devil's advocate. He was excellent at the game, but she was tired of playing it.

Wearily she said, "I don't know who you are, Tierney, or what you're about, but I don't think your intention is to end my life or I would be dead."

He relaxed his posture. His expression softened. "You're right to trust me, Lilly."

"I don't trust you at all. But you saved my life."

"I guess that counts for something."

"At the very least it keeps you out of handcuffs."

"But it didn't get us back to where we were that day on the river. What do I have to do? What will it take to get us there, Lilly?"

He didn't move. Nor did she. And yet it seemed the distance between them narrowed, and continued to until a log on the grate shifted, sending a shower of sparks up the chimney and dispelling the mood.

He inclined his head toward the door. "It's easier when you hold the door for me."

She operated the door while he made several more trips onto the porch for firewood. On his last trip out, he took a metal bucket with him, one which they had filled with drinking water but which now was empty.

When he returned, the bucket was packed full of snow. "I need a shower." He scraped several hot coals from beneath the grate onto the hearth, then set the bucket on top of them. Rapidly the snow began to melt. "Unfortunately, a sponge bath will have to do."

"Sponge bath?" she said.

"You've never heard that expression?"

"Not since my grandmother died."

"I learned it from my grandmother, too. My grandfather told me it was a whore's bath. Grandma lit into him. She didn't like him saying anything that even smacked of dirty when I was within earshot."

"And how often was that?"

"Every day," he replied. "They raised me."

While she was assimilating that, he disappeared into the bedroom and returned with washcloths and towels. "There are only two towels left without blood on them."

"How does your head feel?"

"Better now. The concussion gave me several bad moments when I was out there," he said, nodding toward the door. He dipped his finger into the bucket of water. "I don't think it'll get much warmer than that. Can you stand it?"

"I thought it was for you."

"You get this first bucketful."

"No thanks."

Her curt refusal exasperated him. "I'll wait in the bedroom until you give me the all clear. Will that make you feel safe from ravishment?" Then he took a deep breath, lowered his head, and shaking it, expelled his breath along with his anger. "I thought you would enjoy washing. That's all."

Feeling chastened, Lilly reached for her handbag. Among the contents was a small plastic bottle of liquid hand soap. She held it out, a gesture of conciliation. "Southern Magnolia. I'll share."

"I accept. Southern Magnolia will be a vast improvement over what I smell like now." He stepped into the bedroom. "Take your time." He closed the door.

She removed all her clothes and washed hastily. Her wet skin broke out with gooseflesh even though she was practically standing in the fireplace. Her teeth chattered uncontrollably. Nevertheless, she put the tepid water, washcloth, and soap to good use, dried herself briskly, then put her clothes on and opened the bedroom door. "All done, and it felt wonderful."

He was wrapped in a blanket he'd taken from the bed, but he was still shivering. He pulled the bedroom door closed. "It's too cold for you in there. Breathing that air could bring on another attack."

"I've taken my meds."

"You're not going in there," he said stubbornly. "Seeing you near death once was enough, thanks."

"I hate for you to miss your bath."

"I won't. I'm not modest."

He carried her bathwater outside and discarded it, refilling the bucket with snow. While he was waiting for it to melt, then heat, Lilly rummaged in the kitchen. "We've got pots and pans. Do you think we could heat a can of soup in the fireplace?"

"Sure."

She glanced over her shoulder and caught him peeling his sweater over his head in the inexplicable way a man does it, making his hair stand on end, and only then pulling his arms from the sleeves.

Not wanting to think of him with that tolerant fondness her sex has for the peculiarities of the other, she crossed to the living room window and pushed aside the drape. "Maybe it's my imagination," she said, "but the snow seems to have let up a little."

"I guess the forecasters were right."

"I guess."

She heard the clank of his belt buckle striking the rock hearth when he dropped his jeans. The whispery rasp of fabric against skin. The soft splash of water as he dipped the washcloth into the bucket.

She placed the tip of her index finger against the cold window-pane, then drew a vertical line in the frost. "I don't believe any of my calls to Dutch got through."

She sensed that he'd ceased all movement and was standing per-fectly still, staring at her back. After several tense moments, she heard the ripple of water and knew that he was resuming his bath.

"Which means that Dutch didn't hear from me that you're Blue. So if Dutch didn't identify you to the FBI, they were seeking you on their own. Why, Tierney?"

"You can ask them when they get here."

"I would rather you tell me."

He didn't say anything for such a long time she thought he was going to ignore her. But eventually he spoke. "That girl, Millicent Gunn. I know her from the sporting goods store where she clerks. I was in there buying socks within days—maybe the very day—of when she was reported missing. I'm sure they're checking out every-one who had any contact with her."

"Is that what they said on the radio, that they were checking out everyone? Or was your name the only one mentioned?"

"I may be the only one they haven't got around to."

That was a reasonable explanation, but if that was all there was to it, why had he become so upset about it? Also, she doubted his name would have been broadcast if the FBI wanted him only for a routine interview.

"If I hadn't been able to etch your name into the cabinet, I suppose I could have written it in the frost on the window."

Suddenly she realized that was precisely what she had done. Like a schoolgirl writing the name of her beau on her book cover, without even being aware she was doing it, she had printed his name in the frost.

Embarrassed and impatient with herself, she swiped the name off the glass... only to see, in the watery smear left by her hand, a reflection of him. Naked, backlit by the fire, his wet skin glistening.

Her lips parted on a swift intake of air. Desire, embedded deep within her center, unfurled and expanded. Unaware of her watching him, he leaned down to dip the cloth in the bucket. He wrung water from it before applying it to his chest, moving it gingerly over his bruised ribs, down his flat belly, then into the shadowy lushness between his thighs.

Lilly closed her eyes and pressed her forehead against the windowpane. Her blood was pumping thick and hot. The roaring in her ears was so loud she could barely hear him when he said, "You could have done that. The oil from our skin leaves marks on the glass that last until the window is washed."

What was he talking about? She couldn't even remember. She raised her head and, to prevent herself from looking at him again, let the drape fall back over the window before she opened her eyes.

"Just about finished," he said. She heard the jingle of his belt buckle when he picked up his jeans. A few seconds later, he said, "You can turn around now."

When she came around, she didn't look directly at him, but out of the corner of her eye she could see him pulling his head through the neck of his sweater. She moved into the kitchen. "I'll get the soup ready." Miraculously her voice sounded normal.

"Good. I'm hungry."

He went outside to empty the bucket. By the time he joined her in the kitchen, she had emptied a can of condensed soup into a pan and added some of their drinking water to it.

"Thanks for the Southern Magnolia," he said.

"You're welcome."

"I hate asking you to do this again, but would you check that gash on my head?"

She had to touch him? Right now? "Of course."

As before, he straddled one of the bar stools. Moving behind him, she parted his wet hair. Wet? His hair was wet? He must have dunked his head in the bucket of water, but to her mortifying shame, she realized she hadn't noticed anything above his neck.

"No fresh bleeding," she said, "but I probably should replace the Band-Aid strips."

She cleaned the wound with one of the antiseptic pads, then they went through the same painstaking ritual as the night before, cutting the adhesive part of the bandage into strips with her manicure scissors, then placing them crosswise over the wound. She tried to perform the task with as much detachment as possible, but her motions were clumsy. Several times she felt him flinch and had to apologize for hurting him.

They heated the pan of soup in the fireplace and ate it sitting cross-legged on the mattress. Discovering they were ravenous, they heated another can.

Midway through the second helping, he said, "Lilly, are you all right?"

She raised her head, startled. "Why?"

"You're being awfully quiet."

"I'm just tired," she lied, then went back to eating her soup.

They prolonged the meal for as long as possible, but after they had finished, they still faced hours of nighttime with nothing to do.

After several minutes of silence, broken only by the crackle of the fire, he said, "Feel free to go to sleep whenever you want."

"I'm not sleepy."

"You said you were tired."

"Tired but not sleepy."

"That's how I feel, too. Weary, but wide awake."

"That long nap..."

"Hmm."

Another silence ensued. Finally she looked over at him. "Why were you reared by your grandparents?"

"My mom and dad were killed in a car wreck. The driver of a semi was going too fast, didn't heed the warning signs of road construction, couldn't slow down in time, literally ran up over them. Pancaked their car. It was hours before they could cut all the body parts out of the wreckage."

His matter-of-fact tone didn't fool her. He couldn't conceal the bitterness underlying it.

"The details were kept from me when it happened," he said. "But years later, when I was old enough to ask about it, my granddad let me read the newspaper write-up about the accident. My grandparents lost their daughter. I was orphaned. The careless truck driver walked away without a scratch."

"How old were you?"

"When it happened? Eight. Mom and Dad had gone away for a long weekend to celebrate their tenth anniversary and left me with my grandparents." He reached for the poker and stirred the fire.

"After their funerals, when I realized that it wasn't a bad dream, that they really were dead, I refused to go back into our house. My grandparents took me home to pack up my things, but I pitched a billy fit in the yard and wouldn't go inside. I just couldn't go into those rooms again, knowing that Mom and Dad weren't there, and never would be."

"You loved them," she said quietly.

He gave a self-conscious shrug. "I was a kid. Took everything they did for me for granted, but . . . yeah, I loved them. My grandparents were all right, too. Even though I must have been a huge inconvenience thrust upon them, they never made me feel that way. In fact, I never doubted they loved me."

"Did you ever return to your house?"

"No."

She propped her chin on her raised knees and pondered his profile. "You stay away from home now, too. You have a career which keeps you away for long periods of time."

He shot her a wry grin. "Bet the shrinks would have a field day with that."

"Was that a subconscious career choice? Or deliberate?"

"My wife thought it was deliberate."

"*Wife?*"

"Past tense. We were married for all of thirteen months."

"When was this?"

"Long time ago. I was barely old enough to vote, much less get married. I shouldn't have. I was selfish and self-absorbed. Not ready to settle down, certainly not ready to account to anybody. My wanderlust was her main complaint. Among many. All deserved," he said with a rueful smile.

The loss of his parents had continued to have an effect on him even into his adulthood, influencing decisions, impacting his marriage. What other emotional and psychological scars had that tragic event left on eight-year-old Ben? Had it warped and deformed his soul? He no longer pitched billy fits, but his pent-up anger might have sought other outlets.

Was he Blue?

The ribbon, the handcuffs, his inconsistencies and evasions were too significant to dismiss. If it had been reported on the radio that Cleary police were looking for him, she could assume that one of her calls to Dutch had gone through. But the FBI? There were essential pieces missing from his explanation of their interest in him.

Yet looking at him, she asked herself for the thousandth time how he could possibly be a man who kidnapped women and in all probability killed them. Surely she would know if a psychopath lived behind his eyes. There was an intensity there, yes. Often they sparked with anger or irritation. But they didn't gleam with the fanatic, fiery madness of a serial killer.

Most convincing of all the arguments was that he hadn't harmed her. Indeed, he had risked his own life today to save hers. It had been his voice, raw with emotion and fear, that she had heard calling her out of that void. Then for hours, heedless of his own discomfort, he had held her in his arms, touched her with such tenderness and—

Her thoughts crystallized around a sudden realization. The caresses that she had believed part of a wonderful dream hadn't been dreamed at all.

As though attuned to her thoughts, he turned his head and fixed his blue gaze on her. "I think it's time we went to bed."

CHAPTER
24

Betsy Calhoun's daughter had little to share with Agents Begley and Wise except cups of hot tea and homemade oatmeal raisin cookies. She explained that her husband was out of town on a buying trip for their office supplies store on Main Street. She wept when she told them about the last time she'd seen her mother.

"I stopped by her house to check on her. It was three o'clock in the afternoon, and she was still in her nightgown."

As Begley had guessed, Betsy Calhoun was suffering from clinical depression over the loss of her husband.

"She rarely left her house anymore," the woman said. She idly stroked the yellow cat, which had moved from the windowsill to her lap shortly after their arrival. "I encouraged her to get involved in community and church activities, volunteer for charity work, do *something*. But without Daddy, she couldn't be motivated to do anything."

"If I'm not mistaken," Hoot said, "her car was found in the parking lot of the bank."

"That's a mystery. She hadn't been in the bank for months. Since Daddy passed, I've been taking care of all her money matters. I can't explain why her car was there. Except she evidently took my advice to get out of the house more often." She dabbed her eyes with an embroidered hankie. "When they found it with that awful blue ribbon tied to the steering wheel, I knew something horrible had happened."

"Could she have met someone there in the parking lot?"

"Like who?"

"That's why we're asking," Begley said with uncharacteristic patience. "In the hope of learning who that someone may be."

"I've racked my brain, believe me. I can't think of anyone. Mother just isn't a social, people person." Indeed, Betsy Calhoun's circle of friends was limited to the ladies in her Sunday school class.

"With all due respect to her and your father's memory," Hoot said hesitantly, "is it possible she's been seeing a gentleman friend and keeping it a secret?"

She shook her head adamantly. "Not Mother. She's had the love of her life. She's actually shy of other men. I don't think she's ever even been on a date with anyone except my father. Mother's only outings are to the hair salon every Friday morning, church on Sundays, and an occasional trip to the market."

To her daughter's knowledge, she'd never had reason to go into the sporting goods store. "What in the world for?"

They asked if she knew Ben Tierney. "Who's that?"

Hoot gave her a brief description, but she shook her head and told them she could safely vouch that her mother wasn't acquainted with any such individual.

"I just want her to be found and brought home," she said, sniffing into the handkerchief. "If God doesn't grant me that prayer, at least I'd like to know what happened to her." Looking at them tearfully, she asked, "Do you think you'll ever find her?"

"We're going to do our best," Begley pledged, pressing her hand between his.

A few minutes later, as they pulled away from the cozy cottage, he remarked, "Nice lady."

"Yes, sir." Once again Hoot was shivering inside his coat, waiting for the sedan's heater to warm up. He didn't remember what it felt like to have dry, warm feet. "Whistler Falls Lodge, sir?"

"For lack of someplace else."

Ordinarily, having to spend the night in one of Gus Elmer's cabins without benefit of public utilities would have been a daunting and dreary prospect, but Hoot was so exhausted he actually looked forward to it. "Do you think he could put together a meal for us?"

The question about dinner didn't register with Begley, who was deep in thought. "Here's the thing," he said, musing out loud, "we've deduced that Tierney is our most likely suspect."

"Why else would he be keeping such close tabs on the disappearance cases, hoarding all that information we found in his rooms?"

"Precisely, Hoot. That certainly lent credibility to your hunch about him. We've also surmised—and accurately, I think—that his motivation is to be the savior of women in need. Correct?"

"Yes, sir." Actually Begley had surmised it, but Hoot had agreed, and so far, they'd uncovered nothing that would invalidate that theory.

"This is my problem," Begley continued. "Where would a shy widow lady who only went to the beauty parlor and Sunday school ever meet Tierney? She wasn't a kayaker, that's for damn sure."

"No, sir."

"Mrs. Calhoun has a small number of acquaintances, and her daughter had never heard of Tierney. So how did he get to know Betsy Calhoun well enough to select her as his next victim? Two diverse people like that, where did their paths cross?"

"I think that could be asked of all the victims with the exception of Torrie Lambert, whom he literally happened upon, and Millicent Gunn."

"Carolyn Maddox is plausible," Begley said. "A stretch, but plausible. Maybe he met Laureen Elliott in the medical clinic where she worked. He could have had the flu or something. But a timid widow and an adventurer?" Begley shook his head. "Doesn't compute."

Not in Hoot's mind either. He mulled it over for several minutes. "Suppose Tierney read her husband's obituary in the local newspaper. Remember the transponder he ordered from the catalog? Maybe he surveilled Mrs. Calhoun and realized what a lonely and dejected lady she was." The explanation sounded lame even to him. Begley wasted no time shooting holes in it.

"He's too active a man to keep surveillance over someone. Besides, that would take a lot of time, and he's not always here. I suppose he could have bumped into her in the parking lot of the bank. Maybe her car had stalled and he rendered help. Something like that. Saw instantly her loneliness and need. She was another random selection, like the Lambert girl." It was credible, but there was no conviction in his voice. He stared through the windshield while tapping his left hand fingers on the console between the seats.

"Are you having second thoughts about him, sir?"

"I don't know, Hoot," he grumbled.

"If he's not Blue, how do you explain all the materials he's collected on the disappearances?"

"First thing I'm going to ask him." He smacked his lips with irritation and muttered something about the goddamn case, and why the fuck couldn't he get a handle on it. Hoot didn't catch every word, but that was the gist of it.

Suddenly Begley turned to him. "Heard any more from Perkins?"

"No, sir. But trust me, he's on it. As soon as he learns something, he'll be in touch."

Begley gazed up at the sky. "I hope to hell a chopper can get here tomorrow. I don't know how long I can keep our jealous police chief at bay." He snorted his contempt for Dutch Burton. "However, as long as that road is blocked, he can't get any farther up the mountain than we can."

"And Tierney can't get down."

"Right, Hoot. We've got that going for us. And that's the sum to-tal of anything good I can say about this whole frigging mess."

Wes went into the high school gym's weight room ahead of Scott. They had to rely on the windows for light. The gloom was oppres-sive. There were no soft surfaces to absorb the cold. "Once you get going, you'll warm up." Wes's voice bounced off the tile walls, mak-ing it inordinately loud.

Scott remained moodily silent as he shrugged off his outer coat, then unzipped the jacket of his sweat suit and took it off. Beneath it he was wearing a tank top.

Wes took a moment to admire his son's physique. It was that of a natural athlete. He was long waisted and long limbed. His body fat was maybe ten percent, if that. Each muscle was well developed and perfectly toned, impressively delineated beneath his skin.

Wes envied Scott's near-perfect structure. He hadn't been that lucky. Thanks to his mother, his legs were shorter than ideal, and he had a propensity for osteoarthritis that had come to him via his old man's family, most of them bent and bandy-legged by the time they were fifty.

But Scott had been genetically favored with the best of Wes's and Dora's genes. He had inherited strength and stamina from him, grace and coordination from her.

Watching him now as he approached the weight bench, Wes thought that if only he'd been blessed with Scott's body and natural ability, he could have made it into the pros, he could have made it big.

Scott could if he wanted to, but that was the hell of it. The desire, the drive, the bloodlust for competition wasn't automatically issued along with physical superiority. Scott hadn't been born with the determination necessary to make a good athlete into a champion, but Wes was going to make damn certain that he acquired it. He was going to build a fire in the boy's belly if it was the last thing he did.

Scott was hardly on fire now. The effort he was putting into the free weight warm-up was uninspired. "None of those weights have the heft of that chip on your shoulder," Wes remarked.

Scott looked at him in the mirrored wall behind the bench but didn't respond.

"What's the matter with you tonight?"

Scott continued doing alternating biceps curls. "Nothing."

"Are you mad because I made you come here and work out instead of letting you go over to your friend Gary's house?"

"Gary's a jerk."

"So what's the problem?"

Scott propped the weights on his shoulders and began a set of squats. "Nothing's the matter. Everything's wonderful."

"Then why are you sulking like a four-year-old?"

"Gee, Dad, I don't know." He returned the weights to the rack, keeping his gaze locked with Wes's in the mirror. "Do you think it could be a mood swing because I'm being pumped full of steroids?"

Wes grabbed him by the arm, spun him around, and roughly pushed him backward against the mirror. He thrust his finger into Scott's face. "You smart-talk me like that again, and I'll whip your ass."

Scott only laughed. "Like I'd care."

"When I got finished with you, you'd care. Believe me, you'd care." Wes glared at him angrily, then flung his arms out to his sides. "I don't get you, Scott. I don't get your ingratitude. You think I want to give up my evening to be here spotting you while you work out? I'm doing all this for you."

"Who do you think you're kidding?" Scott shouted back. "You're doing it for *you*."

Wes knew from experience that Scott had inherited not only Dora's supple musculature but also her tendency to become mule-headed when pushed too far. He felt like smacking his son for talking back to him. But he reined in his temper and kept his voice at a reasonable level.

"You're wrong, son. Okay, sure," he said before Scott could interrupt, "I'll admit that it does my ego good to know that you're the strongest, the fastest, the best, but—"

"But you don't give a shit about me."

Wes was genuinely dismayed. "How can you say that after every-thing I've done for you?"

"You didn't do anything for me today, did you? When those FBI agents asked why Millicent and I broke up, I was the one in the hot seat, not you. I stuttered some stupid explanation while you sat there and didn't say a single goddamn word."

Speaking softly, Wes said, "Would you have rather I told them the truth?" He saw a flicker of uncertainty in his son's eyes and took advantage of it. "We've never talked about it. Would it have been a good idea for us to thrash through this for the first time in front of them? In front of your mother? Wouldn't it have embarrassed you just a lit-tle for them to learn that your girlfriend preferred me to you?"

"She didn't."

Wes chuckled. "That's not what she said. You were there. You saw. Did it look to you like she was having just a so-so time, or like she was so into it she was about to buck me off her?"

He saw Scott's hands ball into fists at his sides. His face was flushed, and not because of any exertion he'd put into his warm-up. He was enraged. His breaths were shallow and quick, as if he was on the verge of erupting.

Wes wished he would. He would have liked nothing better than for Scott to lay into him and fight with all his might to win. It would be good for the boy to vent some spleen. He wanted to see him act like a man rather than the sniveling titmouse Dora would have pre-ferred him to be.

But to his vast disappointment, almost disgust, he saw tears welling in his son's eyes.

"You set me up to see you together," Scott accused.

Wes didn't deny it. "It was time someone woke you up to the fact that the girl you'd become so ga-ga over was a slut."

"That's not true. You . . . you . . ."

"I dropped a few suggestive remarks, and she recognized them for the come-ons they were. This was no innocent virgin, Scott. I didn't force her. Hell, I didn't even have to try hard. She knew damn well what she was getting into when she came to my office that evening. Getting into her pants was as easy as one, two, three. Truth is, she wasn't wearing pants, and she made sure I knew it.

"If you would stop being mad at me long enough to think about it, you'd realize what that says about her. She'd been toying with the idea of having both the son and the father before I ever touched her."

"You're disgusting."

"Me? I'm disgusting? Why am I the bad guy? She was the one who did it for the novelty, for the fun of it. I did it for you."

"That's...that's bullshit!" Scott sputtered. "You did it to show me you *could.*"

Wes tried to lay his hand on Scott's shoulder, but when Scott threw it off, he said angrily, "Look, if I had come to you for a father-to-son heart-to-heart, and had told you that your sweetheart was a whore, you wouldn't have believed me, would you? Well? Would you? No. In order for you to believe it, you had to see it for yourself. I knew if you saw us together, that would be the end of it."

"Mission accomplished." Scott sneered.

"Goddamn right. You were well rid of her for a lot of reasons. I did you a favor."

"You fucked my girlfriend as a *favor* to me?"

Wes sighed. "I can't discuss it if you're going to twist everything I say."

"How many times?"

"What?"

"Don't play dumb. You heard me. How many times were you with Millicent? Just that once on top of your desk? Or did I just happen to catch you at it, and now you've made up this swell story about doing me a favor?"

"Scott."

"How many times?"

"Several, okay?" Wes shouted back. "I didn't keep count. It doesn't matter. You're refusing to—"

Scott reached for his sweat suit jacket and shoved his arms into the sleeves, then snatched up his overcoat and headed for the exit.

"Get back here, Scott," Wes ordered. "We're not finished."

"Oh yeah, we are."

"Where are you going?"

Scott kept walking and didn't answer.

"If this is your way of getting even—"

Scott stopped in his tracks and turned. Looking Wes straight in the eye, he smiled. "I already got even. With both of you."

CHAPTER
25

WHEN TIERNEY SAID IT WAS TIME FOR THEM TO GO TO BED, he meant it literally. Leaving her to sit in front of the fire, he got up, gathered all the blankets, and heaped them on the mattress.

He caught her watching him curiously. "I'm not going to sleep on the sofa," he stated definitively. "I don't fit on it. I'm battered and beat up, and I need what creature comfort I can get. You can have an extra blanket to tuck around you so there'll be no chance of us touching, even accidentally."

"All right."

She got up and went to the bathroom. He didn't have to caution her to hurry; it was frigid in those rooms.

When she returned, he was piling fresh logs onto the fire. "You lie here, nearer the hearth." She moved to where he indicated, but she didn't lie down until he had disappeared into the bedroom. At his suggestion, she tucked a blanket around herself.

He was back in a few minutes. She saw him hesitate and glance down at the wet legs of his jeans. She said, "Do you want to take them off?"

"Yes, but I won't." He lay down on top of the blanket with which she'd covered herself and pulled the others over them both. He groaned as he settled himself onto the mattress.

"Are you hurting?"

"Only when I breathe. You? Are you comfortable?"

"Fine."

"You haven't coughed in over an hour."

"I'm much better."

"Sounds like it. You're barely wheezing."

"Sometimes it's worse at night. I hope it doesn't keep you awake."

"Same goes for my snoring. If the fire burns down, just nudge me awake. I'll get up and add more wood."

"Okay."

On their backs, nowhere close to touching, they stared at the ceiling. The firelight cast dancing shadows across the exposed beams. Ordinarily the interplay of light and darkness would have been hypnotic and sleep inducing. But she lay rigid and tense, light-years away from sleepy.

"Do you think they'll come tomorrow?" She wasn't sure who she was referring to by "they." Dutch and a local rescue team, or the FBI. Both perhaps.

"I figure someone will set out to try," he replied. "That is, if the forecast holds and the snowfall stops."

"*And* if Dutch got my first voice mail message. He may think I've been safely back in Atlanta all this time."

"Maybe."

"If he didn't get that voice mail, he doesn't even know you're here with me."

"No."

But intuitively Lilly felt that Dutch did know, and the strain in Tierney's voice indicated he thought so too. "If the weather clears," she said, "we'll have cell phone service again."

"When we do, who will you call, Lilly? The FBI or Dutch?"

"I haven't thought about it."

"You'll call Dutch."

They were quiet for a moment, listening to the pop of the burning logs, then, turning onto her side to face the fireplace and stacking her hands beneath her cheek, she said, "Good night, Tierney."

"Good night."

There would be no nudging him awake because he didn't fall asleep. She knew this because she didn't fall asleep either. There were several reasons for her insomnia. The long nap that afternoon. The firelight flickering on her closed eyelids. The uncomfortable bulkiness of her clothes and the weight of the blankets. The recollections of her terror during those last minutes of the asthma attack.

But the primary reason for her wakefulness was Tierney, lying an arm's length away. After telling her good night, he hadn't uttered a sound, he hadn't moved, and yet she knew that he was as alert and as aware of her nearness as she was of his.

When he turned onto his side to face the fire, as she was doing, she lay in agonizing expectation of a touch that never came. Impossibly, though neither moved a muscle or made a sound, the tension between them wound tighter with each passing second.

Easily an hour after they'd exchanged their awkward good nights, he spoke. He didn't ask first in a whisper if she was asleep. Even though she was facing away from him, he knew she was still awake, just as she'd known he was. His soft, low voice came as no surprise. However, what he said staggered her.

"He hit you, didn't he? Dutch. He hit you."

She swallowed but remained otherwise motionless. "Where did you hear that?"

"Nowhere. It's just that I've observed him enough, it's reasonable to assume. To some cops violence becomes commonplace. It starts to seem the normal solution to every problem. Especially to a man who's emotionally fractured and drinking too much."

She said nothing.

"And," he added in an even lower pitch, "I don't think you would have given up on your marriage for any lesser reason."

She'd never told anyone, not her friends and business associates who had recognized her emotional turmoil for what it was and urged her to confide in them, not even her grief counselor, to whom she had laid bare every other aspect of herself. It felt right to confide it to Tierney simply because he'd been the only person perceptive enough to figure it out.

"It only happened once," she said quietly. "He'd raised his fists before, as though he wanted to strike me. I warned him that if he ever did, our life together would be over. That's what I told him. No, that's what I *promised* him."

She closed her eyes for a moment and took a deep breath. Even now it was difficult to think back on that terrible night. "Either he didn't listen, or he didn't believe me, or he was too drunk to remember my warning. He came home very late. He was belligerent, defensive before I even accused him of anything. Spoiling for a fight.

"Because I'd had a lengthy budget meeting that day, I was exhausted. Rather than engage in one of our famous rows, I tried to avoid him, but he wouldn't let me. He wanted a fight and wasn't going to be satisfied until he got one.

"He cornered me in the bedroom. Literally backed me into a

corner and wouldn't let me go past him. He accused me of causing Amy's death. It was my fault we'd lost our daughter, he said. Her brain tumor was God's way of punishing me for going back to work after my pregnancy leave, rather than staying at home with her."

"That's insane."

She gave a mirthless laugh. "That's what I said. In those exact words. Dutch didn't take it well. He hit me in the face with his fist, hard enough to force me into the wall. I banged my head against it so hard, it almost knocked me unconscious. I slumped to the floor and covered my head with my arms.

"And all the while, I was thinking, This cannot be happening. Not to me. I, Lilly Martin, cannot be cowering in a corner of my own bedroom trying to protect myself from my husband.

"This happens to people you read about in the newspaper, I thought. Poor or ignorant or otherwise disadvantaged people who grew up in violent homes and continue the cycle. My father never even paddled me, much less raised his hand to my mother. It would've been unthinkable."

She paused and took a breath. "Dutch came to his senses. Immediately, he began apologizing, weeping, justifying what he'd done. He blamed it on the pressure he was under at work and his heartache over Amy. I could have argued that I also was under pressure at work, that I had experienced a heartache as deep as his. But I knew further argument would be pointless. We were long past quarreling. And at that point, I was beyond forgiving.

"Without a word, I pulled myself off the floor, left the house, and checked into a hotel for the night. I contacted a lawyer and filed for divorce the following day. For me, there was no going back."

"How bad did he hurt you?"

"I was bruised, but not broken."

"Did you file charges?"

"My attorney urged me to, but I opted against it. I just wanted out, Tierney. Dutch was sinking into despair as though he had an anvil strapped to his ankle. I didn't want to be dragged down with him. A legal involvement would have postponed my getting free from him. Can you understand?"

"Yes. I don't agree. He belonged in jail. But I do understand why you decided against it."

"I told my staff I had the flu and sequestered myself in the hotel. I stayed until the bruises and swelling went away. When I checked out, it was a symbolic moment. As of then, my new life without Dutch Burton commenced."

"Not completely without."

It was a mumbled remark. She wasn't sure she was supposed to hear it. In any case, she didn't acknowledge it.

After a brief silence he said, "I'm sorry it happened to you."

"I'm sorry, too, but more for Dutch than for me. I recovered. Dutch won't. My bruises disappeared. His will remain on his soul forever. He'll never be free of the guilt."

"Don't expect me to feel sorry for the bastard. In fact I'd love to give him ten times over what he gave you."

"Please don't. Not that you actually would."

"The hell I wouldn't. I'd welcome the chance."

"Please, Tierney. Say you won't."

After a short silence, he said softly, "Okay, I won't. Anyway, after tomorrow, I won't be in a position to challenge anybody, will I?"

She didn't reply to that. "One more thing?"

"What?"

"Don't tell anyone about it."

"Why should I protect him?"

"Not him, me. For my sake, don't tell anyone. Please."

"All right."

"Promise?"

"You asked me not to tell, Lilly. I won't tell."

She believed that. "Thank you."

"You're welcome." A few moments lapsed, then he said, "Now sleep."

She settled herself more comfortably and pulled the blankets up to her chin. But her eyes refused to close. She watched the fire eat away at a log until a charred piece of it broke off and fell into the embers. She continued to stare at it. She watched it take on heat and begin to glow hotly, turning red as it smoldered; then suddenly it rekindled and burst into flame.

She turned, bringing herself face-to-face with Tierney.

His eyes were open and watching her.

She whispered, "I don't want to sleep."

Scott depressed the doorbell out of habit before remembering that the electricity was off. He knocked hard several times and heard footsteps approaching. The door was pulled open. "Hello, Miss Ritt."

"Scott," Marilee exclaimed, evidently surprised to see him there. "Did I forget a tutoring session?"

"I came to see Mr. Ritt."

She glanced over her shoulder toward the kitchen, where Scott could see William seated at the candlelit dining table. "We're just finishing our dinner."

"I can come back later."

"No, no, come in." She moved aside and waved him in. He stamped snow off his boots before stepping into the tiled entryway. As she closed the door behind him, she looked toward the curb. Seeing no car, she said, "You walked over?"

"Yes, ma'am."

"Who is it, Marilee?" William called from the kitchen.

"Scott Hamer."

William came from the kitchen, his napkin still tucked into his collar, lying like a bib over his narrow chest. "Good Lord, Scott, what's brought you out tonight of all nights? Is your mother having another migraine?"

"No." Scott darted a look toward Marilee, then said to William, "I need to talk to you in private."

William studied him for a moment, clearly as puzzled by the unannounced visit as his sister was. "Of course." He motioned Scott toward the living room, where a fire was blazing in the neat, brick fireplace. "Please excuse us, Marilee."

"Can I take your coat, Scott?" she asked.

"No, I'm fine."

"Would you like something to drink?"

"No thank you, Miss Ritt. I won't be here that long."

Plainly her curiosity was killing her, but she smiled pleasantly and said, "Well, let me know if you change your mind."

William waited until she had closed the door to the kitchen before indicating a chair. "Have a seat."

"I'll stand."

William gave him a measured look as he pulled the napkin from his shirt collar and carefully folded it before setting it on an end table. "You sound out of sorts."

"I'm not going to take any more steroids."

Taken aback, William said, "Really? Are you noticing side effects since we began stacking?"

They had started Scott out with oral steroids. Dissatisfied with the results and impatient to see improved performance more quickly, Wes had begun adding injections. While injections bypassed the metabolic process and alleviated some side effects, there were still serious concerns. Any usage could damage the taker's body as well as alter his behavior. Scott had read about the particular dangers of combining or "stacking" the injections with steroids taken orally.

"Increased sexual desire but decreased erectile function, eh, Scott?"

William's sly expression was not only infuriating but repugnant. What did this weird, creepy runt know about erectile function?

Then William winked and laughed nastily. "Judging by your popularity with the ladies, I don't believe sexual dysfunction is the problem. Are you worried about a few pimples?"

Scott refused to be goaded. "I'm not taking them anymore. Not the shots and not the pills. My dad is paying you a lot of money for them. He's paying you even more to keep your mouth shut about it. But it stops as of now."

Unruffled, William sat down on the upholstered armrest of the chair. "Have you discussed this decision with Wes?"

"I don't need to. I'm an adult."

"There's more to being an adult than achieving your eighteenth birthday."

His tone was so condescending Scott wanted to punch him.

"Forgive me for stating the obvious, Scott, but Wes will be opposed to this decision of yours."

"If he forces the issue, I'll rat him out."

"To whom?"

"For starters, the school board. Newspapers. Believe me, I'll make myself heard."

"That would end his coaching career."

"That's the idea."

"You're doing this to ruin your father?"

"He ruined himself."

William pursed his lips as though he were thinking that over. "I see your point." Then he raised his shoulders in a shrug. "But I'm confused. This sounds like a problem between you and Wes. Why are you here?"

"One of your sugar tits is about to be cut off. You'll lose money. I'm here to tell you not to butt in."

"Oh, I get it now," he said with a laugh. "This is a threat."

"Whatever you want to call it."

"Scott," he said in a patronizing tone, "Wes doesn't need me to supply him with steroids. They're easily obtainable. If I don't provide them, he'll get them from somewhere else. He can buy them online, for chrissake."

"Not without risk of being found out. There would be records. You've made it easy for him. I'm here to tell you to stop."

"I suppose there's an 'or else.'"

"Or else I'll tell the state board that you dispense pharmaceuticals without prescriptions."

"You can prove this?"

"By clearing out my mother's medicine chest." That struck home. For the first time Scott saw a glint of apprehension in William's eyes. He pressed the advantage. "If you and my dad give me a fight over this, I'll expose you both. He'll have to stop coaching, and your pharmaceutical license will be revoked."

"Oh, I doubt you would do anything that extreme." His voice reminded Scott uneasily of a snake slithering through tall grass. "The repercussions would be too, too great."

"I don't give a damn about the repercussions."

"No? Are you sure?" William stood up and gave him a sad smile. "What about your mother?"

That was the one disturbing hitch to taking a stance against his dad. What would it mean to his mom if the real Wes Hamer was exposed, with all of his artifice, deceit, and bullshit stripped away? She would suffer public ridicule, and that would be painful for her.

But Scott reasoned that by saving himself from Wes, he would be releasing her, too. No doubt she knew about his dad's infidelities, and looked the other way in order to keep the family intact, or simply because she didn't care. This afternoon, when she had learned about the steroids, she'd stood up to Wes. His mom had more backbone than people gave her credit for. Especially his dad.

"My mom is none of your business."

William regarded him closely for a moment, then reached out and touched Scott's hand. Repelled, Scott snatched it out of his reach. William merely smiled, but it wasn't a warm expression. The opposite in fact.

"I caution you to reconsider, Scott. If you begin revealing secrets, you're likely to create a lot of unpleasantness for yourself. Exposing secrets tends to have a snowball effect. Once one is exposed, others inevitably follow, and each becomes larger and more destructive. Are you sure you want to start that ball rolling in your direction?"

Scott tried to keep his alarm from showing. He must not have been successful, because William chuckled. Leaning forward, he whispered, "You *do* have a dirty little secret, don't you, Scott?"

"No."

"Of course you do. It involves Millicent."

CHAPTER
26

I DON'T KNOW WHAT YOU'RE TALKING ABOUT."

Scott turned to leave, but William grabbed his arm and whipped him around. Ordinarily the druggist wouldn't have stood a chance against Scott's athleticism. Scott could have broken him over his knee like a brittle stick. But he was so surprised by William's aggressive and sudden move, he didn't resist.

"Then allow me to make myself perfectly clear to you, Scott. I'm talking about Millicent's affair with Wes, although the word *affair* lends their fuckfests a romantic connotation that's misleading."

Blood rushed to Scott's head. "You don't know—"

"But I do, Scott. I do. See, your dear dad has twin compulsions. One is to screw every woman he can. The other is to boast about it. Surprising, isn't it, and rather reckless, that he hasn't realized the two traits are incompatible. It's a fascinating psychological tendency that really should be examined.

"But I digress. Where was I? Oh yes. Had there been any romantic love between him and Millicent, it would have been a Greek tragedy. A messy ménage to say the least. As it was, to hear Wes tell it, their entanglement was purely physical. He once referred to her as being constantly 'in heat.'" William grinned. "Imagine. And this was going on while she was officially your sweetheart. Practically under your nose."

Scott's heart was thudding. He was producing saliva at a vicious rate and couldn't swallow it fast enough. A tide of heat rushed through his system, bathing him in sweat.

"So, Scott, I advise you not to come to my house threatening me with exposure ever again. You've got far more at stake here than I."

Tilting his head to one side, William said, "You know, you're very much like Wes, whom you seem to dislike. I didn't realize until just now how similar you are.

"Like him, you think your handsome face and powerful body entitle you to bully people. Wise up, son. There are various kinds of power, and one of the most effective is knowing things about people they would rather not become known.

"For instance, I don't think you or Wes would enjoy my telling those FBI agents, who coincidentally were at your house today, that he was fucking your girlfriend at the same time you were.

"They may conclude that such an unsavory situation had created ill will among the parties involved. They may think—heaven forbid—that such a primal rivalry between a father and son could lead to all sorts of mayhem, including, but not limited to, disposing of the problem, which in this case happens to be Millicent."

"Oh, God," Scott groaned. The toe of his boot caught in the rug as he spun around, causing him to stumble on his way to the entry. He wrestled with the doorknob in his haste to open it, then bolted through the door without even bothering to close it. The frigid air was bracing but not cold enough to stave off the nausea. He barely made it to the hedge that separated the Ritts' house from their neighbor's before he vomited.

The spasms were violent, forcing him onto all fours in the snow, his head hanging between his shoulders. Even after his stomach was empty, he continued to heave painfully.

Eventually the spasms subsided. He cupped a handful of snow into his mouth, let it melt, spat it out. He rubbed another handful over his feverish face. His sweat was making him chilled. He shuddered uncontrollably and clenched his teeth to keep them from clicking together.

"Scott?"

He raised his head and looked toward the sound of the voice. Marilee Ritt was standing poised on the back porch, about to pick her way down the snow-covered steps.

"Go back," he shouted.

"You're sick."

His legs felt like jelly as he struggled to stand up. She was halfway down the steps now. "Go back inside." His voice sounded hoarse and panicky. Turning his back to her, he threshed his way through the dense hedge and cut diagonally across the neighbor's front yard, wading through snow, responding blindly to the instinct governing him—escape.

* * *

"Hey."

Dutch, who'd been dozing in his chair, jerked awake, removed his feet from the corner of his desk, and automatically stood up. Assuming the worst, he said, "What now?"

Wes waved him back into his seat. "Nothing. That I know of." He removed a bottle of whiskey from his coat pocket and set it on Dutch's desk, then took off his damp outerwear and hung the garments on the wall rack near the door. He blew on his cupped hands as he sat down across the desk from Dutch.

"It's stopped snowing," he said. "But the windchill is still a few degrees below zero. They say it'll get even colder when the clouds clear. Tonight will be one for the record books."

"Want some coffee?" Dutch asked.

"No, thanks. I've drunk so much today, I may not sleep till June. I brought my own refreshment." He nodded at the bottle of Jack Daniel's. "Pass me your cup."

Dutch shoved his empty coffee cup across the desk. Wes uncapped the bottle, poured whiskey into it, pushed the cup back toward Dutch. He drank straight from the bottle. After each had taken a few belts, he gave Dutch a critical once-over. "You look like shit."

Dutch was aware of that. His raw, swollen face looked like a pack of wild dogs had been gnawing on it. "That ointment Ritt sent over by you is worthless."

"Those cuts are gonna get infected if you don't have them seen to. Want me to drive you to the hospital?"

"No."

"Ritt's house?"

"Hell no."

"He said he had something stronger if you needed it."

Dutch shook his head.

"Have you had anything to eat?"

"Snacks here and there."

"Dora could put together—"

"I'm not really hungry."

Dutch assumed that Wes would get to the point of his visit sooner or later. In the meantime, he wished he would go away and leave him alone. He resented being mothered. He didn't feel like making casual conversation. He wanted to wallow in his misery alone, thank you. If that sounded paranoid and self-persecuting, too bad. That was how he felt.

And why shouldn't he? He couldn't make anything happen.

Nothing he did turned out right. In fact, each action he took ended in disaster. His aborted attempt to take Cal Hawkins's rig up the mountain road would probably result in several lawsuits. Hawkins might press criminal charges against him.

On top of that debacle, his authority had been repeatedly challenged. Defying Begley's warning, he'd driven out to Whistler Falls Lodge but had been stopped before he could get inside cabin number eight to see for himself the kind of evidence against Tierney the feds were guarding.

He was the primo, number one law enforcement officer in this burg, yet Begley had burst out of old Gus Elmer's cozy office and confronted him, accusing him of jeopardizing an ongoing federal investigation and talking down to him like he was nobody. Even his own men had grown surly and mouthy every time he gave them an order.

"Dutch?"

He snapped out of the vexing reverie and focused on Wes. "What are you doing here?" he asked querulously. "Why aren't you at home cuddled up with your wife?"

Wes snorted and took another drink from the bottle. "I'd rather cuddle up with that flagpole out there. It's a hell of a lot warmer and cuddlier than my wife."

"What's the matter?"

With a dismissive gesture he said, "PMS, a headache, who knows? Who cares? Her panties are always in a wad over something."

"How's Scott? Has he said anything about the meeting this afternoon with Begley and Wise?"

"Why?"

Judging by Wes's knee-jerk reaction, the FBI interview was a sore spot. "No particular reason. Just wondering how Scott felt about it." Dutch took a sip of his whiskey, eyeing Wes over the rim of the cup. "Scott seemed a bit hesitant with some of his answers to their questions. Was he lying?" He picked up a paper clip and reshaped it, then held it up to Wes. "Or just bending the truth."

"Look at it from his standpoint," Wes said. "He was surrounded by five grown-ups, all authority figures, asking questions about him and his girlfriend. At his age, would you have been straightforward with them about your sex life?"

"I wouldn't be straightforward with them now."

Wes chuckled. "Well, there you go." He stacked his hands behind his head, propped his ankle on the opposite knee, and settled back into the chair, looking like he didn't have a care in the world.

Dutch suspected otherwise. Wes hadn't come here to pass the time. Nor was he concerned about sepsis on Dutch's face or when he'd had his last hot meal. The whiskey was a nice, friendly gesture, but Wes wasn't that thoughtful a friend. He had an ulterior motive or he wouldn't be here.

Dutch's gut clenched when he considered what the purpose of the visit might be. Maybe the whiskey was for easing the pain. If so, he'd just as soon suffer it sooner rather than later.

"Did you come here to fire me, Wes?"

Wes's sputtering laugh appeared genuine. "What?"

"Are you the self-appointed committee representing the city council?"

"Jesus Christ, Dutch. You are one paranoid son of a bitch, you know that? Where'd you get a wild notion like that?"

"From what you said last night. Don't you remember? You reminded me that you'd put your neck on the line when you hired me. You said that my failure would reflect poorly on you."

"Aw, hell. We were tired, edgy. Our nerves were shot. You were going a little bit round the bend on the issue of Lilly, and her being in the cabin with this guy. As your friend, I was only trying to shed a different perspective on things. Get you back on track. But you know," he rushed to say when he saw that Dutch was about to interrupt, "over the course of this day, I've come closer to your way of thinking."

Dutch eyed him warily. "What do you mean?"

Wes shot a glance over his shoulder at the closed door. He sat forward and lowered his voice. "You think as I think—hell, as the *feds* think—that this Tierney is our culprit, right? He's kidnapped five women and done God only knows what to them. And that blue ribbon shit? How creepy is that?"

Dutch gave a terse bob of his head, unwilling to commit more than that until he knew where Wes was going with this.

"And your wife—the *ex* being a minor detail—the woman you love is trapped up there with him. I admire your self-restraint, buddy. I really do. If I'd been in your shoes today, I would have killed anybody who tried to keep me off that peak."

"I nearly did."

"Hawkins doesn't count."

Dutch took another sip of whiskey. Each swallow had gone down smoother, tasted better. "What are you leading up to, Wes?"

"Let's go get Tierney. You and me."

"Begley has a chopper—"

"Forget that," Wes said impatiently. "If they get to him before we do, we'll never see him. He'll be hustled away to Charlotte, put under lock and key. Even if he's indicted, his lawyer will cause delay after delay, and five years from now we'll still be trying to bring this psycho to trial and get justice for these ladies and their families. That's not the law of the mountains, not the kind of law our daddies and granddaddies believed in."

Wes had a valid point. Dutch knew from his days on the APD how slowly justice was won, if ever.

"I never have understood how the feds got involved anyway," Wes said.

"Kidnapping is a federal crime."

"Yeah, yeah, but that's a technicality."

"A pretty damn important one."

Wes scooted forward until he was sitting on the edge of his chair. Propping his forearms on the desk, he leaned across it. "Cleary is your jurisdiction, Dutch. This is your town, your people, and the victory should go to you. Not to Begley or that four-eyed yes-man.

"You drag Tierney down Main Street, parade him in front of the Gunns and relatives of the other victims, bring him to trial in this county, and you'll be the local hero. You'll be the bad-ass, don't-fuck-with-me-or-my-town cop who solved the biggest crime in the town's history." He sat back and smiled complacently. "And I'll be the one who had the smarts to hire you for the job."

The pep rally speech was effective. Wes had painted an exciting picture, with Dutch as its focal point. He wanted badly for it to become a reality. But he'd been crushed by disappointment too many times to trust the flurry of optimism he was feeling. He was afraid even to hope that this time, when the stakes were incredibly high, he might finally catch a break.

"Only a crazy cop would arrest someone without evidence," he said. "I don't have any on Tierney. It's all speculation and hearsay."

"The feds—"

"Aren't sharing. Begley threatened to lock me in my own jail if I went into Tierney's cabin out at Old Man Elmer's place."

"He can't do that."

"Doesn't matter if he can or can't. Right now, I don't know what they've got on Tierney, so how can I arrest him and make even a minor charge stick?"

"Do you think Begley would be guarding his rooms so closely if there wasn't incriminating stuff in there? Bring the guy in and then worry about the evidence."

"We have constitutional rights prohibiting that, Wes."

"I know, but isn't there a term for apprehending somebody believed to be..." He waved his hands as though trying to grasp the words.

"Probable cause."

"That's it!" he said. "Say the robbery alarm at the bank goes off, and you see a guy in a mask running out of it. The money bag isn't visible, but you go after him anyway. You don't wait to gather evidence."

Dutch left his chair and paced a slow circle around his desk. The whiskey had helped dull the throbbing pain of his face, but another dose of ibuprofen tablets wouldn't hurt.

"I agree with what you're saying, Wes, but it's impossible. Begley's ordered the chopper for tomorrow morning. If it's clear, if the wind dies, if the pilot makes it as far as Cleary, chances are good he'll be able to take it up to the peak. But it'll take days for us to get enough equipment and manpower in here to clear up that mess on the road."

"The mess on the *main* road." Wes was grinning like he'd just pulled the winning ace from his sleeve. "But what about the other one?"

It took Dutch a moment to catch his meaning. When he did, he barked a laugh. "The road on the mountain's western face? That's little more than a cow path."

"A cow path covered in a foot and a half of snow, which levels it out and makes it easier to navigate."

"If you're a penguin."

"Or a snowmobile."

That checked Dutch's next argument. He stopped and thought about it. "Can a snowmobile get up an incline that steep?"

"Worth a try. Besides, the inclines are more gradual on that road because of all the switchbacks."

That was true. Dutch remembered taking a date up to a popular parking spot when he was in high school. By the time they'd reached the romantic lookout at the peak, she was green with car sickness, so ill he hadn't made it even to first base with her.

"Okay, but who has snowmobiles?"

"Cal Hawkins."

Dutch laughed so hard it made his face hurt worse. "Oh, that's great. Just my luck. He's the last person in the world who would invite me to use his snowmobiles."

"He has no say in it. His old man bought four of them a few

years back to rent to winter vacationers. The bank repossessed them after Cal put them up for collateral on a loan he didn't pay back."

"Again, great."

Wes was still grinning. "I haven't come to the best part yet. The bank is keeping them in storage. Guess where? In the school bus garage."

Dutch was beginning to see the light. "To which you have a key."

"Riiiiight," Wes drawled. He toasted Dutch with the whiskey bottle and took another drink from it. "I also have a key to the office where the keys to all the Cleary Independent School District vehicles are kept."

"How come you're just now thinking of this?"

"Cut me some slack, will ya?" Wes said around a burp, sounding offended. "There's been a lot going on."

"Why didn't Cal suggest we use the snowmobiles?"

"Because his brain is mincemeat. Besides, they've been out of sight, out of mind for over a year. He's probably forgotten all about them. The bank, too, more than likely."

"Let's not remind anyone of them," Dutch said, growing increasingly excited. "We need to keep this quiet. If Begley gets wind of it, he'll stop us."

Wes nodded. "Tonight, gather up everything you think you'll need. Have you still got ski clothes?" Dutch nodded. "Good. Let's meet just before daylight at the garage, ready to go. We'll start up the mountain as soon as it's light, before Begley has a chance to launch his helicopter."

"We'll have to go through town to get to the western face. What if somebody sees us or hears us? Those things are loud. What excuse will we give for taking them out of the garage and using them without the bank's permission?"

"Dutch, for godsake, you're the chief of police," Wes said with annoyance. "If somebody questions you about it, you say you commandeered them to assess what's needed to clear the road, to check out downed power lines, to rescue a cat. Christ, I don't know. You'll think of something."

Dutch gnawed on his lower lip while reviewing the plan from several angles. He didn't see a downside. Taking and using property belonging to someone else was glorified theft, but Wes was right. Who was going to challenge the chief of police for doing what was necessary to apprehend a suspect?

And doing something, even something shady for which he could later be reprimanded, was better than sitting here watching his face fester and letting the FBI humiliate him.

For the first time in two days he felt in control, and Jesus, it felt good.

He raised his cup. "Meet you at four-thirty."

CHAPTER

27

"THERE MUST HAVE BEEN SOMETHING TERRIBLY UPSETTING about that conversation," Marilee said to her brother.

"How many times do I have to tell you—"

"Until I believe you, William."

She had made coffee in an old-fashioned percolator that heated on the gas range. They were having it in the living room, sitting in chairs they'd moved close to the fireplace for warmth and light. For half an hour she'd been trying to get information out of William about his unprecedented and secretive conversation with Scott Hamer. She had yet to get a straight answer.

"Scott threw up before he got out of the yard. What were you talking about that was so awful?"

"If it had been any of your business, Scott wouldn't have asked to speak to me alone. Take the hint, Marilee, and stop asking me about it. You're becoming a nag."

"And you're a liar."

"I haven't lied," he said smoothly.

"Why would Scott seek a private conversation with you?"

"Me of all people, you mean?"

"Don't put words in my mouth, William. I wasn't implying—"

"Of course you were." He narrowed his gaze on her. "You know what I think this is about? Jealousy."

"Jealousy?"

"It's killing you that I'm more important to one of your pupils than you are."

"That's ridiculous!"

He studied her for a moment, his smirk indicating he believed otherwise. "Well, the cause for your interest really doesn't matter, because as I've said, *repeatedly,* the topic of our conversation was private and no concern of yours."

"When one of my students vomits in my yard, it's my concern." She hesitated, then asked the question she had dreaded asking. "Was it about Millicent?"

His expression shifted. He looked at her with curiosity of a different sort. Speaking slowly, he said, "How odd that you would mention her."

"Not that odd, since you were speculating on the reason for their breakup earlier today."

"But Scott didn't know that."

"*Did* you talk about Millicent?"

He hesitated, then said, "Her name came up."

"In what context?"

"In the context of Scott's relationship with Wes."

"Wes? What does he—"

"More than that I can't say without violating confidences, Marilee." He set his coffee cup on the end table and announced that he was going to bed. "I'll be leaving early to open the store. Don't bother getting up to see me off."

"I had no intention of getting up to see you off." It was a cheap shot, unworthy of her. William didn't even acknowledge it as he left the room.

Because of the power outage, there would be no school tomorrow. She should be looking forward to another free day. Instead, she was deeply troubled.

Wes, Scott, and William. The chemistry of that trio made Marilee uneasy. Beyond living in the same town, they had nothing in common except furtive conversations about something that William refused to discuss, when ordinarily he loved being the purveyor of information and gossip. His reticence was annoying. It was also unsettling, especially since Millicent Gunn seemed to factor into it.

Marilee's uneasiness kept her awake for hours, even after she'd gone to bed. She didn't realize she'd fallen into a restless sleep until she was awakened by her lover. He was in bed with her, caressing her through her nightgown.

"Oh, I'm glad you're here," she said, lightly touching his face.

Within seconds he had the nightgown off her, holding her tightly against him, his penis hard and insistent. She placed her thigh on his hip, took him in hand, and guided him into her. But tonight he didn't want fantasies or finesse. He pushed her onto her back. His thrusts were hard and fast, almost angry.

Afterward, he lay across her, heavy with exhaustion, his head on her breasts. She caressed the back of his neck, relieving the tension that had collected there. "You've had an awful day."

He nodded.

"Talk to me about it."

"I just want peace. I want you."

"Me you have," she whispered and folded her arms around his head.

"Can you *believe* this?"

"Shh, Dutch. You're going to wake up the whole neighborhood."

"So what? I don't give a damn who hears me now. We're screwed." He slammed one fist into the palm of his other gloved hand. "I can't buy a break."

Wes shared Dutch's exasperation, but one of them had to hold it together, and it wasn't going to be Dutch. The guy had been clinging to his reason by his fingernails. This most recent obstacle just might cause him to lose it altogether.

Wes couldn't let that happen. He needed Dutch. He needed the authority of Dutch's badge even more. It was imperative they get up that goddamn mountain and arrest Tierney. Better yet, kill him. For reasons of his own, Wes had become as dedicated to that goal as his pal Dutch was.

Now they'd been dealt a setback, but it didn't have to be as catastrophic as Dutch was making it out to be.

As arranged, they'd met at the school bus garage at four-thirty, both of them bleary-eyed from lack of sleep, jazzed on caffeine, and freezing their nuts off even though they were dressed like Eskimos.

The snowmobiles were where Wes had last seen them, parked out of the way in a far corner of the garage, covered with dark green tarpaulins. So far so good.

It was when they began looking for the keys to them that they ran into difficulty. They turned the garage office inside out but couldn't find them. The keys to all the vehicles belonging to the Cleary ISD were labeled by license number. There were no keys for the snowmobiles.

Finally Wes gave up the search. "If they're here, they're well hidden, and we're wasting time looking. We've got no choice but to go ask Morris where the hell the keys to these things are."

Karl Morris was president of Cleary's only bank. "At this hour?"

Wes said, "You have between here and his house to think up a convincing story, Chief. Create an emergency that couldn't wait for daylight."

They'd had to knock on the door several times before it was answered by Mrs. Morris, who was wrapped chin to ankles in some kind of horse blanket–looking thing, the ugliest robe Wes had ever seen. She had a face to match, made even uglier by her inhospitable scowl.

Dutch begged her forgiveness for the intrusion, saying they had to speak to Mr. Morris immediately. It was an emergency. She closed the door and went to get her husband, leaving Dutch and Wes to wait on the porch in the frigid temperature.

Eventually Morris came to the door, looking no more cordial than his wife. Dutch told a tale about some family being stranded in their car and how he desperately needed to use the snowmobiles the bank had repossessed from Cal Hawkins.

"I'd be glad to let you use them, Chief Burton. If they still belonged to the bank. We sold them, hmm…let's see. Before Christmas, if I remember. We posted a notice about the auction of repos. Guess you missed it."

"Guess so. Who bought them?"

"William Ritt. He got permission to leave them there in the school bus garage until he could move them, but he took the keys along with the bill of sale."

They apologized again for getting him out of bed and thanked him for the information.

Now, as they were wading through the snow back to Dutch's Bronco, he was in a high snit.

Wes's patience with Dutch's chronic pessimism had worn thin. "For crying out loud, Dutch, would you get a grip? This doesn't have to be the end of it. We go to Ritt."

"Right. Cleary's information highway of renown."

They climbed into the Bronco, and Dutch revved the motor, which he'd kept idling. "What choice do you have?" Wes asked. "Other than letting Special Agent in Charge Begley steal your suspect along with your thunder?"

Cursing, Dutch put the truck in reverse and backed out of the banker's driveway.

They arrived at the drugstore five minutes later. There were no lights on inside, of course, but William's car was parked in a slot at

the curb next to Marilee's, which had been there overnight. "Told
you he'd be here," Wes remarked.

The bell above the door jingled merrily. William was behind the
lunch counter, boiling a pan of water on the propane stove. The only
sources of light were the blue flame beneath the pan and a votive can-
dle William had placed on the counter. It smelled like apples.

He greeted them with a cheery good morning. "You two are the
only other people I've seen out this morning. Would you like some
coffee? It's freeze dried, but that's the best I can do."

Wes sat down on one of the chrome bar stools and removed his
gloves. "As long as it's hot, I'd love some."

"Me too." Dutch sat next to Wes.

"Your face doesn't look too good, Dutch."

"Yeah, I think I may need some stronger antibiotic cream."

"Then you've come to the right place. I'll get it for you as soon as
the coffee is ready." Their unusual attire hadn't escaped him. He remarked on it as he spooned instant coffee crystals into three mugs.
"Are you going skiing?"

Wes glanced at Dutch, yielding the floor to him. Before they got
there, he had coached Dutch on the best way to approach William
Ritt. "He's a nerd. He's always been a nerd, an outsider who wanted
to be in our circle when there wasn't a chance in hell of his ever getting in. So flatter him. Make him feel that he's on our team and essential to our plan."

"He *is* essential to our plan," Dutch had said. "That's the hell
of it."

Dutch hadn't been at all happy about having to suck up to a
weasel like William Ritt. Now that it was time for him to make his
pitch, Wes held his breath.

Dutch began by coughing behind his hand, then assuming a
grave expression. "I didn't come here this morning for coffee or
medicine for my face."

"Oh?"

"This may seem like an odd request, William," he continued in
the same solemn voice. "In order to even ask it, I must take you into
my confidence about an official matter."

Excellent, Wes thought.

"You know I'd never betray your trust," William said.

"We need to use your snowmobiles."

"Thought you'd never ask."

If he had said he'd once been a body double for Tarzan movies, they couldn't have been more stunned. Dutch was the first to find his voice. "Excuse me?"

William smiled. "As I was driving here this morning, thinking how bad the roads still are, and how long it was going to be before I could get back up to my folks' place on the mountain and resume my restoration, it suddenly occurred to me that I don't need a car to get up there. I can take one of my new snowmobiles. It then occurred to me that I could offer them to SAC Begley—"

"Not Begley."

Wes had to curb the impulse to lay a restraining hand on Dutch's arm. He'd spoken too sharply. William's ears perked up. They needed a quick save, and Dutch didn't have the reflexes for it. Wes said, "This is where the confidentiality comes in. No one's supposed to know this, but Begley has ordered a helicopter up here later today."

"Why isn't anyone supposed to know?"

"Hell, his case got blown yesterday by those yahoos on the radio. Can't begin to tell you how pissed he was over that snafu. Imagine what would happen if word of a chopper got out. One equipped with all the high-tech gewgaws the FBI has at its disposal, guys in black suits and ski masks, automatic weapons, ropes and stuff. Begley would be up to his armpits in gawkers who would endanger themselves as well as his rescue operation."

"I see what you mean."

"This morning Begley and Wise will be busy organizing that mission," Dutch said, having caught on to the manipulation tactic. "Wes and I are serving as an advance team. That is, if we can use your snowmobiles."

"Certainly. I'm only sorry I didn't think of them yesterday. You could have been spared that disaster with Hawkins."

"Yesterday it wouldn't have been safe to drive them. It was snowing too hard, and that road is tricky on a clear day."

"I'm glad to make them available to you now."

Wes's shoulders relaxed. "Are they ready to go?"

William nodded. "Before I bought them, I had a mechanic check them out. They're in showroom condition. The keys for them are at my house. We can pick them up on our way to the garage. While I'm changing clothes, Marilee can make coffee for us to take along."

"You're not going."

Wes kicked Dutch's leg beneath the bar to prevent him from saying anything more. He flashed his best smile at William. "We wouldn't even have the nerve to ask that of you. It's going to be a miserably cold trip. Besides..." He glanced at Dutch and gave a sympathetic wince, then lowered his voice and said to William, "We're not sure what we'll find when we get up there."

"Of course. There's that." William gave Dutch a smile that even a blind man couldn't mistake for sincere. "I'm sure she's fine."

"Yeah. Thanks. But Wes is right. We won't know what we'll be walking into until we get up there. We must assume that this Tierney character is armed and dangerous. I can't ask you to share the risk."

"You didn't ask. I volunteered."

"I realize that, but—"

"I know the road, Dutch. Better than you. Better than anyone. I drive it several times a week and have since I learned to drive."

"All the same—"

"They're my snowmobiles."

The statement was a threat. Veiled, but a threat nonetheless. Wes could all but feel Dutch's hackles rise. "That's true, but I could impound them for taking up space in a garage paid for by taxpayers."

"I have permission."

"Not from me," Wes said. Arguing hadn't worked with the little bugger. Maybe two strong arms of authority would. "I'll ask Dutch to impound your snowmobiles."

"The school board said I could keep them there indefinitely."

"I have more authority than the school board. They do what I tell them to."

William shifted his angry gaze from Wes to Dutch. He stewed for as long as thirty seconds. Wes gave him the glare he gave to the running back who'd fumbled on the five-yard line. Dutch's expression was similarly daunting.

Finally he said, "You give me no choice."

Dutch came off his stool. "We'll follow you to your house."

William turned off the flame beneath the pan of water, which had almost boiled dry. "I'll ask Marilee to make coffee. It'll be better than this."

"No need to get Marilee up," Wes said.

"I'm sure she won't mind."

Dutch and Wes went out and climbed into the Bronco. Wes grinned. "Congratulations, Chief. You've got your snowmobiles."

They watched William Ritt get into his car and back it out of the slot. Dutch followed him down Main Street. Thumping the steering wheel with his gloved fist, he growled, "After all this rigamarole, I had better get my crack at Tierney."

"That's the plan."

"I want him to bleed, Wes."

"I hear you. If he's been boinking Lilly—"

"What?"

Wes looked over at Dutch with misapprehension. "What?"

Dutch said, "I'm worried he's killed her."

Wes moved his mouth, but for a moment no words came out. "Well, sure, Dutch. Naturally that's what we're all worried about."

"Do you think they—"

"Look, I don't know. All I'm saying is that anything you do to him, it'll be justified for whatever he did to or with Lilly."

Dutch squeezed the steering wheel. "I want him to bleed."

CHAPTER
28

I DON'T WANT TO SLEEP.

As though Lilly's simple statement had snipped a thread holding Tierney in check, he moved. Somehow the blanket separating them was cast aside and he was on her, his mouth fastened to hers even before his arm went around her, before his other hand slid up into her hair.

His tongue was strong and bold, delicious with the taste of him. It was a potent kiss that freed her memory of ever having kissed anyone else. The sexiness of it was intoxicating, making her feel as if her bones were melting.

He raised his head and looked into her eyes. She met his gaze without fear or misgiving. Never breaking eye contact, he reached between their bodies and unfastened her slacks, worked his hand inside. Her panties were damp with wanting him. He lowered his head and flicked his tongue against her parted lips. Through them her breath was coming hot and rapid.

He slid his hand inside the silk and fit his palm over her mons. His fingers tapered into her cleft. And then he just held her like that. While they kissed. Nothing more. Only their tongues sliding against each other as though mating, while her sex pulsed inside the warm security of his hand.

Maybe he took his cue from the subtle arching of her back that pressed her more tightly against his palm. Or from the moan of heightened arousal that vibrated through her throat. Or maybe his own desire caused him to wedge his knee between hers, separating them. He levered himself up on one arm so he could get to his belt.

He unbuckled it, unbuttoned his jeans, while she slipped out of her slacks and underpants.

Then in a single movement as supple as a ballet, he relaxed his arm, lowered himself onto her, pushed into her, sheathed himself with her. She made an inarticulate sound of pleasure that he echoed, and then they were quiet except for their heartbeats. Their breath mingled to create clouds of vapor above their heads.

After a time, he began to move. At first it was no more than a slow rocking, his hips against hers. But then he drew out further, pushed higher. The tempo increased gradually but steadily, until with a low growl, he suddenly stopped. She slid her hands past his waist, splayed them over the cheeks of his butt, and pulled him deeper into her.

He groaned, buried his face in her neck, and came.

When the crisis passed, he relaxed. Totally. She absorbed all his body weight. But only briefly. He gave himself scarce moments to recover before levering himself up several degrees.

Watching her expression with fierce intensity, he slowly reached behind him and slid his hand along her thigh until he reached her knee. Folding his hand around it, he guided it back until it was even with his shoulder, resting on her chest. He did likewise with the other knee. Her sex flowered open, exposing the tender center of it. He slid his hand between their bellies, into the damp where they were connected. The pad of his thumb found what it sought. His touch was delicate, but a jolt of sensation shot through her.

She almost sobbed as his thumb tantalized her with small, slippery circles. He lowered his head to her chest, raked his teeth across her nipple so she would feel the caress through all the layers of clothing. Ever so slightly he increased the pressure of his thumb.

The pleasure built and built until every nerve ending in her body buzzed and tingled, from the top of her head to the soles of her feet. Her nipples strained to the point of near pain. A scream was trapped inside her throat as it arched high against his waiting lips. The walls of her body milked his penis, still buried deep inside her, ample even in its softness.

The aftershocks of the orgasm continued for several minutes. When finally they ceased, Tierney kissed her lips lightly and gathered her beneath him.

Neither made a move toward disengaging themselves.

Not a word had passed between them.

They hadn't even disturbed the blankets covering them...

* * *

Lilly came awake with the memory of last night intact, every detail having replayed in her mind even while she slept. Her body felt languid and heavy, chafed by lust, drowsy with satiation. Tierney was curved around her, the fronts of his thighs aligned with the undersides of hers, her bottom snugly tucked into the concave warmth of his lap.

When she tried to move, he grumbled a protest and gently tightened his arm across her waist.

"Bathroom," she whispered.

"Hurry back."

"Save my place." As she slid away from him, she glanced over her shoulder. His eyes were closed, but there was a smile on his lips.

In the fireplace, only a few live coals were glowing beneath a deep layer of ash. The room was frigid. She pulled on her coat as she tiptoed to the bedroom door. The hinges squeaked when she pushed open the door; she halted, looked over her shoulder. But Tierney had gone back to sleep. His even breathing continued uninterrupted.

She hoped he would sleep for several more hours to make up for yesterday's exhaustion. His body needed rest in order to heal.

The bathroom was impossibly cold. She finished her business quickly and returned to the living room. Tierney still slept. As quietly as possible, she placed the two remaining logs on the grate and stirred the smoldering coals beneath, adding a few splinters of kindling to spark flames.

Soon they would need more wood. She debated only a moment before going in search of her scattered clothing. She found her underpants and slacks beneath the covers, pushed to the foot of the mattress. The rest lay scattered across the floor or on pieces of furniture where they'd been tossed.

When she had assembled the articles, she dressed hurriedly. Her boots had dried. The leather was stiff but no longer cold and damp. She put on her gloves and wound Tierney's scarf around her throat.

The last thing she did was use her inhalers.

When she stepped out onto the porch, she immediately noticed that the clouds had cleared. Although the sun was well below the mountain peak, the eastern horizon was a golden pink color. Overhead the sky was spattered with stars, still visible against the deep indigo blue. Gauzy clouds scuttled above the peak, carried by a wind strong enough to bend the treetops and toss about branches.

Despite the wind, the day held the promise of rescue.

Nevertheless, they must prepare as though help would be unable to reach them today. The logs in the stack of firewood on the porch were thick. Without being split, they would be slow to catch fire. Tierney had managed to split smaller ones with the hatchet, but it would be useless against the wood that remained.

She looked across the clearing in the direction of the toolshed. It hadn't snowed that heavily since Tierney's return late yesterday afternoon, so the path he had cleaved was still discernible.

She'd used her inhalers. It wouldn't take her but a few minutes to walk to the shed and back. Despite his insistence that the ax wasn't in the toolbox, she knew it was. He'd just overlooked it.

She wasn't foolish enough to try to split the logs herself. She'd save that chore for him. He wouldn't be pleased with her for fetching the ax, but after he'd saved her life, the least she could do was spare him this one task. The fresh air felt good, even if she had to breathe it through Tierney's scarf. She also welcomed the chance to stretch her legs after being cooped up for the better part of two days.

Before she could talk herself out of it, she went down the steps and started along the narrow path that Tierney had made through the snow.

Tierney. Strange she had never called him Ben. Even that day on the river, she'd used his first name only once, and then he had corrected her. "Everybody calls me Tierney." It suited him.

Stirred by the memory of how many times she'd spoken his name last night in passion, she hugged her coat about her and buried her smile deeper inside his scarf. His scent seemed to have been woven into the wool fibers. She relished it.

Happier than she'd been in a very long time, she crossed the clearing without mishap.

And then she entered the woods.

William Ritt led Dutch and Wes from his carport to the back door of his house, then through the kitchen into the living room.

"There are still some live coals. I'll have a fire going soon." He crouched in front of the grate and went to work.

Dutch was wild with impatience. Every minute he spent idling in neutral worked to Begley's advantage. He didn't need a fire. He didn't want a fire because of the time it would take to build one.

Still, he was hesitant to bully William to the point where he would defy Dutch's threat of impounding the snowmobiles and withdraw his offer of their use. So he stood by and watched as William added logs to the grate and stirred the coals.

Before it slipped his mind, Dutch took a two-way radio transmitter from one of the zippered pockets of his ski suit. He nudged Wes and pressed it into his hand. "In case we get separated up there. Remember how to use it?"

Wes nodded. "Press the button to talk, release to listen."

"Right. It's good for up to seven miles."

The logs had caught. William stood. "There, that's better. I'll get Marilee up to make some coffee."

"We really don't have time," Dutch said. "Just give us those keys and we'll be on our way."

"It won't take but a few minutes. She'll fill a thermos for you to take along." He motioned them closer to the fire. "Make yourselves at home."

"Really," Wes said, "I hate for you to disturb Marilee on our account."

"She won't care," he said and started down the hallway.

Dutch, figuring he might just as well take advantage of the warmth while he could, approached the fireplace and extended his hands toward the flames. Out of the corner of his eye, he saw William approaching a door midway down the hall.

Even if Dutch didn't have a deadline, he would still be against waking up Marilee. That would be an additional person who knew his and Wes's plan, and the more people who knew about it, the better the odds were of having it screwed up.

Too late now.

William tapped twice on the bedroom door before pushing it open. Then he just stood there, arms at his sides, staring. Why was he standing there staring into his sister's bedroom, acting weird even for William Ritt? Dutch wondered.

Unless what William was staring at had rendered him unable to move, unable even to react.

Dutch's cop instincts kicked in. He spoke William's name with a question mark behind it, but already he was moving down the hallway. He wouldn't be surprised to see blood spatters on the walls and a dismembered body.

"What the hell's going on?" asked Wes, who also must have noticed William's strange behavior and was following close on Dutch's heels.

In the few short seconds it took to reach the bedroom, Dutch's adrenaline was pumping in cop mode. Mindful not to rush into the room and destroy or compromise crime evidence, he drew up short at the doorway and pushed William out of his way.

There were no blood spatters. Marilee had not been dismembered. She was sitting bolt upright in bed, covers drawn to her chin, staring at him, shocked speechless by the intrusion.

Beside her in bed, equally shocked, was Scott Hamer.

"Oh, shit." Dutch spun around, hoping to block Wes from getting any closer, but he was already there.

He shoved Dutch into the room, then stood with his hands braced against the doorjamb as though he needed them for support. "What the hell is *this*?" he boomed.

"Wes." Dutch reached out to lay a cautionary hand on him, but Wes knocked it aside as he angrily lumbered toward the bed.

Scott threw off the covers and scrambled out of bed. He was buck naked. But far from ashamed. He faced his father belligerently. "It's exactly what it looks like. *Dad.*" He attached the name like an epithet.

Dutch guessed that Wes was furious as much over Scott's defiant attitude as over catching him with his pants down. But it was to Marilee that he directed his furious glare. "You couldn't get a *man*, you pathetic old cunt."

Scott sprang forward and rammed into Wes like a linebacker, driving his head into his father's belly and propelling him back several feet. He crashed into an old-time cheval glass. Wood splintered, and the mirror shattered into a thousand shards. That didn't stop Scott. He was pummeling Wes with his fists and yelling how dare he talk to Marilee like that?

Dutch could see that both of them would be sliced to ribbons by broken glass if he didn't intervene. Glass crunching under his boots, he grabbed Scott around the waist from behind and hauled him off Wes, who was winded and panting.

Dutch slung Scott toward the other side of the room. "Simmer down and put your clothes on, Scott. Wes." With his head, he motioned him toward the door. Wes shot one murderous look toward Marilee, then stepped into the hall. Dutch followed, pulling the door closed behind him.

Wes paced the hallway like a caged lion. Dutch turned to William, ready with a suggestion that they return to the living room to await an explanation when he realized that William didn't need an explanation. He was wearing a self-satisfied smirk. And suddenly it all made sense to Dutch. William's insistence they come to the house and wake up Marilee, that had been a ploy. He'd staged this scene. "You son of a bitch. You knew."

William didn't even try to hide it. "My sister is a noisy lover. To say nothing of Scott."

Marilee stepped out of the bedroom, remarkably composed, wrapped in a robe, her hair pulled back in its customary ponytail. "Scott has left," she said. "He's extremely upset."

Wes bore down on her. "He's upset? *He's* upset?"

"Yes, and he is my only concern."

"Well, you'd better be concerned about future employment. Your teaching career is over."

"I realize that, Wes, so you can stop yelling at me. I'm not afraid of you. Nothing you threaten me with will hurt or matter."

"How many other boys have you taken to bed?"

"Scott is not a boy."

"Don't smart-ass me. You should be begging my forgiveness."

"For sleeping with Scott?"

"For fucking him."

"How is that worse than giving him steroids?"

Dutch reacted with a start. He shot Wes a look of dismay, but Wes didn't see it. He was so angry, he was shaking. At his sides, he was clenching and flexing his fingers as though preparing to wrap them around Marilee's throat.

Impervious to his seething, she turned to her brother and looked at him with contempt. "This is what you've been savoring. All the innuendos and smug gibes. References to a non-existent infatuation with Wes. This is what they've been about."

"I hoped to appeal to your conscience, get you to break it off before it came to this."

"No you didn't," she snapped. "Far from it. You wanted a scene like this because you're small, and peevish, and cruel, William."

"Forgive me for pointing out, Marilee, that you're in no position to call me names."

"What will you do for entertainment now, I wonder. Not that I care. I'll be moving away as soon as I can make other arrangements. You can go to the devil." Then she turned and retreated into the bedroom, gently closing the door behind her.

Wes confronted William. "You knew about this and didn't tell me?"

"And spoil the surprise?"

Dutch clotheslined Wes across the chest as he lurched toward the man. William was a third Wes's size. It would be murder. "Leave it for now, Wes." When Wes backed down, Dutch took a step toward William. "Give me the keys to the snowmobiles."

"I can't think of a reason why I should."

Dutch took a step closer. "How's this for a reason? If you don't give me those keys, I'll unleash Wes to rearrange the bones in your face, and you'll be slurping your food through a straw for the rest of your cocksucking life."

William sniffed as though indifferent to the threat, but he reached into his pants pocket and withdrew a heavy key ring, which he'd had in his possession all along.

Dutch snatched it from him. "You coming?" he asked Wes.

Wes didn't reply but followed Dutch through the house and out the back door.

They didn't speak again until they were in the Bronco, headed toward the garage. "If word of this gets out, do you know what will happen to Scott's chances of getting a scholarship? They don't want college freshmen humping their professors."

He banged his fist on the dash, several times. Bam, bam, bam. "And that son of a bitch Ritt. I'd like to make gravy of that sniveling little bastard's bowels. He set us up to find them, didn't he?"

"He set us up."

"Why?"

"Payback."

"For what? What did I ever do to him?"

Dutch frowned across at him.

Wes had the grace to look chagrined.

"He wanted to get back at you for all the slights over the years, real and perceived. I don't know why he'd want to humiliate Marilee, though." He thought a moment, then said, "Scott's just a kid. He'll take pussy where and when it's offered, even from a teacher. But Marilee? I'm shocked. Who'd have thought she was capable of this?"

Wes gave a scoffing laugh. "Oh, they're all capable of it. Didn't you know? They're all whores at heart."

It was probably one of his many aches that woke him up. That, and being cold now that Lilly had left their nest. Keeping his eyes closed, Tierney burrowed deeper into the covers and let his mind drift. To last night. To Lilly. To that first time, to that sweet, silent, fluid, ebb-and-flow fuck. He couldn't have wished for it to be more perfect.

They hadn't spoken a word. They hadn't had to. Touch became their language, and it was a dialect in which they'd both been fluent. With millennia of instinctual behavior guiding him, he'd claimed ownership of her, made the body he so desired his. And Lilly, in the mystical and knowing way of woman, had allowed him the self-deception that *he* had been the one to possess *her*.

After that first time, when he finally had rolled off her onto his side, he carried her with him, so that they were lying face-to-face. He'd wished he could read her mind, wished he knew if he had regained her trust. As he'd stared into her eyes, they appeared trustful. Or maybe the lambency was a remnant of her orgasm.

He'd brushed several strands of hair off her damp cheek. Touched her lower lip with the back of his index finger, run his knuckle along her teeth. "You know I didn't use anything."

She nodded.

"You should have made me pull out."

She gave him a look.

"I swear I would have if you'd asked me to."

"But I didn't."

"No. You didn't." He curved his arm around her waist, placed his hand on the small of her back, and drew her against him until his cock was nestled in the vee between her thighs. They kissed. Sexily. Her mouth was hot and eager, wet and receptive. Just thinking about the possibilities it afforded made his blood flow like lava.

Laughing softly, he broke the kiss. "I can't believe I'm saying this, but I'm burning up."

She smiled. "So am I."

They took off their clothes.

Lilly naked. Jesus.

He finally got to see her, and he couldn't look enough. She was beautiful. Her breasts lay soft against her chest. Firelight waltzed across her skin, forming erotic tongues of shadow that seemed to lick at her nipples.

"Last summer, whenever you got wet—"

"I know what you're going to say," she interrupted. "I was embarrassed."

"I knew you were. So I tried to be a gentleman and keep my eyes above your neck. It wasn't easy." He strummed the center of her chest with the backs of his fingers.

"You touched me today," she said in a voice that was low and husky. "While I was asleep."

His gaze flickered up to hers, then away. "Not much. A little."

"I thought I was dreaming."

"I thought I was too." Then he looked into her face again. "If I'm dreaming now, don't wake me up."

"I won't."

Her nipple hardened at his touch. His thumb made several passes across it, then he gently pressed it between his fingers.

Her reaction was to gasp his name. Then she said, "Put your mouth on me."

He lowered his head and rubbed his lips across her nipple. "You've been cheating."

"How?"

"Window peeping on my fantasies."

An involuntary groan issued from Tierney's chest now as he relived taking her nipple into his mouth. His tongue well remembered the texture of it, the taste. He opened his eyes, smiling when he realized that his recollection had evolved into a dream when he lapsed back into sleep.

But he was fully awake now. All of him. He had a painful erection.

"Why should that be the only part of me not aching?" he muttered. Grimacing from various aches, he sat up and rubbed the sleep from his eyes. "Lilly?"

He threw back the blankets and stood up. Or tried. He was on his feet, but his body was bent at a right angle. From there, he eased himself to his full height, every bone, joint, and muscle protesting. His skin broke out in gooseflesh. He shivered against the cold. Grabbing the top blanket, he wrapped it around himself.

"Lilly?" When she didn't answer, he headed into the bedroom.

Lilly paused on the edge of the forest to enjoy the breathtaking scene. It looked like a three-dimensional Christmas card. The boughs of the evergreens were heavily laden with snow. The naked branches of the hardwoods looked nearly black in contrast to the white backdrop. The dawn shone only on the very top branches of the trees, which swayed in the erratic wind currents. But on the floor of the forest it was dark and still.

It was a natural cathedral, a place of worship. She wished she could linger and enjoy the hushed serenity. But it didn't take long for her toes to become numb inside her boots, reminding her that, as pretty as it was, this was still the wilderness, deadly if one didn't take precautions.

Sticking to the crude path, she arrived at the shed. Snow had formed deep drifts against the exterior walls, but when Tierney had forced open the door, it had pushed aside some of the drift, leaving the doorway partially clear.

She waded through the snow that had accumulated since he'd been there and gripped the door latch. She pulled hard, but the door didn't open. In fact, it didn't budge. She tugged on it several times, but it seemed unmovable. Putting all her strength into it, she tried again. When it did give way, it did so suddenly, startling her. She fell back a step and almost lost her balance.

Laughing at her clumsiness, she entered the shed. It was darker inside than she had expected. She chided herself for not bringing the flashlight because she wanted to find the ax quickly and leave. There were always spiders in the shed. Probably mice. She'd never gone into it without the fear of disturbing a snake.

Although all sensible creatures were snug in their beds today, the dank environment alone was enough to give her the willies. It also had the unpleasant, musty odor of enclosures with earthen floors.

She gave her eyes time to adjust to the gloom, then took a glance around. The ax was nowhere in sight, but she remembered it being in the toolbox.

The sound of her own breathing was loud. It wasn't a bona fide wheeze, but it was getting close. Maybe she'd made a careless decision by walking here. Ordinarily, that amount of exercise wouldn't have been harmful or particularly taxing. But in light of yesterday's severe asthma attack, as well as the subfreezing temperature, she probably shouldn't have done anything this strenuous. All the more reason to retrieve the ax quickly and return to the cabin. To Tierney. To bed with Tierney.

She didn't remember the lid to the large wooden box being so heavy. Her first attempt to lift it failed. She managed to raise it only an inch and was winded by the strain. If she had an attack out here, Tierney would never let her hear the end of it.

She bent her knees and placed the heels of both hands against the edge of the lid. By straightening her knees and pushing with all her might, she managed to raise the lid and push it up. When it was perpendicular, its own weight caused it to fall against the wall behind it before Lilly could catch it.

It landed with a racket that she never heard.

Because she was staring down into Millicent Gunn's dead, milky eyes.

Breath was expelled in a rush, but when she tried to suck it back in to form a scream, her bronchial tubes had already constricted. All that came out was a thin whine.

Mindlessly she backed away from the horrifying sight, instinctively seeking escape. She spun around but froze when she saw Tierney standing silhouetted in the rectangle of light formed by the open doorway.

She took everything in at once. He'd put on his jeans and boots, but beneath his coat, which hung open, his chest was bare. It was rising and falling rapidly. He was out of breath. He'd been running.

"Tierney," she gasped. "Millicent..."

"You weren't supposed to see that."

And then, in a blinding instant of clarity, she understood why his features were hard and set, why he had raced to the shed after her, why he wasn't at all astonished by the sight of Millicent's body, which had been crammed without any care or respect into a rough, crude box of rusty tools.

He was coming toward her with his long-legged stride, closing the distance between them rapidly, yet Lilly couldn't move. She'd been stricken with paralysis, the kind experienced in nightmares when one is confronted with mortal danger yet is helpless to outrun it.

But at the last possible second, she discovered she could move. When he grabbed her by the shoulders, she fought him with every resource she had—nails, teeth, flailing limbs.

She left ribbons of fresh blood on his cheek before he wrapped his arms around her tightly, pinning her arms to her sides. "Lilly, stop it!"

He was grunting and gasping.

No, that wasn't Tierney making that awful noise. It was her own asthmatic wheeze.

"Goddammit, Lilly! Give it up!"

"You're a murderer!"

Then she saw his hand descending with lightning speed toward the side of her neck.

It didn't hurt at all.

CHAPTER
29

SPECIAL AGENT CHARLIE WISE SPRANG UPRIGHT WHEN HIS CELL phone rang.

Blindly, he fumbled for it among his keys, change, badge wallet, and eyeglasses, which he'd left on the nightstand when he went to bed. He'd slept like a dead man, but the chiming ring of his cell was as effective as the piercing shriek of a fire alarm, unmercifully yanking him out of unconsciousness. He could very well suffer cardiac arrest for being awakened so abruptly, but before he did, he must answer this call.

He flipped up the phone and pressed it to his ear. "Wise."

"Mornin', Hoot. Did I wake you up?"

It was Perkins. The connection crackled with static, but he could hear if he strained. "No," he lied as he slid on his glasses. "I'm just surprised. Didn't realize cell service had been restored until the phone rang."

"Chopper ... about ... ago. Weather's iffy ... says ..."

"Hold on. Perkins, you still there? Hold on." Hoot bicycled his legs to push off the covers. He clambered out of bed and rushed over to a window, hoping to get a clearer signal. "Perkins?"

"You're breaking up, Hoot."

"Give me the basics."

"Chopper. ETA in Cleary ten hundred hours. Three-member search-and-rescue team. One former sniper from HRT." Hostage rescue.

"Good news. Anything else?"

"Yeah, on Tier ... got ... night. Get to it ... away ... something ..."

Frustrated, Hoot turned his head about, trying to find the sweet spot in the atmosphere that would improve their connection. Then he realized that it had been broken altogether. He checked the readout. His service indicator was blank.

"Hoot?"

Begley was standing in the doorway to the guest room in which Hoot had slept. He was holding his Bible, his place marked with his finger. He was dressed and looking fresh as a daisy, making Hoot painfully aware that he was shivering in his drawers. "Morning, sir. That was Perkins. The helicopter will be here at ten o'clock."

"Excellent." Begley checked his watch. "As soon as you're dressed..."

"Yes, sir."

Begley backed out of the doorway and pulled it closed behind him.

Luckily Gus Elmer's hot water heaters ran on propane, so Hoot showered again, even though that was the first thing he'd done last night after they'd checked in and were assigned cabin number seven. Begley wanted to be close to number eight, not trusting Dutch Burton to stay out of it.

Since there was no electricity, he'd been unable to turn on Tierney's computer, which frustrated Begley. He was eager to get into Tierney's files. Hoot was secretly grateful for the delay. He was cross-eyed with fatigue and doubted he'd have been able to concentrate enough to crack Tierney's security codes.

Their cabin was the only other in the compound that had two bedrooms separated by a living area and small kitchen. They managed to function with light from the fireplace, candles, and a kerosene Coleman camp stove. After eating the canned chili Gus Elmer was happy to provide—for a price—Hoot had showered and practically sleepwalked from the bathroom to the bed.

Now, five minutes after being awakened, he joined Begley in the main room. "I boiled water for coffee, but I don't recommend it. The police department's coffee is better than this. Let's go wait for the chopper there. I suppose we also owe Burton the courtesy of letting him know about the chopper's ETA."

"I agree, sir." Hoot pulled on his coat and gloves.

"Where did Perkins say the chopper will set down?"

"He didn't. We didn't get that far before our service was interrupted."

Begley checked his own phone and cursed when it registered no service. "It's still going to be dodgy, I'm afraid."

"I'll call Perkins back as soon as we get to the police department."

They rode in silence for a time, then Begley said, "Lilly Martin. Do you think she's still alive, Hoot?"

"I believe so, yes."

"Why?"

"Because he knows she called Burton and told him they were together."

"I hope you're right."

As they approached police headquarters, they were stunned to see civilian vehicles, most of them four-wheel trucks, parked in front of the squat brick building. Those that the parking lot wouldn't accommodate were parked along both sides of the street.

"What the hell?" Begley asked rhetorically.

Inside, the anteroom was crowded with men wearing camouflage print hunting garb or similar clothing. Most were armed with rifles. One, Hoot noticed, had a sophisticated bow and a quiver of evil-looking arrows. Everybody was talking at once, and all appeared agitated.

Begley tried to elbow his way through the throng in the general direction of the dispatcher, who seemed to be the target of the malcontent. After several failed attempts, the SAC put his fingers in his mouth and gave an earsplitting whistle. It instantly silenced the babble. Weatherproof boots sounded like a stampede on the hardwood floor as they shuffled one hundred eighty degrees.

With every eye in the room on him, Begley identified himself in a voice that could have cut glass. He was standing with his feet planted wide apart, his hands on his hips. Later, Hoot would confide to his co-workers that the nutcracker had never been more effective.

"I want somebody to tell me what the hell is going on here," he bellowed.

The crowd parted for the man pushing his way through. Although he was dressed for the Iditarod, Hoot recognized Ernie Gunn. "Mr. Begley, Mr. Wise. These men here are some of the volunteers who'd been searching for Millicent until the storm forced them to stop. Word spread yesterday about the guy who took her. We've assembled this morning to help capture Ben Tierney."

Immediately after his meeting with them, Gunn must have notified all his friends that Ben Tierney was the culprit who had taken his daughter. Those friends had told their friends. Hoot looked into the faces of the armed men and saw the resolve of vigilantes bent on getting their man and meting out their own brand of justice.

Begley ignored the others and addressed Gunn. "I understand your desperation—"

"With all due respect, Mr. Begley, you can't. You've got your girl safe and sound at home."

"I stand corrected," he said, speaking humbly. "I can *appreciate* your desperation to find Millicent. I also commend these concerned friends and neighbors who've volunteered their time to search for her. I mean that." He included every man in his sweeping gaze of the room.

"But, gentlemen, this morning you're reminding me of a lynch mob. At this point, Mr. Tierney is not a suspect. We have no hard evidence against him. I want to emphasize that. Folks heard his name mentioned in connection to our visit here, gossip spread like wildfire, it went out over the radio, and things got blown all out of proportion. We came to Cleary only to question him, to have him clarify some issues in order for us to eliminate him as a suspect."

An unidentified voice spoke from the back of the group. "That's all we want to do, too. Question him." The tongue-in-cheek remark was met with snickers.

Begley, clearly irritated by the interruption, said, "You don't need rifles with scopes to talk to a man. A helicopter is due to arrive within an hour. I intend to take it up to the peak. If Tierney is indeed in the cabin recently owned by Chief Burton, he will be asked to cooperate with us and will be questioned according to jurisprudence. He will be afforded his constitutional rights.

"Now, that's how it's going to be. That's the *only* way it's going to be, Mr. Gunn. If you and your friends attempt to compromise our mission, or take matters into your own hands, I will use whatever means I deem necessary to subdue you. This is a police matter. As such—"

"Then where are the goddamn police?" Gunn asked angrily.

"Excuse me?"

Gunn flung his arm wide. "These men came here this morning to offer their time and services to you and the police. But our chief of police is nowhere to be found."

Hoot shared Begley's astonishment. "What do you mean he's nowhere to be found?"

"Just what I said," Gunn replied. "His own men haven't seen or heard from Dutch since late last night, when he told the dispatcher he was going home for some shut-eye."

"He told us to come get him if we needed him." Officer Harris materialized out of the crowd. He'd replaced his uniform with an insulated jumpsuit and a fleece-lined hat with earflaps like most of the others were wearing, making him indistinguishable until now. "I just got back from his place. Looks to me like nobody's been there in a long time. Not even any ash in the fireplace."

Begley cut a worried glance toward Hoot. "Perhaps Wes Hamer..."

Before Begley could finish, Harris was shaking his head. "He's AWOL, too. I stopped at his house on my way here. Mrs. Hamer said Mr. Hamer came in late last night, slept for a couple of hours, then left again before dawn."

"Did she know where he was going?"

"Said she didn't."

Hoot didn't like the feel of this, not at all. Judging by Begley's dark expression, he didn't like it either. He pondered it for several tense moments, then said crisply, "Officer Harris."

"Yes, sir?"

"In the absence of your chief, and until further notice from me, you are in charge of coordinating these men. I want them organized into an official search-and-rescue battalion. Your immediate job is to make certain they have the gear and supplies they'll need. And I'm talking everything. Ammo. Extra clothing. Compasses. Food. Water. Lots of water. I won't be responsible for somebody fainting out there from dehydration."

"Right, sir."

"I want them ready and standing by to go at a moment's notice."

"Yes, sir." Then the young man's eyes clouded with confusion. "To, uh, to do what, sir?"

"I won't know that until I've reconnoitered the area in the chopper. We'll stay in contact through the police radio, so I suggest you remain here. Use this as your base of operation. Other volunteers may straggle in, and we'll need every man we can recruit. If I may make a suggestion?"

"Uh, yeah. Sir."

"I've found that dividing my units into smaller groups and appointing group leaders is an efficient way to coordinate men who've had less training. But choose those leaders carefully, as they'll be reporting only to you. Just a suggestion. You may, of course, manage it as you see fit."

"Yes, sir."

"Agent Wise." Begley did an about-face and strode toward the door. Hoot lunged forward to open it for him, then followed him out. As soon as the door closed behind them, they dropped the pretense. "Do you think they bought that bullshit?"

"Difficult to say, sir," Hoot replied.

"Well, trying to make sense of it will keep them occupied for an hour or so, especially choosing the group leaders. Hopefully by the time they've sorted that out, we'll have rescued Ms. Martin and taken Tierney into custody." Begley paused. "Crap. You didn't get to use the phone."

"Perkins hasn't paged me. If he's got something urgent, he'll contact me that way. In the meantime I'll keep trying to reach him by cell phone."

"What do you make of Burton and Wes Hamer having gone missing, Hoot?"

"No idea, sir."

"I don't like it. Not a fucking bit."

Hoot opened the driver's door. "Where to, sir?"

"The drugstore. That seems to be their hangout. Let's start looking for them there." Before getting into the car, Begley looked up at the clear sky. "Never thought I'd say this, but I almost miss the snow. At least when it was snowing I knew where everybody was."

Marilee didn't think it was possible for matters to get worse. She was wrong.

Dora Hamer showed up on her doorstep, looking like an escapee from an insane asylum, dressed only in a bathrobe, the hem of which was wet from dragging through snow. She wore only house slippers. Her bare feet were raw looking and red. Marilee had never seen anyone in such a distraught state.

The instant Marilee opened the door, Dora cried, "Is Scott here?"

"No."

"Do you know where he is? Please, I beg you. If you know where he is, tell me."

Marilee reached for her hand and pulled her inside, then ushered her toward the fireplace. "Sit down and tell me what's happened."

Dora didn't sit down, she paced, tearing at her hair while one hand clutched a piece of lined paper. The left margin was ragged, like it had been ripped from a spiral notebook. "What's that?" Marilee asked.

"A note I found in Scott's room. A policeman came to the house a while ago."

"Policeman?"

"One of Dutch's men, looking for him and Wes," she said impatiently. "That's not important. After he left, I looked into Scott's room to check on him. The room was empty. I found this." She shook the note at Marilee. "Is it true?" she asked, tears streaming down her cheeks. "You're his *lover*?"

With no thought of denying it, Marilee answered quietly. "For the past several months."

Dora stopped ranting and gaped at her. "How could you? What's wrong with you?"

"Mrs. Hamer, please," Marilee said gently. She was more concerned about the other woman's mental state than she was about the accusations sure to be flung at her. Dora appeared on the verge of emotional collapse. "I'll tell you anything you want to know about my relationship with Scott. But I can't while you're screaming at me. Please?"

She motioned toward one of the two chairs in front of the fire, but Dora swatted her hand aside. The blow stung, but Marilee kept her composure, knowing that one of them must. "What does the note say?"

"He explained what happened this morning."

"It was very ugly. I won't paint it otherwise."

"Well, you should be proud of yourself," Dora sneered, meaning the opposite. "Your shameless behavior has led to *this.*"

She thrust the note at Marilee. It was crumpled and damp from being clutched in Dora's hand. When Marilee smoothed it out, she recognized Scott's handwriting.

The note was addressed to his parents. The first line alarmed her: "I know you'll never forgive me for what I've done." She read the line out loud, then looked up at Dora. "What does he mean by that? What has he done that's unforgivable?"

"Screwing his schoolteacher, I suppose. I don't know." Dora had resumed pacing and was wringing her hands. "You're the last person I want to be near. I hate being inside your house. But I came because I thought you might shed some light on the note. On where he is now. On whatever is 'unforgivable.' Tell me something," she screamed, her voice shredding on the last word.

Marilee read the line again. "He could be referring to our affair. Or he could mean . . ." She couldn't bring herself to say what else the obscure sentence might signify.

"Is he referring to something that he'll have done by the time we read the note, or something he's done already? Something that he thinks we'll consider unforgivable?"

"I don't know, and I'm afraid to speculate, Mrs. Hamer."

Dora backed into the wall, covered her face with her hands, and began to sob. "Does he mean he's going to kill himself?"

Marilee continued reading, her panic rising. The words had the tone of a suicide note, although Scott hadn't specifically said he intended to end his life. However, when he'd left her bedroom through the French doors this morning, barely taking time to dress, he'd been terribly upset. Although she'd begged him to stay, he wouldn't be persuaded.

He ran out and must have stopped at home only long enough to compose the note. Whatever course of action he'd decided on, he'd decided very quickly. The rashness of it terrified her. He wasn't thinking clearly or rationally. "Did he take anything with him when he left?"

"I don't know." Dora's reply was desultory, as though she was so lost in her misery she wasn't really listening.

Marilee took her by the shoulders and shook her. "Was anything missing from the house?"

Dora's vision cleared. "Like what?"

Like a gun. Before Marilee could vocalize her thought, there was hard knocking on the front door. Both women reacted with a start. They stared at the door for several seconds, with shared but unspoken fear.

Marilee was the first to gather her courage. She crossed the room and opened the door.

"Ms. Ritt, we met yesterday."

"I remember. Special Agent Wise."

"Yes, ma'am. And Special Agent in Charge Begley."

"Come in."

She moved aside, allowing the two FBI agents to step into the entry. They stopped short of entering the living room when they saw Dora Hamer cowering against the wall. To his credit, Begley pretended not to notice her dishabille and acted as though he'd bumped into her at a tea party. "Good morning, Mrs. Hamer."

Her eyes were wide with fright. All color had drained from her face. "Have you come about Scott?"

"Scott? No."

Wise sensed their alarm. "What's the matter?"

Dora left it to Marilee to answer. "We don't know that anything is. Why are you here?"

"Actually, we hoped to find your brother at home," Wise replied. "We went to the drugstore first. No one was there."

At the mention of her brother, Marilee felt the muscles of her face solidify. She was still trying to absorb the full enormity of his treachery. His delight in hurting so many people was incomprehensible to her.

If he'd truly been worried about her moral turpitude, he would have confronted her with her transgression privately, encouraged her to seek help from a counselor or minister, or even threatened her with exposure if she didn't immediately end her affair with Scott.

Instead, he had harbored the secret, baiting her with innuendos, until a time when springing the trap would do the most damage and give him the most satisfaction. The God Marilee believed in would regard William's malicious intent a far greater sin than her loving Scott.

The agents were waiting for her answer. "William left about an hour ago." She'd waited in her bedroom until she'd heard him leave the house and his car drive away. "I assumed he was going to the store. If he's not there, then I can't help you. What did you want with him?"

"Actually, we were looking for customers of his. Your husband for one, Mrs. Hamer." Turning to Dora, Wise said, "Can you tell us where he is?"

"I have no idea."

"He and Dutch were here earlier," Marilee said. "With William. I overheard them talking about snowmobiles. William recently purchased some at auction."

The muffled conversation in the hallway had reached through her bedroom door. She'd been too disconsolate over Scott to pay attention to the raised voices, and she cared little what the three of them had to talk about, but that word had registered with her. "Now that I think on it, Wes and Dutch were dressed for skiing."

The look that Begley exchanged with Wise made her uneasy.

"Please, gentlemen, what's this about?"

"Cleary Peak," Begley said.

"And Mr. Tierney?"

"Did they mention him or the peak in their conversation with your brother?" Agent Wise asked.

"I don't think so."

"Are you familiar with the peak, Ms. Ritt?"

"Very. I grew up on it, just below the summit actually, on the western side."

"Western side? How do you get there from town? Does Mountain Laurel Road wind around?"

"No. There's another road that snakes up the western face. But it's not much of a road any longer. Sections of it were washed away in a mudslide several years ago. The road is so rarely used that it hasn't been repaved."

"But snowmobiles could get up it?"

"I don't know anything about snowmobiles, but I suppose it's possible." She divided a look between the two agents. "You think Wes and Dutch have gone up there after Mr. Tierney?"

Although Begley didn't answer specifically, he said, "We're waiting on a helicopter from Charlotte. Hopefully we'll get up there before anyone who has a mind to take the law into his own hands."

He looked at Dora. "Would you be willing to call Mr. Hamer and advise him not to take any foolhardy action?"

"I'd be willing, but I've already tried to reach him on his cell and couldn't get through. I was frantic to tell him about Scott, but—"

"What about Scott?" Begley's piercing stare was so daunting, Dora actually recoiled from it. "Mrs. Hamer," he said, "did the questions we asked Scott yesterday about Millicent upset him to this degree?"

"No."

Her response was weak and had no substance, and Begley seized on that immediately. "Frankly, we felt that Scott, indeed all of you, were withholding information that could be valuable to our investigation."

Wise said, "Perhaps he knows more about Millicent's disappearance than—"

"His emotional instability has nothing to do with Millicent," Marilee said, interrupting. The men directed their attention to her. "I can't let you waste time on something that's irrelevant." She hesitated, then said, "Scott is upset because his father and my brother have been giving him injections of steroids. He wants to stop taking them and knows he'll get a fight from Wes if he does. Further..."

She stopped, took a breath, clasped her hands together. "Furthermore, Scott and I were caught in bed together this morning." Reading the shock in their expressions, she added, "Everything you infer from that is correct. Scott and I are lovers.

"He left a disturbing note in his room this morning." Marilee didn't ask Dora's permission before passing the note to Begley, who read it, then handed it over to Wise. Begley's expression wasn't encouraging.

Wise was the first to regain his voice, and even then he cleared his throat delicately before speaking. "Do you think it's your, uh, relationship with him to which he's referring in the note?"

"I assume, but I don't know for certain."

"Suicide is implied, but..." Dora was unable to continue. She began to cry softly.

"We'll put out a bulletin on his car," Wise said. "He can't have gone too far on these roads."

Dora shook her head. "He didn't take the car."

"Are you saying he's on foot?"

"He's an avid hiker. He even hikes on Cleary Peak."

Begley and Wise exchanged a significant look, then the senior agent addressed Marilee. "How long have you and Scott been in this relationship, Ms. Ritt?"

She appreciated him for not posing the question with censure. In fact, he seemed halfway apologetic for asking. "Since September."

"And during that time, did Scott ever confide in you why he broke up with Millicent Gunn?"

"He never talked about his former girlfriends, and I never asked."

"You didn't?"

"No."

"Never?"

"No."

"You weren't in the least bit curious?"

"No."

"Then you are truly a remarkable woman."

Or a liar. That was what Begley was implying. Oddly, it was less his hard stare than his soft voice that broke her restraint. Her shoulders slumped, and she let go a long sigh. "Last night. We talked about it last night for the first time. He told me why he and Millicent stopped seeing each other."

They waited, but when she said nothing else, Begley prodded her. "Well?"

"I won't tell you that, Mr. Begley. Not at the present time. I'll tell you only if and when it becomes necessary for you to know."

"We need to know now," Wise said.

"I'm sorry."

Wise was about to say more, but Begley held up his hand. Marilee listened and identified the sound at the same time Begley said, "There's the chopper." He headed immediately for the door.

"Wait!" Dora cried. Begley came back around. "If Scott's up there—"

"I'll do everything within my power to return him to you safely, Mrs. Hamer. I give you my word."

The room felt very cold after he and Wise closed the door behind their hasty departure. Marilee went to the fireplace, rearranged the burning logs with a poker, then sat down across from Dora, who said, "They're convinced Scott had something to do with that girl's disappearance."

Marilee hugged her elbows to ward off the chill. Perhaps it was also a subconscious gesture, an attempt to hold on to her flagging hope that Scott's note didn't imply suicide—for reasons she didn't allow herself to contemplate.

"From Millicent to you," Dora said scornfully. "I don't know which of you is worse."

"I don't expect you to understand."

"Well, thank you," Dora said with a bitter laugh. "Because I don't understand how a decent and responsible person, which you've always seemed to be, could seduce a boy. You're an authority figure. He looked up to you. Admired you."

"He still does."

Dora didn't acknowledge that. "You're the reason he's been sneaking out of the house at night. He came to you."

"Yes."

"Do you realize the danger you placed him in?"

"Yes," Marilee replied, her voice soft with contrition. Staring into the flames, she added, "The risks were incredibly high for both of us."

"Yet you lured him into your bed."

Marilee raised her head and looked across at Dora. "Do I look like a femme fatale capable of luring any man, Mrs. Hamer?" She smiled with self-deprecation. "Hardly. Scott responded to me in the same way I responded to him. We recognized a matching need."

"For sex."

"Yes. There was passion." Ignoring the other woman's wince, she continued. "But we were drawn together by more than that. Both of us lacked something essential that the other was willing—no, glad—to provide."

"Oh, I'm sure you gladly provided an outlet for my eighteen-year-old son's lust."

"I did," she admitted without a qualm. She wondered how much she should say. Should she tell her that she had become Scott's sounding board last night when he finally opened up to her and railed against the steroids Wes had forced on him?

That was the least shocking thing he'd told her, but wouldn't it be cruel to tell Dora about Wes's treachery concerning Millicent? Perhaps she already knew. But if not, she was in no state of mind to hear the story now.

Besides, Marilee wasn't a hypocrite. Who was she, having been caught in bed with her student, to cast stones at Wes or anyone? She stuck to the facts but veiled them. "I also gave Scott relief from the pressures imposed on him by your husband. I listened to his opinions, his thoughts and dreams, where—"

"Don't whitewash it, Marilee. Priests who abuse young boys also hear their confessions and give absolution. You're nothing but a sexually repressed old maid who finally found a willing partner."

"You're right, of course," she admitted sadly. "On every point. My only saving grace is that Scott is beyond the age of consent. So far as the law is concerned, I didn't have sexual congress with a child. But from an ethical standpoint, it was…" She wouldn't say it was wrong. She would never think of it as wrong. She finished by saying "Unacceptable."

They stared into the fire for several minutes. Then Dora leaned forward and placed her elbows on her knees. She rested her face in her hands and remained that way for a long time, time enough for the logs to burn down to charred sticks that needed stoking.

Then she lowered her hands and turned her head toward Marilee. "You love my son, don't you?"

"With all my heart," she replied quietly. "But don't be distressed, Dora. You don't have to worry about me ruining Scott's life. Before it started, while he was still just a lovely daydream, I knew that if anything were to develop between us, it would be temporary. I recognized that it couldn't, and wouldn't, and shouldn't last. I planned all along to quietly exit his life one day so that he would be spared any embarrassment or guilt over us."

She turned her head and looked wistfully into the fire. "I knew this day would come. I knew it would break my heart in two, and possibly break Scott's as well, although I hoped to avoid that.

"In anticipation of this day, I treasured every moment we were together. I knew that if our affair was discovered, I would be reviled for the rest of my life. I didn't care. For once in my life I disobeyed the rules. I lived in the moment and tried not to let the dread of the inevitable outcome spoil the time I had with him. I gave him everything

I had within me to give." She shifted her gaze back to Dora. "And I would do it again, without a grain of regret."

The two women looked at each other with complete understanding. It was hard to say who moved first because it seemed that they simultaneously reached across the space between the two chairs and clasped hands. They clung tightly to each other, because neither had anything else to which she could cling.

CHAPTER

30

W INDOW PEEPING ON MY FANTASIES."
He closed his lips around her nipple and sucked it into
his mouth, rubbing his tongue against it until she thought
she would die of the pleasure. As he moved to the other breast, he
whispered, "Naked is so much better than through clothes."

"But even fully dressed, you managed to find everything."

"I have a built-in heat-seeking device."

"You certainly do." Smiling seductively, she slid her hand down
his belly, closed her hand around him, and began to massage. "I saw
you washing," she confessed in a whisper.

He looked at her inquisitively.

"In the window glass. Your reflection. It was only an accidental
glimpse, but..."

Placing his lips against hers, he murmured, "But what?"

"I got all hot and fluttery."

"What you're doing now has got me hot and fluttery."

Squeezing and stroking, she had brought him to full erection
again. As she rolled her thumb over the smooth tip, pressing it where
it was most sensitive, he groaned, "Christ, Lilly."

"This is a lovely device."

"It's not the only one."

In the tangle of blankets, she lost track of exactly how he came
to be lying between her thighs, his hands beneath her hips, tilting her
up toward his mouth and that other heat seeker, his tongue. It
treated her to carnal sensations she didn't know were possible and
acquainted her with a level of intimacy she hadn't realized two separate individuals could share.

Did she actually cry out his name? Or did she only think she did? Either way, it echoed loudly inside her head, her heart.

Moments later, when he was buried deep inside her again, she gazed up at him, her eyes telegraphing a million things she wanted to say but had no words for.

He smiled tenderly. He understood. Tierney understood everything.

When Lilly came to, she was back in the main room of the cabin. A fire was burning in the grate, so she wasn't cold. Welcome sunlight was streaming in through one of the windows, where the drape had been pushed aside. Her neck was sore, but it was no more painful than a crick.

And she was handcuffed.

Tierney!

God, she'd been dreaming about him, about last night, about making love with him. A sob of humiliation and outrage escaped her, but she wouldn't indulge those feelings now. She would save them for later. Assuming she survived.

She looked wildly about the cabin and listened for sounds of him moving around in the other rooms but quickly determined that she was alone. She was seated on the floor beneath the bar that divided the kitchen from the living area. Her hands had been secured to a metal support bracket on the underside of the counter. Her hands had gone to sleep from lack of circulation, and it was probably that discomfort that had brought her out of unconsciousness.

She came up onto her knees to give her arms some slack and much relief. Her inhalers had been placed on the seat of the bar stool nearest her, within reach if she stretched out her fingers. A cup of water was also there. How considerate. Tierney wanted her hydrated and breathing well when he killed her.

What choice did he have? She had sealed her doom when she found Millicent's body.

He was Blue.

His explanations for the handcuffs and all the rest had been, indeed, as false as they'd sounded. Probably he'd been on the mountain to dispose of Millicent's corpse when the storm had forced a postponement. He'd stashed her body in the most convenient hiding place—her toolshed. As he was making his way back to his car, Lilly had intercepted him on the road.

All his actions and evasions since then seemed indisputable signs of guilt. How could she have believed him innocent even for an in-

stant, much less for an entire night? The answer was simple: She had
wanted to.

She had desired him. His self-sacrificing, life-risking kindnesses
toward her yesterday had seemed incompatible with a man who
would then wish to destroy her.

What a clever modus operandi. He befriended his victims. Ro-
manced them into a sentimental stupor. Made sweet love to them.
But at some point, the tender lovemaking turned violent.

She'd had only a glimpse of Millicent's face before turning away
in horror, but the sight was branded on her memory. Millicent hadn't
died in the throes of passion. She had been choked until her tongue
protruded from her lips and her eyes bulged from their sockets. Her
killer had been cruel and merciless. She hadn't died quickly. It had
been slow and awful.

Thinking of it filled Lilly with terror, but also with a determination not to be Tierney's next victim.

Where was he, and how long till he returned? Was he disposing of
Millicent's remains before coming back to deal with her? Whatever
he did, he would have to do it swiftly. He was under a deadline. He'd
said himself that Dutch or someone would try today to reach them.

When, when, when?

She yanked hard on the cuffs, knowing even as she did that it
was futile to try to break free from them. If Tierney couldn't do it,
what possible chance did she have? God, had she really kissed the
skin he'd rubbed raw on his wrists and the scratches her nails had left
on the back of his hand?

She couldn't think about that now. Nor about anything else
they'd done in the dark warmth beneath the blankets. That was last
night. This was today. She wouldn't die of shame. She wouldn't die,
period. She would survive.

Reaching up, she fingered the screws securing the support
brackets to the underside of the counter. If she could loosen them
enough to pull the brackets out of the wood, she could at least slip
the cuffs free. Her hands would still be cuffed together, but she
could run.

She tested the screws. There was no give in any of them, but she
attacked them anyway. She broke her nails and abraded the pads of
her fingers as she tried to twist the screws. After five minutes, she admitted that it was hopeless. She hadn't loosened one of them. All
she'd accomplished was to make her breathing more difficult and her
fingers bleed.

Unless she could devise another means of escape—and nothing

came to mind—she would have to rely on someone coming to her rescue. What kind of scenario would be played out?

Would Tierney kill her quickly and flee? Would he hold her hostage while negotiating the terms of his surrender? Whether he left her alive or dead, would he try to avoid arrest and get gunned down in the process?

Would she die while looking into his face, her eyes imploring him to spare her life, just as they had implored him last night to make her feel alive again after a four-year grieving slumber?

Or would she watch him lying motionless in a bank of snow that turned red as the life flowed out of him?

She wasn't sure which of those two images caused her to start weeping.

But the tears ceased abruptly when her cell phone rang.

"Dammit!" Dutch cursed. "Got her voice mail. Why isn't she answering the phone?"

The trip up the mountain was taking longer than anticipated, and Dutch's patience was long since spent. He knew the basic route of the road, but the surface was covered with several feet of snow, icy in patches, making each yard of it hazardous. The short straightaways were no safer than the hairpin curves. Neither he nor Wes had a lot of experience with snowmobiles. In his opinion, they were unreliable and unwieldy vehicles.

His ski goggles had dug deep impressions into the puffy skin of his face. It was so swollen that his nose blended into his cheeks without any differentiation. Some of the cuts had developed pus. To relieve the throbbing pain, he'd taken off the goggles, but the sun's glare on the snow had made his eyeballs ache so bad he'd put them back on.

Here on the mountain's western face, the wind was much stronger. It whipped snow into icy dervishes they couldn't always avoid. The temperature was impossibly cold, although the heated grips on the snowmobiles kept their hands from freezing. They had to ride single file, so they'd taken turns in the lead.

Wes, who was presently leading, had signaled him that he was about to stop. "I need to take a piss."

Dutch had been annoyed by the delay but had used the opportunity to check his cell phone. When he saw that it was registering service, he hastily pulled off his glove and punched in Lilly's number.

Wes had finished peeing and was plowing his way over when he heard Dutch ask rhetorically why she wasn't answering her phone. "Try it again," he said.

Dutch redialed, with the same unsatisfying result.

"Don't jump to conclusions, Dutch. Just because she's not answering her phone, doesn't mean... well, you know. It could mean a lot of things."

Dutch nodded agreement, but his heart wasn't in it.

Ever the optimist, Wes said, "Maybe she's tried to call you."

Dutch shaded his phone with his hand so he could read the LED. There were no calls from Lilly's number but three from police headquarters, coming in at one-minute intervals. His officers would be wondering where he was. Reluctantly he dialed the number. It was answered immediately, but background noise made the poor connection even worse.

"Chief?" his dispatcher said. "Can you hear me?"

Was he kidding? They could have heard him in China.

"... looking for you. The... BI helicopter has set down... school football field... quick or else... gonna... without you."

Dutch clicked off. Later he could claim he'd lost the signal, hadn't understood the message for all the breakups, hadn't heard the part about the chopper's arrival.

"Begley's got his helicopter," Wes said, having overheard the dispatcher's excited voice.

Dutch nodded grimly as he tried Lilly's number one more time and cursed when he heard the start of her voice mail message again.

"I don't get it," he said irritably. "Isn't she anxious to be rescued?"

"She doesn't know that Tierney is Blue," Wes reminded him.

"I know, but she's been—"

"Listen!" Wes raised his hand. "Did you hear that?"

"What?"

"Shh!"

Dutch lifted his cap away from his ear and listened hard. But all he could hear was the whistling of the wind and the occasional clump of snow landing on the ground after being blown from an upper tree branch. After thirty seconds, he said, "I don't hear anything."

"I don't either now. Thought I did."

"What did it sound like?"

"Like these."

"Snowmobiles? Can't be. Not Ritt's anyway. I had the keys to all four of them." On the key ring that William had given him were four keys for four snowmobiles. At the garage, it had been a quick process of elimination to see which two keys they needed for the snowmobiles they'd taken out. He still had the key ring in a pocket of his snowsuit.

Wes shook his head. "Guess it was my imagination. These things are so damn loud, they could do funny things to your ears. Anyhow, you were saying that Lilly's been..."

"She's been up there for two days. Stranded. Without power. Why wouldn't she have her cell phone in her hand, willing it to ring, trying to call out?"

"You'd think," Wes admitted. "But maybe she's not getting cell service up there. Maybe her battery is dead."

"Or maybe *she* is."

"Dutch—"

"Or maybe she's hurt." Or maybe she was snuggled up in bed with Tierney and resenting the intrusion of the ringing phone. They might not find her injured at all but rosy with health and purring with sexual satisfaction. He looked at Wes and knew that he was thinking the same thing.

"If she could get through, she'd be trying to call you, Dutch. I'm sure of it."

Before he yielded to the temptation to push Wes over the cliff for patronizing him like he was a mental patient, Dutch pulled his ski glove back on. "If you're gonna lead, step up the pace."

Wes started walking toward his snowmobile. "I can't go any faster. These switchbacks are brutal."

"You knew that when you volunteered to come along. And by the way, why did you?"

Wes stopped in his tracks, turned back. "What?"

Dutch pushed his goggles up to his forehead and gave Wes a long, appraising look.

"*What?*"

"Why are you doing this, Wes? Don't get me wrong. I want a crack at Tierney whether or not he's Blue. But what's your stake in this?"

Wes shook his head with misapprehension. "I don't follow."

"Yeah, you do. Don't play stupid. You did everything but lick my dick last night to talk me into going after Tierney myself. I want to know why."

"I explained why. You deserve the glory for capturing him, not the FBI. I'd bask in the glow of your success. Nothing wrong with that, is there?"

"No, there's nothing wrong with that. But I think you have another motive. And I think it has to do with Scott."

"Scott?"

"You should know, Wes, that the more innocent you act, the more suspicious I become. Are you manipulating me? As I said, I want to take care of Tierney anyway. I'd just like to know before I do that I haven't been played for a chump." He gave Wes a hard look. "Did Scott have anything to do with the disappearances of those women?"

"Right. Yeah. Like he had the hots for Betsy Calhoun. Support stockings have always been a huge turn-on for him."

"I'm not kidding."

"Then if you're not kidding, you're crazy. That shrink in Atlanta should have booked you for a few extra sessions."

"Something's up with your kid."

"He's slipping it to his English teacher! That would make him a little fidgety, don't you think?"

"Is that all?"

"Isn't that enough?"

"Did he do something to Millicent?"

"How can you think that? You've known him since he was born."

"I've known you longer." Dutch's eyes narrowed. "Tell me the truth, Wes. Is Scott our culprit?"

"I'm not even going to honor that with—"

"Are you protecting him?"

"No!"

"I know you, Wes."

"You don't know shit!"

"You're covering for somebody."

"I'm covering for *me*!"

Dutch staggered back a few steps and gaped at his oldest friend with disbelief. His mouth went dry.

Wes blew out a gust of air, stared toward the tree line at the right shoulder of the road, then brought his gaze back to Dutch. "I was fucking her, all right?"

"I know you, Wes. I gathered that much."

"Yeah, well." Wes gave him a shorthand account of his brief affair with Millicent, and the consequences of it. "Scott wouldn't have anything to do with her after that, so my plan to end their romance worked like a charm. What I didn't plan on was Millicent up and disappearing.

"I didn't have anything to do with it. Scott didn't have anything to do with it. But I gotta tell you, pal, that this investigation into her disappearance has made me nervous, because assholes like Begley are looking at her life under a microscope, searching for secrets.

"It would be damned inconvenient to my way of life if our threesome became a public scandal. And that's not the end of it. I wouldn't want the feds, her folks, or anybody else to discover that one of us—or maybe even some other guy, who knows?—had knocked her up.

"Doesn't matter who it was, it was me she came to whining about it and claiming the kid was mine. I had the fattest checkbook, see. And the most to lose if I didn't pay up. Scott doesn't even know about the kid. Thank God, she lost it, on account of the anorexia, before she could carry out her threat to bring it all out in the open. Scott, me, her, the whole shebang."

"Jesus."

"Right. It would have been bad enough if word of this had got out last spring. But can you imagine how much shit would hit the fan if it came to light now? Even if I escaped Ernie Gunn's wrath—and he's damned handy with a firearm—Scott and I would surge to the top of the FBI's list of suspects.

"We'd eventually be cleared, of course, but the damage would be done. It would ruin my marriage and my coaching career. No matter how many district championships my teams win, the school board would frown on me screwing a cheerleader."

"Millicent wasn't the first."

"Probably not the last either. I'm man enough to admit to my weaknesses." He frowned with distaste. "But this one got out of hand. Millicent was also Scott's girlfriend, she got pregnant and miscarried, and she's missing. Which spells disturbing any way you look at it. That's why I'm anxious to get this Blue case resolved and put an end to all this nosy probing into poor little Millicent's life."

He paused to take a breath. "That's it, Dutch. That's my vested interest in this matter, beyond wanting to help out my oldest buddy and best friend. Feel better now?"

Dutch shook his head and gave a sardonic laugh. "I should have known it was something involving your dick."

Wes spread his arms wide and flashed his most guileless grin. "What can I say?"

"I won't fool you, Wes, you had me scared."

He slapped Dutch on the shoulder. "Let's go get this bastard."

But when Dutch turned away to mount his snowmobile, Wes's easygoing grin collapsed.

* * *

Lilly wanted to scream with frustration when her cell phone started to ring for the second time. It had been left on the end table, within sight but well out of reach. Tierney had made sure of that.

If Dutch had received her scanty message two nights ago, he would be frantic to reach her, knowing she'd spent all the time with Blue.

Or maybe it wasn't Dutch calling at all.

Maybe her call to him hadn't gone through and he'd never received her message. As she had said to Tierney last night, perhaps Dutch thought she'd been safe at home in Atlanta for the past two days. She had made it plain to him that their life together was over. If he had taken her at her word this time, he would no longer be concerning himself with her.

But when her cell phone began to ring for the third time, she prayed that it was Dutch, or someone, anyone, who would reach her before Tierney returned.

Tierney's breathing was loud and labored. The vapor it formed in front of his face was sometimes dense enough to obscure his vision. His heart seemed to have inflated to fill his entire rib cage.

He had resolved to ignore the sprain in his ankle, but in this instance, mind-over-matter determination wasn't working. The ankle had become weaker and more painful with every step. He could withstand the pain only because he was running for his life.

The minute his name had gone out over the airwaves, he became a target. Every man, woman, and child in Cleary would be out for his blood, and they wouldn't hesitate to defy the authority of the FBI to get it. If Dutch Burton had received the message that Lilly was trapped with him, he would be at the forefront of this bloodthirsty band.

That was why Tierney had stayed off Mountain Laurel Road and was keeping to the woods. If an armed search-and-rescue party from Cleary was coming after Lilly—and Blue—the main road would be the route they'd take.

From yesterday's experience, he had known what to expect when he set out. But knowing how arduous it was going to be didn't make it any less so. He had to move both speedily and carefully, and those two modes were irreconcilable. He feared another injury, but he feared a fire-breathing mob of sharpshooters even more.

Eventually he reached his first destination—the road on the mountain's western face. Relieved that he'd made it this far, he leaned against a tree trunk and sucked in huge drafts of oxygen, even though the air was so cold it hurt to take it in. He drank from the small plastic bottle he'd filled with water before leaving the cabin.

He'd driven this road only once before. Knowing that it was rarely used because of its disrepair, and that it would be virtually impassable now because of the accumulation of ice and snow, he figured it highly unlikely that anyone would be on it today.

Another advantage was that it didn't intersect with Main Street, as the other road did. When he reached the end of this road at the foot of the mountain, he would be several miles from the center of town and less likely to be spotted before he could get someplace where he could think about what to do next.

He removed his cell phone from his coat pocket. Although it registered that he had service, his battery was dead. It had run down during the two days he'd left the phone on. He couldn't make a call. But since service had been restored, others could. That was to his disadvantage.

Time to move.

He stepped out from the cover of the trees and onto the road. The going was rough, but nothing compared with the difficulty of trekking through the woods. He ducked his head against the fierce wind that cut through his inadequate clothing. The glare was so intense he had to squint his eyes nearly shut in order to see at all. He concentrated on nothing except placing one foot in front of the other. He could favor neither his left nor his right side because both hurt equally.

He tried not to think about Lilly.

Doing so made him second-guess his decision to leave her behind. He'd had no choice, really. He couldn't have brought her along.

Goddammit, why had she ventured into the shed and looked inside that box? She—

He stopped in his tracks and paused to listen, hoping that his ears were deceiving him. Over the loud soughing of his own breath and the howl of the wind, he picked up another sound. An approaching motorized vehicle. A snowmobile? No, not just one. Two at least. Growing louder, coming closer.

No, not closer. *Here!*

CHAPTER
31

THE ROTORS CREATED A CYCLONE OF SNOW AND ICE PELLETS. Out of it materialized a man dressed in a black Nomex tactical suit and boots that looked like they meant business. Grit and Determination could have been his middle names. He marched toward Begley and Wise, who were standing on the Fighting Cougars' sideline at the thirty-yard line.

"Good morning, sir," he said to Begley, shouting over the helicopter's noise.

"Collier," Begley said, shaking hands with him.

Hoot knew Collier by reputation. He was a respected agent who'd undergone hostage rescue and tactical training at Quantico last year. It was rumored he'd applied for the Critical Incident Response Group. Only the best and baddest of the badasses got selected for the elite CIRG.

"Do you know Agent Wise?"

"Only by sight."

Hoot's hand was clasped by one wearing a black leather rappelling glove with the fingers cut out to facilitate trigger pulling. It was the closest Hoot had ever come to such an article of clothing.

"Special Agent Wise has maps and topographical charts of the peak," Begley told him.

"Thanks, sir. We've brought our own, too."

"How many onboard?"

"Two men from my team plus the pilot. He's one of ours."

The Bell helicopter belonged to the Charlotte PD. They'd used it before, and Begley liked it. It was fast, maneuverable, safe. He knew it was a seven-place chopper, counting the pilot. He did the math. If they picked up Lilly Martin and Tierney, there wouldn't be enough space for everyone on the return trip. Somebody would be left for later pickup. But it would be such a short trip, he didn't see a problem with that.

Collier said, "I understand the mission is to pick up a female civilian and one hostile?"

"We don't know that he's a hostile. Right now this is a rescue mission only. We'll see what happens when we get there."

"We?"

"Hoot and I are going."

"No need, sir. We can communicate—"

"Negative," Begley said even before he'd finished. "We're going."

Everyone in the bureau knew you didn't argue with an SAC, who would assume jurisdiction and command, requisition helicoptersp and recruit assistance from other agencies, and do whatever was necessary to complete a mission successfully and safely, answering only to headquarters if it failed.

Collier looked at their overcoats and dress loafers. "We didn't bring any extra gear."

"We'll go as we are."

"It's freezing, sir."

"And we're wasting time." Begley fixed him with a nutcracker, and Collier, for all his badassness, caved.

"Right, sir, but be aware. These wind currents are tricky. It's gonna be a bumpy ride."

"Thanks for the warning." Sidestepping Collier, Begley strode toward the helicopter. Hoot and Collier followed at a trot. Collier glanced over at Hoot, sizing him up and obviously finding him lacking. "I didn't know you'd had any training."

"For what?"

"This kind of mission."

"I haven't."

Hoot could lip-read the profanity that slipped past Collier's frown. Having an untrained man at his back was the quickest way for a SWAT officer to die in the performance of his duty. "None?"

Hoot shook his head.

"Then stay out of our way, and don't fuck up."

"I don't plan to."

"You scared?"

"Shitless," Hoot shouted as he ducked under the whirling blades. "Of Begley."

*　*　*

Wes stopped again. Dutch, riding close on his tail, almost rear-ended him. "What the hell, Wes?"

"I saw something. Up ahead. Dodging into the trees."

Dutch scanned the forest. "Are you sure?"

"Through there." Wes pointed.

"A deer maybe?"

"Not unless it was a two-legged one. It was a man, Dutch. I'm sure of it. Just as I rounded the bend, I saw him disappear into the trees. Left of that boulder. Do you think it's Tierney?"

"Show me the spot."

They guided the snowmobiles toward the boulder. It had a frozen waterfall coming over the top of it. "I was right," Wes said, pointing.

The footprints in the deep snow followed the road as far as the next switchback before disappearing around the bend. Here, they veered sharply into the woods, as though whoever had made the tracks had heard their approach and immediately sought cover in the trees.

"It's got to be Tierney," Wes said, his breath gusting with excitement. "Who else could it be?"

Dutch was prone to agree. Simultaneously they cut the engines and climbed off the snowmobiles. They began removing their rifles from the soft-sided gun cases they'd been carrying on their backs. Although he'd checked his weapon thoroughly before they left, Dutch checked it again. It was loaded. Ready. Wes was going about the same procedure, executing it like the skilled hunter he was. Dutch also checked his nine-millimeter pistol and chambered a bullet.

There was no doubt in his mind now that Tierney was their culprit. Wes had explained his personal interest in Millicent's disappearance case. Dutch really had never believed Scott capable of committing a felony. He suspected the boy, despite his brawn, was too gutless and insecure to pull off any crime, much less five kidnaps. All the same, Wes's explanation had relieved Dutch of any apprehension. Tierney was their man.

If not, why had he run into the woods just now? He'd been marooned for two days. His resources would have been limited, and he was supposedly injured. Shouldn't he be running *toward* them, flagging them down, glad to see them, grateful that help had at last arrived? Why would he be avoiding rescue unless rescue also signified capture?

Dutch was ready. He turned on the transmitter of the two-way radio. "Have yours handy in case we lose each other in there."

Wes patted down his pockets, then looked at Dutch with consternation.

"What?"

"I think I left the thing."

"You're kidding."

Wes took off his gloves and slapped his bare hands against all his pockets. "I must've set it down, either at Ritt's house or in the garage. I remember trying out the volume dial right after you gave it to me. After that—"

"Doesn't matter. Let's go."

Wes went first, stepping off the road and scrambling up the steep embankment. Using the ice-covered boulder for support, he turned to give Dutch a hand up. Tierney's trail was clearly marked in the deep snow. Wes said, "He's not even trying to hide his tracks."

"He couldn't if he wanted to." Dutch looked at Wes and, for the first time in days, smiled. "Are we lucky, or what?"

They had the advantage of being fresh. Tierney was aware of this and redoubled his efforts to keep well ahead of them. He'd left the cabin over two hours ago. Except for that one brief rest, he'd been hiking in the worst possible conditions and was battling profound fatigue.

He hadn't paused to identify the two men on the snowmobiles before dashing into the forest. He'd guessed who they were, and he'd been correct. They'd called out to him periodically, and he recognized their voices. Dutch Burton and Wes Hamer. Both of them were strong and athletic. He was also reasonably sure that in the last forty-eight hours neither had been struck by a car, suffered a brain concussion and a gash on the head, or sprained an ankle.

Probably neither had made love most of last night, either.

Strength-wise, they definitely had the advantage over him. But they certainly didn't outsmart him. In fact, they weren't very bright at all. Good trackers would have kept their yaps shut, so as not to alert him to their position or distance from him. Despite their boasting of hunting skills, they had a lot to learn about stalking prey. Maybe they thought human prey responded differently to noise than animal prey.

But make no mistake. Tierney, he thought to himself, *you* are *prey.*

Any doubt of that had been dispelled by Wes's taunting catcalls and Dutch's dire threats, which echoed eerily through the snow-cushioned forest. Just as he had feared, they wanted Blue, dead or alive. He strongly suspected they favored the former, particularly

Dutch Burton, who had shouted more than a few obscene allegations regarding him and Lilly.

Dutch wore a badge, but Tierney knew that wouldn't prevent him from blowing his heart out if given the chance. In addition to being a law enforcement officer, sworn to uphold the law and protect an individual's civil rights, Dutch was a husband scorned whose ex-wife had spent two nights in isolation with another man. If he got Tierney in the crosshairs of his scope, he would pull the trigger and exult at doing so.

They sensed that he was weakening, and that served to spur them on. He didn't stop to look back, but he could tell they were gaining on him. Sounds of their passage through the forest came ever closer. They had it easier than he did. He had to forge the trail. All they had to do was follow it.

He considered taking cover and making a stand against them. He had the pistol, and it was still loaded, missing only the bullet that Lilly had fired at him. However, its respectable range was nothing compared with that of a rifle. And there were two of them. One could keep him under cover while the other sneaked around and flanked him.

He was also afraid that, if he stopped, he would never be able to get up again. His stamina was depleted. He'd thought it had been exhausted yesterday when he went after Lilly's medication, but today he truly was on the verge of collapse. Only sheer willpower kept him on his feet.

Just as he had decided that, in order to have any hope of survival, he must keep moving, he saw a branch near his head splinter. A millisecond later he heard the crack of a gunshot.

He dived into the snow and rolled behind a boulder.

"Tierney, you might just as well give up," Dutch Burton shouted.

He wasn't foolish enough to raise his head above the boulder in order to pinpoint their position, but he could sense them darting between the trees, moving nearer. One was advancing on his right, the other on his left. The important thing was, they were advancing. He was trapped.

Now that he had stopped, he realized how much he hurt. Every cell in his body was screaming in agony. He was short-winded. He was hungry.

"We know you're Blue. The FBI nailed you with stuff they found in your cabin at the lodge."

Tierney had already figured that out. It was circumstantial evidence, but all the justification a jealous ex-husband would need to take him out and worry later about the fallout over his breach of legal procedure.

Tierney didn't dare speak and make himself an easier target. He hardly breathed. He heard nothing from them, either. They had stopped moving. They must have decided to wait him out. For several minutes the three shared the absolute quiet.

A noise eventually broke the silence, and Tierney identified it as another snowmobile. The sound came from a distance, and because it had a million surfaces off which to ricochet before reaching his ears, it was impossible to tell from what direction.

Though they didn't speak, he sensed that Dutch and Wes were listening to it too. Had someone on foot come along and availed himself of one of their snowmobiles? Were they wondering how they were going to transport his dead body back to town if, between them, they had only one snowmobile?

They would be stupid not to take advantage of the distracting noise.

Never accuse them of being stupid.

Above the diminishing buzz of the snowmobile, he heard the unmistakable sound of a twig snapping underfoot. One of them was closing in on his right. Thirty yards away, maybe more. Maybe less. Even a lousy marksman couldn't miss at that distance.

A more subtle noise came from his left. A patch of snow falling with a soft plop onto the ground. Had the wind blown it down, or had one of them disturbed a lower branch and knocked it loose?

He held his breath, listened. The snowmobile could no longer be heard. He couldn't even hear his own breathing. He'd covered his mouth with his scarf so the vapor of his breath wouldn't give away his position.

Wherever they were, however far from his hiding place, they seemed content with their positions. They weren't moving. They could wait.

Again they did. The three of them. Silently. Waiting for someone to make a move.

And then another sound rent the silence. The clatter-clap of helicopter blades. Cleary's police department sure as hell didn't have a chopper. It had to be from a state agency or the FBI. In any case, Dutch wasn't going to shoot him in cold blood in front of witnesses. Wes Hamer didn't count. He would back up his buddy, lie under oath in his defense, no matter what. And vice versa.

Till now, the forest had protected Tierney by providing good cover. But suddenly that advantage had shifted to Dutch. He could shoot now and explain later that Tierney had resisted arrest, leaving him no choice except to stop him with a bullet. Or he could attest that Tierney had charged them, forcing them to protect themselves. Either way, he'd be dead, and they'd be vindicated.

No, in order to survive Lilly's trigger-happy ex, he must get into the open, where he could be seen by whoever was in that chopper.

Conjuring up a map of the peak in his mind, he mentally juxtaposed the two roads, the main one and the one on the western face. He'd been running away from the westernmost, in the general direction of the other. But how far had he gone? How much farther would he have to run before he reached Mountain Laurel Road? Whatever the distance, could he make it with the strength he had left?

He had to try. Dutch and Wes were stronger and better armed, but he had two distinct advantages. His innate sense of direction. And his will to live.

Before he could talk himself out of it, he came up onto his knees. His muscles, particularly the sprained ankle, protested even that. But he forced himself into a crouch and set off again, keeping as low as possible and trying not to give his movement away by disturbing branches or making noise.

He hoped Dutch and Wes would waste time creeping toward the boulder in order to surprise him, only to be surprised themselves when they discovered he wasn't behind it.

It was too much to wish for.

"Dutch, on your left!" he heard Wes shout.

Tierney sprang to his feet and began running. Or tried to. His legs churned through the snow that in places came almost to his waist. His arms thrashed through snow-shrouded brambles. He stumbled over hidden tree roots and undergrowth. Ice-encased branches whacked his face.

But if the grunts and groans of those tracking him were any indication, they were having just as difficult a time as he. Tierney sensed the desperation that propelled their chase and knew his deduction had been correct—Dutch Burton wanted to dispatch him before another law enforcement agency's arrival prevented him from doing so.

As before, the road found him almost before he found it.

With little warning, he reached the edge of the embankment. Quick reflexes saved him from plunging down it this time. He sat on his butt and worked his way down.

The sunlight was bright on the undisturbed ribbon of white. After the shadowed forest, he was momentarily blinded by the glare.

Shading his eyes, he frantically searched the sky for a sign of the helicopter. It was so loud, one would have thought it was directly overhead, but he couldn't see it.

"Ben Tierney!"

Wes and Dutch had emerged from the woods and were standing on the edge of the embankment. Two rifles were aimed at him. Their long, sleek barrels looked menacing in the harsh sunlight. Dutch had both eyes open. So did Wes. These guys knew how to shoot. How to hit. How to kill.

Like shooting fish in a barrel.

He could almost hear his grandfather saying the adage as he raised his hands high above his head. He dropped the pistol and kicked it away. "I'm unarmed!"

"Perfect." He read the word on Dutch's jeering lips just before he squeezed the trigger.

"There's the cabin, sir." Collier spoke to Begley through his headset. Hoot had also been provided one. As a courtesy, he was sure. Not because he had any strategic reason for being here.

"What do you know? They made it," Begley said, pointing out the snowmobile in front of the cabin. "At least one of them did." Addressing the pilot through the headset, he said, "Can you set this thing down?"

"The clearing is small, sir. In this wind, it'll be difficult."

Collier said, "Get us low enough, we'll use the ropes."

But just as he suggested it, the chopper was broadsided by a gust of wind. Acting quickly, the pilot prevented the craft from being swatted to the ground. As the chopper swung around, Hoot felt his pager vibrate against his hip.

He fished inside his coat and removed the pager from his belt. Perkins had punched in their code, indicating urgency. Hoot dug out his cell phone and hit the auto dial he'd assigned to Perkins's number.

"In here! I'm in here!"

Lilly had been shouting since she'd first heard the approaching snowmobile. Knowing she couldn't possibly be heard above its noisome whine, she continued shouting anyway until it stopped.

"In here," she shouted into the sudden silence, her eyes trained on the door.

"Mrs. Burton?"

She didn't bother correcting the name. "Yes, yes. I'm in here."

The door was pushed open, and a man swaddled in ski clothing rushed in. "Thank God you're all right."

"Mr. Ritt!" she exclaimed.

He pushed back his fur-lined hood, removed his gloves, crouched down in front of her, and looked at the handcuffs. "Dutch and Wes haven't been here?"

"No."

"They were coming after you and Tierney."

"He's Blue. As I think you must know. He said he heard it on the radio."

"Who said?"

"Tierney."

"So he knows they're after him?"

"Yes. Do you see the key for these things?"

As he moved about the cabin searching for the key to the handcuffs, she asked how Tierney had come under suspicion.

William Ritt gave her a rushed account of the two FBI agents coming into his drugstore the day before. "I'm not sure what kind of evidence they have on him, but it must be incriminating. They kicked into high gear when they learned you were trapped up here with him. A rescue party was organized, but there was an accident, and the road became hopelessly blocked.

"This morning I volunteered my snowmobiles. Wes and Dutch took off on them, but they left this behind." He took some sort of transmitter from one of his pockets. "It's a two-way radio. I heard Dutch say they'd need it to stay in contact with each other. So I followed, thinking I'd catch up with them."

"But you didn't?"

He shook his head. "Only the snowmobiles. They've been abandoned on the west road. It looks like they set off on foot. Do you think they went after Tierney?"

"Possibly. The only way he could get down the mountain is on foot. Both our cars..." She shook her head with impatience. "It's too long a story."

"Dutch and Wes must have spotted him." He stopped his search for the handcuff key. "I don't see it anywhere. He must have taken it with him."

"It's okay. Now that someone's here, I can stand it."

"Did he hurt you?"

"Not really. Except for knocking me out this morning." She closed her eyes briefly, then said, "I found Millicent Gunn's body in our shed."

"Oh. Gosh, how awful."

"I think she'd been dead for several days. The storm probably prevented Tierney from disposing of her body." She told him about striking Tierney with her car and returning to the cabin to wait out the blizzard. "He was concerned about our survival, certainly. He seemed nice, nonthreatening. But some things he said didn't add up."

"Like what?"

She gave him several examples of Tierney's half-truths. "I got suspicious and searched his backpack. I found these handcuffs and a length of blue ribbon." She motioned with her chin. "There."

William picked up the backpack and withdrew the blue velvet ribbon from one of the zippered compartments. "This is definitely evidence against him."

"Indisputable evidence."

"So why did he leave it here?"

Before Lilly could arrive at an answer to what was a very good question, her ears picked up a sound. "Is that a helicopter?"

"That was the FBI's plan."

A tide of relief surged through her. She'd been glad to see William Ritt and to learn that Tierney's capture was imminent. But if he'd somehow managed to elude Dutch and Wes and return to the cabin, the pharmacist would've posed no threat to him.

William moved to the door and stepped onto the porch, but even before he reentered the cabin, Lilly realized he'd reacted too slowly.

"They're circling away," he said. "But they must've seen my snowmobile."

"They're probably looking for a place to set down. Thank God they're here."

"Amen. Do you realize how lucky you are to have escaped Blue? None of the others did."

"Millicent's death mask." She shuddered. "It was terrible."

"I can imagine how awful it must have been for you, finding her body in the toolbox that way."

She nodded. "But I suppose it was a good thing that I discovered it. By now Tierney has probably moved it, maybe even buried it while I was unconscious. I should have known something wasn't right. He acted so touchy when I mentioned the ax to him after he went for the—" She broke off abruptly.

"Went for the what?"

"Wood," she replied hoarsely. "He went for firewood." She tried to lick her lips, although her mouth had gone dry. "Mr. Ritt?"

"Yes?"

"How...how did you know about the toolbox in the shed?"

"Hoot?"

"You'll have to shout, Perkins. We're in the chopper."

"*You?*"

"What have you got?"

"Tierney..."

The rest of it was lost as the pilot executed a pivot that pinned Hoot more securely to his seat while his stomach remained airborne. "Say again, please," Hoot shouted.

"Finally made contact with Mrs. Lambert."

"Torrie Lambert's mother?"

"Affirmative. Brace yourself."

Hoot asked Perkins to repeat his message three times, until he was certain he'd heard it correctly. He ended the call with a terse thanks. Then, speaking into the headset and interrupting the tactical guys' discussion on how best to get on the ground, he addressed Begley.

"Sir," he shouted, "Ben Tierney was not, repeat *not*, Torrie Lambert's abductor."

Begley's head swiveled around.

Hoot looked straight into the nutcracker. "He's her father."

CHAPTER
32

WILLIAM RITT REMAINED UNRUFFLED. "PARDON ME?"

Lilly's mouth was as dry as a husk. She had to push the words out. "I told you I had found Millicent's body in the shed. I didn't say anything about the toolbox. How did you know there was a toolbox in the shed?"

His feigned misapprehension lasted only a moment longer, then he shook his head with chagrin. "It wasn't very clever of me to make that slip. But it was even less clever of you to bring it to my attention."

She tried to swallow but couldn't.

"You know, Mrs. Burton, or Ms. Martin, or whatever you go by these days. You know what this means, don't you?" His voice had changed as radically as his demeanor. There was nothing ingratiating about him now.

"You're..."

"Blue. Yes. Although I'm not very fond of that silly nickname."

The crack of a rifle shot surprised them. Both looked toward the door, although it was obvious that the sound had come from a distance.

Several seconds later, William said, "Only one shot. Dutch claims to be an excellent marksman. Seems he is."

She sucked in a wheezing breath. "Tierney?"

"Tierney. Dead now. What a stroke of good luck."

He took the transmitter from his pocket and turned it on. It squawked loudly. He lowered the volume.

"What are you doing?" Lilly asked. "Who are you calling?"

"Watch. I think you'll like this. Well, you won't actually like it. But you'll have to agree that it's brilliant."

Bringing the transmitter to his mouth, he depressed the button on the side of it. "Dutch? Dutch?" he shouted frantically. "Can you hear me?"

He released the button and stared at her while he waited for a response. For several moments there was nothing but the hiss of amplified air, then Dutch's voice filled the room. "Who's this?"

He depressed the button. "It's William. I heard a shot. Did you get Tierney?"

He broke off when Lilly opened her mouth to scream. He must have been anticipating that she would try something like that, because he acted swiftly, covering her mouth with his hand.

"Ritt? Where are you?"

Lilly struggled to turn her head and free her mouth. When that didn't work, she tried biting his palm. He only pressed his hand more firmly against her mouth, holding her head against the wall beneath the bar, his fingers digging painfully into the soft tissue of her cheeks.

He picked up the transmitter, depressed the button, and faked a sound that was half retch, half sob. "Dutch, I'm here, in the cabin. Did you get Tierney?"

"Yeah, yeah, he's down. Is Lilly all right?"

For effect, he made his voice crack. "No, your wife is dead. Dead! Tierney killed her!"

Tierney was lying flat on his back. When he opened his eyes, the glare of sunlight reflecting off the snow caused a piercing pain to shoot out the backs of his eyeballs straight into a nerve center inside his brain.

Dutch, I'm here, in the cabin. Did you get Tierney? No, your wife is dead. Dead! Tierney killed her!

The voice sounded tinny, unnatural. Where was it coming from?

"The son of a bitch murdered Lilly!" Dutch Burton's roar was loud enough to shake minor avalanches of snow from tree branches.

"He's moving, Dutch!" Wes shouted. "You only winged him."

Suddenly Tierney remembered why he was lying flat on his back, why his shoulder hurt like hell. All the elements came together in a flash of clarity, the worst of them being that someone was claiming Lilly was dead and he had killed her.

Who would say something that categorically wrong?

Only someone trying to protect himself.

Christ, he had to get back to her.

He struggled to sit up. A surge of nausea filled his throat, but he managed to swallow it. There was a shocking amount of blood on the snow. His face was bathed in a cold, clammy sweat, while his shoulder felt as if it had been branded.

What seemed like a lifetime must have been only a few seconds. When he opened his eyes again and tested them against the glare, he saw Dutch Burton toss aside the transmitter of a two-way radio, which explained the origin of the tinny voice.

Dutch launched himself off the embankment as though he were about to fly. He landed hard on the roadway, but that didn't slow him down. Tierney barely had time to raise his one useful arm before Dutch was on top of him, pounding him with his fists.

"Listen, Dutch." Tierney was surprised by the raspy weakness of his own voice. He doubted Dutch could even hear it. In any case, he was in no mood to stop and listen.

The police chief let fly with a right hook that caught Tierney in the cheekbone. He heard his skin split. His blood spattered Dutch's face. *What the hell was wrong with his face, anyway?*

Tierney deflected a second blow. "Lilly—"

"You killed her. God damn you!"

"No! Listen to me."

But Dutch was beyond listening. His eyes were ablaze with unmitigated hatred. There was no doubt in Tierney's mind that if he couldn't defend himself, the crazed son of a bitch would kill him.

Drawing from resources he had believed were used up, he began not only to defend himself against the attack but to fight back. He had several grudges against Dutch Burton, and they fueled him with renewed strength. He managed to wedge his knee between himself and Dutch. He pushed with all his strength.

Dutch rolled aside long enough for Tierney to reach for the pistol he had dropped earlier. But reflexively he reached with his right arm, which was hanging uselessly from the shoulder socket that had been shattered by the rifle bullet.

He screamed in pain and struggled to stand up, then managed a few stumbling steps.

Dutch grabbed him by his sprained ankle and yanked his foot out from under him. He went down like a sack of cement. Dutch flipped him over onto his back like a fish he was about to gut. Once again he was on top of him, this time with both hands wrapped around his throat, thumbs digging into his Adam's apple.

Dutch's clenched teeth were smeared with blood, and Tierney was glad to see it. At least he'd landed a few awkward left-hand punches.

"Did you fuck her?"

Any compunction Tierney had had against fighting Dutch ended there. What kind of man who had just heard that his wife was dead asked *that*? He was more concerned about his own damn pride than he was about the fate of a woman he professed to love.

"Did you?" he bellowed.

"Dutch, the helicopter."

Tierney heard Wes Hamer's warning shout as though from a great distance, but Dutch seemed not to have heard him at all, or if he did, he wasn't heeding him. Saliva, blood, and sweat dripped from his face onto Tierney's. The cerulean sky overhead was growing dark around the edges. Tierney blinked but couldn't get rid of the black dots that sprinkled his narrowing field of vision.

He was going to die if he didn't do something. And *now*.

Dutch was straddling his waist, putting all his weight behind his hands. Tierney's right arm lay useless at his side. His left was almost as ineffectual. The feeble blows it was delivering didn't faze Dutch.

Tierney took the only chance he had. Raising his knee, he paused to channel all his strength into his quadriceps, then slammed his knee into Burton's exposed crotch, hoping to catch him beneath his scrotum.

Dutch howled. Immediately his hands fell away from Tierney's neck. Tierney bowed his body and threw the other man off, then rolled on top of him, successfully reversing their positions. He pressed his left forearm across Dutch's throat like a crowbar.

With more coordination than he believed he had in his right arm, he picked up his pistol and fired it at Wes Hamer, who was charging across the road toward them. The blast caused Wes to skid to a halt. "Throw down the rifle or the next shot counts."

It was a weakly issued threat, but miraculously it worked. Wes dropped his rifle.

But then Tierney realized that Wes wasn't afraid of him. It was the helicopter, getting louder, coming closer, carrying witnesses.

"Who was that on the radio?" he asked Wes in a breathless pant.

"Ritt. William Ritt."

Ritt? Pale, scrawny, William Ritt? That weasel?

Tierney would sort out the whys and wherefores later. Right now, he bent back over Dutch, whose face looked like that of the villain in a slasher movie, a mix of blood and pus and blind fury. He jabbed the barrel of the pistol beneath Dutch's chin. "I've got several good reasons to kill you. The first being that you hit Lilly. The only reason I'm not going to hurt you is I promised her I wouldn't."

Using the man's wide chest for leverage, he pushed himself to his feet, staggering in search of equilibrium. Raising his left hand, he pointed at the approaching helicopter. "Either of you shoots me in the back, they're going to see it."

Then, knowing he'd squandered a valuable ten seconds on Lilly's worthless ex, he clapped his right arm tightly against the side of his body and began a lurching run up the road in the direction of the cabin.

As they were making tight spins around the cabin, one of Collier's men shouted, "Eleven o'clock."

The pilot banked the chopper, and Begley saw what the SWAT officer had spotted—three men in the center of the narrow road. Until now they'd been blocked from sight by a hairpin curve. The chopper swept the treetops toward them.

Burton was lying on his back. Hamer was standing several yards away. Ben Tierney was leaving a wide trail of blood as he struggled up the incline, away from the other two.

Collier slid open the door of the chopper and took up his position. "I'll take the mover," he calmly said into the headset as he sighted Tierney in his scope.

"Hold fire," Begley barked. "That's not our man."

"He's got a handgun."

"Not our man," Begley repeated.

Begley looked from Tierney to Wes Hamer, who'd run over to Burton and knelt on one knee. Burton shoved him aside and sent him sprawling. Burton scrambled to his feet, then ran around in what appeared to be frantic circles until he bent down and recovered a semi-automatic rifle lying in the snow. He fired a shot at Tierney without taking aim. Tierney never even slowed down. He kept running.

"Hit the PA," Begley ordered the pilot.

Wes Hamer had regained his footing and started toward Burton again.

"Keep him out of the way." Begley issued the order to no one in particular, but one of the tactical officers fired several rounds at Hamer's feet, sending up geysers of snow. Hamer came to a dead standstill and raised his hands high.

Burton raised his rifle to his shoulder and put his eye to the scope, a practiced move that took him possibly two seconds.

"Chief Burton! Hold your fire!" Begley's voice boomed out of the speaker and could be heard above the clatter of the rotors. "Hold fire!" he shouted again.

Burton's head snapped up and around.

Collier was sitting in the open doorway, his feet on the skid, his scope now trained on Burton. Begley was right behind him, leaning out the open door, testing the limits of his shoulder restraint.

He could see Burton clearly and read by his expression that the police chief had been unaware of the chopper until that moment. Begley also read something else in the man's expression that made him ask Collier if he had a clean shot.

"Got him."

Begley shouted, "Burton, hold your fire! Tierney is not Blue! He's not our man."

But Burton didn't heed him. Instead he aimed the rifle at Tierney's retreating back and peered through his scope again. "Son of a bitch! Is he deaf?" Begley yelled.

An innocent man was about to be blown to hell and back, and he would bear the responsibility for that for the rest of his life. In less time than it took him to process these thoughts, he said, "One in the calf."

Collier responded, firing instantly. Dutch Burton's left leg crumpled beneath him. Begley could see the rage in his eyes as he swung the rifle up over his head and fired.

Collier fell backward into the chopper. The bullet hadn't pierced his vest, but it had packed a painful punch.

Burton fired again. The bullet missed Begley by a hair.

He heard the pilot swear elaborately as he swung the chopper around. Begley felt the pull of his seat belt against his middle and the countertug of gravity through the open door.

"I lost my shot," he heard one of the others shout into the headset.

The third tactical man had lost his balance when the chopper ascended sharply. He was clambering to regain a semistable firing position. Collier still lay stunned, half in, half out the door.

Begley was looking down into the bore of Burton's rifle. He shouted, "Don't shoot me, you motherfucker!"

Burton's face was a mask of agony and madness. "Fuck you!"

Begley saw the words form on Burton's lips a millisecond before the bullet pierced his forehead and the back of his skull disintegrated, spraying the snow behind him with a red mist. He fell backward, spread-eagle, a snow angel with a red halo.

Begley whipped his head around to thank the expert marksman.

Charlie Wise slowly lowered the sniper rifle from his shoulder and handed it back to Collier. Calmly he replaced his eyeglasses.

Begley swallowed hard in order to push his heart back down into his chest, where it belonged. "Nice shot, Hoot."

"Thank you, sir."

William Ritt removed his hand from Lilly's mouth, switched off the transmitter, and set it aside. "I told you it was brilliant."

"Why?" Lilly asked on a filament of breath.

"Why did I claim that Tierney had left you here dead? Isn't the answer obvious?"

"No, why did you kill them?"

"Oh. That." William wrapped the ends of the ribbon around his hands and tested its strength with firm tugs. "I could blame my dysfunctional parents, or low self-esteem, but those are such hackneyed excuses. Besides, I'm not insane. I kill them because I want to."

She kept her features composed, but her mind was reeling. Was Tierney dead? Dutch had shot him, that she knew. But he'd said that Tierney was "down." He hadn't said that he was dead. If he were alive, he would come back for her. She knew it.

Until then, what could she do to help herself and keep William Ritt from killing her? She couldn't get away from him. For hours she had tried and failed to free her hands from the cuffs.

To show fear would be to give him exactly what he wanted. Instinctually she knew that he enjoyed killing. It gave him an identity, a standing in the community that he wouldn't otherwise have. He was Blue, the most feared, the most wanted. The persnickety, busybody pharmacist's alter ego was a lady killer. What a head trip that must be for him.

He claimed to have low self-esteem, but she thought just the opposite. He had an inflated ego, believing himself intellectually superior. For two years he had outsmarted everybody, but thus far he'd been unable to brag about it. She would give him a chance to boast. Her only chance of surviving was to keep him talking until help— *please, God, let it be Tierney*—arrived.

"How did you choose your victims? That's one thing that's baffled investigators. The missing women seemed to have nothing in common."

"Me," he said, giving her a chilling smile. "They had me in common. They were all looking at me when they died. Soon you'll have that in common with them, too."

Don't give him the satisfaction of showing your fear. "Besides you, what did they have in common?"

"That's been the beauty of it. Criminal profilers look for patterns. With me, there isn't one. I killed all of them for different reasons."

"Such as?"

"Rejection."

"Torrie Lambert?"

"Long before her."

"There was another?"

"A young woman at college."

"A girlfriend?"

"No. I wanted her to be, but she laughed at me when I asked her for a date. She'd assumed I was a homosexual. Her teasing was cruel. I . . . snapped. I guess that's an accurate word for what happened. She was laughing. I was trying to stop her.

"When I realized she was dead, I wasn't sorry, but naturally I feared being caught. I made it look like a mugging. Her wallet and jewelry are in a keepsake box under my bed at home. To this day, that homicide is in the cold case file."

"No one ever suspected you?"

"No one. I was so insignificant, you see. Still am in most minds."

"Marilee never suspected?"

He made a scornful sound. "My sister has been too busy guarding her own dirty secret to pay much attention to me. I wish I had killed her when we were children. I thought about it once or twice, but never got around to it."

He tested the strength of the ribbon again. "I wonder where Tierney happened upon this."

He was still kneeling in front of her, and even though he hadn't yet laid a hand on her, she was quaking with fear. How much longer could she keep him talking? Where was the helicopter? Where was Tierney? She refused to believe he was dead.

"You were telling me how you chose your victims. I understand why you killed the girl who laughed at you. But you didn't know Torrie Lambert, did you?"

"Not until that day. She'd ventured away from the group and was quite a distance off the trail. I spotted her walking along the western road, near our old homestead, where I happened to be working that day. I engaged her in conversation, listened to her tale of woe, dispensed advice, and then when I tried to comfort her—"

"Comfort her?"

"Touch her. She wouldn't let me."

"Did you rape her?"

His eyes flashed angrily. "I can get it up. Have no doubt about that. If we had more time, I could prove it to you, Ms. Martin."

His reaction made Lilly believe the opposite of his claim, but she wasn't foolish enough to contradict him.

"To her everlasting regret, Torrie Lambert called me a weird little creep."

He was breathing heavily, with agitation. Or possibly excitement, which was even more terrifying. Quietly, she said, "Her hair ribbon became your trademark."

"For lack of a better word, yes."

"You took it into Tennessee to throw off the trackers. Correct?"

He frowned with chagrin. "I didn't realize I'd crossed the state line. It all looks the same. But, yes, I transported it out of the immediate area to throw off the trackers."

"Tell me about the other four. Were they also random?"

"No, they were definitely planned."

"How did you choose them?"

"You have it reversed. They chose me."

"I don't understand."

"Carolyn Maddox's young son is diabetic. She couldn't afford his insulin, and she couldn't get health insurance. She came to me practically begging for help."

"You gave her the medications her son needed."

"Along with comfort and encouragement. But nothing I said or did was ever enough to make her like me. Not that way," he said, his implication plain. "She had time to stop by the store to pick up her kid's medicine for free but never enough time to see me alone.

"She made time for one of the guests at the motel where she cleaned, though. Oh, yes, she had time for him. I saw them together in his car, right there in the parking lot, pawing each other. It was disgusting. She didn't make it home that night."

Her car with the ribbon in it had been found at the side of the road, halfway between her apartment and the motel. Lilly remembered that the motel guest had been questioned, then dropped as a suspect.

"The nurse?"

He sneered. "Laureen. Another story entirely. She was fat. I didn't like her, but I took pity. Call me a softie. I gave her free samples of every diet product to come along. She misinterpreted my kindness and made a pass. Her overtures were blatant and borderline vulgar. I couldn't imagine touching those revolting globs of flesh and was insulted by her assumption that I would want to. Well, you can figure out the rest."

Before she asked, he told her about Betsy Calhoun, who according to him was popping antidepressants at the rate of eight to ten a day. When her prescription ran out and her doctor refused to refill it, she asked William for more.

Where was the helicopter? Why hadn't it come back?

"I agreed to meet Mrs. Calhoun at the bank parking lot. It was really a mercy killing. I put her out of her misery. Unlike all the others, she put up no resistance. Doped up as she was, she was the easiest to kill. But Millicent was the most enjoyable." His narrow lips formed a cruel, reptilian smile.

"Tell me about her." Was the helicopter transporting Tierney's body off the mountain? They would think they had Blue. Rescuing her could wait.

"Millicent was a vain little slut," he said. "She relied on me to supply her with contraceptives so she could fornicate to her heart's content—and then she was careless with them. Who did she come whining to when she got pregnant? Me.

"For years I'd been giving her diet pills and amphetamines to keep her from gaining weight, but she took my generosity for granted. She flirted and teased. Once, just before closing, we were the only two people in the store. She came behind the counter and sidled up to me, rubbed herself against me, and asked if I had any flavored condoms. She said she was tired of the same old rubbery taste. 'Think about it, William,'" he said, imitating a girlish, taunting voice. "Then she laughed and skipped away, like she'd been awfully clever and cute. The last time I saw her, she wasn't laughing."

He stared into near space for a moment, lost in his reverie. "Right up to the end, it was all about *her*. She kept crying, saying, 'Why are you doing this to me? I thought you liked me.'

"As I was driving her up to the old house, I tried to explain that she was a horrible person, that she used people, hurt their feelings for no reason, played games with their emotions. I told her that she was destructive and therefore deserved to be destroyed. But"—he sighed—"I don't think she ever understood."

He was reflective for a moment, then said, "I was about to bury her when I received a call from an electrician that I'd been trying to get up to the house for months. He told me he was on his way. I had to stash her somewhere before he arrived. I knew you had sold this cabin, had overheard Dutch say you'd already cleaned out the shed.

It was the closest and most convenient space I could think of on such short notice.

"I met with the electrician and walked him through the projects I needed him to do. By the time we finished, it was getting dark and I had to return to town. I decided Millicent could spend a day or two in your shed. I didn't get back up here before the storm moved in."

Suddenly, they heard several more bursts of gunfire. No closer than before.

"Now I wonder what that signifies?" William asked rhetorically.

Lilly wondered, too. She groped her mind for another question that would keep William talking. Before she could form one, he asked one of his own. "Is it true that you and Tierney met months ago?"

"Last June."

"Dutch was right to be jealous, wasn't he? I can see it in your face every time I mention Tierney's name. You go all glassy-eyed and wistful." He glanced toward the rumpled blankets on the mattress in front of the fireplace. When his gaze came back to her, he frowned with contempt. "Beautiful people. You always find each other, don't you? Never looking twice at the rest of us."

"I've never been unkind to you."

"But if you'd been stranded in this cabin with me, that bedding wouldn't stink of copulation."

"William—"

"Shut up! I'm talking."

She shut up and let him talk.

"It's ironic, and sort of romantically poetic, the way it's going to end, with both of you dead and everybody thinking that he killed you, when actually he was your lover. See the twist? Isn't that rich? But one thing puzzles me. Why did he leave you here handcuffed?"

To keep me from trying to fight him, or trying to run from him when I saw Millicent's body, she thought. Tierney hadn't wanted her to do something that would precipitate a fatal asthma attack. He'd made a desperate and time-effective move to guarantee she didn't. She understood that now. She understood a lot. She was in love with Tierney and had been since the day they met. Furthermore, she realized that he loved her.

Softly, very close to tears, she said, "He was trying to save my life."

"Unfortunately for you, he didn't try hard enough."

Moving so quickly she couldn't react, he slipped the blue ribbon around her neck and pulled it taut.

"No! Please!"

He smiled at her cruelly and pulled the ribbon even tighter. "I'm certain you realize the futility of begging. I'll tell you what I told all of them. You're about to die."

She tried to kick him, but he sat on her thighs, anchoring them to the floor while he increased the pressure of the ribbon. "It won't take long. Your asthma will speed it along. But if you could please accommodate me by dying quickly, because I hear the helicopter returning."

Indeed Lilly heard its approach, but it could still have been minutes away. The ribbon was biting painfully into the skin of her neck. Her fingers flexed and clenched as she struggled for breath. Her body arched as her lungs sought air.

Was this how she was doomed to die after all? Unable to breathe?

With no warning, no sound, nothing, Tierney bounded through the bedroom door. Before William Ritt had time to register his unexpected appearance, Tierney kicked him in the head.

CHAPTER
33

THE KICK LIFTED WILLIAM OFF THE FLOOR LIKE A CHARACTER in an animated cartoon. He landed three feet from Lilly, rolled onto his back, and tried to sit up. The side of his head just above his ear was bleeding. He slapped his hand to it and gaped at Tierney as though he had come back from the dead.

He did look like a survivor of the apocalypse. His right arm was hanging at an odd angle from his shoulder. His clothing on that side of his body was saturated with blood. His face was as gray as death except for a bleeding cut on his cheekbone. His eyes were sunken and darkly shadowed, and he never took them off William Ritt.

He must have found an unlocked window in the bedroom, knowing that it would be a surprise attack if he came in that way.

"Lilly?" His voice was gravelly.

"He's Blue."

"I figured." Keeping his eyes trained on William, he bent down and placed his pistol in her cuffed right hand. "Got it?"

"Yes."

"If he gets the best of me, kill him. Without a moment's hesitation." He pulled the ribbon from Lilly's neck.

His gait was gawky and uneven, but he bore down on William, who had regained some of his wits and was trying to scramble away. Tierney reached down with only his left hand, grabbed a handful of William's parka, and hauled him up, then let go just long enough to smash his fist, still holding the ribbon, into William's face. The blow spun the pharmacist around. He stumbled and landed hard, facefirst, against the wall, then practically bounced off it.

Tierney covered the back of the man's head with his wide hand

and slammed his face into the wall. Twice. He punched him once in the kidney, causing William to scream, then grabbed his shoulder and turned him around, stapling him to the wall with the fingers of his left hand around his neck. The ribbon was still entwined in Tierney's fingers. It trailed down William's chest.

His face was a bleeding pulp. His eyes were wild with fright. Tierney said, "I ought to wrap this ribbon around your own fucking throat and choke you very slowly."

His voice was weak. Blood was puddling around his feet. He paused to take a breath, but his grip on William Ritt remained inescapable.

"God knows I want to kill you. I want to tear your heart out with my bare hands. But I won't because I don't want you to get off that lightly. You don't deserve a quick death.

"No, I want you to live a long time. I want you to rot in a cell for decades. I want you to stay locked away in anonymity, getting raped every day by bull queers who don't enjoy it until they see you bleed. That's what they do to child killers in prison, you know. And Torrie was only fifteen. Fifteen!" His voice cracked. "And when you die, at what I hope is a ripe old age, you'll go straight to hell and burn for eternity, you miserable piece of shit."

Tierney was barely able to stand. He was swaying on his feet when he opened his hand to release William's neck. The little man slid to the floor and slumped to one side.

Tierney stood over him for a moment longer, then turned and started walking back toward Lilly.

"Tierney!" she cried.

He spun around just as William uncapped a syringe, which he must have had secreted in a pocket of his parka. But it wasn't intended for Tierney. He jabbed the needle into his own neck.

Tierney was on him in an instant. William was trying to depress the plunger and inject air into his vein; Tierney was fighting to keep him from doing so. With his left hand, he caught William's wrist in what must have been a bone-snapping grip. The man cried out, not only in pain but in frustration and outrage, because somehow Tierney had managed to pin his other hand to the floor with his knee.

The cabin door burst open and crashed against the interior wall. "FBI! Don't anybody move!" Two men dressed in full SWAT gear and black ski masks swept the room with their rifles, then trained them on Tierney and William.

"Drop the weapon!" ordered a stern-looking man who had entered behind the others. He was dressed in an ordinary overcoat, but

Lilly was so impressed by his authoritative air, it took her a moment to realize that he was addressing her. She opened her hand and let go of Tierney's pistol. It clattered onto the floor.

Another agent, who was younger and slimmer and wearing eyeglasses, had a pistol aimed at the back of Tierney's head. "Release him, Mr. Tierney."

"He's got a syringe in his neck, trying to kill himself."

The intimidating gray-haired man strode over to them, bent down, took a moment to assess the situation, then unceremoniously yanked the syringe out of William's neck. "Cover him," he said to the man in the glasses.

"He's Blue," Lilly said in a rush. "His name is William Ritt."

"I know his name," the agent said.

"He's the man you want, not Tierney. William Ritt is Blue."

"How do you know?" he asked.

"He told me. He was going to kill me."

During this rapid exchange, Tierney had braced his left hand against the wall and used it for support as he stood up. The older agent took a large white handkerchief from his back pants pocket and wordlessly handed it to him. "This might help with the bleeding."

Tierney took the handkerchief and pressed it into his shoulder. "Thanks."

"So." The agent nudged William with the toe of his shoe, but he was looking at Tierney when he said, "You finally found Blue."

Tierney nodded.

Lilly looked from one to the other with confusion.

The federal agent turned to her. "Ms. Martin, I'm...Oh, my apologies. Hoot, search Ritt for the key to those cuffs."

"He didn't handcuff her. I did."

The older man looked at Tierney with surprise.

"The key is in my coat pocket. It's zipped. I'm not sure I can—"

"Allow me." He unzipped the pocket Tierney indicated and withdrew the small key. "I'm Special Agent in Charge Begley. That's Special Agent Wise." He knelt in front of Lilly and unlocked the handcuffs, then assisted her to stand.

"Pleased to meet you." She pushed past him and rushed to Tierney, who was still holding himself up against the wall. Her hands moved over him, although inches away from actually touching him out of fear of hurting him more. "Lord, Tierney, look at you."

"Did he hurt you?"

"What?" She looked up into his sunken eyes, then shook her head. "No."

"But I did. In the shed—"

"Doesn't matter."

"I had to do it."

"I understand. I *do*."

For several moments their attention was riveted on each other, but they simultaneously became aware of their audience. She addressed the senior agent. "Tierney arrived just in time to stop William Ritt from killing me. Millicent Gunn's body is in the toolbox in the shed. I found it there this morning." She looked at Tierney. "You found it the night you went for wood and searched for the ax. That's why you were so brusque."

He nodded. To Begley he said, "Like Lilly says, I found the body night before last. I didn't touch it, so it's just as I found it. Unless Ritt moved it when he got up here."

"I don't think he did," Lilly told them. "He came straight into the cabin."

"Where's this shed?" Begley asked.

She told him. "William admitted to me that he killed Millicent and hid her body there temporarily. He confessed to—boasted of—the other killings as well."

"Get him out of here." At a nod from Begley, the two tactical officers seized William under the arms and dragged him facedown toward the door. He hung limply between them, as though he'd finally passed out from the beating Tierney had given him.

"Restrain him, put him in the chopper. Wait for me there."

"Yes, sir."

"Hoot?"

"Sir?"

"Call the nearest RA. We need a crime scene unit up here ASAP. Remind them they'll need a chopper."

"Right, sir."

Agent Wise got on his cell phone. Begley turned back to them. "How's the shoulder, Mr. Tierney?"

"Busted."

"I'm surprised you haven't gone into shock."

"Any minute now."

"Want to sit down?"

He shook his head. "You'd never get me back up."

"We set the chopper down in the road about fifty yards from here," Begley said. "Followed your blood trail the rest of the way up. Our pilot already radioed for a CareFlight helicopter to pick you up. It should be here momentarily."

"Thanks."

"Feel like talking?"

"Talking may keep me from passing out."

Begley grinned as though he understood that logic. Then his expression turned serious. "I owe you an apology, Mr. Tierney. We didn't learn until minutes ago that you're Torrie Lambert's father."

Lilly looked up at Tierney, speechless.

"Her mother and I divorced when Torrie was an infant," he said, addressing his explanation to her rather than to the FBI agent. "Her stepfather adopted her, gave her his name. But she was my daughter."

"Which explains a lot," Begley said. "Obviously, you didn't trust us or the local police to solve the case, so you've been doing your own sleuthing over the past two years."

"That's right."

Begley harrumphed and looked at Tierney wryly. Lilly got the impression that, had it been his daughter who was missing, he would have done the same. "Whose handiwork is that in the kitchen?"

He was referring to the message she had scratched into the cabinet. It seemed he missed nothing. "Mine," she said. "For a time, I thought..." With remorse, she motioned toward Tierney.

"Well, you weren't alone in that assumption," Begley said. "Mr. Tierney, were you on to William Ritt?"

"No. I thought it was Wes Hamer."

"Wes Hamer?"

"I became acquainted with Millicent by shopping in her uncle's store," he said. "She developed a...a...an attachment to me."

A crush, Lilly thought.

"This was during my trip here last fall. One night I returned to the lodge, and Millicent was there waiting on me. It made me uncomfortable. I didn't invite her inside my cabin, but she started unloading a very sordid story about her, Wes, Wes's son, a pregnancy and a miscarriage."

Lilly had always thought Wes Hamer was a colossal jerk. According to Tierney's story, he was considerably worse than that.

"When she returned from the clinic for eating disorders, she wanted to get back together with Scott, but he would have nothing to do with her. She asked for my advice." He shook his head ruefully. "I had my own agenda and sure as hell didn't want to get mixed up with anything like that. But then, when she was reported missing last week, well, I thought that maybe Wes had disposed of a problem, and that his crony Dutch was covering for him."

Turning to Lilly, he said, "That's why I didn't tell you what I was doing. If I explained myself, I was afraid you'd feel honor bound to tell Dutch, and he would protect his pal Wes. Even if Wes had turned out not to be Blue, my cover would have been blown, and Dutch would have found a way to block my amateur efforts to find my daughter."

"What were you doing on the mountain the day of the storm?" she asked.

"I never gave up trying to find a trace of her on one of these hiking trails. The day of the storm, I discovered..." He paused, cleared his throat. "Graves. Four of them, and a fresh one dug for Millicent. The shovel used to dig it had been stashed in some underbrush."

"The handcuffs?"

"Those are mine."

"You also bought a transponder," Begley said. "For tracking purposes, I presume."

He nodded, looking abashed. "I never got to use it, but obviously you did your homework."

"Actually, that credit goes to Special Agent Wise," Begley said, indicating the other agent.

He had ended his cell phone call to the RA, whatever that was. He'd been listening to Tierney's story and now stepped forward. "I also owe you an apology, Mr. Tierney. On paper, you looked like a viable suspect."

"On paper, I suppose I would. Why were you looking at me in the first place?"

"Your initials appeared several times in Millicent Gunn's diary. She indicated that you were nice to her."

Tierney shrugged but didn't comment on that.

"About the graves?" Begley prompted.

"I tried not to disturb the area around them, hoping they would provide forensic evidence. Whoever Blue turned out to be."

Begley asked for directions. Tierney told them where they could find his car. "They're about a hundred fifty yards north-northeast from where it's parked. It's a rugged climb, but obviously doable, even for a man carrying a body."

"The ribbon?" Lilly asked. It was still lying on the floor at their feet, stained with his blood as well as William Ritt's.

"Just as I told you. I saw it fluttering on a branch. Ritt must've dropped it when he was digging the grave. I took it because I was afraid a valuable piece of evidence would blow away before I could lead somebody back up there."

To Begley he said, "I used latex gloves when handling the shovel.

It's in the trunk of my car. Hopefully you'll lift Ritt's fingerprints off it." Lilly saw that tears had glossed his eyes. "You'll at least find my daughter's remains."

His voice had grown even more thready with the telling of his story. Considering how much blood he'd lost, Lilly didn't know how he was remaining upright. She slid her arm around his waist. "Why don't you sit down at least?"

He smiled down at her. "I'm okay."

"It was Dutch who shot you, wasn't it?"

He looked into her face for a moment, then turned to Begley. "What about him and Wes Hamer?"

"Collier, one of the tactical team, stayed behind with them." Begley glanced at her uneasily, then asked Tierney, "Is it as Ms. Martin says? Chief Burton shot you?"

"I threw down my pistol," he said bitterly. "It didn't matter."

"He shot you, knowing you were unarmed?"

"That's partially my fault, Ms. Martin," Begley said in response to her dismay. "Chief Burton considered Mr. Tierney a dangerous criminal."

"I knew that." Tierney explained how he'd heard over her car radio that he was wanted for questioning. "When I saw Dutch and Wes Hamer, I figured they were a hunting party out to capture me, dead or alive."

"He was also angry over the two of you being up here together," Begley said. "A bad combination of vigilantism and jealousy."

"That's why I took off running when I saw them," Tierney said. "I hoped to contact you—the FBI—before they got to me. I figured I would have a better chance of explaining myself to you. I doubted I'd have the same luck with them, and I was right."

He paused for breath. "But I couldn't outrun them. They caught up with me, shot me. Seconds later I heard Ritt over the radio transmitter telling them he'd found Lilly here in the cabin, dead. I knew then that something was terribly wrong. I think you can piece together the rest." He slumped against the wall.

Handling him gently, Lilly guided him down until he was sitting on the floor, his back against the wall. "I can't believe Dutch did this to you." Looking up at Begley, she said, "He'll have to face criminal charges, won't he?"

"No, ma'am, he won't."

She was about to ask why not when suddenly she knew. She could see the answer in Begley's sympathetic eyes, and sense it in Agent Wise's averted gaze, and hear it in Tierney's muttered curse.

"I'm sorry, Ms. Martin," Begley said gently. "He gave us no choice. He shot one of my men. It would have been fatal except for his vest. Chief Burton tried to shoot Mr. Tierney in the back, and would have shot me. We gave him repeated warnings. He persisted. In order to save our own lives—"

"You don't have to explain," she said, her voice soft and sorrowful.

Tierney reached for her hand and clasped it.

A cell phone rang. Agent Wise turned his back on them and answered the call as unobtrusively as possible.

There was increased noise and a flurry of motion outside. Begley stepped onto the porch, then returned almost immediately. "Care-Flight chopper is here, Mr. Tierney."

"Will I be able to go with him?"

"I'm afraid not, Ms. Martin," he said. "We'll need you in Cleary."

She nodded, but reluctantly.

"I'll go back with the first group and oversee Ritt's incarceration. You'll stay here under Agent Wise's watch until the chopper can return for you. Today Hoot has proved himself to be most capable," he said, almost tongue in cheek. "Shouldn't be more than half an hour."

"I'm sure I'll be fine."

A team of paramedics rushed inside pushing a gurney. In a matter of minutes Tierney had been strapped to it, hooked up to an IV, into which several bottles of solution were being dripped, and fitted with a nose cannula supplying him with oxygen. Despite the activity around him, he didn't let go of Lilly's hand and never took his eyes off hers, nor did hers stray from his.

She followed the gurney as far as the porch, where she was forced to release his hand. The sun had sunk below the tree line to the west, creating a false twilight. Already the absence of sunlight had caused the temperature to drop dramatically. Hugging herself for warmth, she remained there, staring after Tierney, until the helicopter lifted off.

"Where's he being taken?" she asked Begley, who was ushering her back inside.

"Asheville."

"He's lost so much blood."

"He seems tough enough. He'll be all right." He touched her arm for reassurance. She smiled at him. He smiled back.

"Sir?" They turned in unison to face Agent Wise.

"What is it, Hoot?"

"They found Scott Hamer."

When word reached Dora, she was still with Marilee.

They'd remained together all day, bolstering each other through the hours that Scott was unaccounted for. Dora had cell phone numbers for only a few of Scott's friends, but word quickly spread that his mother was anxious to speak to him. None of the friends Dora reached had heard from him.

Her attempts to reach Wes on his cell phone met with no success. Either his service hadn't yet been restored or he was ignoring her calls.

The two women waited, their distress mounting.

It was Officer Harris who finally found Scott. "He's on his way to the hospital." He refused to tell Dora any more than that over the telephone.

When she and Marilee reached the emergency room, they were almost afraid to hear what the admitting nurse had to tell them. Well acquainted with the Hamer family, the nurse was reluctant to be the messenger of bad news. "The doctor wanted to speak with you directly, Mrs. Hamer. I'll get him," she said and disappeared through a set of double doors.

It was a full ten minutes before a young man in a lab coat emerged. To Dora he looked very young. He divided a look between them. "Mrs. Hamer?"

"I'm Mrs. Hamer."

"Dr. Davison." He shook her hand, which felt cold and clammy in his. "Apparently Scott was climbing the rope in the high school gymnasium, lost his grip, and fell. He was alone. No one there to spot him. He hadn't put a mat under him either, so he landed hard. We're trying to get him stabilized so he can be transported to a major hospital."

Dora would have collapsed with relief had not Marilee been supporting her. "But he's alive?"

"Oh, yes. Forgive me, I thought you knew that much. His injuries aren't life threatening. His vitals are good. But I don't want to minimize the extent of the damage. Both his legs are broken in several places. He's being X-rayed now to check for internal injuries. I don't think we'll find any, but that's routine when the pelvic bones are involved. There appears to be no spinal or head injury. That kind of drop, he was lucky." He paused to let all that sink in before continuing.

"Excuse me, Mrs. Hamer, but I need to ask. Has he been taking steroids?"

"He's been *given* steroids."

"They may have contributed to his injuries, and will make his recovery harder. Steroids strengthen muscles, but not the tendons and ligaments that connect them. They actually become weaker from the additional stress placed on them. I'm afraid Scott's in for a rough time."

"But he's alive."

"Yeah, he's alive. But we need to get him to a hospital that has a trauma unit. Unfortunately, the roads are still icy, and another patient who's had a major blood loss got first dibs on the CareFlight."

"Did they capture Mr. Tierney?"

"I don't know his name," the doctor replied to Marilee's question. "All I know is that they captured Blue, and it was bloody. So it may be a couple hours before Scott can be transferred. In the meantime we'll keep him as comfortable as possible and monitor him closely."

"Can we see him?"

"As soon as he's out of X-ray." He hesitated, then said, "I saw him play football last season. He had a lot of talent. You may want to start preparing him for a disappointment."

A half hour later, the nurse came to usher Dora into the ICU.

Dora extended her hand to Marilee. "Come with me."

"I can't," she said, her voice husky with emotion.

"He'll need you."

"No, he won't." She smiled through her tears. "He did, but he won't anymore. Tell him . . ." She paused, then shook her head sadly. "Never mind. I think it's best if you don't tell him anything."

Dora searched the other woman's eyes, then gave a slow nod. "You're a remarkably unselfish person. And an incredibly brave woman." She hugged Marilee quickly, then rushed through the double doors.

He'd been given painkillers intravenously, so he was groggy, but he knew where he was. As she approached the bed, he smiled wanly and whispered, "Hi, Mom."

Dora clasped his hand and didn't even try to stem her tears. "Hi."

"My legs are fucked up really bad, aren't they?"

"Yes. Really bad."

Scott closed his eyes and expelled a deep sigh through a faint smile. "Thank God."

EPILOGUE

"Ms. Martin, Mr. Tierney is here."

Lilly's assistant knew who Ben Tierney was from all the media coverage of the events that had taken place in North Carolina three months ago. Although William Ritt's capture had been the focus of the stories, there had been a lot of speculation around the *Smart* watercooler about what had transpired inside that cabin for the two days that she and Tierney had been isolated.

No one on staff had had the temerity to ask, especially since there had been no further contact between her and Tierney. Until yesterday. He had called and asked for an appointment this morning.

Lilly knew that word of the upcoming meeting had spread through the offices like wildfire. This morning everyone was on red alert and vying to catch the first glimpse of him.

Her assistant's nonchalance was faked.

It was impossible for Lilly to fake it.

Her voice sounded nothing like her own when she said, "Please send him in."

Heart thumping, she stared at the door. He opened it and walked in, closing it behind him. He was dressed in slacks and a sports jacket. She'd never seen him in anything other than kayaking shorts and the jeans, sweater, and coat he'd been wearing in the cabin.

Well, and nothing.

"Hello, Lilly."

"Hello."

"I'm glad you had the time available today."

"I make it a point to have a follow-up visit with every man with whom I'm trapped in a mountain cabin for forty-eight hours during a blizzard."

He was a little thinner, a little paler, but the smile was endearingly familiar as he took the chair facing her desk and gave her an unhurried once-over. When his eyes reconnected with hers, he said, "You look great."

Then why did you let ninety-four days go by before contacting me? That was what her mind was screaming. What she said was "How's your shoulder?"

"Brand-new. They had to replace the old with a plastic one, reputably durable, virtually indestructible."

"Does it bother you?"

"Not too bad."

"You say that about every injury."

He held her gaze for a moment, then said quietly, "Some hurt more than others."

She turned her head aside to avoid the magnetism of his blue gaze. Countless times she had asked herself what she would say and do when she saw him again—*if* she did.

Well, she knew she would see him at least once more. She had to. But after that, she didn't know what to expect.

She had scripted several ways she would play this scene, ranging from cool detachment to passionate abandon. Now she couldn't remember a single clever line from any of the imagined scenarios.

"I suppose you had to have physical therapy for it."

"I was in a rehab hospital for several weeks."

"The inactivity must have been maddening for you."

"It was. But I was so much better off than most of the patients there. Scott Hamer for one."

"Yes, I heard about his accident."

"It wasn't an accident." Her surprise must have shown. "He and I had some heart-to-heart talks in the hospital. He told me he let go of the rope on purpose."

"Why?"

She listened with increasing dismay as he told her about the steroids Wes had been giving Scott. "That in addition to sleeping with his girlfriend," she remarked, shaking her head. "Wes Hamer is a despicable human being."

"I agree. They're keeping the scandal with Millicent under wraps. Not to protect Wes but to spare her parents. Why add to their pain?"

"He deserves public censure, but I understand that reasoning."

"The scuttlebutt is that he's been humbled, not only by Scott's accident but also by what happened on the mountain."

"He was only following Dutch's lead."

"Not exactly, Lilly. According to Scott, Wes admitted to egging Dutch on to come after me."

"What did Wes care?"

"For a time he feared that Scott might be Blue."

"Scott?"

"He had motive. At least Wes thought so. Wes tapped into Dutch's jealousy of us and talked him into doing what he wanted to do all along—get me for being with you. It was an easy sale for Wes, but it wound up getting his best friend killed. He'll carry the guilt of that to his grave."

"Why does she stay with him, I wonder?"

"Mrs. Hamer? After she learned about the steroids, Scott says she was ready to leave him. Wes begged her to stay. He professes to be a different man. Turned over a new leaf. To demonstrate his change of heart, he's even quit coaching. Started selling sporting goods."

"For Millicent's uncle?"

"He's not *that* reformed," Tierney said with distaste.

"What about Scott? What's in his future?"

"He's still in a wheelchair, but once he's completely healed, he wants to continue his education as planned."

"But no athletics."

"No. He won't be playing any more competitive sports, and he couldn't be happier about it."

"He must have been a terribly unhappy young man to go to such extremes to get out from under Wes's thumb."

"He's still unhappy," Tierney said, frowning thoughtfully. "Scott bared his soul to me about a lot of stuff. He's relieved that he doesn't have to perform athletically. But there's something else he's holding back.

"He says it's too personal to confide, that he's not ready to share it yet. I had a lot of time to observe him while we were in the hospital together. He reads. Classics mostly. He sits and stares into space for hours at a time. He's an extremely sad young man."

"Perhaps over Millicent?"

"He regrets what happened to her, of course, but after she and Wes . . ." He let the rest remain unspoken. "Something else—or someone else—has broken his heart. Maybe one of these days he'll feel comfortable enough to talk about it. He promised to stay in touch."

"I'm sure he appreciates your friendship."

"He's a good kid."

After a short silence she said, "I'm sure you know that William Ritt pleaded guilty to all the charges."

Tierney's lips formed a harsh line. "Five consecutive life sentences. That's still too good for him."

"I couldn't agree more."

"At least he saved the taxpayers the cost of a trial."

"He was never liked," she said. "By anyone. In my own experience, the chummier he tried to get, the more off-putting he was. Now even his own sister has abandoned him. I don't know Marilee well, but she was always pleasant to me. Can you imagine how mortified she must be? I sent her a card of encouragement, but it came back unopened."

"I heard she's moved away from Cleary and left no forwarding address. Probably best," he said.

"Probably."

Having exhausted those topics, they grew quiet. She was aware of him staring at her. She kept her gaze fixed on the stack of mail on her desk. In anticipation of his arrival, she'd been unable to concentrate on it. Finally, when she could stand the tension no longer, she looked at him.

"Lilly, I didn't call you before now because—"

"I didn't ask."

"But you deserve an explanation."

She got up and walked to the window. The worst storm of the past hundred years had marked the end of winter. Spring had arrived and was edging toward summer. Twenty stories below, Atlanta's streets were basking in the sunshine of a mild afternoon.

"You switched hospitals, Tierney. You instructed the FBI office in Charlotte not to give anyone, including me, any information on how to contact you. I got the message."

"Obviously you didn't. It wasn't that I didn't want to see you."

"Wasn't it?"

"No."

"Then what?"

"You had to bury Dutch," he said. "And I had to exhume Torrie."

Her pique deflating, Lilly turned to face him. "Forgive me. I haven't told you yet how sorry I am about her."

"Thank you. Finding out what happened to her was both a relief and a finality. Good on the one hand. Terrible on the other."

She almost went to him then, but she didn't. "I'd like you to tell me about Torrie. If you feel like talking about it."

"It's not a pretty story, but you need to hear it."

She motioned for him to go ahead.

He took a deep breath. "Torrie was only a few months old when I went on an extended trip to Africa. I was under contract to cover the continent for a travel magazine. What was supposed to take a few weeks turned into months. Many months. I missed Thanksgiving. Christmas. Lots of things.

"In my absence, Paula—Torrie's mother—met and fell in love with another man. When I finally came home, she slapped the divorce papers on me before I had unpacked. Paula and her husband-to-be wanted me to abdicate all parental rights to Torrie, saying that he'd spent more time with her than I had.

"At the time, I talked myself into believing that it was the right and decent thing to do. Lambert loved Paula. He treated Torrie as his own. I figured it would be better for my daughter if I simply bowed out and let them have their life without any interference from me."

"At the time," Lilly said quietly. "That's a crucial qualifying phrase."

"Right." He stood up and moved to a wall where some of the magazine's more notable issues had been framed for display. He looked at them individually, but Lilly didn't think he was actually reading the copy or taking in the cover photos.

"They never stopped me from seeing her. In fact, they encouraged it. But the visits were always awkward. We didn't know each other. I was a stranger the poor kid was forced to see now and then. I would enter stage left, say an appropriate line or two, exit stage right, disappear into the wings for another year or so. This was my daughter's *life,* and I played a walk-on role in it. As years went by, I didn't do even that. The visits became more infrequent."

He moved to another cover, studied it. "I was on the Amazon when word reached me that she was missing. She had disappeared without a trace and was believed to have been kidnapped. It took me two weeks to get back to civilization and return to the States.

"I hadn't seen her for years. I'd been notified as a courtesy, nothing more. Paula was surprised when I showed up on their doorstep in Nashville, which in itself says a lot about me and my priorities, doesn't it? But rather than comfort her and do whatever I could to make the situation easier for her and Lambert, I acted like a jackass.

"I had the gall to criticize them for not staying longer in Cleary and insisting that the search continue. Winter had set in. It wasn't feasible that they keep hundreds of people combing that mountain. But I refused to accept that there was nothing more to be done than hope that Torrie would turn up somewhere, someday. I couldn't settle for her picture on a milk carton and a plea for information."

He turned around to face her. "Lambert tossed me out of his house, and I don't blame him. I checked into a hotel. And in that impersonal room, where nothing except a duffel bag of clothes belonged to me, I suddenly realized that I was utterly alone.

"Paula and her husband had each other to lean on, cry with, cling to for support. I didn't have anybody, and I was the reason why. It occurred to me that I had given away the only other person on the planet who shared my blood. That's when I came face-to-face with what a selfish bastard I'd been.

"Giving up Torrie hadn't been a sacrifice. That's what I'd told myself, but it wasn't true. It had been self-serving, not some grand gesture of self-denial for my child's sake. I'd wanted to globe-trot. I'd wanted freedom to pack up and leave without having to take my family into consideration. In that empty hotel room, I saw myself for what I was. Or at least for what I'd been. It was time to make restitution.

"That night, I resolved to learn what happened to Torrie or die trying. That was one responsibility I would not shirk. It would be the last thing I ever did for my child. The *only* thing I ever did for her." By the time he finished, his voice was rough with emotion.

"I saw it through to the end, Lilly. I had to crawl out of my hospital bed, but I was there when the forensic specialists conducted the exhumations. I was with Paula when our daughter's remains were positively identified. We held a small memorial service and a proper burial for her in Nashville."

He turned away from his inspection of the magazine covers and looked at her. His eyes were misty. "I had to put closure on all that before I could come to you. Do you understand?"

She nodded, too emotional to speak.

"After hearing it, you may not want to have anything to do with me, but I hope you will."

"Do you think..."

"What?"

"That day we kayaked the river, do you think you sensed in me the same kind of emptiness and loss you were feeling? I'd lost Amy. You'd lost Torrie. Did you recognize a—"

"Kindred spirit?"

"Something like that."

"I'm certain of it," he said.

"Oh."

"Wait, are you wondering if that's what attracted me to you? The only thing that attracted me?"

"Was it?"

"What do you think?"

The intensity of his stare was like a caress. It answered the question for her. She shook her head. "No. I think we both knew when we said good-bye that day that it wasn't an ending, only a postponement."

"The time we've spent together can be counted in hours," he said, "but I feel like we know each other better than most couples ever do."

"Are we a couple, Tierney?"

He came to her then and cupped her face between his hands, tilting it up to within inches of his. "God, I hope so." His eyes lighted on every feature of her face before they settled on her mouth.

"Want me?" she whispered.

"You have no idea."

Then he lowered his head and kissed her. His tongue slipped between her lips, gently at first, but instantly the kiss turned wet and hot, infinitely sexy, brimming with evocative promise.

Movement of his right arm was still limited, but he curved his left one around her, and with a move she remembered well from their first kiss, he placed his hand on the small of her back and drew her up flush against him.

They kissed for endless minutes, never breaking contact. When they finally broke apart, he smoothed her hair away from her face. "No longer afraid of me?"

"Only afraid that you'll disappear from my life again."

"Then you've got nothing to be afraid of." He kissed her lightly to seal the promise, but when he raised his head, his expression was serious. "I'll be better at it this time, Lilly. I swear to you. I'll love you like you've never been loved."

"You already have. You risked your life for me. Several times."

"I didn't know how to love before, but—"

She laid her fingers against his lips. "Yes, you did, Tierney. You couldn't have done what you did, giving up more than two years of your life, and nearly dying for Torrie's sake, if you didn't love her."

"But she died without knowing it."

"I don't think so. She knew."

He looked skeptical, but she could tell that he desperately

wanted to believe it. "Paula told me she read all my articles. Kept all the magazines in her room and wouldn't throw any of them away."

Lilly folded her hands around his head. "She knew you loved her."

"If I had it to do over again, I'd make sure of it. I'd tell her every day. I'd do it differently. I'd do it right."

Lilly hugged him tightly, laying her head on his chest so he wouldn't see her secret smile. Today was theirs alone. There would be time enough tomorrow to tell him that, although he had lost one child on the mountain, he had created another.

Already he had been granted a second chance to do it right.